"TWO NOVELS IN ONE...gripping and action-packed."
—*Chicago Tribune*

"EXTRAORDINARY."
—*The New York Times Book Review*

P9-DMV-221

PQW766016

"[A] CAN'T-MISS DOUBLE-THRILLER."
—*The Jackson (MS) Clarion-Ledger*

"BARR IS AT HER BEST...
She writes as though she's held her breath to the
limit, as Pigeon does, to dive deeply at a reef."
—*Boston Herald*

"Barr has given us two novels in one as she skillfully switches the story from the twenty-first to the nineteenth century . . . [She] perfectly captures the time periods in alternating chapters and makes each story as gripping and action-packed as the other."   —*Chicago Tribune*

"[An] extraordinary setting . . . a lyrical evocation of the natural landscape . . . Anna [has] force as a woman of inner strength and ironclad sensitivity."
—*The New York Times Book Review*

"When Pigeon faces the elements or evildoers, Barr is at her best, using her talent for linking the physical scene with suspenseful action. She writes as though she's held her breath to the limit, as Pigeon does, to dive deeply at a reef . . . for an outdoorsy mystery that makes you feel you're in the scene, this is it."   —*Boston Herald*

"Although the present mystery is taut and tense, Barr does a fantastic job with the second, historical narrative . . . Readers will feel as if they picked up one book but wound up with two . . . a slam-bang denouement . . . one of Barr's finest."   —*Milwaukee Journal Sentinel*

"Barr weaves together two separate narratives, and does so with no decrease in suspense. Quite the contrary; she shifts gears smoothly between past and present, involving the reader in both. Add to this two attractive protagonists and a behind-the-scenes portrayal of the National Park Service and you have a novel with something for nearly everyone."
—*The San Diego Union-Tribune*

continued . . .

"Vividly captures the majestic and hidden beauty of the keys . . . The award-winning author uses the unique environment as a backdrop for a solid, complex plot as concerned about nature as the nature of man."

—*Fort Lauderdale Sun-Sentinel*

"The world of underwater sea, coral and fish provides a brilliant backdrop to [Anna's] adventures."

—*Hartford Courant*

"[A] can't-miss double-thriller . . . *Flashback* is Barr's most confident, surprising, and locale-driven mystery to date. Unforgettable characters . . . will keep fans talking for days."

—*The Jackson (MS) Clarion-Ledger*

"A web of intrigue . . . Barr's richly worded descriptions leave the reader yearning to visit wherever it is Anna Pigeon happens to be stationed . . . [She] has developed into one of modern fiction's most three-dimensional sleuths."

—*The Columbia (SC) State*

"When it comes to a vibrant sense of place, Barr has few equals . . . Those who already admire the doughty National Park ranger will rejoice in this double-layered story with its readable setting, passionately rendered; new readers have a treat in store."

—*Publishers Weekly*

"The most grandly scaled of her eleven adventures."

—*Kirkus Reviews*

More praise for Nevada Barr's award-winning
Anna Pigeon mysteries . . .

"Well-baited suspense."   —*People*

"Gripping adventure . . . [an] exceptional series."
                                          —*The Denver Post*

"Nevada Barr writes with a cool, steady hand about the
violence of nature and the cruelty of man."
                                   —*The New York Times Book Review*

"A truly harrowing series of tight squeezes."
                                        —*Chicago Tribune*

"Heart-pounding . . . Barr combines primo mysteries
with what always feels like a virtual reality tour of one of
the parks . . . There is beauty here. Still, Anna never loses
her edginess in a world where your life depends on having a backup light for your backup light."
                                       —*Detroit Free Press*

"Evocative and suspenseful . . . Thoroughly satisfying—
thanks to the writing and plotting talents of a master."
                                —*Publishers Weekly* (starred review)

"Barr's descriptive prose is a constant source of pleasure."
                                    —*San Francisco Chronicle*

"From the fabric of fiction she creates real worlds, sometimes beautiful, sometimes terrifying, but always convincing."   —*The San Diego Union-Tribune*

"Nevada Barr is one of the best."   —*The Boston Globe*

Flashback

NEVADA BARR

BERKLEY BOOKS, NEW YORK

If you purchased this book without a cover, you should be aware that this book is stolen property. It was reported as "unsold and destroyed" to the publisher, and neither the author nor the publisher has received any payment for this "stripped book."

This is a work of fiction. Names, characters, places, and incidents either are the product of the author's imagination or are used fictitiously, and any resemblance to actual persons, living or dead, business establishments, events, or locales is entirely coincidental.

FLASHBACK

A Berkley Book / published by arrangement with the author

PRINTING HISTORY
G. P. Putnam's Sons hardcover edition / February 2003
Berkley mass-market edition / February 2004

Copyright © 2003 by Nevada Barr.
Excerpt from *High Country* by Nevada Barr copyright © 2004 by Nevada Barr.
Cover illustration by Rob Wood.
Cover design by Wood Ronsaville Harlin, Inc.
Interior map copyright © 2002 by Jackie Aher.

All rights reserved.
This book, or parts thereof, may not be reproduced in any form without permission. The scanning, uploading, and distribution of this book via the Internet or via any other means without the permission of the publisher is illegal and punishable by law. Please purchase only authorized electronic editions, and do not participate in or encourage electronic piracy of copyrighted materials. Your support of the author's rights is appreciated.
For information address: The Berkley Publishing Group,
a division of Penguin Group (USA) Inc.,
375 Hudson Street, New York, New York 10014.

ISBN: 0-425-19449-3

BERKLEY®
Berkley Books are published by The Berkley Publishing Group,
a division of Penguin Group (USA) Inc.,
375 Hudson Street, New York, New York 10014.
BERKLEY and the "B" design
are trademarks belonging to Penguin Group (USA) Inc.

PRINTED IN THE UNITED STATES OF AMERICA

10 9 8 7 6 5 4 3 2 1

FOR JOAN, who helped me with the plot twists
of life and literature during the writing of this book

Due to the isolated locale and complex nature of Dry Tortugas National Park, this book could not have been written without the cooperation of the people who work at Everglades and Dry Tortugas National Parks. My thanks go out to Superintendent Maureen Finnerty, Chief Ranger Bill Wright, Linda Irey and, most especially, Supervisory Ranger Paul Taylor, who took the time to show me all the nooks and crannies above and below sea level; Captain Cliff Green and First Mate Linda Vanaman, who shared their stories, expertise and wonderful attitudes toward all things fishy; Al Riemer, who let me hang around his shop and gossip; and Mike Ryan, who made the history come alive through his knowledge and research.

HISTORICAL NOTE

In 1865, Dr. Samuel Mudd was tried and convicted for aiding and abetting John Wilkes Booth after the assassination of President Lincoln. He received a sentence of life imprisonment to be served at Fort Jefferson in the Dry Tortugas, Florida. Two years later, during a yellow fever outbreak at the prison, Dr. Mudd acted courageously, using his medical skill to treat the sick. Acknowledging his services, President Andrew Johnson pardoned him in 1869. Though there has been a great deal of discussion over Dr. Mudd's guilt or innocence, the device of the doppelgänger was a complete fiction created for this story.

A month after Dr. Mudd was pardoned, Samuel Arnold's case was reviewed. President Johnson found there was sufficient doubt about his participation in the conspiracy to pardon him as well. After his release, Mr. Arnold lived a quiet life of seclusion on his farm in Maryland. In 1906, at the age of 72, Samuel Arnold died of consumption at his home. His wife and children were at his bedside.

Throughout their lives, both men maintained their innocence of any crime connected with the death of Mr. Lincoln.

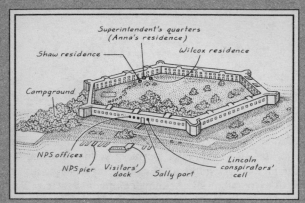

Superintendent's quarters
(Anna's residence)

Shaw residence

Wilcox residence

Campground

NPS offices

NPS pier

Visitors' dock

Sally port

Lincoln conspirators' cell

Fort Jefferson on Garden Key

Gulf of Mexico

TORTUGAS BANK

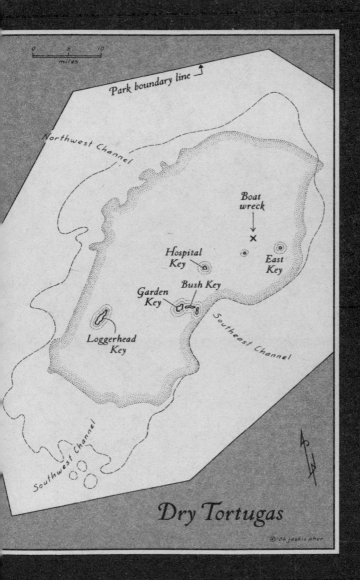

Dry Tortugas

Until she ran out of oxygen, Anna was willing to believe she was taking part in a PBS special. The water was so clear sunlight shone through as if the sea were but mountain air. Cloud shadows, stealthy and faintly magical at four fathoms, moved lazily across patches of sand that showed startlingly white against the dark, ragged coral. Fishes colored so brightly it seemed it must be a trick of the eye or the tail end of an altered state flitted, nibbled, explored and slept. Without moving, Anna could see a school of silver fish, tiny anchovies, synchronized, moving like polished chain mail in a glittering curtain. Four Blue Tangs, so blue her eyes ached with the joy of them, nosed along the edge of a screamingly purple sea fan bigger than a coffee table. A jewfish, six feet long and easily three hundred pounds, his blotchy hide mimicking the sun-dappled rock, pouting lower lip thick as Anna's wrist, lay without moving beneath an overhang of a coral-covered rock less than half his size, his wee fish brain assuring him he was hidden. Countless other fish, big and small, bright and dull, ever more delightful to Anna because she'd not named them and so robbed them of a modicum of their mystery, moved around her on their fishy business.

Air, and with it time, was running out. If she wished to live, she needed to breathe. Her lungs ached with that peculiar sensation of being full to bursting. Familiar desperation licked at the edges of her mind. One more kick, greetings to a spiny lobster (a creature whose body design was only possible in a weightless world), and, with a strong sense of being hounded from paradise, she swam for the surface, drove a foot or more into the air and breathed.

The sky was as blue as the eye-watering fishes and every bit as merciless as the sea. The ocean was calm. Even with her chin barely above the surface she could see for miles. There was remarkably little to soothe the eye between the unrelenting glare of sea and sky. To the north was Garden Key, a scrap of sand no more than thirteen acres in total and, at its highest point, a few meters above sea level. Covering the key, two of its sides spilling out into the water, was the most bizarre duty station at which she had served.

Fort Jefferson, a massive brick fortress, had been built on this last lick of America, the Dry Tortugas, seventy miles off Key West in the Gulf of Mexico. At the time construction started in 1846, it was the cutting edge of national defense. Made of brick and mortar with five bastions jutting out from the corners of a pentagon, it had been built as the first line of defense for the southern states, guarding an immense natural—and invisible—harbor; it was the only place for sixty miles where ships could sit out the hurricanes that menaced the Gulf and the southeastern seaboard or come under the protection of the fort's guns in time of war. Though real, the harbor was invisible because its breakwaters, a great broken ring of coral, were submerged.

Jefferson never fired a single shot in defense of its country. Time and substrata conspired against it. Before the third tier of the fort could be completed, the engineers noticed the weight of the massive structure was causing it to sink and stopped construction. Even unfinished it might have seen honorable—if not glamorous—duty, but the rifled cannon was invented, and the seven-to-fifteen-foot-thick brick-and-mortar walls were designed only to withstand old-style cannons. Under siege by these new weapons of war, the fort would not stand. Though destined for glorious battle, Jefferson sat out the Civil War as a union prison.

Till Anna had been assigned temporary duty at the Dry Tortugas, she'd not even heard of it. Now it was home.

For a moment she merely treaded water, head thrown back to let the sun seek out any epithelial cell it hadn't already destroyed over the last ten years. Just breathing—when the practice had recently been denied—was heaven. Somewhere she'd read that a meager seventeen percent of air pulled in by the lungs was actually used. Idly, she wondered if she could train her body to salvage the other eighty-three percent so she could remain underwater ten minutes at a stretch rather than two. Scuba gave one the time but, with the required gear, not the freedom. Anna preferred free diving. Three times she breathed deep, on the third she held it, upended and kicked again for bliss of the bottom.

Flashing in the sun, she was as colorful as any fish. Her mask and fins were iridescent lime green, her dive skin startling blue. Though the water was a welcoming eighty-eight degrees in late June, that was still eight point six degrees below where she functioned best. For prolonged stays in this captivating netherworld she wore a skin, a lightweight body-hugging suit with a close-fitting hood and matching socks. Not only did it conserve body heat, but it also protected her from the sometimes vicious bite of the coral. Like all divers who weren't vandals, Anna assiduously avoided touching—and so harming—living coral, but when they occasionally did collide, human skin was usually as damaged as the coral.

Again she stayed with and played with the fish until her lungs felt close to bursting. Though it would be hotly debated by a good percentage of Dry Tortugas National Park's visitors, as far as she was concerned the "paradise" part of this subtropical paradise was hidden beneath the waves.

Anna had never understood how people could go to the beach and lie in the sand to relax. The shore was a far harsher environment than the mountains. Air was hot and heavy and clung to the skin. Wind scoured. Sand itched. Salt sucked moisture from flesh. The sun, in the sky and again off the surface of the sea, seared and blinded. For a couple of hours each day it was heaven. After that it began to wear one down as the ocean wears away rock and bone.

Two dive sites, twenty dives—the deepest over forty feet—

and Anna finally tired herself out. Legs reduced to jelly from pushing through an alien universe, she couldn't kick hard enough to rise above the surface and pull herself over the gunwale. Glad there were no witnesses, she wriggled and flopped over the transom beside the outboard motor to spill on deck, splattering like a bushel of sardines. Her "Sunday" was over. She'd managed to spend yet one more weekend in Davy Jones's locker. There wasn't really any place else to go.

The *Reef Ranger,* one of the park's patrol boats, a twenty-five-foot inboard/outboard Boston Whaler, the bridge consisting of a high bench and a Plexiglas windscreen, fired up at a touch. Anna upped anchor, then turned the bow toward the bastinadoed fortress that was to be her home for another eight to twelve weeks. Seen from the level of the surrounding ocean, Fort Jefferson presented a bleak and surreal picture: an overwhelming geometric tonnage floating, apparently unsupported, on the surface of the sea.

Enjoying the feel of a boat beneath her after so many years in landlocked parks, Anna headed for the fort. The mariners' rhyme used to help those new to the water remember which markers to follow when entering heavy traffic areas rattled meaninglessly through her mind: *red on right returning.* Shrunken by salt and sun, her skin felt two sizes too small for her bones, and even with dark glasses and the sun at her back, it was hard to keep her eyes open against the glare.

The opportunity to serve as Interim Supervisory Ranger for the hundred square miles of park, scarcely one of which was above water, came in May. Word trickled down from the southeastern region that the Dry Tortugas' Supervisory Ranger had to take a leave of absence for personal reasons and a replacement was needed until he returned or, failing that, a permanent replacement was found.

Dry Tortugas National Park was managed jointly with southern Florida's Everglades National Park. The brass all worked out of Homestead, near Everglades. Marooned as it was, seventy miles into the Gulf, day-to-day operations of the Dry Tortugas were run by a Supervisory Ranger, who managed one law enforcement ranger, two interpreters and an office administrator. Additional law enforcement had been budgeted and two rangers hired. They were new to the service and, at present, being trained at the Federal Law Enforcement Training Center in Georgia.

"Supervisory Ranger" was a title that bridged a gray area in the NPS hierarchy. For reasons to which Anna was not privy, the head office chose not to upgrade the position to Chief Ranger but left it as a subsidiary position to the Chief Ranger at Everglades. Still, it was a step above Anna's current District Ranger level on the Natchez Trace. To serve as "Acting Supervisory Ranger" was a good career move.

That wasn't entirely why she'd chosen to abandon home and hound for three months to accept the position. Anna was in no hurry to rush out of the field and into a desk job. There'd be time enough for that when her knees gave out or her tolerance for the elements—both natural and criminal—wore thin.

She had taken the Dry Tortugas assignment for personal reasons. When she was in a good frame of mind, she told herself she'd needed to retreat to a less populated and mechanized post to find the solitude and unmarred horizons wherein to renew herself, to seek answers. When cranky or down, she felt it was the craven running away of a yellow-bellied deserter.

Paul Davidson, his divorce finalized, had asked her to marry him.

Two days later, a car, a boat and a plane ride behind her— not to mention two thousand miles of real estate, a goodly chunk of it submerged—she was settling into her quarters at Fort Jefferson.

"Coincidence?" her sister Molly had asked sarcastically. "You be the judge."

The fort had only one phone, which worked sporadically, and mail was delivered once a week. Two weeks had passed in sandy exile, and she was no more ready to think about marriage than she had been the day she left. But, given the paucity of entertainments—even a devotee could only commune with fish for so long—she was rapidly getting to the point where there was nothing else to think about.

Under these pressing circumstances, she'd done the only sensible thing: she stuck her nose in somebody else's business. Daniel Barrons, a maintenance man-of-all-trades and the closest thing Anna'd made to a friend at the fort, had a weakness for gossip that she shamelessly exploited.

He was a block of a man, with what her father would have referred to as a "peasant build," one designed for carrying sick calves into the barn. Perhaps in his late forties, Daniel covered his blunt face with a brown-black beard. On his left arm, seldom seen as the man wasn't given to tank tops, was a tattoo so classic Anna smiled whenever she glimpsed its bottom edge: a naked girl reclining on elbows and fanny under a cartoon palm tree.

Given this rough and manly exterior, tradition would have had him strong and silent. Every time he snuggled down in his favorite position to dish the dirt, elbows on workbench, hindquarters stuck out and usually bristling with tools shoved in his pockets, furry chin in scarred hands, Anna was charmed and tickled.

With only a small nudge, Daniel had assumed the position and filled her in on why she'd been given the opportunity to explore this oddly harsh, boring, beautiful, magical bit of the earth. Her predecessor, Lanny Wilcox, hadn't taken an extended leave willingly. It had been forced upon him when he'd begun to come unglued.

"His girlfriend, a little Cuban number as cute as a basket full of kittens, ran out on him," Daniel had told her, his voice low and gentle as usual. He consistently spoke as if a baby slept in the next room and he was loath to wake it.

"Lanny was a terrific guy, but he was getting up there, fifty-one this last birthday. At his peak he couldn't a been much to look at. Hey, I like Lanny just fine, but, well, even he knew he was about as good-looking as the south end of a northbound spiny lobster. Five, six months ago he hooked up with Theresa. She's not yet thirty, smart, funny and a nice addition to a bathing suit. Next thing you know, she's living out here. When she cut out, Lanny just sort of lost it."

From what Anna had gathered, the old Supervisory Ranger's "losing it" consisted of increasingly bizarre behavior that revolved around the seeing and hearing of things that no one else saw or heard. "Ghosts," murmured a couple of the more melodramatic inhabitants of the fort. "Hallucinations," said the practical ones, and Lanny was bundled up and shipped off to play with his imaginary friends out of sight of the tax-paying public.

On first arriving, struck by the beauty of the sky and sea, the fishes and the masonry, Anna couldn't understand what stresses could possibly chase even a heartbroken man around the bend. Piloting the *Reef Ranger* into the harbor, the glow of her swimming with the fishes burned and blown away, she realized that after a mere couple of weeks of isolation, wet heat and scouring winds, she was tempted to dream up companions of her own. She needed a sense of connection to something, somebody to keep her on an even keel.

She laughed. The sound whipped away on the liquid wind over the bow. Soon she was going to have to relinquish her self-image as a hermit. Paul—or perhaps just the passage of years—had socialized her to some extent. Molly would be pleased. Anna made a mental note to tell her sister when next she phoned. It could be a while. Not only was the fort's only phone in much demand, but it also had a one-to-two-second delay, like a phone call from Mars, that made communication an exercise in frustration.

Red on right.

Anna slowed the *Ranger* to a sedate and wakeless speed as she entered the small jewel of a harbor on the east side of Garden Key. Eleven pleasure boats were anchored, two she recognized from the weekend before, *Moonshadow* and *Key to My Heart,* both expensive, both exquisitely kept. They were owned by two well-to-do couples out of Miami who seemed joined at the hip as their boats were joined at the gunwale, one rafting off the other. Anna waved as she passed.

At the end of the harbor away from the tourists, as if there were an invisible set of tracks running from Bush Key—Garden's near neighbor—to the harbor mouth and they had been condemned to live on the wrong side of them, two commercial shrimpers cuddled up to one another.

Commercial fishing and, much to the shriek and lament of the locals, sportfishing were banned in the park, but right outside the boundaries was good shrimping. The boats stalked the perimeters, the honest—or the cautious—keeping outside the imaginary line established by NPS buoys. Perhaps a few sought to poach, but there were plenty of shrimp outside. Most came for the same reasons ships had been coming for two hundred years, the reason the fort had been built in the middle of the ocean: the natural safe zone of flat water the coral reefs provided.

Shrimp boats, their side nets looking like tattered wings falling from a complex skeleton of wood and metal, were a complication Anna'd not foreseen. They sailed from many ports, most in the south and southeast, following the shrimp: four weeks in Texas, then through the Gulf to the Keys. Some boats were family owned, most were not. All were manned and kept in a way unique to an idiosyncratic and inbred culture. Daniel called them "bikers of the sea." Having spent an unspecified and largely undiscussed number of years in the land version of that violent fraternity before, as he put it, "breaking my back and seeing the light," he would know.

The shrimpers were a scabrous lot, not just the boats, which reeked of dead fish, cigarette smoke and old grease—part cooking, part engine—but the sailors themselves. The family boats were crewed by men and women, three or four to a boat. The others were all male, but for the occasional unfortunate who, like a biker chick out of favor, was passed from boat to boat, usually fueled for her duties with drugs and alcohol.

Anna had yet to see a shrimper with all his or her teeth. The violence of the culture coupled with months at sea away from modern dentistry marked their faces. A lot of them went to sea to kick drugs and found more onboard. A startling percentage had felony records.

This borderline lifestyle would not have affected Anna had not a symbiotic relationship sprung up between them and the tourists and park employees at the fort. Fresh gulf shrimp were delicious. The shrimpers where glad to trade a few for the culinary delight of those in the park. The problem was that the currency was alcohol—mostly cheap beer, but enough whiskey to make things interesting. Drunk, the shrimpers lived up to Daniel's name for them. They came ashore; they yelled, disrupted tours, urinated in public, knocked one another's few remaining teeth out, beat their women and occasionally knifed one another.

Her third day at Fort Jefferson Anna had been made painfully aware of a few administrational oddities of Dry Tortugas National Park: there was no place to hold prisoners and, though they were legally allowed to make arrests, it was highly discouraged by headquarters in Homestead. Two law-enforcement rangers keeping drunken violent shrimpers under guard in the open air for hours till the Coast Guard arrived wasn't a great idea. Transporting them three hours one way to Key West and so leaving the park without law enforcement or EMTs for a day didn't work either.

The best they could do was separate the combatants, bind the ugliest wounds and shoo the lot of them back onboard their boats.

The two shrimpers anchored in the harbor as Anna motored in were family owned. They'd never caused problems, and the lady on one of the boats had a terrific little dog she let Anna pet. Tonight should be quiet. Anna didn't know if she was grateful or not. With only one other ranger—Bob Shaw—in house, neither ever truly had a day off but slept with a radio ready to serve as backup for the person on duty. Quiet promised uninterrupted sleep. Anna supposed that was a good thing. Still, she would have welcomed something to do.

As she backed the *Reef Ranger* neatly into the employee dock, Bob Shaw walked down the weathered planking. Opposite where Anna tied up, on the far side of the park pier with its public bathrooms and commercial loading area that the ferries from Key West used, the NPS supply boat, the *Activa,* was moored. Like Christmas every Tuesday, but better, the *Activa* arrived with supplies, groceries, mail and Cliff and Linda. Cliff was the captain, Linda the first mate. New blood was as exciting to the inhabitants of Fort Jefferson as fresh food. The crew of the *Activa* could be counted on to bring the latest news and gossip along with other treats and necessities.

"Teddy took your stuff up to your quarters for you and stuck the perishables in the refrigerator," Bob said as Anna cut the engine. She tossed him the stern line and he tied it neatly to the cleat on the starboard side. Wind was more or less a constant on DRTO, and the NPS boats were tied to both sides of their slips to keep them from banging into the sides of the dock. Fenders could only do so much when the winds flirted with hurricane force.

"I'll be sure and thank her. Is Teddy in the office?" Anna asked. Teddy, short for Theodora, was Bob's wife.

"Till five, like always." He stood stiffly to one side as Anna heaved towel, fins, snorkel and water bottle onto the dock.

Bob was a strange fit with the park. He'd been there for eleven years and clearly loved the place. He said, and Anna believed him, that he never wanted to work anywhere else and intended to serve out his remaining six years till retirement at the fort.

Anna suspected his desire to remain in this isolated post was due only partly to his love for the resource. A good chunk of it, she theorized, was because nowhere else could he live such a rich and rewarding fantasy life without coming head-to-head with the cynicism of his fellows.

Fortunately for her, Bob's particular brand of psychosis made him a great ranger.

Swearing he was five-six, though Anna, at five-four, could look him in the eye in flat shoes, he seemed bent on being the poster boy for a benign version of the Napoleon complex. Now, as he readied to go on his evening rounds—showing the flag, boarding boats he deemed suspicious, handing out brochures to newcomers and checking the boundaries because they were there—he wore full gear: sidearm, baton, pepper spray, cuffs and a Kevlar bulletproof vest. If the man hadn't been such a strong swimmer, Anna's greatest worry would have been that he'd fall overboard and his defensive equipment would sink him like a stone. The only concession he made to the cloying heat was to wear shorts.

Though Anna would never have dreamed of telling him so, they tended to spoil the effect. Not only was he no taller than Anna, but he couldn't have exceeded her one hundred twenty pounds by much. Like a lot of men who take to the water, most of that was in his chest and shoulders. Chickens would have been insulted to hear his legs compared to theirs.

"Anything up for tonight?" she asked as they made lines fast. Mostly she asked for the fun of hearing Bob's answer. His fantasy, as luck would have it, was that he was the sole protector (she didn't count for reasons of gender, and Lanny hadn't counted for reasons Bob clearly had but was too honorable to speak of) of this jewel in the ocean. Like all other great and honorable lawmen of history, Bob was constantly in danger from the forces of evil. Each and every boat could be smuggling cocaine from Panama, heroin from the east, guns from pretty much anywhere. All shrimpers were ready, willing and able to knife him in the back.

Given that he apparently genuinely believed this despite eleven years in a sleepy port, Anna couldn't but admire his stalwart courage in facing each day, never late, never shirking. Having been exposed to this criminal-under-every-bush, Marshal Dillon under-siege mentality the day she arrived, Anna was pleasantly surprised the first time she'd patrolled with him. Part of honor and duty—and natural inclination probably, though his tough-guy image would never let him admit it even to himself—required he be gracious, polite and, when he thought no one was looking, overtly kind. Seeing that, Anna had been quite taken with the man and made it a point to resist the temptation to tease him about the boogeymen that lived under his boat. She didn't even resent his sexism. Respect for a superior overrode it, and it wasn't personal. There were no women patrolling the streets of Dodge City, flying fighters over Nazi Germany or walking shoulder-to-shoulder with Clint Eastwood through the saloon's swinging doors.

Sans petticoat and fan, Anna simply didn't fit into Bob's worldview.

"Did you see the boats on the south side, anchored out a ways, not in the harbor?" Bob asked. He smoothed his sandy-red and handsome mustache with one hand and pointed with the other.

Vaguely Anna remembered passing them, but had paid them little mind.

"I saw them."

"They've been here two and a half days. Never come into the harbor. Never visit the fort. Something's up with them."

Anna'd not noticed those things. And they were pertinent. Most folks, if they bothered to come to Garden Key, made use of the harbor and at least paid a curiosity visit to the fort.

"Good eye," Anna said and meant it. "I'll keep close to the radio."

Bob jumped lightly into the second of DRTO's five patrol boats. Only four were working. The fifth was beached behind the dock up on blocks. Bob took the *Bay Ranger,* a twenty-foot aluminum-hulled Sylvan. He seemed to prefer it to the sturdier

Boston Whalers. Maybe because it was quieter, had a lower profile. All the better for sneaking up on evildoers.

Anna shouldered the net bag she used to carry her dive things.

"Oh," Bob said as she turned to go. "You got a big box from New York waiting for you. Teddy said if there's bagels in it, she'll trade you some of her homemade key lime pie for some."

Anna waved Bob off, then stood a moment, habit demanding she do a visual check of an area after an absence of hours. The campground, with space for only a handful of tents and, other than flush toilets on the public dock, no amenities, was quiet. Because there was so little dirt to be had on Garden Key, overnighters were by reservation only. Picnickers sat at tables nursing beers and sunburns, talking among themselves, families for the most part with lots of little kids scratching at mosquito bites, Kool-Aid smiles adding to the clownish colors of beach towels and bathing suits. Even Bob would have a hard time imagining an evil nemesis in the bunch.

Savoring the fact that she wasn't in a hurry, that, once again, her work for the National Park Service allowed her to rest her eyes and mind on a wonder most people would never take the time to see, she turned her attention to the fort.

Bob's motor's drone a pleasant burr in her ears, as comforting as the hum of bees in summer blooms, she looked across the moat at Fort Jefferson. More than the skyscrapers of Manhattan, the Golden Gate Bridge or all of Bill Gates's cyber magic, it impressed her with man's determination to fight the world to a standstill and then re-form it in his own design.

Seventy miles out in the sea, on the unprepossessing Bush Key, the magnitude of the effort awed her. Jefferson stood three stories high and was topped with earthworks and ammunition bunkers. A coal-black tower, built as a lighthouse but demoted to a harbor light when the taller lighthouse on Loggerhead Key was finished, thrust above the battlements. The black metal of its skin gave it an unearned sinister aspect. A wide moat, meeting the fortress walls on one side and contained by brick and mortar on the other, ran around the two bastions fronting the structure. Beyond was nothing but the Atlantic. At first the moat had amused Anna. Only in the front and along the eastern wall

was it bordered by land. On the two other sides its outer wall
separated it only from the sea.

When she'd first seen it, it had struck her as a conceit, the architect slavishly following the classic castle moat theme though
this fort was set in a natural saltwater moat thousands of miles
on one side and seventy on the other. Duncan, the island's historian and chief interpreter, had disabused her of that notion.
Moats were not merely to keep land troops at bay but ships with
malicious intent at their distance.

Trailing a young couple so in love they didn't notice it was
too hot to be hanging all over each other, Anna crossed the
bridge. As she stepped into the imagined cool and welcome
dark of the entryway she heard the shivery sound of children
giggling and saw a small head vanish into a stone slot. Anna
laughed because heat and boredom had yet to diminish the
childlike glee the fort engendered in her: "secret" rooms where
ammunition had once been stored, dark and twisted caves
where arches met and clashed and crossed at the bastions, designed by an architect who must have foreseen the genius of Es-
cher. The formidable structure was now dissolving back into
the sea with infinite slowness. Lime dripped out of solution as
rain worked its way through ancient mortar. Stalactites formed,
growing like teeth in the long, long passages through the casemates. Standing at a corner and looking down arch after arch
after arch, perspective skewed. It was easy to feel as if one were
falling through time itself.

Anna stepped from beneath the sally port to the edge of the
parade ground. The sun hit her eyes with such force she winced.
Within the embrace of the casemates was a third and different
world: no ocean, no mind-bending arches, just a manageable
patch of sky, horizons close, and the comfort of the man-made
on all sides. Brick arches at ground and second floor, one after
the other in an unbroken line, surrounded an expanse of grass
so dry it crackled underfoot. Twin houses, officer quarters during the Civil War, now served as quarters for the absent Lanny
Wilcox and Bob and Teddy Shaw. Around the edges of the parade ground, inside the heavy walls, were scattered ruins from
when Jefferson was home to troops, prisoners, slaves, cooks,
washerwomen, officers, wives and daughters: the skeletal re-

mains of a Civil War barracks, razed by the NPS when safety
had been a higher priority than preservation; two half-finished
armories, their under-roofs rounded like their later relative, the
Quonset hut; a half disassembled shot oven; the foundation for
what started out to be a church to a soldier's god but ended life
as a belowground cistern for the federal government. All testi-
fied to the hubbub of disparate humanity who had once been
packed within the walls like powder in a cannon's barrel.

Two boys rampaged out from the shadows behind Anna and
ran left past the office to disappear into the first casemate. Anna
turned left as well. The arch of the casemate had been boarded
up to enclose the park's offices. The same treatment had been
used to make employee quarters, some at ground level and
some in the second tier, where cannons and convicts had been
stored during the Civil War.

Anna pushed past the Employees Only sign and pulled the
door shut behind her. Air-conditioning; cool was wonderful.
Dry was even better. Without humidity the air felt pounds
lighter, slid into the lungs effortlessly. The physical ease was a
relief, but as ever in the gullet of bureaucracy, the magic was
gone. The place looked like a hundred other park offices:
vaguely dingy, crowded, metal desks and chin-high partitions
cutting up what little space there was.

Teddy Shaw sat behind the first desk, staring at the now
ubiquitous computer screen. Teddy was younger than her husband by a dozen years or so, thirty to thirty-five at a guess, and
a couple of inches taller, an advantage her posture seemed bent
on rejecting. She probably had at least twenty pounds on him as
well but was nowhere near fat. The euphemism "pleasantly
plump" was apt in Teddy's case. Except for the stooped shoulders, she was pretty in a girl-next-door way, with brown hair
brushing her shoulders and brown eyes that reminded Anna of
her inherited golden retriever, Taco, in color if not softness. Because of her relative youth and uncompromising support of her
husband's John Wayne/Napoleon neurosis, one might have expected her to assume the role of helpless maiden in need of rescue. More than once Anna had thought Teddy would have liked
to be that for him, but a core of inner steel got in her way. Teddy
was as peculiar in her way as Bob was in his. She steadfastly
believed in her husband's heroic potential and seemed mildly

embittered that others did not see him in the same light. Anna
thought Teddy would almost welcome disaster—even at the
cost of a few lives—if her husband would finally be given a
chance to shine.

"Thanks for putting up my groceries," Anna said by way of
greeting. "Bagels, if I got 'em, for key lime pie?"

"Yup. Six."

"Four."

"Five"

"Deal." Anna didn't much care for either bagels or key lime
pie, but she enjoyed the dickering. "Any messages?"

"Two. On your desk."

Anna dumped her bag and threaded her way to the back of
the office. To facilitate climate control and keep out the endless
weeping of moisture and dust from the tiers above, the office
was completely enclosed, walls and ceiling painted white, making it into a box that could have as easily been in a trailer house
in Nevada as a two-hundred-year-old fortress in the Gulf of
Mexico. Off the back of the box were two closet-sized rooms.
One Bob had laid claim to, the other was the Supervisory
Ranger's office. Though Anna's claustrophobia wouldn't allow
her to linger there—and certainly never with the door shut—she
got a kick out of her new office. Behind a door narrower and
shorter than standard issue, the essence of Fort Jefferson again
manifested itself. The outer wall was exposed brick. The one
window, overlooking the moat, was a firing slot cutting through
seven feet of defensive stonework. The only modern touch was
a skinny three-paned window cemented into the slit.

Anna would check e-mail in the morning when she came on
duty. It would be something to look forward to, this far out in
the middle of watery nowhere, though even e-mail was not instantaneous—it took a day or more, as it was routed through
headquarters in Homestead.

The two promised messages were where Teddy said they'd
be. The first was from Alistair Kirk, the Assistant Chief Ranger
of Everglades and Dry Tortugas National Parks. "Tomorrow,
10:00 A.M., you and Daniel call me re: new water treatment
plans." Fresh water had been a problem since the fort had been
built. The original designers had created an ingenious plan
where the top of the fort would collect rainwater, which would

then be drawn down through sand filters built inside the fort's frame and stored in one hundred nine vaulted cisterns built below ground level beneath the casemates. The total capacity was a million and a half gallons.

What hadn't been foreseen was that the fort would be too heavy for the land. When tens of tons of brick began to settle, the cisterns cracked, letting seawater in and rendering them useless for fresh-water storage. They'd been sealed off after the Civil War. Since that time, in addition to what rainwater could be caught, drinking water had been barged to the island in wooden casks and rationed as strictly as rum. In 1935 the NPS had taken over Garden Key. Eventually the cisterns beneath the aborted chapel had been rehabilitated for use. Much of the fresh water was collected during the torrential rains that fell in hurricane season. In dry years a reverse osmosis plant that desalinated seawater augmented this.

The entire system was outmoded and needed to be rethought and rebuilt. It would be a time of great upheaval, and Anna rather hoped she'd be home in Mississippi before the digging and cursing and spending commenced.

The second note was from Paul Davidson. Knowing it was almost impossible to get hold of her, Paul left her messages several times a week and wrote her every day. In her quarters, along with groceries and the mysterious box from Molly rumored to contain New York bagels, would be a packet of letters from him.

In Teddy's crabbed hand, Paul said: "Taco and I arrested your favorite drunk today. All three of us missed you. Taco and I probably more than Barstow. Paul." Clay Barstow was a scrawny, amiable old alcoholic Anna arrested every time she found his battered '57 pickup truck crawling along the Trace at fifteen miles an hour, two wheels off the pavement for guidance. They'd become, if not friends, at least comfortable with their relationship as jailer and jailed. As Sheriff of Claiborne County, Paul must have had to arrest him. Taco, left in Paul's care, rode in the front seat of the Sheriff's car each day. The three-legged dog would be gleefully spoiled by the time Anna returned. She laughed even as she felt the muscles around her heart tighten with an inexplicable pain.

This subtle form of heart attack had been with Anna since

the Friday night Paul had taken her to the Episcopal church in
Port Gibson, where he occasionally fulfilled the office of priest
when Father Sam was out of town and when Paul's duties of ap-
prehending criminals didn't take precedence over his job of forgiving them. It had been late spring. The foliage around the
two-century-old, barn-red church had already matured into a fe-
cund green that whispered of summer. The leaves were so thick
that no sun dappled through.

St. James Church was stuffy and, as churches seem to be between choir practice and Sunday services, preternaturally still;
more than simply an absence of sound, a deepening of silence
until one could almost believe it had become active through the
alchemy of some unseen listening ear. Those who'd been
washed in the blood of the Lamb would probably say it was the
presence of God.

To Anna it had more the feel of the yawning silence of a well
inviting a dark fall that was as seductive as it was terrifying.

Leading her by the hand, Paul took her down the side aisle.
The sun was close to setting. From its place near the horizon
beyond the far bank of the Mississippi River, the rays cut horizontally beneath the protective canopy of antebellum oaks.
Light so saturated with color it collected on the polished
wooden bench in puddles of ruby, emerald, topaz and cobalt
poured through the stained-glass depiction of St. Francis holding a lamb.

Paul ushered her into this rainbow-drenched pew, then
seated himself in the pew in front of her. He twisted around and
put his forearms on the seatback, his eyes level with hers. His
blond hair, not so much going gray as fading at the temples, was
dyed a rich auburn by a fold of St. Francis's robe, and he looked
closer to thirty than fifty. His eyes, customarily a blue that Anna
found varied in hue as much as the sky, depending on his internal weather, showed violet in the strange light.

Maybe because she'd been alone for so many years, maybe
because she'd chosen to be blind to the signs, Anna hadn't
known he'd brought her to St. James to propose. His divorce,
not a particularly pleasant exercise in emotional law, was
scarcely two weeks old. Anna thought she had time.

From his shirt pocket he removed the clichéd black velvet
box. Anna blinked in the manner of an iguana on speed. She

was a trained law-enforcement officer. How could she have missed a clue the size of a two-carat diamond ring box in a man's breast pocket?

It was two carats. Anna asked. She couldn't help herself. It was the biggest diamond she'd ever seen outside a jewelry-store window. Light, green from the grass under the saint's feet, caught in the facets till it glowed like kryptonite. Anna felt her strength being drained away.

Paul held it out to her, but she could not raise her hands from where they rested, palms up on her thighs like fainting white spiders.

"You with me, sweetheart?"

Sweetheart. She'd grown to love the endearments he was so comfortable with. Darling. Honey. She'd not yet been able to say them back, but she planned to give it a shot real soon. Zach had never called her sweet names. He'd called her "Pigeon," and she had thought she loved it.

Anna had not wanted Zach there in the light with her and Paul and fear and hope, and she'd shaken her head to rid her mind of her first husband's face.

"You're not with me?" Paul asked.

"No. It's just that . . . I'm with you." She tried to smile and found it was a whole lot easier than she thought it would be. There was happiness nearby. Anna could feel it rising in place of the listening silence.

Paul looked at her closely, answering her smile with the slow southern warmth that had first warmed her loins and then come to warm her heart. "Good. I brought you to this church, my church, the house of my God, because I know you're not exactly on a first-name basis with the Almighty. Maybe you don't always think he—"

"She."

"—she exists." He reached out, stroked her cheek with such gentleness she felt tears prick at her eyes and confuse her mind. "I brought you here to ask you to marry me because I want you to know my belief is enough. God comes or doesn't, is or isn't, manifests or vanishes according to forces I cannot begin to understand. I have chosen this," and though he didn't gesture at the church, Anna felt as if he had. "What you choose is for you.

I will never push or pry or expect. Freedom of religion. An
American marriage." Again he smiled. Again the kryptonite
flashed. Anna felt a new sort of joy bubbling up around her.
From somewhere in the dark of her mind she heard Zach whisper. "Pigeon, you're my person..." and she found an inner
voice responding to the old litany: "No, you're my..." Again
she shook her head to rattle out the vision, and she wondered
when Zach had changed from an angel to a ghost.

"No. No. Don't say no," Paul was murmuring and reaching
out to take her face between his hands. Dislodged, the diamond
in its box fell into Anna's open palm. A sign.

"A good catch," she argued aloud.

"I am," Paul promised. "I will be."

"I'm sure you would be," Anna said, pulling herself out of
the jewel-lit church and back into the stony gloom of her office
with its firing slit for a window. Born of the flashback—not the
first she had of Paul's offer of marriage—a juxtaposition of joy
and haunting filled her lungs as it had in St. James Church. She
blew it out on a gust of air.

"I'm about to lock up," Teddy called back. "Are you going to
be awhile?"

"No. I'm done," Anna replied, glad to have the impetus to
move. The message about the water-system meeting she left on
the desk. The note from Paul she carried with her. When she got
back to her quarters she would tuck it in a painted box Molly
had brought her from her trip to Russia when Anna was still in
college and her sister was already a rising star in the field of
psychiatry. The box was too full to close, but though she felt
mildly absurd because of it, Anna couldn't bring herself to
throw the notes away.

"Got everything?" Teddy asked, sounding like a kindergarten teacher asking a five-year-old if she went to the bathroom before letting her on the bus for a field trip.

Anna held up her net bag as proof she was allowed to go,
and slipped out into the stark sun and shade of the parade
ground. A brick walk, not original to the fort but added by the
National Park Service, circumnavigated the inner court next to
the casemates.

Anna's temporary quarters were directly across from the

sally port, so one direction was no shorter than the other. The most direct route was across, but the grass was Serengeti brown, the air still and bright and seeming to hold the glare as well as the heat of the day. She turned south, taking the shaded side.

Lanny Wilcox had left or, if Daniel was correct, been snatched away from Fort Jefferson hurriedly. Nothing of his had gone with him but for a suitcase of clothes. As a consequence—housing in short supply in a place so small and so removed—Anna had arrived having no appropriate place to perch. After much discussion (including that of making her roommates with Duncan, the historian and interpreter, his wife and their seven-year-old son—an arrangement that had everyone concerned up in arms) the powers that be had grudgingly allowed her to live in the superintendent's quarters. "Superintendent's quarters" was something of a misnomer. In reality they served as VIP guest quarters. Mostly they sat empty, ever clean, ever ready, on the off chance some senator or congressman should call and want a place for the weekend. The quarters were given to Anna with the caveat that if somebody important were to want them she'd be bumped out to share space with the seven-year-old in a bed shaped like a racecar.

Since that had yet to happen, Anna was pleased enough with her living arrangements. In the second tier, the superintendent's quarters took up two of the old casemates. Like the office, inside it was square, modern and white. To either side of a comfortable living-room-cum-kitchen were two large bedrooms, each with two sets of bunk beds and a small bath.

What elevated it from adequate to grand was the "porch." The prefabricated box that formed the living space took less than half the width of the fort's second deck. The other half was original, with broad, high openings framing views of the Gulf, the lighthouse on Loggerhead Key and every sunset.

Only two picnic tables sat between Anna's front door and an uninterrupted view to the end of the world.

"I'm home," she called as she opened the door to her apartment and banged her snorkel and fins past the screen. Theoretically she was supposed to confine herself to the bunkroom on the left, but she'd opened the door to its mirror image on the other side of the kitchen to make the place larger and more interesting. It had yet to get her forgiven for denying access to the outdoors.

"I'm home. It's me. Come out," she called hopefully. Just as she was beginning to believe he'd reconsidered her reprieve and decided to extend her punishment, Piedmont came trotting out of the forbidden suite, his yellow-ringed tail held high, the end curved just enough to be stylish.

An amber-eyed yellow tiger, found treed by a Texas flash flood, Piedmont probably hadn't a drop of Siamese blood in his veins, but he had always been extraordinarily vocal. As he trotted over to Anna's feet he sounded so much like a fussy old man carping about his day that she laughed and picked him up to rub all the right places under his chin.

She'd wondered whether it was a kindness to drag him to the middle of the ocean but, once the trauma of cat travel was over, she'd congratulated herself every day on the wisdom of her decision. With a cat in it, a home was never empty. Echoes, like mice, were frightened from the corners, and loneliness, though still possible, had blunter teeth.

Mutual admiration firmly established, Anna carried the cat over to the sofa. The living-room–kitchen area was rectangular, with stove, refrigerator and sink along the wall overlooking the parade ground. The "living room" was a chair, couch and coffee table arranged before a huge picture window onto the shaded brick of the casemate and the ragged-edged brick "window" with a view of Loggerhead. The furniture was a cut above standard issue—this was, after all, the superintendent's quarters—made of light-colored wood with white canvas cushions. On the low coffee table was Anna's promised loot: letters from home and the much-discussed box from her sister, Molly.

Unable to enjoy anything till sweat, salt and sand had been rinsed off, Anna showered, slipped on a short rayon dress—a trick she'd learned living through Mississippi summers—and sat on the sofa with Piedmont at one elbow and a glass of iced tea on the end table at the other.

Unopened boxes. Packages that came through the mail. Parcels wrapped in brown paper. She'd always loved them. For a few seconds she just sat enjoying the anticipation. Piedmont meowed and butted her in the ribs, then walked prickly-pawed across her lap, slinking his fat tail beneath her chin.

"You think there's catnip treats in there for you?" she asked, and he meowed again. "Okay. We open it." From long-standing love, she and Piedmont pretended to understand one another's language. After so many years together, maybe they did.

Molly was a belt-and-suspenders sort of woman and had bound the package round with fiber strapping tape as if she shipped hazardous gas over rough terrain. Anna had to cut into the package with a carving knife. When she got it open there was no salt-baked smell of bagels or Styrofoam peanuts heralding fragile toys. In a thick nest of folded newspaper were two bundles of letters tied up with string, and a handful of black and white pictures sealed in a sandwich baggie.

The letters looked familiar. They were addressed in a flowing and faded hand to Peggy Broderick, Warwick, Massachusetts. Anna and Molly's grandmother had been one of eight children, six of them girls. The eldest, Anna remembered vaguely, was named Molly. She had raised their grandmother, Peggy, one of the younger children, after their mother had died. "Unknown causes" was written in the family Bible. Having borne eight kids, Anna guessed she'd just worn out.

The letters and the pictures were in a cedar chest in the attic during the years Molly and Anna were growing up. As the eldest, Molly had inherited this scrap of family history along with the old Bible. They'd probably been moldering in a storage unit in the basement of her West End Avenue apartment building ever since. The old chest, originally a hope chest for one of the girls, had been filled with letters from a time when keeping correspondence was deemed important. These letters must be a small part of that collection.

A crisp, buff-colored piece of notepaper embossed with the initials M.P., MD, rested on top. Stationery was a weakness of Molly's. Even missives as unprepossessing as "don't forget to take out the garbage" were often scrawled on paper so rich and fine Anna could almost smell the sweat of Egyptians laboring in the papyrus.

She took the note out and read it aloud to the cat, who'd taken the split-second opportunity as she unfolded it to leap into the open box.

Dear Anna,

On hearing you were bored and restless, Frederick reminded me how dearly you love corpses, murder and mayhem of all kinds. I'm not sure this will fill the bill but, lacking in blood and edged weapons, it's the best I could do short of coming down there and killing somebody for your amusement. The letters are to our great-great-grandmother, Peggy, from her sister, Raffia, who was married to a captain in the Union Army. For three years he was stationed on that unprepossessing sand spit upon which you've decided to maroon yourself.

In hopes this will pass the time and keep you out of trouble—

Love,
Molly

"Hah," Anna said. "Trouble would have to swim too far to get to me. Out you go, Piedmont."

Not willing to submit to being lifted from the box like a common pest, the cat leapt out. Having landed neatly on the coffee table, he licked a paw to indicate his stunning indifference to the box and its contents.

Anna took out the bundles and, for reasons she wasn't sure of, sniffed them. Maybe there was the faintest scent of cedar or lavender. Because they'd been written when women wore long dresses and carried parasols, Anna's imagination might have created a memory of perfume that had evaporated a hundred years before.

Each had the return address:

> Mrs. Joseph Coleman
> Wife of Captain Coleman
> U.S. Army
> Fort Jefferson

Anna wondered if Mrs. Coleman's address could have been that simple or if she trusted Peggy to know where to write her. Anna had never had much interest in family history, in who had married whom and what year the first had sailed for America.

Letters, handwritten letters, were different. More real because of the immediacy of connection to the hand that held the pen and, so, the mind that directed the hand.

The string binding the bundle was new and undeserving of the care advanced to relics. Molly, in her precise academic way, had arranged the letters, probably by date, oldest last, unless some more abstruse and recondite pattern had seduced her by its mere complexity.

Anna untied the string and draped it over Piedmont's head. The cat continued to wash as if she, the box and the string did not exist.

Having removed the thin pages from the first envelope and unfolded them with care, she began to read.

Dear Peggy,
    Fort Jefferson is the cruelest of places . . .

Fort Jefferson is the cruelest of places. Poor Tilly. I really couldn't blame her—perhaps I should say I could not blame her fairly because, Lord knows, the little beast was getting to be as grating to my nerves as the awful crying she complained of.

"Oh I do wish he'd pass out or something. It'll ruin everything." She said that for the sixth time while bent over my dressing table, dousing herself with face powder that comes dear here in the middle of salty nowhere. Not that I wear it, Peggy, lest you were thinking I had become a fallen woman at the late great age of thirty-seven. No, no such wildness. Not that it would avail me anything on this sand and brick island. Here, thanks to summer storms and high seas keeping the ships from the dock, I shall be glad if I still have my teeth when I turn thirty-eight and don't lose them to scurvy. In spite of heat, dirt and the rest of it she grows more beautiful every day. I couldn't bear it if she lost even a single tooth. Not to mention what Molly would do to me. When she sent Tilly to live with us I'm sure she had a far more glamorous life in mind than that which Fort Jefferson offers. It's no place for a sixteen-year-old girl regardless of how "hoydenish" she was becoming in Warwick.

Just as I was choosing to be kind to our little sister despite her wastrel ways with my face powder, another awful wail came in with the wind. It was as if it were a live thing, one of the ghosts Molly sees and tries to pray back into hell. The window curtains bellied out, the lamps were set to dancing and the most inhuman sound crawled up our backs like dead men's fingers.

"Raffia, can't you get Joseph to do something? Knock him on the head or something? Just till the show's over?" (We were to perform " 'Tis True I Have Flirted," both playing very young girls for comic effect.)

With that compassionate plea, Tilly threw down the powder puff, scattering dust everywhere. I could hear the precious particles hitting the lamp chimney and burning, a whispery crinkle at the edges of my mind. Luanne, the woman that does for us— you remember me mentioning her, a Negro who belonged to Mrs. Dicks, the lighthouse keeper's wife—will be looking at me with dog's eyes when she has to clean it up. Because she was born a slave, Luanne never learned to read the Bible, but she is as good at making me feel guilty as Sister Mary Francis used to be.

"You're a baby," I told her. "And all of us have spoiled you rotten. Joseph can't just give an order like that. Who knows what the man did? If he was caught drinking on sentry duty he could be shot." I have been an army wife for twenty years. Four of those we were at war. Yet I've never served at a place where corporal punishment is so swift and brutal as here. Joseph tells me it's a necessary outgrowth of living at a prison camp. Even here I'd never heard crying of the like gusting into our rooms. It had that anguished animal sound of a wild thing dying in a trap.

"They oughtn't be let drink," Tilly said primly. Oh to be a girl again when right and wrong can be settled by decree. I doubt, were the Union Army comprised utterly of ladies for temperance armed with rifles, they could keep liquor off Garden Key. As it is the soldiers crave drink more than do the prisoners. There's little here for amusement but fishing and becoming drunk.

There came another shriek so sharp and so raw I could not but believe it tore the flesh from the throat of the man making it.

"If he doesn't quit, I'm going to be sorry he wasn't shot," Tilly announced.

Out of deference to Molly and because Tilly can get a bit above herself, I put on my big-sisterly voice and told her: "That was unchristian. You confess that next time Father Burnett comes or you will go to hell."

"I'd probably feel right at home."

The little minx. I almost laughed, but Molly worked so hard to bring us up in the church after Mother and Daddy died, I didn't have the heart.

With my fussing about Tilly I hope you're not getting the impression I am sorry to have her here. I am sorry, but only for her. Tilly deserves more from her sixteenth year than to be marooned on an ugly world full of unhappiness, heat and sickness. Selfishly I am glad she's come. She is so much company for me. As you know, Joseph rarely talks—at least not to me. Saving it for his beloved "men" I suppose. Even the simple right of an army wife to complain about rations and quarters is denied me. When I see the hardship of the prisoners and the soldiers I cannot bring myself to enjoy whining about my lot. The freshest meat and vegetables, the cleanest water (the cisterns beneath the fort are a dismal failure—salt water leaks in—drinking water must be brought by barge) come to the officers.

We do try our best to see that the prisoners' lives are bearable. This war has made us keepers—if not literally, then very nearly so—of our brothers. Joseph's closest friend is one of the inmates here, Colonel Battersea. As fate would have it, the colonel was Joseph's instructor at West Point. They became friends when Joseph was a cadet—the colonel and Mrs. Battersea took him under their wing. Now they are in opposing armies and my husband's old mentor is his ward.

The prisoners of war are to be released, but no one yet knows when. Colonel Battersea's wife has a wasting disease, and Joseph has been trying to affect his early release but has yet to succeed.

Where was I? Ah yes: getting ready for our show. I'd secured the mirror and the lamplight from Tilly and was setting about trying to blot out with the paint pots the ravages of the years. I'm still as slim and upright as when last you saw me (being "condemned to barrenness," as Joseph so kindly puts it, has its compensations). My hair is no longer strictly light brown. There are marked incursions of white. But, by parting it left of center and wearing my braids wrapped round my head I can hide the worst of it. My skin is what gives me away as very nearly forty. Much as I try, the sun has me looking like the self-same field hand Molly used to tell us we'd resemble if we didn't wear our bonnets.

For a time I painted and primped and powdered—my work cut out for me as I've said. Tilly stood at my shoulder burbling with "compliments": "Oh, Raffia, you don't look nearly so *old* with rouge. You know, from a distance, if only there weren't all that gray in your hair, you could *almost* play the part as well as me."

At that, I said, "No thank you. I am perfectly happy to be the shadowy background against which your brilliance can show all the more brightly." That kept her from heaping more coals of kindness on my head for a few minutes while she worked out whether I was being cutting or genuinely humble.

Into my hard-won silence came another of those terrible screams, this one in a dying fall, almost as if it changed after it was uttered from the cry of a human being to the wail of the wind through the casemates. It gave me a turn, I don't mind telling you. I had that sudden cold and shaking sensation Molly told us came when "a goose steps on your grave." This was most definitely a whole flock stomping on mine. Tilly slammed the window and the change in the air upset the light. In the sudden dance of the flames my face didn't look like me.

It frightened me so badly I did the only thing I could think of and yelled at Tilly for closing the sash with such violence.

"I'm going out there," Tilly yelled back. She stepped behind the screen in the corner that I use for dressing. Bits of clothing flew over the top.

"Don't you pull your skirt over your head," I warned her. The amount of paint on her face would ruin the fabric.

She stuck her head out and said: "I'm not having everything spoiled after we've worked so hard." The fright the last cry had given us sliced years off her. She sounded like a peevish little girl again but, even through the stage makeup, I could see, along with fear and selfishness, was compassion.

"No you are not going out there," I snapped back. "This is army business and no concern of ours." I had been of half a mind to go try and stop the wailing myself, and not for the good of our theatrical evening. Hearing myself utter those words: "this is army business and no concern..." decided me. I cannot tell you how many times over the eighteen years I've been married I have heard Joseph say exactly those words. Each time I tried to right some small wrong, help some needful person, or even, God forbid, ask Joseph where he'd been when he came in at two or three or four o'clock in the morning, he said: "it's army business and no concern of yours."

Of all the phrases in language and literature, hearing myself parrot that one upset me nearly as much as anything that had happened heretofore.

"We'll both go," I said.

Most everybody had already gone to the mess hall or was shut up in their quarters getting ready to go on stage. Still I told Tilly to hush. Luanne had been set to watching Mrs. Caulley's three children, and I don't know which of the four shrieked the loudest at not being allowed to watch the entertainment. I was afraid the sound of our voices would start the weeping and pleading all over again.

Tilly promised to be "quiet as a mouse," as she has since she was three, but I took it as a sign she'd matured when she refrained from making those tiny squeaky mouse sounds as she walked.

"We've got to hurry," I warned. "Major Tanner is making his curtain speech at eight, and Joel Lane is singing 'Take Me Home' right after," I said quickly. Calling of Private Lane to mind was oddly prophetic—pathetic—as you shall see if I ever finish this letter-become-tome.

The mention of Joel's singing stopped her planned argument, as I knew it would. In this topsy-turvy place where our enemy prisoners are here for more sanguine reasons than the prisoners of our beloved Union, this story I'm about to tell isn't as peculiar as it might seem.

Both Tilly and I had taken notice of Private Lane, a prisoner, a Johnny Reb and a secessionist, when he was set to hauling crushed shell to refurbish the walkway across the parade ground. Given that litany of his crimes against society, I was yet to find out the worst.

Private Lane is imminently noticeable. Six foot or taller with black hair, blue eyes and a smile with no teeth knocked or rot-ted out of it. Handsome as he is, it's his voice that does the damage. Training or natural talent has turned his native drawl into a weapon I expect few women could resist without effort. I know this because Tilly, being no better than she should, spoke to him.

That might well have been the end of it, but fate chose to make Private Lane a part of our lives. Not two days later, the prisoners, along with the engineers and laborers brought in from New York, were put to hauling eight-inch Columbiads—fearsome cannons—to the third tier. Raising and placing these great guns is something to see. Tilly and I and a couple of the other ladies decided to brave the heat of the day to watch the process.

Because manpower and life are the only things held cheap here, the men were lifting with block and tackle, using ropes, pulleys and the strength of their backs. The heat had melted the rules, and the officer in charge allowed the prisoners to work with their shirts off. As they began lifting the cannon, easily as long as two men put end-to-end and weighing lord knows how much, the confederate soldiers started singing.

I suppose it was a song they'd grown up knowing, a working song used by field slaves. The Negroes on the other lines picked it up, and as they hauled, they sang. A clear tenor rose, singing counterpoint: Private Joel Lane, muscles bunched, half naked, voice soaring.

Well, Miss Tilly's breath sucked in so audibly I thought she'd stepped on a nail or a scorpion till I saw where she looked.

When the cannon was seated and the show at an end, Tilly and I and the rest of the ladies started down the spiral stairway that connects the tiers in that section of the fort. Tilly was just ahead of me, not paying attention, and I was focused on not treading on her skirt tail where she let it drag over the steps. Of a sudden she says in the most casual of ways how intelligent Private Lane looked.

Hah! I, too, admired his "intelligence" till he put his shirt back on.

Three days after this display of Joel Lane's intellect we were to see him again in a more intimate setting.

As I've mentioned, this has been a difficult summer. The end

of the war but prisoners (and soldiers) not yet free, the heat,
endless storms, bad food and water, yellow jack and bone-break
fever rampant, has morale at a dreadful low. I'd not thought it
could get worse when word came that the Lincoln conspirators
were to be sent here to serve out their sentences. Fort Jefferson
is a violent place, but with this unwelcome bit of news, violence, soldiers on prisoners, Negroes on whites, unionists on
confederates, officers on men, has become epidemic.

In an attempt to raise morale, the post surgeon, Captain
Caulley, chose to organize a theatrical troupe. It was an excellent effort. Much of the agony and anger the men suffer is borne
in boredom. I'm sure Captain Caulley's motives were altruistic,
but it also appealed to him on a practical level. It is he and his
corps who are called upon to attend this increase in gunshots,
knife wounds, broken noses, heads, teeth and knuckles. Joseph,
not a lover of the arts in any of their guises, was in favor of anything that would stop activities that keep guards and prisoners
off the work rosters.

In accordance with the surgeon's plan, the call went. Anyone
who had a talent was to report to the officers' mess after parade
the following day. One hundred and fifty-three men and seven
of the women including Tilly and me answered. The men were
excited for the first time in a long while over something other
than gambling or brawling.

Private Joel Lane was among them, with his dark hair and
angel voice and, unfortunately, his shirt. That's the day I
learned the worst of him. The boy is not a deserter, a killer or a
thief, but neither is he the son of a rich plantation owner. He is
an actor. Before the war he traveled with his father's theatrical
company, making his living singing in comic operas and playing the female leads in his father's Shakespearean productions.

Needless to say, Joel was cast in Captain Caulley's production. Because of their matching youth and beauty, he and Tilly
were given a romantic duet in the third part of our entertainment. I immediately volunteered to play accompaniment on the
harpsichord and have watched them ever since with a hawklike
intensity that would do Molly proud.

This, then, is why I'd invoked Private Lane's name to get
Tilly through quarters and to the parade ground quickly and
quietly.

There are no rules about where the women here can go—or very few at any rate. The laundresses often go to the cells of prisoners whose families send them money to pay for laundry and such. The prisoners are, of course, paid for the labor they do in building the fort, and the women will walk to the store on the quay to buy their necessaries. I've never felt any fear moving around the fort, night or day.

This night was markedly different. Perhaps I'd not completely shaken the chill I'd felt at the last cry. Or perhaps it was the edges of the storm that flirted with us, though, Lord knows, I've had plenty of experience with weather of all kinds here. The parade ground was empty. I've seldom seen it empty. On an island not more than ten acres—not large enough for the fort, the moat extends into the sea itself—with eight to twelve hundred souls, there simply is no space where one can be truly alone. This night the parade ground was uninhabited but for the wind, which was fitful and sudden.

The walkway out from the officers' quarters is edged along both sides with whitewashed cannonballs. It can look quite grand—or as grand as we can muster here. Either my fancy or the moonlight twisting through the scudding clouds tricked my eyes and, for a moment, they appeared as human skulls.

Few of the closed casemates showed lights at their small windows, and the open casemates looked blacker than black. The unfinished barracks and armory looked ready to come to life, great unimaginable beasts but with claws and fangs.

Add to this the skittery racket made by the wind through the dry palm fronds tossing in sudden frantic life then falling silent as if the winds of all the world had died forever and perhaps you'll understand my uncharacteristic drama.

"Don't they look like a bunch of skulls all laid out in a line by some demented ogre?" Tilly said.

Hearing her echo my unpleasant thought, I nearly jumped out of my skin. To comfort myself and bring us back to the ordinary, I pinched her arm hard enough to make her squawk. I marched her firmly forward. She balked and said: "Maybe this isn't proper behavior for the wife and sister-in-law of a commanding officer." Apparently I was not the only one suffering from the megrims. I suppose she, too, felt the whispering of demons and bones. However, I had no intention of letting her wriggle out after she had pestered me half to death about the whole thing not three minutes before.

I said, with what I think you would agree was laudable courage, "Let's get this over or it will be you and not the screaming that spoils the show."

Holding on to Tilly both for comfort and control, I hurried us down the walk and into the blinding shadow under the stand of palms between the officers' quarters and the sally port. I had little doubt but that was where the moaning had emanated from. It's there and behind the unfinished armory nearby most of the corporal punishments are carried out.

I'm not sure what impelled me at this juncture. Tilly would have been willing to abandon the project. Certainly I had no notion of righting wrongs, changing army ways or, heavens forefend, be thanked for trying. Base curiosity of the variety that kills cats must account for it.

"Watch your step," I whispered. "With all the construction there's bound to be nails. You don't want to step on one and get lockjaw because—"

"Because you'd have to knock out my front teeth to feed me and, with no teeth, nobody will marry me and I'll end up an old maid like Molly," Tilly finished for me.

I suppose I said some such before, but I'm sure I never added the part about being an old maid. There are worse fates to be sure. Her mimicry of me was so perfect I was hurt despite being used to Tilly being Tilly.

"When did I get so old?" I said. One should never ask a question to which one does not wish to hear the answer.

"It was having those miscarriages one after the other for years and years."

"There'll be the guard now," I said. We were near to the sally port and I had no intention of pursuing the subject of my age and failures. "Hello the gate," I called.

No one responded. The prickly feeling at the back of my neck returned. First the abandoned parade ground, now no sentries at the gate. The moaning began to build after what had been a comparatively long respite. The fretful wind gusted into the stone and brick cavern that provides egress from the fort. Flames in the lamps secured there jumped then died. In that brief flash I saw—or thought I saw—what caused the crying.

I ceased to wonder the sounds seemed inhuman. The mouth that made them was not a human mouth.

Tilly started toward the wavering light. I grabbed her. "Stay back," I hissed. I was not quick enough.

```
┌─────────┐
│         │
│         │
│    3    │
│         │
│         │
└─────────┘
```

Anna laid the curling pages on her knees. The paper was as thin as dried leaves, and she'd been holding them too tightly. Her thumb and forefinger had pinched a faint crease in the upper right-hand corner. For a moment she sat without moving, without thinking, just taking in the space: Piedmont asleep at her side, throat up, eyes covered with his paws, the sharp contrast of blinds and sunlight striping the window over the sink, the smooth glow of terra-cotta floor tile unifying the living spaces. A sense of having awakened from a strange dream and not knowing where she was pervaded her. Quietly she waited till reality—or the reality the National Park Service paid her to inhabit—reformed around her.

When the room had solidified, she rose, careful not to disturb the sleeping cat, and crossed to the window that looked down on the parade ground. For a fleeting instant she was surprised that the enlisted men's barracks were gone, the officers' mess, the formal walk with its edging of cannonballs. The moment passed and she was relieved to see the tree-spotted expanse of sunburned grass, the casemates, arches open to the parade ground, gun ports opening on the sea, filled with nothing but light and shadow.

The park had a permanent, live-in staff of seven people.

There'd been days Anna couldn't stand the crowd and fled to
the sea. In 1865 there'd been eight to twelve hundred people in
residence. The thought, filling her mind as it did with unwashed
bodies and gabbling voices, made an involuntary shudder run
through her. Perhaps some race memory of the place had come
down through her maternal bloodline.

She ate apples and peanut butter for supper and went to bed
at eight-thirty. Outside it was still daylight.

Her great-great-aunt Raffia's letter followed her into sleep
and manifested itself in confused scenes of Jefferson by torch-
light, actors in blackface, her teeth falling out to scurvy and,
once, the pounding whump of cannon fire that brought her close
to consciousness till the ill-lit and flickering past dragged her
down into sleep again.

Anna woke because somebody was in her room. Out from
the darkness a voice whispered, "Anna, Anna, Anna." Furtive
fingers jabbed at her arm and shoulder. Perhaps Anna was slow
to wake from reverie, but from sleep, never. Fast as a fish flipping on a line, she was off her stomach and half sitting. The poking hand had been caught at the wrist and bent back. The
whisper shifted to: "You're hurting me. It's Teddy, Teddy Shaw."

Anna let go of her gentle marauder and switched on the
lamp by the bedside. Opposite, on the top bunk, she could just
see Piedmont's orange eyes from behind a bulwark of pillows.
Some watchcat.

"What're you doing? Why didn't you knock?" Anna grumbled as she pulled a tee shirt from the floor and dragged it on for
decency's sake.

"I didn't want to startle you," Teddy said, rubbing her wrist.

On the island, Anna'd never thought to lock her doors to protect herself. Maybe she would start locking them to protect others.

"What is it?"

"Bob's not back."

Anna plucked up the black plastic travel alarm that lived on
the bed stand. Four forty. "He was off duty—"

"At midnight. He was off at midnight. He's not back. Four

hours and forty minutes. He's not back. I just woke up and was still by myself."

"Did he call in?" Anna picked her radio up out of the charger behind the clock, and clicked down the mike button.

As Teddy was saying, "He last radioed around eight," Anna was calling "Five-eight-one, five-eight-zero." Three times she repeated first Bob's call number and then her own.

"No answer," she said unnecessarily. "Did you try calling him after eight?"

Teddy had seated herself, not on the bunk opposite but on the foot of the narrow bed Anna slept in, apparently needing to be close. Her wide bottom pinned down the covers, trapping Anna's legs, and she had to make a conscious effort not to kick free.

Teddy shook her head. "No. Bob doesn't like me calling him unless it's an emergency because he could be in the middle of something and me calling might compromise it. And when he's watching something he'll turn his radio clear off. You know how it is. A call at the wrong time could blow your cover."

In her years—and years—with the park service Anna'd only had a "cover" a couple of times. Bob evidently found, created or imagined such situations often enough he and his wife had developed a system for handling them.

"Better let me up," Anna said, nudging to be free of the mummy bag Teddy had inadvertently made of her covers. Teddy stood obediently. Anna got up and began dragging on the pieces of her uniform that were scattered on bunks, floor and bedposts.

"What did he call in at eight for?" Anna asked. She must have heard the call but she had no recollection of it. Chances were, absorbed in her great-great-aunt's letter, part of her mind had registered that the call was not for her and filtered it out as background noise.

"He said he had something going and wouldn't be home for supper." Teddy's voice was muddled. Anna stopped fussing with the Velcro-on-Velcro adjustment of her duty belt and looked up. The woman's face was muddled as well. Fear and pride and quirks of what could be defiance or dishonesty banged into each other till Teddy wore the face of an angry child who sees a treat and cannot choose between wailing or snatching.

Anna stepped into her deck shoes. "Did he say what he had going, boat names or where he was located?"

"He wouldn't have wanted that transmission intercepted," Teddy said, pride momentarily winning out over whatever else boiled beneath her skin.

"Well nobody did, at least not us," Anna said bitterly and pushed down a number of derogatory comments about Buffalo Bob that came to mind. No sense in beating up the man's wife. "I guess we start our search at the dock.

"I'm going to get Danny and Mack up," she told Teddy. Mack was the island's other maintenance man and the one in charge of keeping the six big generators running so the fort had lights, air-conditioning, water pressure and phone service. Both he and Daniel were good boatmen and held mariner's licenses.

"You get on the radio and call the coast guard. Tell them we've a boat and ranger five hours overdue and to please stand by. Tell them we are starting a rudimentary search now."

"Rudimentary?" Teddy's back went up as she prepared to do battle for Bob's right to a full-scale operation, and Anna realized she'd gotten caught up in logistics and forgotten that the object of this exercise was Teddy's husband.

"Sorry to be barking orders," she said, masking her need to be moving with gentleness. "Rudimentary is because of the darkness. We won't be able to see much—just maybe a boat if it's disabled or something like that. But I don't want to wait till first light to move on this."

"I'll get on to the coast guard." Teddy left two steps ahead of Anna. Before rejecting the mainstream for the Dry Tortugas and Bob Shaw, Teddy had been head nurse in an emergency room in Miami. Anna had never seen her under pressure before. Admiring her control and competence, she could see why she'd risen to the top of her profession at a relatively early age. Because of her background and training, Lanny Wilcox had gotten permission to let her set up the fort's "hospital," a room with a clean bed, a sink and what emergency medical supplies they had. It crossed Anna's mind as they clattered down the wooden staircase into the parade ground to tell Teddy to make sure the hospital was ready to receive Bob, should he need medical attention, but she thought better of it. It would only alarm Teddy unnecessarily and, if she hadn't kept the hospital stocked and functioning before now, it would be too late.

"You wake up Cliff and Linda," Anna named the captain and first mate of the *Activa*, the NPS supply boat that had come in that afternoon. "Tell them we need eyes. Tell them to get their dive gear off their boat. We may need it when it gets light."

"Then call the coast guard," Teddy said without slowing or turning around.

"Right."

Off the last step, Teddy broke into a jog as she cut across the parade ground. The moon was just coming on full, and the dry grass shone light as beach sand. The fort walls were silvered, and the empty arches so black the shadows looked to be made of solid matter.

Anna turned right, following the brick path along the ground-level casemates. The southern side of the fort was closed to visitors. The open casemates contained machinery and supplies needed to keep the fort up and running. Three were dedicated to Mack's generators, and two had been enclosed to make employee quarters. Danny lived in the first of these. The two he inhabited had the arches walled up with lumber weathered and in need of paint. A hopelessly modern door with a screen finished off the defacement of history. Anna banged on it soundly.

A moment or two and a dim light appeared in the kitchen window, probably from Danny's bedroom. Not more than thirty seconds passed, but Anna was about to knock again when he opened the door. In place of a standard bathrobe, the maintenance man wore a Japanese kimono, black koi on a field of white that gave his stalwart form the look of a particularly deadly samurai.

"Yeah. What is it? What time is it?"

"The middle of the night," Anna said. "Bob never came home from his shift. I need you to take out one of the boats. We'll be looking for big stuff, the *Bay Ranger* or chunks of it. At first light we'll get a better idea. You dive?"

"Not on purpose."

"Okay. I'm getting Mack. Meet us at the dock."

"Got it."

William Macintyre's quarters were next, nearer the office by the generator rooms. His lights were on. Anna hoped he wasn't up because he was drinking. She didn't know Mack well—he'd been on vacation the first eight days of her stay at Jefferson— but she'd served in enough isolated posts to know that alcohol was a fairly standard form of entertainment in National Parks.

He answered at her first knock. But for shoes and socks he was dressed in a pair of Levi's torn out at the knee and a tee shirt. Mack looked the part of a mechanic. His hands and forearms were scarred from years of working with engines. Black grease was ingrained in the flesh around his nails and the cracks across the pads of his fingers. His clothes smelled faintly of burnt oil and stale gasoline. Like Daniel, he wore a full beard but kept his close-cropped over a box-and-bone jaw. Hair grew in white in places as if it covered old injuries. Though not yet forty, he was nearly bald. The fringe of hair remaining was scraped back into a stringy ponytail.

"You're up late," Anna said.

"What of it?" His voice cracked as if his mouth and throat had gone dry.

Anna looked past the hostility in his light brown eyes. He was cranky but apparently sober. She explained the situation.

"I'm taking the *Atlantic Ranger.* Nobody screws with it but me."

"Okay," Anna said neutrally.

He started to make more demands but instead let his square jaw break in a smile, and his fingers ran over his scalp, remembering the hair that had once flourished there. "Hey. Sorry. Don't think I'm always such an asshole. Bad night's all."

He wanted Anna to ask him why "bad" but she had neither the time nor the inclination. Warm and fuzzy wasn't a management style she had much truck with.

"They happen. Meet us at the dock. Five minutes."

"No problem."

Before his door closed, his sudden rudeness and equally unexpected capitulation were forgotten. Anna's brain was churning out lists of equipment needed. Her eyes saw only the black water and the grid search she drew over it, dividing it into sectors, one for each of the boats.

The office door was ajar, light pouring out. Anna stepped inside. Teddy was just returning from the gloomy recesses where the main radio was housed. The handhelds hadn't the power to reach the mainland. Those calls had to be made from the office, where the radio was hooked to the repeater atop the fort's walls.

"The coast guard has a cutter two hours north of here. It's heading this way," Teddy said.

"I said stand by," Anna replied sharply.

Teddy was not intimidated.

"They were scheduled to hit Key West tomorrow. They started early is all."

"You'll ride with me. You need anything not in the first-aid kit on the *Reef Ranger*, get it now and meet me at the dock."

Teddy swung an orange medical kit out of the shadows at her side. She'd anticipated and done her packing.

The men were already at the boats. Mack had the *Atlantic Ranger*'s engine running and was perched on the bench in front of the wheel, putting on his shoes. He must have sprinted barefoot to reach the water before Anna.

She was unimpressed. "Not a fucking footrace," she muttered.

"What?" Teddy was at her heels.

"Nothing." Anna made a mental note to calm down, breathe. The situation was crawling up her spine. She didn't want it fogging her thinking. Intentionally slowing her pace, she arrived on the dock, breathed in and out slowly, and took stock of her resources.

Danny was there, bulky and reassuring. Cliff, the tall, lean, gray-haired, gentleman-captain of the *Activa*, sat on a piling looking alert and interested, his long-fingered hands folded serenely in his lap. Cliff had the most boating experience of the group. Anna'd never asked his age, but it was probably closer to seventy than sixty. For all his years on the sea, he looked more like an English professor than an old salt. Everything about him suggested the hush of libraries and leather-bound books. Linda, the *Activa*'s first mate, stood next to him, her short blond hair in spikes. She was no taller than Anna but probably a good deal stronger. Linda was the best diver the park had, and it showed in the sculpt of her shoulders and calves. Too many years under a tropical sun had tanned her skin like fine saddle leather.

First order of business was to catch Mack's eye and draw her finger across her throat. He cut his engine as if he'd been expecting the request. Despite the heat, faint wraiths of steam rose from the *Atlantic*. In the back of her mind, Anna made a note to have Danny check it. Clearly it was running too hot. She gave the quiet a moment to settle their scattered thoughts, then spelled out what she needed.

The *Bay Ranger*, the boat Bob took on patrol, was not in its slip. The first question was answered: Bob had not returned to the fort. If they found him, it would be at sea.

The *Reef* and *Atlantic Rangers*, both twenty-five-foot Boston Whalers, and the researcher's boat, the *Curious*, a twenty-foot Maco, would be captained by Anna, Mack and Danny, respectively. Running the spotlights and acting as a second pair of eyes: Teddy on the *Reef* with Anna, Cliff with Mack and Linda on the *Curious* with Daniel.

One hundred square miles: on the map it didn't appear that sizable. For three small boats searching at night, the area was formidable. Anna divided it into rectangles, east, central and west. She and Teddy went west; Mack and Cliff took the middle; Danny and Linda the eastern third. The plan was simple: mentally lay a grid over the sector and drive the boats in a zigzag pattern along imaginary lines.

Having cleared the harbor, Anna pushed the throttle till the boat planed, and steered southwest past Loggerhead Key.

The search was to be blessed with absolutely flat water. The air was so still and warm and wet it felt as if it had knit together, forming a heavy blanket that crushed the movement of the ocean. The Atlantic lay still as a pool in a deep cavern. Water and sky were tropical ink, the stars and the moon startlingly bright by contrast.

Teddy stood beside Anna. The moon was several days past full, but with clear sky above and glittering sea below it gave the illusion of much light. Its cool silver touch thinned Teddy's face and collected in shadows under her usually invisible cheekbones. Straight, proud, grim and unspeaking, her hair slipping behind her in a wind of their own making, she looked every inch the courageous yet tragic heroine. Anna wondered if she played out a role in the fantasy she and her husband so assiduously cultivated. The uncharitable thought that the Shaws, craving heroics and acts of derring-do, had staged this whole disappearance for the twisted fun of it—a ranger version of Munchausen's syndrome—crossed Anna's mind.

They reached the buoy marking the southwestern boundary of the park. Anna cut her engines and showed Teddy how to work the searchlight, moving it in slow arcs aimed low to pick up shadows of anything floating on the water's surface. Then, engine just above idle, they started the painstaking process of searching.

Twice they spotted floating objects. Both were lobster traps. Outside park boundaries, lobster fishermen laid their lines; traps on the ocean floor tied one to another with floating buoys to mark where they lay. Storms, faulty lines and ships' propellers routinely set the traps and buoys free to drift into park waters. Anna dutifully hauled them onboard. Disposing of them was problematical. Already Fort Jefferson had a pile the size of a Sherman tank in one of the casemates. The only way to get rid of the Styrofoam floats was to get somebody to haul them to the mainland. Cliff and Linda weren't anxious to add garbage scow to the *Activa*'s resume.

Lobster traps were the sum total of excitement until they'd worked north past Loggerhead and a faint green-gray light on the eastern horizon suggested sunrise. Then they got a call from Danny.

"Got something," he said succinctly.

"What?" Anna radioed back.

Never particularly disciplined on the airwaves, Danny replied: "A whole shit-load. Oil. Flotsam. We're about three-quarters of a mile west of East Key. Better get on over here. We'll flash our light."

"Oh, God," Teddy murmured. Her stoicism evaporated and, with it, Anna's doubts about the veracity of Bob's disappearance. Had the Shaws planned a bit of theatrics, oil and flotsam obviously hadn't factored in.

"Easy," Anna said. "We don't know what Danny found. Could be a spill from a passing tanker." *Lame,* she thought and pushed the throttle forward heading east. Within minutes, Teddy spotted Danny's light flashing. Anna adjusted her course accordingly. Over the radio, just under the burr of engine noise, she heard Danny calling Mack to make sure he and Linda had gotten the message.

As they neared the *Curious,* she slowed to a crawl and told Teddy to work the searchlight. Faint and iridescent, a sheen of oil spread across the water, breaking into toxic rainbows in the wake of the *Reef Ranger.* Pieces of flotsam running with petroleum-induced colors floated in the mess, as did other, less identifiable bits of what had presumably been a boat.

"Holy smoke," Anna muttered. "It didn't just sink, it was blown to kingdom come."

Teddy had her knuckles shoved in her mouth to stop her emotions from bleating forth. In the backwash of the light Anna caught the liquid glitter of tears. Teddy's eyes glowed, large and unsettling, like an animal's in the night.

Anna put the engine into reverse and stopped their forward motion. The engine stilled, she took the searchlight from Teddy and began slow, sweeping arcs across the greasy black water. From Danny's boat Linda let her searchlight follow Anna's, doubling the wattage. The sheen of oil was thin and would dissipate in an hour or more, scattering itself till it would be detectable only to sensitive instruments. That it was still obvious to the naked eye could be accounted for by the fact that sea and sky were preternaturally still. The disturbance from the *Reef Ranger*'s arrival continued to move under the mess, though at a greater distance now, like ripples on a pond.

"Not much left," Danny said of what they were assuming had once been a boat.

Though the *Reef* and the *Curious* were fifty or sixty feet apart, in the absolute silence he sounded so close Anna's skin twitched like a horse's when a fly alights.

"Not much," she agreed.

The lights were picking out only bits and fragments: fiber-glass, wood. A ship's line, made to float and bright screaming yellow, caught the light so suddenly it seemed to snake through the oil.

"Line," Linda said unnecessarily. To Anna's knowledge the first mate neither smoked nor drank strong liquor, but her voiced rasped, bourbon over gravel, like a skid-row actor.

"I see it."

"We got a piece of hull," Danny said. "See if you can spot it for 'em, Linda. It wasn't one of ours. Not white. Green. Kind of a glittery metallic bottle green like those newer speedboats got. I don't think it was Bob went down."

Beside her Anna heard a low mewling cry, barely audible and the first sound Teddy Shaw had made since Danny radioed.

"Look." Linda pointed with her light south of the circle of oil. "Not the hull but something." The sun had crept closer to the horizon, chasing faint pink-and-gold light ahead to reflect off the water. Against this backdrop, Linda's keen eyes had spotted a shape.

The *Reef* was closest. "I'll get it," Anna said.

Having started the engine, she backed slowly away from the slick, wanting to disturb things as little as possible. She motored up close, and Teddy lifted the thing out of the water with a boat hook and dropped it on deck. "A life jacket," Anna called to the *Curious*.

"Not one of ours," Teddy said, and Anna could hear the relief Teddy'd not had the courage to feel till tangible proof it was not her husband's boat was in her hands.

"Whoever it belonged to wasn't wearing it. Straps are intact, buckles unbroken," Anna said. "Probably shoved under a seat and blown free in the explosion."

"Bob always wears his. Always," Teddy said. Hope was added to the relief, and Anna was glad for her.

Bob religiously wore a personal flotation device. It wasn't standard issue but one of those sleek little jobs that rest at the small of the back. It would keep him afloat but had to be deployed. If he were unconscious when he hit the water it would prove nothing but an additional anchor dragging him to the bottom.

The hum of an approaching boat caught Anna's attention. She threaded back around the cabin to the radio and called the *Atlantic Ranger.*

"Mack," she said when he'd answered. "We've got oil and flotsam. Looks like a boat blew up, burned to waterline and sank. It's not the *Bay Ranger.* No sign of Bob or his boat. You and Cliff keep looking. Linda and I'll dive on this as soon as the light gets a little stronger."

Silence followed, then a couple clicks of the mike as Mack fingered it. "We'll need to give you a hand with that," he said finally.

"Linda and I'll take a look. If we need you or Cliff to help with the underwater work, I'll give you a call."

Another silence, then: "Ten-four." The National Park Service had abandoned the ten codes years before, choosing plain speaking for their radio communications, but some of the numbers, ten-four for "okay" and ten-twenty for "location," had become so ingrained in everyday language that they persisted.

Anna could understand Mack's reticence to continue the search. In a post so isolated the arrival of groceries and mail was considered a grand occasion it would be hard to be turned away from a bona-fide adventure. Quicker than thought, she sent a prayer down to Poseidon that this would prove to be the peak of the day's excitement and that Bob would turn up unharmed and with a good excuse for his nocturnal wandering. She doubted her prayer would be heard. Bob was a stickler for rules. If he were alive, he would have radioed in. The usual reasons for a man staying out all night didn't apply at Fort Jefferson. The only single women near enough for an assignation were the lighthouse keepers on Loggerhead Key and Donna and Patrice not only outweighed and towered over Ranger Shaw but had eyes only for each other.

For the duration of the dive, Anna abdicated leadership to Linda. For Anna, scuba diving was a sport. On several occasions, the most notable being in the icy waters of Lake Superior, she'd gone on difficult or dangerous dives, but compared to the first mate of the *Activa* she was a neophyte. Linda had participated in and led dives all over the world. She had rescued other divers, recovered bodies and searched for sunken treasure. Treasure was one of the lures that had brought her, finally, to the Dry Tortugas, a major shipping lane during the days when Spanish galleons were heavy with gold plundered from the Incas and the Aztecs.

Today would have more to do with bodies than booty, Anna suspected. Or, worse, pieces of bodies. Whole corpses didn't bother her much, but bits here and there were a tad unsettling. And, though she would never admit it even to herself, she

wasn't all that gung ho to go flippering around in what might
amount to fisherman soup.

The *Reef* was rafted off the *Curious,* and Anna and Teddy
joined Linda and Danny on the research boat. Danny had
backed it up to be well clear of the oil slick so the divers
wouldn't foul their gear or get petroleum on the neoprene of
their wet suits when they went over the side. As Anna and Linda
donned dive suits and scuba gear, the sun sprang from the sea.
In these latitudes there was little twilight; day and night were
sudden and complete. While Anna buckled and tugged and
checked equipment, Linda went through her safety spiel.
Wrecks, especially recent wrecks, were notoriously unstable. It
was possible parts of it could still be burning. The women took
a moment to rehearse the rudimentary hand signals: help, look
and go to the surface. Then they rolled off the gunwale into the
water. Because the air temperature had yet to rise with the sun,
the water was a few degrees warmer and the initial plunge felt
good, like the first immersion in a warm bath. Suddenly weightless and warm, Anna felt her muscles relax and her mind empty
of the surface's fussy thoughts.

The sun low, water made murky by the recent disturbance,
the bottom was a mottled dark area seen through a fog of particulate matter. Anna guessed the depth at around thirty or forty
feet. The boat they sought had gone down in what was considered deep water in the shallow, reef-filled park. Just to the east
of the boundary line the ocean floor dropped thousands of feet
down a sheer wall.

Quicker to get oriented, Linda gestured "follow me." Her
fins, long and sleek, were of that strange neon color cities had
taken to painting fire trucks in the late seventies, a shade between yellow and lime. Not pretty but surprisingly visible.
Anna followed their flicking toward where the boat had exploded, burned and, presumably, sunk.

Visibility got worse, but not by much. A lot of the particles
had settled. The blast must have come early on, between midnight and two or three in the morning. Any earlier and someone
at the fort would have heard and reported it. Swimming along in
this sea of thoughts and other flotsam it occurred to Anna that
someone had heard it. She'd heard it. It had almost awakened

her. Tangled in dreams of the Civil War brought on by Great-Great-Aunt Raffia's letter, her unconscious mind had transmuted it into cannon fire. There was no way to prove that had been the case but, looking back, Anna was pretty sure it was. The knowledge was of little practical value. Not having fully awakened, she had no idea what time she'd heard the explosion.

Doesn't matter, she told herself. Boat fires were stunningly fast. Even if she'd leapt from her bed and sprinted to the *Reef Ranger,* this boat would have burned to waterline before she could have reached it.

And Bob?

That thought Anna pushed away. Too little information yet for self-recrimination.

The iridescent fins ahead of her stopped. Anna kicked to where Linda hung, suspended fifteen feet above the ocean floor. Beneath them was what remained of the boat whose blood sheened the surface. Guessing from the mess scattered over broken coral reefs, it had been a cigarette-type boat, long and lean and fast; basically huge engines and fuel tank housed in a bullet-shaped fiberglass body. This one was larger than most Anna had seen; maybe thirty feet long when it was in one piece. At present, fragments of it were strewn over an area three times that.

It looked as though the blast had been centered around the engine compartment. The stern had been severed from the rest of the hull and lay at an awkward angle against a coral boulder. The living coral was gouged by the impact and scored by propeller blades. Jagged chunks of ripped and melted fiberglass reached around what had been a bench seat and was now a lump of charred plastic. A bright orange personal flotation device was tethered to it. Buoyant innards trailed out like intestines from a mutilated trunk. One of the straps had caught on the twisted fiberglass, condemning the float to death by drowning.

Thirty feet away was the foreshortened bow section. Two cabin doors of clamshell design like those in cowboy saloons had been ripped away. One lay on the sand near the wreck, the other was still attached by a length of metal or fiberglass. The rectangle opening into the boat's low-ceilinged cabin was twisted until it resembled a door drawn by a very small child; the lines bent and blurred, none of the corners square. A scrap of cloth—pant leg or sleeve—reached out from the dark interior. Because the water was still, it did not wave or sway but stood out, a flag in a still life.

Surrounding the two major pieces of the wreck, lying on white sand, scattered across coral, sea fans, sponges and stone, were the shattered remains of the boat's midsection. Much of it was mangled to the point that it was unrecognizable. Here and there were the bizarre anomalies that often accompany tornadoes and explosions. A boat hook, purposely blunt and attached to a long pole, had been thrown clean as a javelin into the sand, its haft sticking up, a piece of paper neatly skewered by the head. The lens of a running light, detached from the hull but otherwise unharmed, lay fifteen feet from the main wreck gleaming ruby-bright, dead center in a circle of green coral.

The Dry Tortugas' underwater camera rode in a zippered nylon pouch attached to Anna's web gear. She took it out. Even from a distance of twenty feet the photos would not be good. The water was cloudy and the light weak. Later she would take clearer shots, but she wanted to record the lay of the wreck in case anything should shift once they began fiddling with the pieces.

After the first couple shots Linda tugged her wrist and pointed. Anna's gaze followed the other diver's finger to the forward section of the wreck. The small movements of their fins had moved through the viscous world and finally reached the frozen flag flying from the ruined cabin doorway. The fabric, mottled black and yellow, possibly partially burned, was waving ever so faintly. The motion had disarranged the original drape, exposing what looked very like a forefinger and thumb.

The two of them began swimming slowly in the direction of the bow. Anna dearly hoped the hand was connected to an arm and the arm to a body with another arm, legs, head and whatnot attached. And she wished she had diving gloves; there was probably going to be slimy bits coming up.

They stopped again, hovering just above and in front of the door. Linda touched Anna's shoulder, pointed to the wreck and waggled her hand back and forth, reminding Anna that the pieces of the boat were possibly unsteady and could fall, crushing or tapping an unwary diver.

Linda's short blond hair stood out from her head, moving with strange life lent by the sea. Her mouth was distorted and swollen with the froggy humanness shared by the creature from the black lagoon and scuba divers with their mouthpieces in place. Her light blue eyes, crinkled by lines that usually reassured Anna of a life led in sunlight and laughter, were exaggerated by her mask. A slow leak pooled salt water—an ocean of tears—high on her cheeks.

For an instant, no less powerful because short-lived, a cold fear swept through Anna; a child awakening in a nightmare made more real by the light of day.

Anna watched her own hand float up, finger and thumb making the okay sign, letting Linda know she'd gotten the message. The rift between the dimension of Dean Koontz and Jacques Cousteau was healed as quickly as it had formed. The fear was gone.

Rough night, Anna excused it to herself. *Overtired.*

She kicked once and moved to the segmented hull. At a show of her palm, the universal signal for halt, Linda stayed back. Because of Linda's superior skill in the water, Anna had been glad to abdicate leadership during the diving. When it came to risk taking, she couldn't. Storms, currents and reefs were Linda's nemeses. At present, this tippy, murdered vessel with its one flailing human arm was Anna's responsibility.

Reaching the top left corner of the cabin, Anna steadied herself on the wreck and looked toward the bow. Keeled over, tilting cabin and deck at a sixty- or seventy-degree angle up from the sandy bottom, the bow was wedged between two upthrusts of coral. From the damage both to the animals and the boat's underside, Anna guessed she had been driven between the coral boulders with a degree of force, enough to shove the bow into the sandy bottom.

Anna shook the boat experimentally. It didn't budge. She pushed it from several more angles without dislodging anything. Partially reassured it wasn't a death trap just waiting to slam shut on her claustrophobic little self, she swam back to the cabin door, to the fingers protruding from the torn fabric. Linda still hung in the water fifteen feet away. A first mate—and cap-

tain when Cliff was sick or on vacation—she was good both at
the giving and the taking of orders.

Anna removed the camera from its pocket and clicked pictures: north, east, south and west of the bow section and one
close-up of the finger-fringed fabric floating in front of her
nose. Record made, she returned the camera to its niche and
kicked a bit closer to examine the beckoning flesh. "Finger-
fringed" was unpleasantly apt. What they'd seen was not a
thumb and forefinger but a ring finger and the avulsed half of
the middle finger. The yellow was not a sleeve but possibly the
torso of a tee shirt peeled from the body by the blast and blown
out along the arm. There was a wrist, Anna was relieved to note,
and part of a forearm leading back to an anchor of some sort. A
body, it was to be hoped. Gently, Anna turned the new-made
relic. From the look of it, the arm had belonged to a man. Much
of the flesh was burned or excised by the explosion, but the ribbons remaining were coarse-skinned and the few hairs not
scorched off were coarse and black.

Bracing herself against the cabin, she reached toward the underwater light at her waist. Head bent toward the hook connecting the flashlight to her buoyancy compensator, she sensed
rather than saw darkness descending, an eclipse of the pale watery sun. With a grinding noise that was felt as well as heard the
tortured fiberglass fell away beneath her hand. The hulk, steady
moments before, rolled with the impetuosity of submerged matter. Under the grinding filling her ears and grating on her bones
came Linda's close-mouth scream, a weak mermaid's siren.

Pushing at the environment with hands and flippered feet,
Anna scuttled backward in the tradition of octopi but without
the grace. The heel of her right foot banged into coral, and the
cabin rolled down. Through the silt and particles, through the
luminous and shifting green of the sky, a ton of fiberglass, wood
and metal moved. White and bottle green, a wall toppling, a
twisted and melting cliff-face.

Again Anna kicked. Her right leg didn't move but jerked, a
spasm as before sleep. The hull rolled onto her swim fin, trapping it and her toes in a viselike grip. Bubbles, sand, a fog of
minute coral deaths, destroyed her vision. Light and dark remained. Dark was fast falling, the cabin roof closing on the
boulder where Anna wriggled, bait on a hook. Panic tickled in-

side her brain, urging her to rip off the blinding mask, tear away
the regulator with its claustrophobic life support. Training
shaped panic to fear. Fear escalated to instinct.

The flashlight fell into shadow. The dive knife strapped to
Anna's calf found her palm. The blade slid into the top of her
fin and with a slash her foot was cut free. She kicked back and
up. The cabin rolled, keel looming into view sharp as a harrow,
a kaleidoscope of ruin. The hard edge of the still-attached cabin
door clawed at Anna's thigh, scraped down over her knee. Ignoring the pain, Anna pushed off the underside of the wreck.

The moment she was free and safe, the movement stopped.
Panting, bubbles and noise billowing out of her regulator, mask
beginning to fog from internal heat, Anna suffered a horror that
this was personal: the insensate, ruined hulk had wanted to kill
her. Fear, no less intense because unrealistic, pushed up from
her stomach in cold nauseating waves.

Into the glittering cloud of air bubbles came Linda's face,
pulled out of human shape by the dive gear. Thoughts of monsters from the black or any other lagoon were gone; for one rare
moment Anna was comforted just not to be alone. Her heart
slowed, her breathing began to return to normal. The fear was
too much, too hard. Then Anna realized she must have coupled
the rolling cabin with being trapped in the dark under nearly
two hundred feet of ice-cold water nearly ten years before, experienced that fear for this.

As good an explanation as any, she told herself. *Evils sufficient unto the day.*

With the help of Linda's work-lined face, Anna pulled herself rapidly back together. Linda was signing but Anna's brain
was not yet quite right-side up. She made the "okay" with both
hands, hoping that was all the answer Linda required. Apparently it was; the agitated finger wiggling and twitching ceased.
Bubbles returned to their normal noisy bursts. The women
looked down on the offending wreck.

An old hand, Linda hung in the water not moving, weight
and buoyancy perfectly balanced. Anna, her weight belt a tad
heavy, had to kick gently to maintain. Missing the one fin, she
listed slightly.

Yards of beautifully colored, incredibly varied and terribly
fragile living coral had been crushed or scraped away. Anna felt

the loss with greater sorrow than the loss of whoever belonged
to the hairy, yellow-clad arm. She justified her inhumane lean-
ings with the myth that her job inured her to human suffering.

The wreck hadn't completely turned turtle. The coral crevice
it wedged itself into during the original descent had stopped it.
The top half of the cabin door—the left side, had the boat been
upright—was above the coral boulder.

Linda pointed. Down at the bottom, just peeking out of the
crush between cabin and coral, was the finger. An image of the
Wicked Witch of the East, smashed under Dorothy's house,
only her feet protruding, came into Anna's mind, and she half
expected to see the finger and the mangled palm to which it was
attached shrivel and disappear beneath the fallen boat.

At her elbow, Linda was scribbling on an underwater pad.
Finished, she showed Anna: "We go in now?" Anna shook her
head and took the notebook.

"I go for ropes. Replace fin. You stay *out* of boat."

Linda read, then made the okay sign and pointed at Anna's
NPS camera. Understanding was established. Linda would continue to record the wreckage. Anna would refurbish her gear
and get what was necessary to work safely around the sunken
boat.

In the ten minutes it took to return to the *Activa,* collect what
she needed and swim back, the light grew immeasurably better.
The sun had jumped high and sudden above the horizon. Some
of the extra matter put into suspension by the shifting of the hull
had settled out. All in all, with Linda swimming gracefully
about snapping pictures of the kind required on any routine accident investigation, Anna was hard pressed to remember the
alarums of a quarter of an hour before. Probably the facility to
forget was one of the reasons she stayed in the line of work
she'd chosen. Looking back, no matter what had actually transpired, it never seemed all that bad. Still, she was shaken. Not
by the trapping of her fin, but by the sense she'd suffered that it
was *intentional.* This was something she couldn't afford to
think too long on. She purposely wiped the weirdness from her
mind and concentrated on what was in front of her.

While she'd been gone the finger had disappeared. Anna
mentally tipped her hat to L. Frank Baum. Obviously the man
had done his homework.

Linda, good as her word and essentially a cautious woman, had stayed away from the bow section. Several yards from the wedged hull, her back to it, she crouched froglike over a shard of the shattered boat, the camera held four inches from her mask as she framed the shot. Thirty or forty feet out, laden with coiled line, Anna glided toward her.

Movement caught her eye and she looked past Linda. A bubble the size of a beach ball was squeezing out of the cracked keel where the bow had upended when the wreck had shifted. The bubble's elongated shape moved, expanded. It was not clear but filled with roiling sulphurous gray. For an instant Anna's mind froze in wonder. Once before she'd seen a bubble like that. With the speed of thought, the memory came clear. She and Molly, both little girls, had been playing with a length of fuse left over from when their dad, afraid they would collapse and kill somebody, had dynamited unstable caves dug in a sandpit by the local schoolkids. They'd put one end of the fuse in a puddle of water and lit the other. When the fuse burnt to the end, a yellow bubble appeared on the puddle. They popped it and a puff of smoke was released.

The boat was still burning. When it rolled, the flames inside must have found a new source of air and fuel. Dropping the line, Anna kicked hard for the first mate, still oblivious in her concentration. Muted, high-pitched noises reached Anna's ears as she impotently called Linda's name without ungluing her lips from the regulator's mouthpiece.

Intuition or unusually acute hearing brought the other woman's head up, stirring her yellow hair into a mini-nova around her face.

Kicking for all she was worth, Anna pointed. Linda turned to look back. Suspended, weightless, her body rotated with her head. A nightmare sense of slow motion, of trying to run through viscous mud, overtook Anna. A booming—thunder through rain—and the keel of the ship expanded as if it had taken a deep breath. Cracks appeared. Red fire, incongruous forty feet under the ocean, opened, then burst out in gouts of flame. The hull exploded outward, shards of razor-sharp Plexiglas shot like torpedoes in every direction. A bubble of black veined with red blossomed.

Linda, her body half turned toward the blast, was snatched

up by unseen forces. Arms and legs flew out, then were crushed inward, a doll being wadded up, tossed away. Her head snapped out of the circle of flesh. Her mask was ripped from her face. Eyes wide, mouth open, she seemed to be screaming, but Anna heard nothing.

A wave of force smacked into Anna and she felt herself falling. There was no up or down. Just an endless fall into an airless darkness.

4

I cannot say how I knew it was the confederate boy, Joel Lane. The lamps in the sally port were set too far apart for proper lighting. Maybe it was the black hair. Lord knows his hair was the only thing unchanged, the only thing left that was pretty about him.

Still and all, I could see enough of Private Lane's face to know I didn't want Tilly going any closer. But you know Tilly, ever the rusher-in when the angels are thinking twice about treading. She thinks she is so grown and worldly. To Tilly everything is black or white. Having been married to the U.S. Army lo these many years, I have grown accustomed to black and blue and shades of gray.

But even I have never seen a man beaten as badly as this poor boy. Oh, Peggy, even with you seeing Dennis after he died and your work with the wounded in New York, you would have wept for Tilly's soldier. He had been so lovely, and Joseph's guards beat him till he didn't even look human anymore, then strung him up against the stones in the sally port.

Tilly recognized the boy and tore herself away from me. (I had been clutching her rather firmly to my side, anticipating some such end to our outing—though not Joel and not such brutality—usually it's a drunkard who at least doesn't feel his tortures till he's been cut down.) The horrid girl is as strong as she is quick, and I had little choice but to run after her or stay where I was.

Tilly was wailing "Oh no! Oh no!" and, though I believe she was sincerely upset and have pity on that account, she threw her arms forward then clasped them to her breast too much like that picture of that new French actress, Sarah Bernhardt.

Her noise didn't bring the boy's head up or cause him to move at all—which was worrisome—but it brought Sergeant Sinapp out of the guardroom. Though he's one of Joseph's cronies, I have never liked the man. Sinapp is too thick. His lips are thick. His fingers blunt and so thick it's a wonder he can make a fist—though that seems to be the one thing he excels at. Even his ears are thick. "Cauliflowered," they call them. It comes from fighting. His neck is so thick it really cannot be said to exist, there being so little differentiation between the bottom of his ears and the top of his shoulders.

Tilly was brought to a sudden stop by Sinapp. Behind him the guardroom was brightly lit, cards no doubt being more important to keep an eye on than murderers, thieves and enemy soldiers. He moved his thickness to one side, and the light shone full on Tilly.

She was a pretty picture: face caked with makeup like a you-know-what, hair all up on her head, hands clasped beseechingly. The wind blew Tilly's cotton skirt against her body. The little minx was not wearing her petticoats. It was clear to me and to the disgusting Sergeant Sinapp that she'd not even bothered with pantaloons. Every line of leg and thigh was clearly delineated. Sinapp actually licked his lips. Licked his lips! His great pale tongue poking out like a lizard seeking an ant. In an instant more I expect he would have begun smacking and drooling like a starving hound. I did hear a low moan and I don't think it was from the unfortunate Private Lane.

"Sergeant Sinapp," I barked. I've not been an army wife all these years without having learned the voice of authority. Tilly broke from her pose, thank God, and turned so the wind no longer played its trick with her dress. Freed from what could only be lust in that paralyzing form that sometimes takes men,

Sinapp sucked his tongue back in and stood as close to attention as his tree-trunk body would allow.

"What is the meaning of this?" I demanded. My appearance from the shadows startled him, and his recent thoughts had evidently been so wicked it didn't occur to him that he well might ask that question of Tilly and me.

For a moment, while guilt and confusion rattled around in his very small brain, I thought I could get past him easily. Unfortunately, as with many men accustomed to few emotions and comfortable with none but anger, he got mad. Had I not been his captain's wife I expect he might have overstepped the bounds of common decency.

"You got no business—"

I could see his slow mental processes, so recently scrambled, lining themselves back up. Right quick before he could bluster himself back into some semblance of a sergeant at arms, I stepped up close and sniffed.

"You've been drinking," I said with all the disapproval I could muster. Whether he'd been drinking or not, I couldn't tell. Amid the swamp of odium that drifted from him, sorting out a single scent was past even my bloodhound abilities. The laundresses at Fort Jefferson often take home three times as much pay as their soldier husbands each month. They are grossly underpaid. Woolen uniforms in the sodden heat of July wring much in the way of bodily effluvia from men far less unpalatable than Sergeant Sinapp.

"Have not!" he countered, sounding so much like your Leonard did when he was three and into breaking things and pestering the dogs that I nearly laughed.

Tilly had taken this moment out of my control and the sergeant's thrall to scoot her unpantalooned self behind my back and into the sally port where her pet rebel was.

The sight of young Joel Lane robbed me of any rebuke I might, for Molly's sake, have given Tilly. Lips and eyelids were swelled, the skin stretched so tight I feared it might burst and spill the blue-black blood pooled beneath. The once-clean line of his jaw was blurred, misshapen, and his neat close ears puffed, red, angry and probably never to resume their pretty shape.

It is common practice to punish prisoners and union soldiers alike by tying their hands behind their backs and hoisting them up till their toes barely touch the ground. As vicious as this practice is, it evidently wasn't sufficiently cruel for Sinapp. Private Lane had been strung up by his thumbs; this I have never seen but only read of in books of medieval tortures.

The poor boy's thumbs were the size and color of plums. Tilly slid to her knees and began to cry. This time I saw nothing of theatrics in her. I often forget how young she is—or I choose to forget how inured to brutish behavior I have become.

"Cut this man down," I commanded the sergeant, hoping he was still cowed by my previous accusation of imbibing.

He'd had time to reinsert his spine and gather his few thoughts.

"I can't do that, ma'am. This ain't no place for you to be. This here's army business.

"That man was talking traitor talk. Going on about Mr. Lincoln like his foul murder was a right and good thing. That's why he got himself strung up. I'm making no apologies that he got what was coming. When he gets cut down he'll be put to carrying shot—a hundred and twenty-eight pounder or my name ain't Cobb Sinapp."

During the rehearsals I have gotten to know Joel somewhat, and he didn't strike me as a political man, certainly not one to speak out if it would get him beat half to death which surely even the dullest reb here must know could happen with tensions so high. Joel was more likely a reckless young man who had joined the war against the union because that's what the young dandies in his circle were doing. Still, I cannot completely discount Cobb (what a ridiculous name, undoubtedly he was called after the kind of pipe his mother smoked in the birthing room) Sinapp's words. Who knows what strange twists might exist in the mind of a southern boy, and an actor to boot?

"Cut him down at once," I insisted. "Or I'll—"

"I'll scream," Tilly said, and I've never seen that exquisite face of hers look so hard. "I'll scream and I'll go on screaming until the whole fort comes down around us."

I must say I was relieved at her interruptions. I had no idea what my threat was to have been. I certainly couldn't threaten to tell my husband. Sergeant Sinapp knows in what high regard Joseph holds me, though he'd never dare speak of it or show any overt disrespect.

Tilly's threat sounded childish to my ears, but it put the fear of God into the wretched Sinapp.

"Now no need for that kinda talk, missy. What with them murderin' cowards, this place is already a..."

I suppose he was searching for a metaphor: powder keg, hornets' nest or some such, but the limitation of his intellect stopped him. However, much as I dislike admitting it even to you, the most forgiving of souls, Sergeant Sinapp had a point. The "murderin' cowards" to whom the sergeant referred are the Lincoln conspirators. Not the man who shot him, of course, or that woman who was put to death, but Samuel Arnold, Edward Spangler and Dr. Mudd, who is said to have set John Booth's leg after he broke it leaping to the stage. As if we weren't enough on edge, knowing that those who were at least in part responsible for the death of the president are to be with us soon has brought the hatred to the surface.

"Cut him down, cut him down," Tilly began. A smallish boy-faced fellow emerged from the guardroom behind Sinapp and proffered his knife. Sinapp cut Private Lane down, letting the boy fall all in a heap on the stone. Had Tilly not gotten in the way, I expect Joel Lane's skull would have been cracked open when he hit.

The boy-faced soldier had the good sense to vanish after that, but the sergeant stood around being of no use to us but needing to vent his frustration. He threatened to tell Joseph, which I'm sure he will, and I will have to answer for Tilly's soft heart. Joseph won't do much but to yell. He learned a long time ago, the first time he struck me, that he had but three options: to kill me outright, never to strike me again, or to sleep with one eye open for the rest of his natural life.

Without help there was sadly little Tilly and I could do. Private Lane was too heavy for us to move. We asked the sergeant to help us but he would not so much as fetch water to wet the boy's lips or bathe his poor ruined face. Between us, Tilly and I made him as comfortable as we could there on the stones of the sally port and got him to drink a little water I fetched myself. Then we had to leave him.

Tilly begged Sinapp prettily to be compassionate, and I made a number of threats I have no authority to carry out, that if Joel Lane was further damaged when we returned, much in the way of ill luck would befall whomsoever mistreated him.

We'd stayed too long as it was—the theatrical would have started and only by rushing would Tilly and I be back in time for our entrance. The drama of the situation outweighed the artificial drama of our little play, and I had to all but drag our little sister from the rebel's side. Many evils are bound to come from this act of kindness, not the least of which is Tilly, playing at Miss Nightingale, will probably feel obliged to fall in love with her patient, or fancy she has.

On the way back, as we ran in a most undignified fashion across the parade ground toward our bows and pinafores, Tilly suddenly said: "Our duet!" (They had adapted "Somebody's Darling" for two parts.) "We can't do it, his being gone. And I looked so pretty in that blue silk robe." I took heart from that. If the baggage is still thinking of her own self and vain pursuits, we can hope tonight's debacle hasn't damaged her spirit too badly.

For a time the excitement of being in a theatrical production gave us respite from the sad state of the rebel soldier we'd left quite possibly dying, but I dared not even think of that. I suppose it's unchristian, but I think the bright lights and tumultuous applause took our minds completely. The stage—built by the prisoners—is small but utterly delightful. I continue to be amazed by the varied talents one can garner simply by imprisoning a section of the American armies. Which side they fought for doesn't seem to be a factor. The fort boasts several excellent carpenters; the lights (every candle and lamp on the key was pressed into service) had been cunningly shaped and aimed by a union deserter from New York. Before the war he worked for a clothier in the city of New York, and one of his tasks was to provide attractive lighting for the window displays and the live mannequins. We even had an exquisitely painted backdrop provided by a burglar-cum-muralist from Philadelphia. War and theater seem to be good bedfellows.

Despite this "innocent maid" being rather long in the tooth and not a maiden by any stretch of the imagination, Tilly's and my " 'Tis True I Have Flirted" was very well received. I do be-

lieve we would have gotten a standing ovation had I not insisted
Tilly put her underskirts and knickers back on in spite of the
heat. What the girl was thinking, I cannot say. Under the bright
lights burning all round our makeshift stage she would have
looked like a burlesque queen.

Both of us had a wonderful time. Tilly can be excused by her
youth, I suppose. As for me, I must simply be a vain and shallow creature for all the thought I gave that battered boy during
my brief moment of glory. I did happen to notice that the fort's
surgeon had not abandoned his seat in the center of the third
row despite the fact we had sent a boy with a message about
Joel. Evidently he didn't feel the health of one rebel soldier—
and one reputed to have celebrated our dear Mr. Lincoln's
death—was worth missing an entertainment.

I think the evening would have been an unqualified success
had not a minor riot broken out. Two numbers after Tilly's and
my triumph, as a magician was pulling two rats from an old hat
(rabbits being hard to come by in the middle of the ocean and
rats, he assured us, being really rather clever creatures), there
was a great hullabaloo from the parade ground.

The men in the audience grew restive, and a handful of the
officers stood up and left. My stage business being finished but
for the curtain call, I slipped out the back of the mess hall behind the stage and hid myself in the shadows of the new construction to see what the noise was about. Soldiers being so
outnumbered by prisoners, we live with the fear of an uprising,
though the unfortunate wretches condemned to serve their time
here have shown no such inclination. At first I thought this
long-held fear had come to pass. The parade ground, so ghostly
and quiet when Tilly and I went out earlier, was teeming with
men in various states of dress. Some carried lanterns, a few
with torches or candles, all were grumbling or shouting, creating a noise that was truly frightening.

I was standing behind a pile of bricks the engineers were to
use for the barracks's foundation and thought myself alone.
When I felt someone grab my shoulder, I screamed. In the general hubbub, all was confusion, noise, fire and darkness, and no
one heard me. When I found Tilly had followed me out, I was
so angry and relieved I nearly slapped her. I think only knowing

how it feels to be on the receiving end of that sort of hurt stopped my hand.

Guns began to fire, at what or who was unclear, but the reports were loud, echoing as they do in the enclosed space of Fort Jefferson. Those who'd been invited to the entertainment in the mess hall poured out across the gravel. Many had snatched lanterns from the footlights and the walls.

The lights crossed and moved, making each man into four and casting wild shadows. Suddenly Tilly and I were illuminated, and I heard Joseph's familiar bellow.

"Christ on the cross, you stupid woman!"

That, of course, would be me. He came at us at a run, and his face was twisted with anger.

Tilly must have thought he was going to attack us. She shrank down and clung to my skirts like she used to when she was a little girl.

Joseph did lay hands on me but only to give me a shake and vent his anger. "The whole God damn fort is up in arms. You get yourself and your sister back in quarters and bolt the door or I'll beat you till you can't sit down for a month of Sundays."

There are times I do believe he loves me. Oddly enough that was one of them. Tilly, though, was frightened out of her wits and began to sob. Long ago I learned that there is nothing Joseph so hates as a weeping woman. He left the lantern he'd carried on the ground, grabbed a handful of Tilly's pinafore in one hand and my arm with the other and all but carried us back into the officers' mess. I was reminded of my husband's strength of back and of purpose. I suppose it's why his men love him. As I did once and do again from time to time.

He hurled us at his petty officer with dire threats and not a few expletives, and we were marched up to my quarters like naughty children and a soldier stationed outside our door at my husband's order to see that we stayed there.

Though angry at having been bundled away and locked in, I felt safer, partly for myself and a great deal for Tilly. Once the door was slammed behind us we went to the window. The noise, the running, had grown worse.

"An uprising? A lynching?" I said, forgetting I was not alone and very probably infecting Tilly with my fears.

"Lynching?" she repeated "Private Lane? For what they say he said about the president?"

I said nothing, but that had been my first thought as well.

5

From a place above and just outside Fort Jefferson's walls, Anna watched soldiers, small and silent as black ants, scurrying across the parade ground in the moonlight. In clots and trails they moved toward a confused flashing of lanterns near the sally port. Though logic told her she could not, she saw, too, Raffia and Tilly behind a locked door in the officers' quarters, an armed guard to keep them in. The vivid colors of their bows and pinafores came to startling life when they neared a lamp, only to return to gray as they passed from its circle of influence. The vision was very real; she was there and she was not.

Then a force she could not see clamped over her face, something hard and foreign was forced into her mouth. Air rushed into her lungs, a sudden hammer blow banging out her ribs. The fort, the soldiers, the women, receded to a pinpoint then burned out in a tiny noiseless explosion, and Anna was alone.

Darkness coiled around her body and mind. She flailed but touched nothing. Down and up ceased to have meaning. For a moment of blinding panic she believed she was dead and this suffocating nothingness was eternal afterlife.

Another monstrous struggle with unseen forces determined to invade her very being for all of time, and again air thundered into her lungs. She could hear it passing through her trachea; marbles pouring down the narrow neck of a glass jar.

Without conscious thought, air changed from invader to the single most important thing in life. Anna gulped and floundered. Darkness began to recede, edges first, turning green then sifting in toward the center.

Underwater. She was underwater. A hand was on her waist, a regulator held in her mouth. This knowledge didn't speak to the rational part of her brain, it was merely an observation. A watery world made as little sense as the silent scream of the black vortex had moments earlier.

Rising. Breaking the surface. Sunlight. More of the marvelous air. Anna remembered now: Fort Jefferson, the hunt for Bob Shaw, cutting away her trapped fin. After that there was only the darkness and Great-Great-Aunt Raffia.

She spit out the regulator and fought the arm across her chest feebly. A strong swimmer towed her toward the NPS boats: hers, Mack's and Daniel's. She knew names. A good sign.

"Stop wiggling," came a command and Anna obeyed, lying in the water, face to the sky, being reeled in like the day's catch.

"What happened?" she asked.

"Later. Onboard. Be quiet."

For reasons she was unsure of—and uninterested in—Anna was content to be a package with no thoughts and no responsibilities other than to shut up and lie still.

The idyll was short-lived. As her rescuer floated her inert body close to the nearest boat, shouting and clattering dinned in her waterlogged ears. "Is she alive?" was hollered more than once so Anna knew her lost minutes had been of the dangerous sort. When the answer was in the affirmative, somebody said, "Hallelujah!" so she knew she was among friends.

Her birth from the warm amniotic sea and the odd drift of mind was sufficiently violent with hauling and pushing and dragging her corpus over the gunwale and flopping it onto the deck that she was reborn, not only into the world of the living but into her old life with its dues and responsibilities.

"What happened?" she demanded.

"You're welcome," she heard a voice murmur. Teddy Shaw,

dressed in a dripping blouse, underpants and fins, a snorkel and mask the sum total of her dive gear, sat beside her on the box covering the engine of the Boston Whaler. Teddy had saved Anna's life. Since Danny didn't dive, she must have shucked off her trousers at the first sign of a problem and free dived unknown territory to bring Anna out.

"Oh. Right," Anna said. "What happened?" Then, more sharply: "Where's Linda? I was diving with Linda." She stood quickly with the half-baked idea of going back down. Dizziness smacked into her. Teddy caught her before she toppled over the side.

Teddy gently pushed her head down. Blackness receded. "I know what you did for me," Anna said. It came out in a creaky little whisper. "I am grateful. But I'm in a hurry. Where is Linda?" She pushed herself upright, but this time had the good sense to remain seated. Fainting was embarrassing, and as the shock of being alive wore off, her entire body had begun to hurt.

"She's okay." Danny knelt in front of her, the gesture of an adult soothing a child.

"Where?"

"On the *Atlantic Ranger*. There." Daniel pointed. "Right after the explosion I radioed Mack to get another diver over here. Rather than wait, Teddy went over the side in a snorkel.

"Mack got here a few minutes ago, just as Teddy broke surface with you. Linda'd come up a minute or so before. She's on board with Cliff now."

"She's okay?" Anna asked.

"Shook up. Bruised. She was closer than you but didn't seem as hard hit. The hull must have aimed the explosion up and out where you were. She got cut up pretty bad on the coral but managed to keep her regulator in her mouth and never lost consciousness. The blast stirred up the bottom and knocked you clean out of her sight. She'd come up to see if she could see your bubbles, but Teddy'd already gone down."

Explosion. Blast. Anna remembered none of that. For a second she just sat, watching the water on the deck around her feet turn pink.

"Guess I'm bleeding," she said. "What blew up? The boat?"

"The boat," Daniel confirmed.

"How could the damn thing blow up?" Anna asked nobody in particular. "It'd already blown up. There were pieces scattered all over hell and back." For some reason the image of the damaged fingers beckoning from the misshapen cabin door flashed behind Anna's eyes. Terror seized her: fear the finger belonged to the grim reaper himself, that he stalked her and, having missed this time, would try again, and soon. The horror was so intense and unexpected Anna sucked her breath in.

"What's the matter? Are you okay?" chorused in her ears, and she was pulled out of her paranoia.

"Must have broken a rib," she lied. Raw fear born of a mental-picture-become-real was as frightening as the false hell of the image.

It was insane.

Anna rubbed her face hard with both hands, scrubbing away the disease.

"Extra fuel tanks in the bow, is my guess," Daniel said, returning to her question of how a boat could explode twice. "That or explosives of some kind."

"Fire," Anna said. "Just before nothing, I saw a bubble full of smoke leaking from the hull."

"An explosive detonated by fire," Daniel amended his earlier supposition.

While she'd been sitting, gathering what wits were left to her, ignoring Teddy, her savior, and making demands for information, the *Atlantic* motored over to raft off the *Curious*, and Teddy and Daniel had divested her of tank, weight belt, fins and snorkel.

Anna reached down to retrieve the heavy buoyancy compensator—BC—that held tank and regulator. "I'd better go back down," she said. "Figure out what the hell happened."

"That might not be the best idea."

Cliff, with his kindly professional face and quiet voice, leaned on the gunwales where the two boats touched. "Might want to rethink that one. Linda's not going back down. Not today."

Anna's vision, narrow and inward for the few minutes she'd been out of the water, opened to include sky, ocean and this handful of people floating in between. Linda, free of dive gear

as she was, sat in the *Atlantic*'s bow. Mack was cutting her tattered dive skin off of her. The exposed flesh oozed with cuts and
scrapes, one or two quite deep, bleeding freely, though not life
threateningly.

"Are you okay, Linda?" Anna asked.

"Better than you. And I've got sense enough to call it a day.
I hurt too bad not to be stupid down there."

Anna hadn't taken time to assess herself, but she did so now.
Like Linda, her dive skin was torn in dozens of places. Blood
mixed with water was staining the deck around her feet. When
she breathed, her ribs hurt—probably not broken but badly
bruised. There might be other injuries not so readily apparent.

"Good point," she finally agreed. "Teddy might not take
kindly to having to save my life more than once a day."

"I'll go down in half an hour or so," Cliff promised. "Let the
dust settle a bit."

Anna thought for a second and was pleased to note that her
ability to reason seemed to have returned. "Okay," she said.
"You stay here, Mack. Dive with Cliff. Stay clear of the wreck
if anything looks like it could turn on you. I'll leave my gear
and the camera." It occurred to her then that the camera had
been with Linda. She looked at the other diver, naked now but
for the bottom of her two-piece bathing suit. The top lay in
pieces on the deck. Ugly scrapes raked across her left breast.

Linda pawed through the refuse of her gear and held it up.
"Can't promise it'll still work."

"Bob—" Teddy began.

Anna overrode her. "Daniel, take the *Curious* and continue
the search. Teddy, me and Linda will go back to the fort, get
patched up, then join you."

With a minimum of fuss, they divided themselves among the
boats and, Teddy driving, the women motored back to Garden
Key.

The more time that passed, the more Anna's body made its
complaints heard. By the time they docked, she had stiffened up
and was hard pressed to find any part of her that did not ache.

Linda looked just as miserable. "Why don't you lay low for
a while," Anna suggested. "Teddy'll do the driving. I'll sit still
and look." That would be about all she could do, but Anna
chose not to put it into words.

Ever practical, Linda accepted.

Anna showered quickly. Naked, she could see the toll coral and trauma had taken. She'd sustained no deep cuts as Linda had, but contusions, burning and itching from the coral's defensive toxins, marked her so that she looked as if she suffered from some vile and highly contagious disease.

Choosing comfort, she set aside the National Park Service's uniform code and donned another short loose dress. She wanted as little touching her skin as park rules and regulations would allow.

She made herself a peanut butter sandwich, poured a glass of sparkling water that tasted flat though she'd just opened it, and sat on the couch next to a sleeping Piedmont to eat. The coffee table was strewn with Great-Great-Aunt Raffia's correspondence to her sister Peggy. Perhaps because of the dreams she'd had the night before or the moments without oxygen when she'd hovered above the western ramparts watching the last letter she'd read come to life, Anna felt a connection to Raffia and Tilly that was more than family ties. The fear that touched her onboard the *Curious* when her mind took her back to the beckoning finger again rubbed at the edges of her mind.

"I feel funny," she said to the cat. "My mind isn't working right." The admission, spoken aloud even to a sleeping cat, disturbed her. This was not the kind of thing she wanted to become public knowledge.

"It'll pass," she said to the imaginary jury in her head. Leaving the sandwich half-eaten, she grabbed a daypack she'd stuffed with needful things and left the cat to his nap.

Anna'd been raised on cowboy-and-Indian stories. At least conceptually she was no stranger to the phrase "skinned alive." Having been rudely scraped over the coral, she suffered a new and deeper understanding of the old torture. It hurt to walk. The dress chafed. The sun poked red-hot rays into her. Because they were abraded by living coral, the wounds itched. Scratching them was brutal. The only good thing she could say about the contusions, had she been mad enough to want to play the Pollyanna Glad Game, was they took her mind off the aches the tumbling had engendered, the nausea from swallowing salt water and the persistent cough left over from trying to breathe underwater.

She was in no shape to head up a search for Ranger Shaw but, until the coast guard arrived, she was the only game in town. Letting Teddy go alone was a bad idea. Doing nothing when Bob might be alive and in need was unthinkable.

For twenty minutes she and Teddy continued working the grid from the north-south axis to the west of where Cliff and Mack had quit. Anna tried with very little success to stay in the shade of the Boston Whaler's one pitiful awning. She'd been too scraped up to make herself spread on sun block, and the sun burned her raw flesh.

In the midst of a fantasy about parasols, the radio crackled. Cliff had resurfaced. The bow of the boat had been destroyed by a second and more violent explosion. The beckoning finger was gone, as was every other part of the individual whose remains had hidden in the drowned cabin. Danny's guess that stored fuel had exploded due to fire left burning from the first conflagration amidships was ratified by the remnants of auxiliary fuel tanks stowed, presumably, belowdecks in the fore cabin.

"And I got lucky," he finished. "Got something you need to see."

"What?"

"Come on over. It can wait a few minutes."

His reluctance to deliver the news over the airwaves scared Teddy. Blood drained from her face, leaving it the faded gray-gold of winter grass. Anna knew they shared the same thought; *you don't tell a woman you've found her husband's corpse over the radio.*

Bob Shaw's body wasn't waiting for them. Not quite.

"Found this about sixty feet south and a bit east of the wreck," Cliff said as Teddy tied their boat to the *Curious.* He held up what first appeared to be a clump of seaweed—Anna's mind trying to make seaworthy sense of what her eyes saw.

"A duty belt," she said after a moment. "Bob's." Teddy made a small sound, a muffled squeak. Given there was nothing she could do for the woman who'd saved her life but find her husband—or his body—Anna chose not to notice.

She took the gun belt from Cliff's hands and lifted it over the gunwale to examine it. Bob's semiautomatic was snapped into the holster. Spare magazines were full, as was the magazine in the SIG Sauer; cuffs and pepper spray were in place. Because the belt Velcroed closed instead of buckling, it was impossible to tell if it had been removed intentionally or torn off with violence. What with one thing and another, Anna had allowed herself to believe Bob's disappearance and the sinking of the green go-fast boat were separate, unrelated incidents. Boats burned for many reasons, most having nothing to do with AWOL park rangers. Factoring Bob back in changed things. Now it was not just the death of a stranger but, perhaps, a man she liked.

"Anything else?"

Cliff shook his head then said: "I don't know. There might be. I figured you'd want to know soon as could be, so I marked the spot, brought the belt up and called."

Technically, he should have left it where it lay, but under the circumstances that seemed a moot point.

"You up for another dive?" Anna asked.

"Sure. It's less than thirty feet for the most part. I shouldn't have any trouble."

"We," Anna said. "I'm going with you."

"Do you think that's a good idea?" Diving experience, age, years of captaining boats, of commanding, made his softspoken question something to be seriously considered.

Anna did so. After a moment she said honestly: "Not a great idea, no. Maybe not even a good idea. But I'll be okay, if that's what you mean. All I intend to do is be a floating pair of eyes."

Satisfied, Cliff nodded. "We stay together," he said neutrally, aware Anna was the captain of this particular ship.

"We stay together," she agreed.

For just such emergencies Anna kept an old swimsuit in the storage bin in the compartment under the bridge. It stank of mildew and bagged in the seat but would suffice to keep her legal. Putting on BC vest and tank wasn't as bad as she'd feared. Though she was bruised from being batted about the ocean floor, the heavy nylon mesh of the vest and the metal air tank had protected those portions of her anatomy from the cutting edges of the coral.

Side by side, she and Cliff rolled backward off the gunwale. When she hit the water Anna would have screamed had her mouth not been full of rubber. Seawater bit into each and every cut and scrape, rubbing salt into her wounds. The shock made her feel faint and disoriented. Pain and the wooziness faded as skin and mind adapted to the new realities of life.

Cliff hung in the water nearby, as comfortable and perfectly balanced as Linda had been. At his "follow me" signal Anna kicked into motion. Once the initial sting had passed it felt wonderful to be underwater. The freedom and weightlessness of diving was the closest thing to flying unaided Anna would ever experience. It was good to stretch her bruised muscles; good to have the weight off her scraped buttocks. And it was good to be doing something other than gridding the ocean with a potential widow and finding nothing.

As they swam past the wreck, she was fascinated by the new configuration the second explosion left behind. The stern, still of a piece, had been shifted, and the floating life jacket, instead of straining for the surface, was half buried beneath. The bow section no longer existed: no structure, no cabin, just pieces blown out in a rough cone shape pointing in the direction from which Anna had been swimming. It was easy to see how Linda, much closer to the bow of the boat, had fared no worse than she had. For all their might, explosives could be aimed and channeled by containers no more substantial than wax. What had aimed this, Anna couldn't begin to guess and doubted it mattered. She had not been the target. Nor had anyone else.

Further on Cliff stopped, hovering several feet above the bottom. They were about twenty-five feet down. The ocean floor was devoid of vegetation, though not of life. Without trying, Anna found two tiny fish. One no bigger than her thumbnail vanished into a burrow in the sand at her approach. A red flag, like a surveyor's flag on an eighteen-inch wire, had been stuck in the sand. This, then, was where Bob Shaw's gun belt had been found. With a fingertip, Anna drew a spiral out around the flag, pointed to herself then Cliff. He made the okay sign with thumb and forefinger. Staying ten feet apart the two of them began swimming in an ever-widening circle with the red flag at its center.

The small desolate plain of sand and dead coral gave way to an underwater meadow of what looked to be grasses covered with fur. Soon, on the northern edge of their circle, they swam over the remnants of the sunken go-fast boat. Because of the boulders of coral, they were forced to swim nearer the surface.

On the fifth circuit, more coral intruding with its cacophony
of color and confusion of life, they found Shaw's deck shoes.
Twenty feet apart and tumbled into a forest of hot pink
anemone, Anna was surprised they had spotted them. After the
location of the second shoe was marked with another of Cliff's
flags, Anna stopped. Hanging in the water, clear now that they'd
moved away from the area of disturbance, she looked back
across the imaginary circle till she found the red flag marking
where the gun belt had been found. A compass reading from the
line between shoes and flag read NNW. Turning, Anna followed
a SSE heading, continuing the line.

Approximately three hundred feet farther she came upon
what she'd known must be there: the *Bay Ranger*. A jagged hole
in her bow, she lay on her side in a patch of sand beneath twenty
feet of clear, still water. Had the wreck of the go-fast boat not
stopped them, Danny and Linda would have found her in the
next couple of passes. Already, curious fishes had come and
swam languidly around the control panel and its sunshade.

The little Sylvan runabout had no cabin, no belowdecks.
Anna and Cliff could see at a glance that Bob was not onboard.
Had Bob been on one of the other patrol boats—both Boston
Whalers—like Molly Brown, he would have been unsinkable.
A Whaler would float even when cut in half, and run if you hap-
pened to be on the half with the engine. She hoped Bob's love
affair with stealth hadn't killed him.

Because she'd be a fool not to, Anna swam around the boat
to be sure a corpse was not pinned beneath or thrown nearby.
She knew she would find nothing. Bob Shaw had been alive and
swimming at one point. Either he'd left the site of the *Bay* and
dropped first shoes and then duty belt in an attempt to reach the
boat that had exploded, or he had jumped from the green boat
before it sank and was swimming toward the *Bay*, dropping first
belt then shoes.

Anna guessed it was the former for a couple reasons.
Though they couldn't be sure without further investigation, it
was a good bet that a piece of debris, blasted from the green
boat, was the missile that smashed a hole in Bob's hull. The
other reason was, knowing Bob Shaw, if he needed to offload
weight, his shoes would go before his firearm.

Catching Cliff's eye, Anna pointed up. Together they surfaced. The strain of a long night, a severe pummeling and a near-death experience were catching up to Anna. Removing her snorkel, she whistled high and piercing, two fingers under her tongue the way Carl Johnson taught her in third grade. When Daniel sighted them she waved and was comforted to see him loose the two boats so they could motor over. Anna didn't feel up to swimming back, but, she told herself—as she would tell them—she remained where she was because she wanted them to see Shaw's boat.

Back onboard, scrapes again on fire from various abuses incurred boarding and stripping off gear, Anna shared what she was fairly sure was the good news.

"It looks like when the other boat exploded, a piece of it pierced Bob's hull and the *Bay* sank. Probably very quickly. It's a damn big hole. Bob was either thrown overboard or jumped. My bet is thrown. His radio is still on his duty belt. If he'd had time, he would have radioed for help before the water ruined it. From where we found the deck shoes and the belt, it looks as though, once in the water, Bob swam toward the other boat.

"There were survivors on it, is what I'm figuring," Anna finished.

"Bob died saving someone, or trying to?" Teddy asked. Her voice was vague, seeking her hero husband through darkness and fog, looking for an image to take to bed for a lifetime of lonely nights.

"I don't think he's dead," Anna said flatly. "He was swimming. We know he had a personal flotation device, and he was hale and hearty enough to think about saving someone's skin other than his own." She looked at East Key, a skinny ribbon of sand barely above waterline, a half-mile from the boats. "I think Bob and whoever he swam to save must be there; the closest landfall."

"Bob," Teddy said. It was half a question and half a call to the man she had come perilously close to giving up as dead.

"I *think* he could have tried for East Key." Anna tried to lower what could be false hopes, but it was too late. Teddy was firing up the *Reef Ranger* without waiting for anyone's by your leave. It was a wonder Anna and Cliff threw off the *Reef*'s lines and saved the *Curious* from being bumped and towed alongside.

Anna stepped up to the bench and slid in beside Teddy. "Let me take over from here." Teddy had the boat up to ramming speed and, if the look on her face was any indication, had no intention of slowing down to beach the thing.

For a second Teddy glared at her, feral as any half-starved cat, but reason returned. She turned the boat over to Anna and moved to the bow to be that much closer to the place her husband might be.

Anna felt a pang of envy at the obvious love between the Shaws. So what if it was based on castles built in the sand of the Caribbean? And she dearly hoped she was right about Bob. After the first glad tidings and the departure of the *Reef* an unpleasant thought had darkened her mood. If Bob was on East Key and he was alive, why hadn't he been jumping, waving, signaling two NPS boats a mere half mile out to sea?

Cutting throttle, she let a wave catch and carry the *Reef* onto the sandy shoreline. East Key was concave along its western shore, creating a nice landing place. Teddy leapt ashore yelling, "Bob!" Anna stayed to give the *Reef* an extra pull above waterline. East Key was so small—measured not in acres and miles but yards and buckets—Teddy would either find her husband or know he wasn't there before Anna'd done.

"Bob! Bob?" Then, music to Anna's ears: "Oh, Bob."

Anna turned to follow the joyful noise. Teddy's head popped above a low dune with a prairie-dog quickness that nearly made Anna laugh.

"Bring the first-aid kit," Teddy ordered in a voice that had Anna hopping like one of Teddy's emergency-room orderlies.

The *Reef*'s medical kit slung over one complaining shoulder, she scrambled up the dune behind which she'd seen Teddy Shaw's head. Sand ground into the abrasions on her bare legs and scorched the bottoms of her feet. As she topped the low dune, she forgot her petty concerns.

Ranger Shaw lay on the other side, his lower body sprawled across the legs of a dead man as if he'd lain atop the corpse before his wife turned him face up. Teddy cradled his head in her lap.

"He's not dead," she said fiercely as Anna took in the scene.

"Bleeding out?" Anna asked.

"No."

"Breathing?"

"Yes."

Shaw would live another couple minutes.

"Water," Anna said, dropped the first-aid kit where Teddy could reach it easily, and trotted back to the *Reef*. Shaw had suffered some kind of trauma, swum at least a half-mile if not more, either pursuing or towing another man, then lay in the sun for half a day. Dehydration would be a serious factor.

In the minutes Anna was gone Teddy completed the evolution from wife to head ER nurse. The dead man had been rolled on his side, facing away, to give him his dignity. The medical bag was set to shade Shaw's face, and Teddy had his trouser leg nearly cut off.

Anna joined her, unbuttoned Shaw's shirt, then ran both hands over his head, neck and torso to check for damage. "Back okay?" she asked as they worked.

"Clean," Teddy replied. "He was laying facedown half on the dead guy. I checked his back before I rolled him over."

"Head, neck and chest are okay," Anna said. "Oh, hey, got some eye movement."

"Not surprised. I hurt him. Look here." Below Bob's left knee the white of bone showed through the flesh. "Broken," Teddy said. "Compound. And lost a lot of blood."

"Bob, open your eyes," Teddy said commandingly.

Shaw opened his eyes; blinds going up in an empty room.

"You're okay, honey. We're here. You need to stay awake. We're going to sit you up so Anna can give you a drink."

Shaw came back into himself, his soul back in his eyes. "Water," he repeated. "Good . . ."

Cliff, Mack and Danny arrived. Bob was packaged and Danny and Mack carried him aboard the *Reef*. Mack argued for the *Atlantic* for some reason but was ignored. After the night's terrors and the day's adventures, Anna was going to carry her catch home.

She did give Mack the unidentified corpse. They didn't have a body bag and the remains, made festive by beach towels, were strapped to a backboard.

Teddy stayed at Bob's side murmuring endearments and giving him as many small sips of water as he would take. The bleeding around the fracture had stopped on its own hours before. Compound fractures were always bad, but where the exposed end of the bone had been drying in sun and jammed full of sand for five hours, complications proliferated. Other than rehydration, neither Anna nor Teddy would attempt treatment. Anna radioed Duncan, the fort's historian, to call the mainland for a helicopter. Before the *Reef Ranger* brought her cargo to the dock, he radioed back to let her know one had been dispatched.

Mack and Danny carried Bob to his wife's "hospital." The corpse was housed in the researcher's dorm with the air-conditioning turned as cold as the thermostat had numbers for. The body would fly back to Key West with Bob and Teddy Shaw.

Everyone was anxious to hear Bob's story, but at Teddy's request, they left the infirmary. Mack, more tenacious or more curious, was inclined to ignore requests, and Anna had ordered him out. After that he remembered his manners and left with good grace. Nobody but the Shaws seemed to want to admit the adventure was over.

With water to drink, a saline IV drip to assist, and a cool dim place, Bob regained full consciousness. Anna asked to do the intravenous drip, needing the "sticks" to keep her IV status as an emergency medical technician current. After she failed twice, leaving small bloody prints behind, Teddy snatched the needle away and inserted it neatly.

"I'd have got it in another try," Anna said.

"Bob's suffered enough."

Anna knew that, but "sticks" were hard to come by.

After a shot of Demerol authorized over the phone by the medevac doctor and administered by his wife, Bob bordered on jocular. Sometimes being alive did that to a person.

When Bob was as comfortable as possible, Anna pulled up a stool and sat by the bedside facing him. Several times she breathed in and out, ridding her feverish brain of the strangeness and ghostly half-images that had plagued her since being awakened by Teddy in the middle of the night. Mind clean and open, she was ready to listen.

"So," she said. "Tell me what happened." She half expected

to get a rebuke from Teddy. Though alert and oriented, Bob was in pretty bad shape. Teddy said nothing, and it occurred to Anna that heroes, regardless of personal injury, were expected to make it back through enemy lines to report, even if they had to do it with their last breath.

Bob began his tale with scattered thoughts and broken time lines, stopped, made adjustments inside his skull, and began again, this time at the beginning.

"Just before midnight I was heading in from checking the northwest boundary of the park. Three shrimpers, all outside our waters. Two family-owned. Been here before. Never been any trouble. The third looked like trouble. Details in my patrol log."

Bob's patrol log was providing reading for the fishes, but Anna didn't interrupt.

"As I came past Loggerhead, I caught a glint of something toward East Key. No lights, nothing like that, just a place on the water that didn't match up. I radioed in . . ."

His voice trailed off, and Anna watched his eyes grow dull as he searched his mind for verification of his words.

"You called in," Teddy said, taking the place of memory. "You told me you were onto something and needed radio silence."

"Okay. I radioed in, then turned off my running lights and cruised toward the place on the water. With binoculars I could see it was a Scarab—one of those go-fast boats, like a cigarette boat but bigger and only a few years old. It was black or some dark color, moored in the middle of a coral bed, no lights. Two people onboard. Maybe three but at least two. Could see the lit ends of their cigarettes. Looked hinky.

"About fifty yards out I turned my light on them and hailed. The boat was deep metallic green and rode low in the water like it was loaded to the gunwales. Not usual for a go-fast boat. They'd have heard my motor so my being there was no surprise, but as soon as they realized I was law enforcement, one guy ducks into the cabin and the other fires up the engine. He got panicked or something and didn't take time to turn on the fans to purge the bilge and engine compartment of gas fumes.

"Must have been a spark, because it blew up. A piece of it hit my boat. I was thrown overboard. My boat sank, theirs burned a second then went down."

Bob stopped and rubbed his eyes with both fists like a sleepy child. "God, it was fast," he said, sounding less like a Joe Friday and more like a real person. "Two boats afloat. Bang. Flash. Both boats gone like they never happened. I didn't know they could sink that fast. I might have a funny time sense. I was never out cold, but things were hazy after I went overboard. Just for a couple seconds." This last was to Teddy, who nodded as if she expected no less from him.

"I could see one of the passengers on the other boat—I think the one that started the engine—was still alive but in a bad way. I got my PFD inflated and started to swim over to give him a hand. Till then I didn't know my leg had been hit—it didn't hurt, nothing. Once I knew, it hurt like a son-of-a-bitch. Anyway I swam toward the guy but with my leg it was rough going and I had to drop my duty belt. I lost my sidearm."

Bob looked at his wife, loath to admit this gross failing on his part.

"Only a damn fool would have kept their gun given the circumstances. Anyway, Cliff found it for you," Anna said. "Go on."

"I got to the guy. He was alive but hurting and not able to help himself. I towed him to East Key—and tried to get up a signal fire. I couldn't manage it. By the time the sun came up the guy was breathing bad. I tried to shade him. Then I don't remember anything till Teddy yelling, 'Bob.' " He smiled at his wife and Anna looked away, not to give them a moment's privacy but because their faces had blurred. She rubbed her eyes, wondering if she needed sleep or what. When she looked again they were back in focus.

"The man you saved—"

"He died."

"Still counts," Anna said. "The man never said anything?"

"Not much. He was never fully there, if you know what I mean. He was burned, and I think he'd been struck on the head. Pain and concussion or whatever had him scrambled."

"What did he say?" Anna asked.

"Let's see." Bob closed his eyes the better to recall. "He was scared, wanted to get to dry land. 'Feet on American soil,' he said once. Once he said, 'cold,' and then I thought he was saying 'tree saw' but it made no sense. Nothing he said made sense."

For a minute, or maybe more, Anna waited in case Bob should wish to add anything, but he didn't. "I'll let you rest," she said. "Your ride should be here in half an hour or so. I want to get a look at the man you saved before they haul him off to the knackers."

As she closed the infirmary door it suddenly struck her that Bob had done it. When reality came knocking he'd been able to act out his fantasy. He'd swum over half a mile with a compound fracture dragging behind him a man he'd saved from the briny deep. He'd tried to build a signal fire and, when he felt himself blacking out, his last thought was to fall in such a way as to protect the other guy from the burning rays of the sun.

That made him a genuine, bona-fide hero in Anna's book.

Later there would be time to fête Bob, to wonder why the riders of the green go-fast boat were hovering off East Key, why they panicked sufficiently when they saw law enforcement to forget to clear the gasoline fumes, and why they carried extra fuel in their bow. Right now she had a corpse to examine. The helicopter from Key West would be at the fort in less than thirty minutes to whisk this bit of human jetsam away.

It took her only a minute to fetch a camera and return to the researcher's dorm. Danny and Mack did their work well. All six generators must have been working overtime. The dorm was as cold as a morgue. And as dim. The long narrow room, packed floor-to-ceiling with bunk beds, had but one window facing out on the parade ground, and that was dull with a cataract of mini-blinds.

Having switched on the overhead lights, which seemed to alter the nature of the dimness rather than shed illumination, Anna walked back to the industrial-style kitchen. On the counter, stripped of the colorful towels and covered by a white sheet, was her objective.

As she neared, the sheet, draped over what must have been the man's right hand, stirred; a minute flutter and lift as if plucked up then dropped by restless fingers. A horror movie thrill closed Anna's throat, and she stopped. For an instant the room's walls seemed to waver, start to close in. The sudden panic receded, but not the fear. For a minute or more she watched the shrouded form, but there were no more zombielike manifestations.

"Damn," Anna said aloud and was comforted by the sound of her own voice. The fort, lack of sleep, too much sun, too long underwater, something was playing tricks with her mind. "Okay, buddy," she continued, finding talking brought her out of whatever creepy place she'd glimpsed. "Let's see if you've got anything to tell me."

Pinching the sheet delicately between thumbs and forefingers, she peeled it back. She always took care to respect the dead—an honor she would not necessarily extend were they still living. Dead, a person was evidence at best and the empty valise of someone's memory if nothing else. Anna hoped this dead man would prove a treasure trove of answers. Starting with who he was.

Having taken the sheet off, she put her pocket notebook and pen on the counter by the corpse's right foot, pulled on latex gloves to protect herself as much as any trace evidence, and began. Hispanic—Cuban or Puerto Rican probably—in his late twenties to mid-thirties, black hair cut short and well, the kind of barbering a well-to-do businessman might get. Much of the left side of his face was covered in second-degree burns. The ear had been taken by a third-degree burn. All that remained was a hole surrounded by blackened flesh.

Around his neck was a two-inch gold crucifix—not a cross, a crucifix with the crucified Christ executed in exquisite detail with skill and a joy in the macabre. The chain was fused into the flesh where the fire had hit.

Shirt and pants were burned nearly off the left side of the body, while the right remained relatively intact. He'd been standing to the right of the blast, at the engine. It was probably he who'd triggered the first explosion. Anna checked the rest of him for possible identifying marks. His right pocket contained one hundred fifty-three dollars in a gold or gold-plated money clip with a dog's head engraved on it, a shepherd or wolf or coyote. Other than that he carried no identification. A bird of some kind, maybe an eagle, wings folded, was tattooed on the back of his calf. Possibly he'd been in the service at one time. Her knowledge of the military and its insignias fuzzy at best and gleaned from the movies, Anna couldn't remember which branch, if any, used a bird diving downward as its emblem.

Dutifully, she photographed everything and touched nothing but his trouser pockets and the edge of a torn trouser leg. If there was to be any forensic investigation of the remains, she didn't want it said she'd fouled it up. Odds were good there wouldn't be. No crime they knew of had been committed. He'd killed himself and his buddy in an unnecessary but not terribly rare boating accident.

Probably X rays of his teeth would be taken for identification purposes and, if no one came forward with a missing-persons claim, the body would be held however many days Florida law decreed, then disposed of.

If the man had grown up outside the United States, his dental work would be of little value. The boat might be a better way to trace his identity. If it was his boat. If it had been purchased and/or licensed in the U.S.

Anna clicked a couple shots of the tattoo just to prove she was doing her job, and suffered a moment of compassion for Florida law-enforcement officers of every stripe. Working where several cultures came together, many recent immigrants, many illegal, the twists and tangles in what in Kansas might be a routine investigation became an almost impossible task.

Leaving the makeshift morgue with its sad John Doe, Anna could hear the chop and whuff of the medevac helicopter from Key West. Garden Key had a helipad on a slight rise between the campground and the sea on the old coaling dock used to refuel ships when the fort was a working part of America's first line of defense.

She had no desire to be anywhere near the helipad when the helicopter set down. The mere thought of being sandblasted on top of flayed by live coral made the undamaged bits of her twitch.

The Shaws and the corpse shipped out. The search and rescue had been a success: her ranger was not dead; her administrative officer was not widowed. Further diving was a bad idea—at least until tomorrow. Both Anna and Linda were too tired and beat-up to be safe, and Cliff had done more than his share. Though he would go again without complaint if Anna asked him to, she wouldn't. He was no longer a young man—he was no longer even a middle-aged man unless he intended to live to one hundred and forty. Besides, Anna wanted to see things firsthand. The weather was dead calm; the wreck would still be there tomorrow.

The remainder of the day she spent alone in the office, enjoying the quiet and the protection of walls, cushioned chairs and air-conditioning. When she'd been a Yankee, she'd scoffed at the stale soulless world of processed air. Since becoming a southerner, she'd seen the light. With the top layer of her epidermis scraped away, she was more than content to hide in the safe and comfortable womb of the modern world.

Another of the perks of modern science was instant gratification, this time in the form of a digital camera, the one fitted with an underwater container Anna, then Linda, then Cliff had used to photograph the wreck. Anna'd used it again to take her pictures of the corpse. After she'd written reports on the past twenty-four hours' adventures, she downloaded the photos to Teddy's computer. Anna had taken advantage of Teddy's absence to work at her desk rather than stay locked away in the claustrophobic confines of her own office.

An advantage of the digital camera was that a photographer could take up to twelve hundred photographs before running out of space. The disadvantage was that a photographer could take up to twelve hundred photographs. Because film was not a factor, there was no need to be frugal.

Cliff's photos, taken after the second explosion, were the most interesting. Anna compared before and after shots, but could come up with nothing better than Danny's original suggestion that the go-fast carried extra fuel, and fire from the first blast engendered the second.

When she finally emerged from beneath the virtual sea, the office had grown gray with dusk. She shut the computer down and tried to move, but she'd been turned to stone. An absurd picture of Teddy returning to find her hunched in her chair, back humped, hands shaped like claws, glazed eyes fixed on the screen, tittered through Anna's brain.

Groaning, she loosed the muscles and joints grown stiff. Even her skin had stiffened, or so it seemed, and felt as if it might rip were she to move too quickly.

Getting outside helped. Though the sun had set, it was still close to ninety degrees. After so long in the AC, the heat's first embrace felt grand. Warm, dusk and no mosquitoes: a rare treat for a woman late of Mississippi. The Dry Tortugas were not always so blessed. Often after rains there would be an infestation of the bloodsuckers, particularly if there'd been an open container left out to hold standing water. With the recent drought, the vile creatures were blessedly absent.

Rather than cut across the parade ground, Anna climbed the spiral staircase near the fort's gift shop and took the scenic route home. The stairs were dark enough she had to feel her way up, but the steps were wide—at least at the outer edges—and the handrails in good shape. On the second level she came out into the relative brightness of the open casemates.

To her right, above what had once been the guardroom and was now the Visitors Center and gift shop, was the cell in which Dr. Mudd and one of the other Lincoln conspirators had been imprisoned. To her left was the northeast bastion. Anna turned left. With openings to the sea on one side and the parade ground on the other, the long rows of casemates collected light. On moonlit nights Anna often walked in them, enjoying the silence, the shadows and the sense of human history that mixed with the blood and mortar holding the bricks together. The bastions, with their cavernous rooms and complex system of arches, were her favorite haunts.

Not this night. The northeast bastion's size and depth made it too dark. Usually the dark didn't bother her, but her nerves had been scraped along with her flesh, and the black corners set off internal alarms. Hugging the inner wall, she hurried through and came out into the long passage down the northern edge of the parade ground. Two perfect rows of arches, one small, made for the passage of men, one large for the housing of cannon, unrolled. The arches forced perspective, creating the illusion that the dimly lit vaults continued on to infinity.

Soothed by the uniform light and the fussy mutterings of thousands of sooty terns nesting on nearby Bush Key, Anna drifted through the measured twilight.

Halfway to her quarters she noticed she was not alone. The other's presence was not heralded by a shout or a footstep but by an unpleasant frisson along Anna's spine. At the end of the casemates where the last arch gaped black, leading into the one bastion without a gun port at its end, the one called The Chapel because it was surmised it had been so intended by the fort's builders, stood a woman in white.

Her dress was long, tight-waisted, the sleeves of her blouse oversized at the shoulder and snug from elbow to wrist. For a moment she was still, then she raised one hand and patted her upswept hair as if looking for loose pins to poke in more securely.

"Hey!" Anna yelled. "You!" And she began to run. The woman looked up, then stepped back into the darkness, vanishing from sight. Running quickly and lightly, it was only seconds before Anna reached the place where the woman had stood. She searched The Chapel, the northwestern spiral stairs down to the lower level and the exposed part of the casemates in front of her apartment and that of Duncan and his family, but found nothing.

Shaken, more scared than she ought to be, Anna sat on the picnic table outside her quarters. There were three possibilities: she'd seen a ghost, somebody was messing with her or she was going mad.

6

My Dearest Peggy—

Sorry it has been so long since last I wrote. Things have been a bit mad. Or perhaps I should say a bit madder than usual. The fracas at the sally port turned out not to be the lynching of Private Lane but the arrival through the storm of the Lincoln conspirators. The entire fort was up in arms, our boys literally running about with weapons and anger at ready. The fort crackled with evil the rest of that night and for two days after. Joseph kept Tilly and I under house arrest for nearly forty-eight hours either in fear for our well-being or, more likely, because he forgot to tell our guards to go away and leave us alone. I do know they dearly wanted to be relieved of this most onerous duty.

We did not see Joseph. I don't know where he slept or if he slept at all. I expect he was busy keeping the soldiers and prisoners from using the arrival of the conspirators as a rallying point to express their rage and frustration at the long hot summer with its dry storms and lack of fresh food and water.

Tilly slept with me both nights. The unsettled state of the garrison, along with being under house arrest, had us both on edge. I cannot, however, say that I slept with Tilly. The girl kicks and tosses about just as she did when she was five years old. I don't know that I should have slept a great deal better had she gone to her own bed. The heat is oppressive and having a soldier escort one to the privy is not conducive to the free and easy functioning of the body. Tilly is as out of sorts as I but for different reasons. Singing romantic duets with Private Lane, then holding his bloody head in her lap by lamplight, has unhinged our little sister. I do believe Tilly is in love with the boy or fancies herself so, which amounts to the same thing.

By the afternoon we were released, she had worked herself into a frenzy of worry that Joel had died. My attempts to assure her that the fort's surgeon would have seen to the boy and he was probably resting comfortably in the hospital had little ameliorating effect. Possibly this was because I wasn't sure I believed it myself.

We weren't so much released from our gentle, if humiliating, bondage as simply forgotten. Tilly and I were in my room, sewing a new blouse to replace the one Joel Lane had been so inconsiderate as to bleed all over, when Tilly—who'd done more sighing and fretting than sewing—got up to visit the privy. She returned in moments with the report that our warden had vanished and, the call of nature so urgent a minute before now forgotten, insisted we go in search of Joel.

The storm passed without giving us a drop of rain to fill our cisterns, and the heat of summer, heavy with moisture we can neither drink nor wash in but are condemned to wear like a sweated sheet, filled the parade ground. Still I was glad to be out—or at least as "out" as life on a prison island allows.

The fort was once again in order. Sentries patrolled on the third tier. Work gangs labored at building the enlisted men's barracks. Off-duty soldiers smoked in the open casemates or played at cards or dice. Gambling is second only to consuming alcohol as the favorite pastime, providing at least an illusion of excitement.

Despite this appearance of normalcy, I could feel an undercurrent of tension. Tilly was nearly coming out of her skin, alternately tearing up or giggling as if her poor over-burdened little self could not decide whether we were embarking on a grand adventure or a tragic love affair.

Before the boy had been punished for his "traitorous talk" he'd been lodged along with others from his captured regiment in one of the casemates in the northwest corner over the bakery. Because these Virginia boys are young, for the most part, well spoken and ready to put their backs into any work assigned them, they've been given the best quarters the fort has to offer. The casemate they share is not walled in, and they are afforded the relief of sea breezes.

Ignoring the impropriety of shouting up at the prisoners, Tilly and I stopped beneath their quarters. A pleasant young man with beautiful mustaches that curl to the bottom of his jaw told us Joel had not returned to the casemate after the Lincoln conspirators came. Their captain asked the guards where Joel was. They said they didn't know. He'd either been taken to the hospital outside the fort's walls or been put in another casemate.

As we crossed the parade ground it became clear that the tension I felt was not all of my own making. The soldiers are usually a friendly lot, calling out greetings or wanting to show me a letter from home or some small thing they've carved from driftwood or formed from iron scraps. This day they were quiet or formed into small clumps, backs to the outside world, muttering and whispering to each other. Even the work gangs were silent: no singing, no banter, just the ring of hammers and the repetitive thump of wheelbarrows rolled over uneven ground.

The two biggest trees between the sally port and the open area in the middle of the parade ground had borne ugly fruit. Half a dozen men, some in the battered remnants of the uniform of the confederacy, some union men, had been bound, hands behind their backs, then strung up till their toes barely brushed the earth.

I'm ashamed to admit neither Tilly nor I gave them much thought but to glance at their faces to determine that Private Lane was not among them.

We hated to ask the guard at the sally port the whereabouts of Joel Lane—Tilly, I'm sure, remembering Sergeant Sinapp. Still, we had no recourse but the guard. We couldn't very well wander from cell to cell like Wee Willie Winkie, peeking in the windows and crying at the locks.

By great good fortune Sinapp was nowhere to be seen. Outside the fort a ship had docked for coal, and the bustle and shouting had drawn away everyone not duty-bound to stay at their posts. A fresh-faced boy from New York was manning the sally port, leaning against the stone arch and looking forlornly

at the men loading coal as if they attended a marvelous entertainment to which he was not invited.

Intimidating him was child's play but, as with most things
that come easily, of little value. He did not know Joel by name,
could not separate one bloodied soldier from another after two
days of near-riot and subsequent punishment.

"Maybe Hospital Key," he told us. Hospital Key is nearly a
mile away. There is a makeshift building there—little more than
walls and roof hastily knocked together—where contagious patients are housed. Behind the dreary structure is where we bury
our dead. "Being sent to Hospital Key" is our euphemism for
dying. Perhaps it was because of this association that I felt so
hopeless.

As good fortune would have it, while we were at the docks a
skiff from the hospital landed with two of the "nurses"—unskilled prisoners willing to work with the sick. Even after a
quarter of an hour at sea the men stank of sickness and rot. It
caught in my throat, threatening to dislodge my lunch of beans
and salted pork. Both Tilly and I clutched our handkerchiefs
over our noses to the amusement of the men. One "nurse," a
confederate lieutenant, told us Joel had not been in hospital as
far as he knew, and he served there twelve out of every twenty-
four hours.

Tilly was despondent over the news and became convinced
that her pet Johnny Reb was dead. I admit I was at a loss myself. From the extent of the injuries Joel sustained, neither of us
could believe he would be on any of the work crews. Having no
other options, we walked along the moat back toward the sally
port. There are always magnificent frigate birds soaring there,
immense black-winged creatures which, rather than flap, seem
able to soar indefinitely. Tilly, engrossed in a world built partly
of her love of drama and partly of real fear for Joel Lane, called
them "dark angels." I pooh-poohed her as befits the role of the
older, wiser sister, but I cannot say the description was not apt.

To further dampen spirits already near to drowning, a smirk-
ing Sergeant Sinapp met us at the drawbridge. His uniform,
heavy wool like those of all the soldiers, was dark from armpit
to waist with sweat, and his dun-colored hair stuck to his forehead beneath the brim of his cap in a parody of a little Caesar.

"Mornin', ladies," he drawled. I find it particularly offensive when men from the north affect a southern drawl. It always sounds cruel to my ears. Coming from Sinapp I suspected it was meant to be.

I chose not to reply. Tilly, absorbed in her own thoughts, scarcely seemed to notice him.

Not wishing for the indignity of trying to dodge around him, I hooked my arm through Tilly's to keep her from wandering into the moat in her preoccupation, stopped in front of the sergeant and waited. It was clear I was doomed to endure whatever he chose to consider witty repartee.

"Looking for the boyfriend?" he asked and gave Tilly an encore performance of his leer two nights before. Fortunately she didn't seem to notice.

"Sergeant," I said. "Please excuse us, we wish to pass." I was terribly polite. Molly would be pleased to know I do occasionally use the good manners she was at such pains to instill in us.

The foul man didn't budge. The peculiar fatigue that had descended upon me so abruptly kept me from saying more.

"You been to the hospital?"

I said nothing. My focus had slid from Joel, Tilly and even the odious and odiferous sergeant to a single and greatly desired goal: I wanted to sit down, preferably in the shade.

"You have. I seen you." That was a lie but I left it unchallenged.

Sweat rolled down both sides of his face and into his collar. I was pleased to note he was nursing a particularly nasty boil below his left ear where the wool chafed his neck.

"Your boyfriend ain't in the hospital," Sinapp had to say. "We put him where traitor's deserve to be. Teach him to talk more respectful. Too bad there won't be anybody to hear it where he is."

Too tired to think of a reply, I stood holding up Tilly for a while longer. Either Sinapp grew bored with baiting us or he had exhausted his vocabulary. Finally he stepped aside and let us walk in out of the sun.

The shade beneath the sally port is complete unto darkness—or so it seemed after the glare of the sun—and a breeze off the harbor blows through. I led Tilly to a wooden bench the officers of the guard keep there and collapsed and let the unnerving assault of Sergeant Sinapp and two nights without

proper sleep wash over me. Tilly came out of her stupor, which
should have been a comfort—I had begun to worry—but it was
only to embark on an emotional storm of a different kind. Tears
leaked from her eyes. "He's dead. They killed him," she said in
a tiny voice. " 'There's no one to talk to where he is.'" She repeated the sergeant's words.

What with one thing and another, Tilly was working herself
into a state of hysterics. I know I should have slapped her, but I
doubt Tilly has ever been struck in her life and I couldn't bring
myself to be the first. I like to think it is because I am too good-
hearted, but it may have been that I was simply too tired to raise
my arm.

Instead, I held her and rocked her and murmured, "Shh, shh,
he's not dead," over and over until I convinced myself.

Sinapp's words might have meant the boy had been murdered, but his tone was that of a man enjoying not the memory
of an evil done but an ongoing cruelty. There was such *relish* in
his voice when he spoke of there being no one to hear Joel's
imagined repentance. In the unfinished confines of Fort Jefferson there was only one place I could think of where one would
be truly alone, unheard.

"He's not dead," I told Tilly.

She rebounded from despair as only the young can: in the
time it takes for a tear to be wiped away.

"I must go to him"

I must go to him. What on earth has Molly been letting that
girl read? She was such the tragic heroine I was tempted to administer the slap my inherent saintliness had resisted just moments before. All that saved her from at the very least the acid
of my tongue was the look of genuine anguish on her face.

The young man on sentry duty at the guardhouse moved,
and we realized our teapot tempest had been observed. Eyes
blinded by shade after glare and minds blinded by our own
thoughts, neither of us had noticed him against the stone in his
stone-dark uniform.

"Now then don't you go thinking on that, Mrs. Coleman. It
won't do, you know."

He moved out from the wall to stand before us.

"You knew," I said. I wasn't so much accusing him as
amazed that this callow youth was such a practiced dissembler.

"I apologize, ma'am. But we have orders, and not talking about the Lane boy is one of them."

"You are talking about him now," Tilly said with the inexorable logic of a sixteen-year-old. The guard couldn't have been much older and seemed struck by Tilly's words.

"I am," he said, appalled at his dereliction of duty. A moment was all he needed to justify things in his mind. "But it's different."

I began to suspect this sweet-faced liar was not one of the Lord's brighter creations.

"We'll see him now," Tilly announced and stood up, brushing her skirts straight in a no-nonsense sort of way. "Now."

The soldier shuffled his feet but otherwise stood his ground. "I can't let you do that, Miss. The captain would have my hide."

Tilly began to tremble the way she used to just before she threw one of her terrible tantrums. I decided to step in before she humiliated us both and frightened the guard half silly. "We do need to see Private Lane," I told him, trying to make it sound as if we had orders from on high.

He grew more uncomfortable. His feet stilled, but his eyes fixed on some place of courage on the wall between Tilly and me.

"Come on, Tilly," I said with what I hoped was the voice of age and authority.

"I can't let you do that," he said again and stepped in front of me. I admired him for his courage and attention to duty, but my patience was at an end.

"How will you stop us?" I asked. "Will you throw us to the ground? Lock us in the guardhouse? Both of us?"

Regardless of orders, he was unwilling to lay hands on a woman, particularly not his captain's wife.

"I'll inform the captain," he said finally.

"And abandon your post? If you do that you will end up keeping Private Lane company. Or worse." With that, I took Tilly's arm and we left him standing in his personal quandary. Of course he would hail the first soldier who came within range and send him to fetch Joseph, but I hoped Tilly and I had gained enough time.

Tilly and I scuttled hastily down the row of casemates to the left of the sally port, walking through the narrow arches. In the shadows to our left was a rubble of new brick and gleaming cannon, oiled and ready but so new they'd not been fired. On our right was the brilliant light of the parade ground. I had been to our destination only once before and had not had the cause nor desire to see it a second time. Tilly was not even aware of its existence, and I couldn't really think of any words that might soften what was bound to be a blow.

At last we came to the largest room yet, windowless as were the others with no firing slits or gun ports to let in the day. A wooden door set in the heavy planks that sealed off one of the arches.

"What's that?" Tilly asked, again five years old.

I told her: "It's called the dungeon. It's the only truly secure place in the fort. Joseph puts the most dangerous men here sometimes."

"Oh, look," Tilly whispered and pointed.

I had forgotten, but just above the door were the words, "Abandon Hope All Ye Who Enter Here." Tilly is not the only person on this earth with a love of melodrama.

I crossed the brick floor to peer in the tiny barred window in the door.

Light, leached of its living gold by passage through the single narrow slit in the outer wall, provided just enough illumination I could see a pile of clothing on the floor of the dungeon. All that marked it as a man was a hand flung out and up, turned as gray and devoid of warmth as the light caught in its palm.

A heavy shackle weighed down the wrist. From it ran a chain to a ring set in the wall. In this age of steam engines, universities and travel across the oceans, a sight so medieval didn't seem real. It was as if I peeked through a portal into a barbaric past.

One my husband had created.

Reality came back to me on the terrible odor wafting through the bars. A bucket for waste stood beside the crumpled form, and next to it, much too close for decency, a bucket with the handle of a water dipper protruding over the rim.

Private Lane—and who else could this have been?—could not even move out of his own waste. I do apologize for talking of such a distasteful thing, but the truth of it underscored how like an animal it made the boy seem, and how like mindless beasts the men who had put him there.

"Is it Joel? Is he alive?"

Tilly had crept up in her slippered feet. Her voice so close and sudden nearly stopped my heart.

"I don't know," I said truthfully. "If he is he won't be for long."

She began tugging at the door, but its lock was forged to withstand the strength of even first love.

The ringing of boots on brick in a rhythm I've listened for over half my life stopped us both—her tugging at the lock, me tugging at her.

"Joseph," I said.

7

Anna put Raffia's letter down and sat for a moment staring sightlessly across the narrow sitting room toward the kitchen sink. A grilled cheese sandwich with a single bite out of it lay congealed to the plate beside her on the sofa. On the coffee table, near the box of letters, was yet another glass of flat, unsparkly sparkling water. Her throat had been dry for days, and the water only seemed to make it worse.

The window over the sink had gone dark. An idle part of Anna's brain pondered that for a moment before logic told her night must have long since replaced the subtropical dusk. Even with this scrap of knowledge to cling to she couldn't shake the creepy sensation that, should she look out of that window, she would see soldiers from the Civil War hanging from trees.

It was the battering she'd taken, she told herself: heat, lack of sleep, blunt trauma, contusions, severed fingers, dead Cubans and live heroes.

And that made her see a ghost.

She shook her head as if negating an invisible accuser. She'd endured worse and never once had emanations from the ether plagued her. Though she didn't want to admit it, because to do so was as frightening as the ghost, the woman in white she knew was Raffia had not been a beginning but merely a next step. For a while now, maybe a day, maybe longer—Anna couldn't be sure, memories of sanity being tricky things—the world had started shifting occasionally, reality slipping just a little, just enough that Anna's entire being was suffused with the wrongness of things. It was as if she'd been cursed with the ability to see into another dimension or another time, and she didn't like it.

"Evils sufficient unto the day." She repeated the aphorism to the cat. Piedmont meowed politely but, not being much of a philosopher, chose to lick his hindquarters rather than continue the discussion. He assumed the position that always reminded Anna of a turkey ready for roasting and commenced his bath. Rubbing her eyes hard enough to chase red and black stars across her vision, Anna knew she was desperately in need of something. Sleep maybe. Her mind, the one thing she could count on to consistently work properly, was on the fritz. Molly. She needed Molly, and not as a sister this time but as a mental health professional. She looked at the clock on the front of the stove. The hands indicated one o'clock. Knowing that couldn't be right, she forced her stiff and creaking frame from the couch and went into the bedroom. The clock on the night table suffered the same time warp: one A.M. The sofa, Aunt Raffia, the other dimension she'd been slipping into, had swallowed three hours, and Anna couldn't readily account for them. By the number of pages beneath Piedmont's furry butt she knew she could not have been reading the whole time. Dreaming? Sleeping with her eyes open?

The unholy frisson of fear that had stalked the edges of her consciousness sank its claws in, and she winced with the sudden onslaught of psychic pain. Molly would have to be rudely awakened. She slipped on her flip-flops.

"Don't wait up," she told the cat as she collected the office keys from under the papers he used as a bath mat.

The night was glorious, the air at least eighty degrees and, after the air-conditioning, soothing against Anna's tortured skin. Unimpeded by light pollution or clouds, the moon cast enough light to throw silver pathways through the open casemates. Anna didn't slow down to glory in it but walked across the middle of the parade ground, dry grasses crackling beneath her feet. She looked neither right nor left, not wanting to see what might be beckoning from the seductive black and silver rooms.

The humdrum bureaucratic box that encapsulated the administrative offices, usually a bane to eyes conditioned to historic grandeur, was a comfort. It exuded normalcy. No ghost worth her ectoplasm would deign to haunt such tedious architecture.

Sitting at Teddy's desk, Anna punched in the long list of numbers required to make a credit card call and was further reassured by her besieged brain's ability to recall them.

"Dr. Pigeon," Molly answered on the second ring, sounding alert and geared for whatever emergency the dead-of-night phone call presaged.

"Hello," Anna said. "It's me."

"Hello?"

"Hello."

"Hello?"

The creepy feeling flexed its claws again, and Anna wondered if she'd really dialed, if she'd spoken aloud, if this was all a dream.

"Anna?"

The delay. The phone on this out-of-the-way scrap of sand was subject to one- to two-second delays in transmission. Anna sighed out breath she'd not known she was holding. This phenomenon was merely mechanical. She could deal with that.

"I'm in trouble," Anna said and waited through another "Anna?" while the words made their journey to her sister's apartment on the Upper West Side.

"Start at the beginning," Molly told her when communication had been established.

Though Molly already knew some of it, Anna did as she was told, listing in chronological order the events that could possibly in some way, shape or form be responsible for the all-too-visible heebie-jeebies she'd been suffering. She included the not-totally-unpleasant pressure of Paul Davidson's love letters, the heat, the dryness of her mouth, the boat explosion, feeling the wreck was sentient and malicious, believing the corpse of the Cuban boatman to have moved a finger, each and every wince or advent of the willies she could recall, ending with the startling appearance of Raffia Coleman, the woman in white.

"Wilkie Collins," Molly said.

"Just like that but no veil," Anna replied. Silence came down, a palpable thing, like an iron plug in Anna's ear. She wondered if Molly was thinking of Collins's book, one of the first mysteries ever written. She hoped Molly was forming a perfectly logical diagnosis that would be the psychiatric equivalent of "take two aspirin and call me in the morning." As the silence continued, Anna began to lose hope.

"Okay," Molly said after what Anna felt was a cruel and unusual amount of time. "You say this figure was our great-great-aunt Raffia, the woman whose letters I sent you?"

"Yes."

"Do you just, quote, *know,* unquote, it was Aunt Raffia, or do you genuinely *believe* it was Aunt Raffia?"

Anna let the difference between the two percolate through her brain. "I just know," she said. "I don't believe it. It's nuts. I don't believe in ghosts. Either this was a figment or a fake, though I don't know who but you knows anything about Aunt Raffia."

"Do you lock your door?"

Anna said nothing. It was a rhetorical question. Living in National Parks, Anna'd seldom felt the need. Living in New York, the concept appalled Molly.

"Okay," Anna agreed. "Where does that leave me? Headed for Bedlam or Bellevue or what?"

Again Molly was quiet too long, and Anna felt a fist of panic knuckling behind her sternum.

"Given you don't literally believe the woman was real—or a real ghost—unless it's some kind of bizarre joke by people too long on a desert island, I think there is hope for you."

Anna laughed, wanting that to be all, something a trained psychiatrist would laugh off as normal, but Molly wasn't through.

"However," her sister went on. "Given the clarity and duration of the hallucination, as well as the intense feelings of fear and disorientation you've been having over the last few days, I would like you to see someone."

"Like a shrink?" Anna asked, appalled just as if she'd not been talking to one for half her life.

"A neurologist would be the place to start," Molly said.

"You've had blunt trauma, possibly affecting the head or the inner ear—I don't really know how an underwater explosion works. That could be a factor. But considering you had these feelings earlier—"

"Maybe not," Anna cut her off, trampling her sister's words as they came two seconds late. "I mean, time's relative, and I wasn't seeing things before the explosion. I mean, of course I was seeing things, but I wasn't *seeing* things." Abruptly she stopped. Not only was she babbling, but with her inner ear she could hear Sister Mary Corinne saying: "Thou dost protest too much."

Molly let the silence settle. Anna hoped she was just making sure there were no words left on the time delay and not dialing her cell phone to call the men with the butterfly nets to catch her mad sibling.

"It never hurts to get things checked out," Molly said reasonably. "A CAT scan, a physical, that sort of thing. Once those are ruled out we can take a next step."

Suddenly Anna was sorry she'd called, sorry she'd told anyone. She didn't want to take a first step, let alone a next step.

"Or it could just be one of those things and go away," she said.

"Could be," Molly returned with such studied neutrality Anna grew more alarmed.

To reassure her sister—and herself—she laughed. "Hey, maybe it's in the air out here. The guy before me went nuts and had to be relieved of duty." The instant the words were out of her mouth, Anna was shocked to hear the truth in them.

"My God, Molly. No kidding. The guy's name was Lanny Wilcox. Daniel, the maintenance man here, said Lanny got stranger and stranger and finally started seeing things nobody else saw. I've got to go. I've got to think about this."

"Be careful," her sister warned. "Things we want to be true are incredibly convincing."

"Right."

"Call me," Molly said. Anna heard the words, little and far away, as she returned the receiver to its cradle and forgot them a second later. To escape the air-conditioning that chilled the sweat between the thin dress and her bare skin, she slipped out of the office and sat on the steps, elbows on her knees, temples between her palms, fingers in hair gone mostly gray.

Lanny Wilcox had gone mad. His girlfriend had left him. He'd become distraught, obsessed with this Theresa woman, increasingly erratic. He'd started seeing things. Developed a paranoia probably—no, undoubtedly—accompanied by feelings of anxiety. Lanny had communicated his thoughts—his visions—to his fellow rangers and been bundled off to the mainland, out of sight and possibly out of his mind.

Now she was here, in his place. Her sweetheart had yet to abandon her, but there was a degree of stress in the relationship. Certainly there'd been other stressors: Shaw's disappearance, the sunken boats, reports explaining the loss of a United States Government boat.

Anna'd begun feeling strange, anxious. She was even a tad paranoid—afraid she was going off the deep end. Of course it wasn't paranoia if it was true.

"Stop that," she said sharply.

Then tonight, she'd begun seeing things.

"Not seeing things," she said aloud. "Seeing a thing. One thing."

But it had been a doozy; a flour-colored female in period costume who Anna "knew" was her and Molly's long-dead great-great-aunt.

The aunt part could be put off onto the power of suggestion; Anna's immersion in Raffia's letters. The ghost or hallucination or whatever could not.

The odds of both she and Lanny Wilcox, same job, same location, close to the same age going insane within weeks of each other were slim—at least she guessed they were. A check of medical leaves and absences of Fort Jefferson personnel over the past five years might be a good idea. Perhaps the nut cases one heard of drifting ashore and taking up residence on the islands of the Caribbean had been perfectly normal when they'd arrived. Sand and surf could have an as-yet-unresearched corrosive effect on the human mind. Maybe van Gogh would still have both ears if he'd stayed in France.

"Jesus," Anna whispered and squeezed the heels of her hands together to push her unraveling thoughts back into a thread she could follow.

So. Unless a great number of people on islands in the Caribbean went nuts, she and Lanny were moderately rare. Either a coincidence Thomas Hardy would be proud of had occurred or there were external forces at work. Like somebody... or something—

Somebody wanted the Supervisory Ranger to believe he or she was going mad so... So what? So they would go away? That was scarcely efficacious; the NPS would simply ship another out to fill the post.

A shudder took her from the inside out as though she ridded herself of a blanket of snow. Trying to fix on motive undermined the theory that Anna wanted—needed—to believe. "Two rangers going crazy in a row is crazy," she said. The echo of the word "crazy" scared her. *Therefore,* she pushed her mind on doggedly, if her theory was true—and until the walls started sprouting eyeballs and the lizards holding forth on Eastern philosophy, she had to believe it was—then she was not losing her mind; she was being gaslighted.

As Lanny had been gaslighted? "Yes," Anna hissed. "Move on." Squeezing her skull even more tightly, she continued to build the case for sanity.

Since Anna chose to believe that she was sane—or at least as sane as she'd ever been—the next obvious conclusion was that what she had seen earlier that evening had been real. Closing her fingers into fists, hair sticking out between the knuckles, she tugged gently at her scalp to assist in this rearrangement of theories.

Starting at the point where seeing was believing, it followed that the ghostly woman was real—not necessarily flesh and blood but conceived and executed by someone who was.

Lanny's beloved was an obvious choice to begin the deconstruction of his reality. If the same thing were happening to Anna, why would the perpetrator choose an image of her Aunt Raffia?

It was possible someone—anyone—in the fort could have read Raffia's letters. They needn't even have bothered to; Anna'd been sufficiently fascinated by the story she'd shared parts of it with several people: Duncan the historian, Teddy, Daniel. Pertaining to the fort as it did, the stories would have been repeated, discussed. Fort Jefferson's peak period as a working fort had been during its time as a prison for the Union Army. It was possible—probable, in fact—that anyone designing a haunt for the place would choose a specter from that period. A female in a long white dress not only fit with the history of the fort but was a classic in the ghost world, virtually a cliché like the rattling of chains and the trailing of rotting grave cloth.

The fact that Anna had "known" it was Raffia was neither here nor there. Reading the old letters would easily account for her identification. The brain seeks the familiar, needs to make sense of things.

Creating illusions was a good deal easier than most people suspected, Anna reminded herself. The human brain was excellent in filling in blanks, weaving whole cloth from a few threads. Magicians were masters at suggestion, distraction: a hint and an audience would believe.

If this was what happened to Lanny and was now happening to her, the field was narrowed down to the people living on Garden Key and the two lighthouse keepers on Loggerhead. It was too much of a stretch to believe a regular citizen would boat out the seventy or so miles from the mainland over a six- to eight-week period just to drive the ranger nuts.

The woman in white, seen from a distance and fleetingly, the light poor, the setting perfect, could have been quite simply a real woman dressed and in whiteface, a life-sized drawing, white on black cloth or paper, shown, then whisked from sight. Steeped in the history of the fort and her own family, Anna's mind would have filled in the rest.

She moved. Anna distinctly remembered the raise of the arm, the hand on the hair. She remembered, too, how detailed and specific everything she'd seen had been, but she pushed that memory into the mental file: "Tricks of eye and mind." Examining it too closely would lead her back to the place where madness was the answer.

Duncan's wife was the only woman living on Garden Key who physically resembled Anna's ghost: slender, well proportioned.

A scene of such little importance it had slipped her mind came back with stunning clarity: passing Duncan in the sally port, him smiling as always, his face creased with it till the old saw "wreathed with smiles" seemed sensical, his thinning blond hair as feathery as a baby duck's head, his square, strong body positively springy with vitality and clean living.

"Anna," he'd said, voice rich from years of playing to crowds. "I hear your sister sent you historical gold. Written around when Mudd was incarcerated here. Mind if I look at it sometime? Might be my Rosetta Stone."

Vaguely, she'd been aware Duncan was bent on proving beyond a shadow of a doubt and once and for all and finally (as if reality could ever lay hope and speculation to rest) that Dr. Mudd was guilty of conspiring to murder President Lincoln.

Had Duncan grown impatient, slipped into her quarters and read the letters? Duncan knew his history and was part actor/producer as were all good interpreters and historical reenactors. Other than universal malice, she could see no reason he or his wife would have for such trickery.

Teddy Shaw and Bob? He'd been in the hospital in Key West when Anna'd suffered her visitation, but Teddy'd been at the fort, and Anna doubted Teddy did much without his knowledge and enthusiastic approval. Daniel. Mack. Duncan. His wife. Linda. Cliff. The list was short and absurd. Much as she might wish to stretch things, she couldn't imagine why any of them would have the need or desire to carry out a hoax of such magnitude.

Consciously she breathed out the thoughts. Her mind was running too fast. She imagined she could hear the strain—the same sound as a car engine forced too hard in a low gear—see the needle sliding into the red. Loosing the clamp her fists had on her skull and the busy weaving fetters that tied thought to thought, she leaned back against the office door and let the soft night air in through lungs, eyes, ears and the pores in her skin.

The moon was well on its way toward setting, and the shadows, slightly blacker than she remembered them, had crept out to swallow the two houses, joined like Siamese twins, a screened-in porch at either end. Teddy slept alone in one. In the other Lanny Wilcox's worldly goods awaited his return.

The houses stood where the officers' quarters had been in Raffia's day. Anna pictured what they must have looked like in the moonlight. Three stories high, long covered veranda on the first and second floors onto which the doors opened, palm trees and a path bordered by whitewashed skulls. Cannonballs.

To her the fort, this fort, the National Park Service's fort, seemed small and empty. Though it covered nearly seven acres and walking around it was close to a mile under bricked arches, it didn't seem big enough to hide anyone intent on evil. Without people for crowds or miles and miles of country to hide away in, evildoers would be obvious.

The Fort Jefferson Raffia described in her letters, with its thousand men, carpenters, bricklayers, engineers, guards and prisoners; with its store and construction projects, hospital, bakery and coaling docks visited by great ships, seemed as if it must have been a much larger place. St. John's bread trees with their thick crowns and twisted limbs took the place of the grove of palms Raffia had described. Two Portia trees grew their blood-red flowers, a source of delight in the desiccated parade ground, where the men suffering punishment were hung.

"Shit." Anna jerked herself upright. Raffia's world had begun to manifest again, a mist forming into three dimensions in a time where it did not belong. For a second—just a second—Anna could have sworn she saw a body, arms tied behind, toes barely sweeping the ground, hanging from the boughs of the Portia.

"God damn," Anna cursed herself and scrubbed at her face with her palms in an attempt to reconnect with the corporal world. *I fell asleep. I was dreaming.* "I was dreaming," she whispered aloud to see if the words were more reassuring than the thought. The Truth she'd settled on before the mists or the dreams had come resurfaced. Anna grabbed onto it.

Whatever she saw was real until proven otherwise.

Feeling shaky and naked and little in her short dress with no underpinnings, she pushed up from the steps. Kicking off the flip-flops so their idiosyncratic noise wouldn't alert the fort that she was flapping about, she walked around the perimeter of the open area, staying close to the casemates that she might share their shadows.

The Portia trees were spaced fifteen to twenty feet apart. There were three altogether. No bodies hung from the limbs. Nothing even suggested that shape or mass. This was one of the few times in her years as a law-enforcement ranger that she wished there was a corpse left hanging in the trees.

"Can't even trust the dead anymore," she muttered, then

wondered if talking to yourself was a sign of incipient madness. "I've always talked to myself," she said. *See,* her traitorous mind whispered.

"Fuck."

A light flitted, butterfly-like across the upstairs window of one of the houses between the Portia trees and her quarters on the second tier: Lanny Wilcox's house.

"Fuck," Anna said again for lack of anything more erudite. She didn't move. The thought that she would be pursuing yet another will-o'-the-wisp and would become hopelessly lost in craziness paralyzed her. The light didn't come a second time, though she waited without moving for several minutes.

Standing barefoot in the dark, helpless with indecision, she had a sudden galvanizing thought. What if this precise reaction was what the maker of ghosts and will-o'-the-wisps wanted? A ranger too unsure of herself to do her job? Even as the idea cheered her, it faded. Criminals—real ones—were seldom so crafty as to employ esoteric psychological tortures with uncertain ends. Except in fiction, it was pretty much a smash-and-grab, drive-by-shooting sort of world.

As if in ratification, the unmistakable click of an old-fashioned door closing snicked through the still air. Anna'd been related to a psychiatrist long enough to know that run-of-the-mill hallucinations seldom came with sound. A human being from the twenty-first century was skulking about the Wilcox place in the dead of night.

"Hallelujah!" Anna breathed and, silent as a cat on her bare feet, she ran lightly over the brick path that rounded toward the houses. She made so little noise she could hear a muffled plod that could be the fall of soft-soled shoes on brick.

The pathway was old, the bricks broken in places. Intent on speed, Anna stumbled, her toes catching on a ragged upthrust. Pain was immediate and intense. She didn't cry out but went down on one knee. If the skin was scraped from it, the screaming of the nerves in her toes drowned out its complaint. All she felt was the jar. Her fall made a sound, a small one but on a night so still it might have been enough. Holding her breath, she listened. The footsteps had stopped.

If they'd ever been there. The earlier expletive went unspoken if not unthought. Hallucinations she could live with. Self-doubt was crippling. She stayed where she was, not moving, not thinking, just listening. Mad or not, there was little in this dimension or the next that she could not outwait. The pain in her toes passed, allowing her to feel the burn where brick had abraded the skin from her knee. Compared to the burn of coral it wasn't worth her notice. It was almost a relief to have a scrape that didn't itch while it hurt.

She didn't twitch or scratch or fidget. Stillness grew around her, knit from the night itself. The faintest of skritching noises heralded a lizard, not more than two inches long, who came out from his crevice in the crumbling mortar and warmed his tiny belly on the brick an inch and a half from her little finger and never sensed he was not alone.

Occasionally a recurrence of the idea that there'd been no footsteps drifted into Anna's brain. In stillness she accepted it without fear. Should she be mad, there was no better place to be so than in the quiet darkness with a lizard for company.

After a time she had no interest in measuring, her patience was rewarded. Not a footfall but a splash came to her ears. She rose in one fluid motion and ran quickly around behind the Wilcox/Shaw homes and up the wooden stairs to where her quarters were. The casemates beneath, where she guessed the nightwalker had stopped when he heard her fall, were too dark to walk into alone, half-naked, at night merely because she believed the danger to have passed.

On the second tier she ran to the broken-out gun port forming a ragged-edged window opposite her picnic tables and leaned out to see beyond the thickness of the wall. The casemates on the first floor had like holes punched in their sides. At one time the ports had been enclosed with iron shutters—high-tech for their time—designed to fly open when the canons came forward and slam shut when they recoiled. According to the old military and engineering reports, they'd never worked properly. In the ensuing century those that hadn't been forcibly removed had rusted out. Water had blown into the exposed mortar, and bricks had fallen away leaving great toothy gaps where the ports had been.

Crawling out onto her three-foot windowsill, she studied the

gun ports in the ground-floor casemates. Empty. She'd expected
that. The moat, crystal clear and not more than two- or three-
feet deep on the west side, was empty as well. She'd not expected that. The water was mildly agitated, but that could mean
nothing. Big fish and little waves came in through the break in
the wall to the sea.

On the gray concrete capping the wall separating the moat
from the ocean she saw, not what she looked for, but proof it
had been there. Against the pale concrete, silvered by the moon,
were two dark handprints and a darkened slash. Whoever she'd
heard leaving Wilcox's quarters had stepped into a lower casemate when she'd fallen. Too clever or cowardly to trust her silence, he—or she—had gone out through the portal into the
moat and over into the ocean. The moat wall on the west and
south sides of the fort was high, six to eight feet above water
level in places. Once outside, it could be easy to keep out of
sight of the fort.

Because the moat was unoccupied, at least by bipeds, Anna
guessed she'd not heard the drop from the fort to the moat but
the splash made as the person had clambered out on the far side.
By the time she reached the place the handprints were, whoever
it was would be gone, either back into the campground, out to
his boat or in through another portal and back to his bed.

It occurred to Anna to run down, follow the trail through the
darkened casemate and the warm water just to see if the handprints and the butt slide were really there, feel the dampness
with her own fingers. Instead, she turned and went into her
quarters.

She did not want to arrive on the moat wall to find the prints
were gone, then have to spend the rest of the night wondering if
they'd dried or were never there in the first place.

Too late to sleep, she picked up Raffia's letters and began to
read.

8

My Dearest Peg,

The footsteps we heard were indeed Joseph's. Having had more than ample opportunity over the years to witness his rages, I've come to classify them into red and white. When in a red rage Joseph yells and curses, slams doors and smashes his fists into things—not me, mind you, but walls, bolsters and other pieces of innocent household accoutrements. The white rages are more alarming. These are blessedly rare and marked by tight-lipped control and palpable emanations of violence leashed. I don't fear them as I once did and, in a strange way, have come almost to admire them. Joseph in a rage is a force of nature. I find myself watching him in fascination and awe, much as I would a tremendous hurricane wind.

The day he found Tilly and me outside the door of the dungeon, his rage was white hot. Entering as he did from the direction of the light, the first thing we saw was his silhouette framed in a confluence of dark arches. Joseph is not a big man, but he looked so to us. Tilly stopped her whimpering over her damaged rebel and became absolutely still.

What she did from instinct, I had to learn by trial and error. When Joseph's rage is white, I know better than to so much as utter a single word.

Since he cannot speak when this mood is upon him—due no

doubt to the fact that even the slenderest of syllables cannot
force themselves through iron-clenched jaws and lips com-
pressed to a bloodless seam—our entire drama was enacted in
near silence. Only the ring of my husband's boots on the brick
and the whisper of my skirts entangling with Tilly's told of our
exodus.

Joseph grabbed each of us by the upper arm and marched us
from the door of the dungeon. Struggling would only have
drawn attention to our indignity, so we allowed ourselves to be
escorted ignobly back to quarters. Joseph never looks so handsome as he does when in high dudgeon. His hazel eyes were
sparkling, his dark mustache framing that sensuous mouth and
setting off a nose that must have been introduced into his
French ancestors when they fought the Saracens in Spain. Perhaps I am pitifully like that old dog we used to have. He never
seemed to care if we were yelling at him or stroking him as long
as we were paying attention to him.

That night and the next day I kept myself out of his way, doing housewifely things for his comfort, and left Tilly to bring
him around. Though I know soft ways and womanly wiles are
best, I cannot bring myself to do them. Even after two decades
there is a devil in me that wants to meet the devil in him out in
the open. And, too, I believe our sister could wrap Lucifer himself around her little finger if she set her mind to it.

Even with beauty, cunning and youthful zeal, such is my
husband's inner strength, it took Tilly thirty-six hours before he
would agree to let us tend Joel. The fort surgeon refused to treat
a "traitor," and Joseph refused to order him to do so, but in the
end, I think he does have a heart if not of gold then at least not
entirely of stone and didn't want the boy to die alone and un-
cared for.

Having begged what necessaries we could from the small infirmary in the parade ground—bandages and a blanket were all
they said they could spare—we set off to get the key and then
go to the dungeon.

The passage of another day and the insistence of the Lord in
pouring the rational balm of pure sunlight down from a stunningly blue sky had done much to calm the garrison and return
the soldiers to routine. Just that quickly was Joel not forgiven
but forgotten. None of the guards so much as raised an eyebrow

when we appeared, bandages and buckets of fresh water in hand, to ask for the key.

"He's dead," Tilly whispered when I opened the dungeon's door.

"Hush." Should the boy still live, I didn't want him to hear her despair. He lay, without moving, in his own waste—the reek of it filled the vault. Diffused light from the gun slit showed us a full water bucket and an empty slops bucket. Food had been left for the pleasure of rats and mice, who graciously vacated the area at the noise of our arrival.

Blood and bruising made Joel's flesh the color with his stained uniform, still confederate gray only in the places where rebel insignias had been ripped from it subsequent to his capture.

"He's warm," she said. "That means he's alive."

The vault was near ninety-eight degrees at a guess. Even a cold-blooded creature from the depths of the ocean would have been warm to the touch. I felt for a pulse in his throat just under his jaw and was pleased to tell Tilly: "Yes, that means he's alive."

I could see Tilly was shortly to become useless with the emotion of the past days, so I set her to the task of clearing away the old food and sweeping up the crumbs. When she'd left the cell to fetch broom, dustpan and cleaning rags, I removed Joel's clothing and cleaned him as though he were an infant. Tilly at her tender age did not need to see that part of a naked man, but it was the one part of Private Lane's body that was unhurt and, though my experience is limited to my husband and the boys we used to spy on swimming at the old quarry, Joel is a well enough made man.

The rest of him was painful to look at. There was bruising on his chest so dark and vicious I knew the ribs underneath had to be broken. His abdomen was black and purple as well, but it felt neither terribly hot nor swollen. Had the beating ruptured something inside, Tilly's and my roles as ministering angels would soon have changed to those of undertakers. Ropes had cut both arms, and his thumbs remained so swollen and angry I could not be sure he'd ever have full use of his hands again.

In a previous letter I described the injuries to his face. Suffice to say, though still grim and disfiguring, I did think they looked somewhat better. He looked more man than monster. I felt his face, and the bones had not been broken but for his nose. It will never be so neat and straight as it once was.

As I washed his most delicate areas, his member twitched and started to swell. Modern scientific theory would have it that when people die the heart is the last organ to cease functioning. I believe with men the center of life is located somewhat further down.

"Tina," he whispered. I was so pleased that he had not entirely left this world, I wasn't terribly interested in what past peccadilloes I had inadvertently awakened in memory. And I most certainly will not tell Tilly his first word was not her name.

I left the vicinity where I had been giving such life-affirming ministrations and knelt by his head. "It's Mrs. Coleman," I told him.

"Oh my God," he mumbled and his eyelids twitched. The flesh around them was too battered to allow his eyes to open fully, but even so I could see alarm there. To wake and find oneself being touched intimately by the prison warden's wife must have been jarring to his poor beleaguered mind.

To calm him lest this new horror shake his tenuous grip on consciousness, I told him where he was and why I was at his side doing what I suspect was once the job of "Tina." The alarm faded and he closed his eyes but did not leave me.

"Thirsty," he said.

Holding his head in my lap that he might not choke, I drizzled nearly a cup of water between his parched lips. Having drunk, he seemed much revived, and I sent a belated prayer of thanks to the Almighty for the strength and recuperative powers of the young.

By the time Tilly returned, I had Private Lane as clean as a sponge bath allowed and decently covered from the waist down by the blanket.

I gave her a moment to weep over Private Lane, which I think did him nearly as much good as the water and the "bath," but when she began peppering him with questions that were bound to upset the balance of his humors, I sent her off on more errands.

We stayed, dripping water and encouragement into Joel, for

near two hours. He spoke again several times and seemed clear-headed but fell easily into restless dozing that was tormented by dreams. Finally he fell into what I dearly hoped was a restful sleep and not a return of the unconsciousness that is so like and so near to death.

Tilly and I knelt one to each side of him, my knees aching from so long against the hard floor. Tilly cradled one of Joel's hands in her lap, looking at it as she asked me: "Will he be crippled?"

Honestly, I could not say and didn't wish to burden her with my opinion. "He needs a doctor," I said instead.

Between us lay the hurtful knowledge that the fort's hospital was closed to Joel, and Captain Caulley had hardened his heart against the man who'd spoken traitorously of the murder of our president.

"We'll do our best," I promised.

Tilly said nothing for a minute, then: "There's another medical doctor at Fort Jefferson."

There are no other doctors at Fort Jefferson and for a moment I sorted through my memories in the vain attempt to find one. Then it came to me.

"Oh, no, Tilly."

She said nothing, but by the way she looked at me I could tell neither of us were to have any peace till it had been tried.

9

When her eyes grew too tired to read, Anna returned to the broken-out gun portal. The moon was low, yet she could feel its light upon her skin if she closed her eyes. *My mind is no place to play alone,* she thought and kept her eyes open, her brain focused on real three-dimensional things, things she could touch.

Staying awake in these wee hours wasn't difficult. Sleep seemed like a thing of the past, something she used to do but was no longer necessary. That in itself was odd. Thinking back, she knew that she should have been exhausted—not just mentally but with the body fatigue that demands sleep. No wonder she was getting squirrelly. Had she access to sleeping pills she would have happily drugged her body into submission. As it was, there was no point in going to bed; she may as well stare at the moon as the ceiling. Sitting still she was at least resting.

Unfortunately stillness without exacerbated restlessness within. Her mind with its specters would not leave her alone. The corners of her eyes were plagued with flickerings of almost unseen things flitting from shadow to shadow. Too long staring at the silver track the moon lay across the quiescent ocean and it began to change subtly, to move in sinister ways. The fear that had torn at her earlier when her sister, her *psychiatrist,* for

God's sake, didn't immediately assure her she was sane, that
normal people saw ghosts on a regular basis, returned.

Frank Herbert's Bene Gesserit had it right: fear was a mind
killer. Anna needed a litany of facts to hold the irrational world
at bay.

"Idle mind; devil's playground," she whispered, and res-
olutely turned her mental processes to the events of the night,
something real—or so she had chosen to believe—to let her
gray matter chew on.

A boat had exploded and sunk. This boat was carrying a lot
of extra fuel. An NPS boat had been sunk by a chunk of flying
debris. Bob Shaw saved an unidentified Cuban man. Anna saw
a ghost. There was a light in the upstairs bedroom of Lanny
Wilcox's quarters. A person shut a door. A person crossed the
moat and climbed over the outside wall into the sea.

How these things interrelated—if they did—was lost to
Anna. What she should do about any of it was also a mystery.
Investigation of the sunken boats would continue come sun-up.
Identification of the Cuban man would be done by Florida State
law enforcement. The ghost or ghost-hoax was within Anna's
jurisdiction, but she could not bring herself to venture into the
dark where the nearly unseen skittered about and so that, too,
would have to wait till morning.

Lanny Wilcox's bedroom and her own were the only viable
choices remaining. She chose Lanny's. If one wasn't going to
sleep, surely it was more interesting not to sleep in a man's bedroom than one's own.

With this thought, the image of Paul Davidson sprang clear
and strong behind her eyes: the square shoulders, the slow
smile that never came cold and always reached his eyes, the
southern drawl, the way he called her "darlin'."

A wave of emotion so strong it wrung a flood of tears from
eyes dry an instant before overcame her. Not since the months
after her first husband, Zach, died had she so longed for a man.
Had Paul appeared before her on the moon-swept brick she
would have married him on the spot, abandoned the park service, given her life over to him, and gladly crawled into the circle of his arms, there to hide safe and warm for all the years left
to her.

Davidson did not appear. After a time the disconcerting flow

of tears dried up and she was left with nothing but Lanny
Wilcox's bedroom. She fetched another pair of shoes from her
quarters, running shoes this time, quiet and tightly laced, and
donned a pair of underpants. Creeping about in the middle of
the night seeking unsavory persons was not an activity she
wanted to undertake without panties. Thus sartorially fortified,
she descended the stairs to return to the administrative offices
for the key to the ex–Supervisory Ranger's house.

Her flip-flops were where she'd stepped out of them at the
steps. She took them in and tossed them on her desk, then retrieved the key, along with a heavy six-cell flashlight. Anna was
the acting Supervisory Ranger, there was no rule stating she
could not enter quarters to investigate a suspicious occurrence
yet, for reasons she didn't understand, she knew she would not
turn on any lights in Wilcox's quarters.

Lanny's front door was closed but not latched. She didn't
need the key.

Aware that normal people were abed at this hour and that the
Shaws' house shared a wall with Wilcox's, she moved even
more softly than was her habit, leaving doors ajar lest the click
alarm Teddy, presumably sleeping next door. There'd been no
room on the medevac helicopter and she was to take the sea
plane to Key West in the morning.

Unsure of precisely what she sought, Anna first opened the
refrigerator. The core of people's lives often lay in their refrig-
erators and medicine cabinets. Nothing remained in Lanny's
that could go bad. Someone—probably Teddy—had had the
foresight to remove food that would spoil. A six-pack of Yoo-
Hoo with one bottle missing, an unopened plastic jug of drinking water and a door full of condiments were all that had been
left. The water jug had sprung a leak and about a quarter of its
contents glistened atop the vegetable trays.

The freezer contained nothing but ice cubes and frozen en-
trees. Apparently Lanny ate with the creativity and nutritional
concern of the average bachelor. Anna moved on.

Built over a century before, the house was small to modern
eyes, the rooms cramped, the windows few and high off the
floor. Between the tiny kitchen and a living room not much bigger was a sort of stile: three steps up to a landing from which
narrow stairs ascended to the rooms above and three steps down

the other side to the living area. Having gained the landing, Anna stood still in the chill air—the air-conditioner left running so Wilcox wouldn't return to mildewed goods and verdant walls. Her flashlight soundlessly searched that which was in plain sight. Wilcox was a packrat. The little rooms were crammed with the usual and the unusual garnered from half a lifetime in the parks. The walls were covered with framed pictures. Two posters, one of the Devil's Post Pile, one of Chaco Canyon, bumped frames over a derelict sofa. Photos of rough-clad men and women in hiking boots and packs were scattered around. Mixed in were carved masks, mostly foreign-looking: South American, maybe some from Mexico, one clearly left over from a past Mardi Gras. The floor was equally well covered with books, boots, skateboard, compact disks, unopened junk mail, magazines and dead plants in gaily-painted ceramic pots. Forlorn and useless, a pair of snow skis stood in one corner.

Anna turned her light back the way she'd come. The kitchen side was marginally better: counters were clean and the sink was free of dirty dishes. A small wooden table flanked by two very nice wooden folding chairs, probably from the nineteen forties, took up most of the floor space.

The kitchen walls were more interesting than those in the other room. Wooden boxes of varying sizes, from one no more than three inches square to the largest, probably eighteen by twelve inches, had been mounted on the plaster. The boxes were painted in such vibrant colors that Anna's flashlight seemed to ignite rather than illuminate them. Several had been hung so their lids fell open. Inside were scenes complementing or contrasting those on the outside. The artwork was original and fine.

Anna judged art by several criteria. The first was if she could do it, it wasn't art. That disqualified a whole slew of modern painters who slathered, sprayed, glued, welded or stapled shapes together. These box worlds she could not have created. A woman had done them, she'd have sworn to that. The themes were fierce but intensely female with an undercurrent of medieval Catholicism running through. An angel with a scarred face and broken wings stood between a group of armed men and a donkey laden with palm branches. Inside the box were

flies and white feathers, the angel and ass either dead and
buried or ascended to heaven.

Theresa, the fiancée who had run off with Lanny's heart and
sanity, was probably the artist. For a moment more Anna was
lost to the present as her flashlight fired up one box after another. Each was a miniature theater, the lights just coming up on
the actors in the midst of a dynamic scene. When Anna reached
the last, she felt a sense of both satisfaction and loss, the way
one feels when finishing a good book.

Her brain switched from the divine to the prosaic. She could
understand why a beautiful young artist of such intensely personal yet universal images might abandon any number of men,
but why would she abandon her work? Had it been Anna, these
walls would have been stripped bare, the boxes carefully
packed, before she gave a thought to the clothes she would wear
or her toothbrush beside the sink.

The bathroom at the top of the stairs was no bigger than a
closet. Too small for a bathtub. Toilet, shower and sink were
close enough one could wash one's feet and brush one's teeth
while sitting on the commode. It was the only room in the
house free of clutter. Even a dropped tissue would have been
sufficient to inhibit passage in the confined space.

The medicine cabinet, small and old and standing out from
the wall, was very like the one Anna remembered from growing
up. It even had the same halo of rusty incursions into the reflec-
tive surface where metal edging met the glass.

Anna trained her light inside. Here would be evidence of the
weaknesses of the body: diabetes, dentures, headaches. Most
Americans consumed quantities of over-the-counter drugs, and
one in three was on some sort of prescription medicine all the
time. Lanny was no exception. On the middle shelf were three
prescription bottles: one for high cholesterol, one for high
blood pressure and one Anna had a lifetime experience of, Lev-
aquin, the three magic tablets to banish the misery of a bladder
infection; one of the more splintery crosses women have had to
bear. The prescription had been written six weeks before for
Theresa Alvarez. Anna removed the cap and shook out two
tablets. Theresa had left behind not only her artwork but the last
of her medicine.

Curiouser and curiouser. Anna put the pills back and resolved to check the closet, see if Ms. Alvarez had bothered to take her clothes in what was coming to seem a headlong flight rather than mere abandonment.

The bedroom was jammed with more stuff. No floor space was visible. The walls were lined halfway up with boxes, books, scuba tanks, two backpacks and a lot of other paraphernalia related to outdoor adventure and indoor entertainment.

The closet, the old-fashioned size, built when people had one outfit for the workweek and one for going to church on Sundays, was devoid of women's clothing. Three pairs of high-heeled shoes, obviously purchased before Theresa had taken up living on a desert island, were all that attested to her recent presence.

Gingerly, Anna sat on the bed. Despite what one presumed to be nightly occupancy, it was also covered in piles. After losing Theresa, Lanny had snuggled down each night with laundry—presumably clean since there were no unpleasant odors—magazines and two CD players, one with the lid broken off.

Anna wondered where Theresa had painted. She couldn't imagine works of such detail and clarity being created in the three-dimensional cacophony that was Lanny Wilcox's home.

On reflection, two things surprised Anna regarding Lanny's Theresa: that she'd not left him sooner than she did and, again, that she'd left her artwork behind.

Anna was not an artist. Her creations tended to be big and functional: benches, tables, outhouses. And they were usually painted with a wide brush and any color that was cheap and handy. Even so, when she had put time and effort into making something, she didn't like leaving it with people or in places where it would be abused. If she was disturbed when wicked campers sprayed graffiti on privy walls she'd nailed together, how much more painful must it have been for Theresa to abandon her works to a home where they would eventually be vying for wall space with snowshoes and frying pans?

No answer came. What came was nothing, followed by a short sharp jab of fear. For a moment Anna had absolutely no idea in hell why she'd come to Wilcox's, why she was upstairs in his bedroom with a flashlight.

Flashlight.

Memory rushed back and she laughed out loud with relief. She'd seen a light in the upstairs window. Or thought she had. "Stop that," she said. She'd seen a light. There was no reason anyone whose purposes were legitimate would enter in the night without turning the lights on. The fact that she had done just that wiggled momentarily, but she dismissed it and shone her light around the room. With the plethora of goods crammed into it, she doubted anyone would have been able to find anything and, at a glance, it seemed there would be little to tempt a thief.

The beam raked across the headboard and onto the nightstand. Its surface was the only clear spot in the house. Everything had been wiped from the top of the low table, including reading lamp and alarm clock. In their place a digital camera had been left lying on its side.

Unless Lanny, in a fit of pique, had done it himself at the cost of his lamp, it must have happened after he'd gone, by someone in a hurry, someone who had little respect and no patience for Lanny's stockpile of junk. Maybe somebody who'd been in the house that night, the camera one of the intruder's objectives. Since he or she hadn't taken it with them, they must have been after the pictures stored inside.

Having propped the flashlight on one of the pillows, Anna picked the camera up and turned it on. She hit the eject button. The disk had been left in place. She turned the knob to "retrieve" and began going through the images. They looked as if a child had taken them—or a man testing a new camera under various light and movement conditions. Lanny had no children that she knew of, and the camera was several years old and had the look of a piece of equipment much used, so neither explanation fit. Photo after photo of the corners and walls of the rooms Lanny lived in, flash photos, taken by night, of uninteresting twists and turns within the casemates. Close-ups of what could be anything: cannon barrels, dock pilings, the flagpole.

Anna clicked through, wondering what it was her phantom intruder had sought, which picture incriminated, embarrassed, compromised or exonerated.

After several dozen views of Lanny's kitchen closet, she realized what she was looking at. Not pictures of walls, floors and shelves of canned goods. These were pictures of what Lanny

saw, visions he'd tried to validate digitally. Pictures of things
that weren't there.

She set the camera back where she'd found it. She needed to
get out of that claustrophobic house, away from unseen things
that drove men mad.

Such was her need to breathe untainted air that she fled, not
home to her bed, but out into the middle of the parade ground
where she could stand beneath open sky. There she stared at the
stars, sucked in lungfuls of warm, damp air and yearned for the
sweet purifying oxygen of her western mountains. Something
was terribly wrong: with Fort Jefferson, with Lanny Wilcox,
with her. Tears of self-pity stung her eyes, and she wondered if
she should take Molly's advice and go to the mainland, to a
hospital, get a CAT scan, see a head shrinker. At the moment
being in a clean modern room in the solicitous care of professionals didn't seem such a wretched alternative.

Temptation was shouted down by duty. Bob was out of the
running; Lanny was gone. Without her the fort would have no
law enforcement. Anna pulled herself together, stopped gulping
air and breathed slowly, deeply. When her heart ceased to race
and her mind to gabble, she turned to go back to her quarters.

A light from the southern casemates stopped her. This was
not the ephemeral will-o'-the-wisp she'd spent the shank of the
night chasing but the solid reassuring yellow glow of electric
lights shining from the archway into the maintenance shop and
the long row of generators that provided the fort with the stuff
of the good life: light, heat, air-conditioning, radio to the mainland and water pressure.

Instead of being alarmed by yet another nocturnal manifes-
tation, Anna looked forward to a confrontation with a live,
flesh-and-blood human being, evil or not.

The bringer of light was Daniel Barrons. Anna watched him
for several minutes before he knew she was there. Clad in khaki
shorts, bedroom slippers and an uncharacteristic tank top that
unveiled his tattoos; not only the classic tattoo of the naked girl
under the palm tree but a number of others which, screened
from view by a prodigious nest of chest and back hair, she
couldn't make any artistic sense of. Daniel moved down the
line of roaring generators, opening panels and fiddling about inside. It wasn't until he'd visited all but the one beside which

Anna stood that he noticed her. When he did he squeaked loudly and threw up both palms shoulder high, reminding her of an illustration in a turn-of-the-century acting book her husband had found at The Strand in New York. The photograph was a graphic lesson on how the thespian should indicate surprise. She and Zach had laughed at it then. Those were the days when The Method was the rage. Seeing "surprise" produced so spontaneously, Anna wished Zach had lived to share the joke.

Anna hadn't thought of her dead husband in days. Since giving up carrying the torch a few years back, occasionally as much as a week would pass during which she wouldn't say his name to herself. Remembering him after the night she'd just had was oddly comforting. Perhaps being insane in the company of actors wasn't as stigmatizing as it would be in law-enforcement circles.

"Jesus H. Christ," Daniel bellowed over the din of the six generators. "You scared the shit out of me."

"You screamed like a girl," Anna said, uncertain whether she wished to provoke or was merely being accurate.

"Swear to God I thought you were a ghost. We got 'em, you know. And I did not. If anything I squealed like a stuck pig."

Again Anna was unsure if the statement that Daniel would rather be likened to a pig than a girl was meant to provoke or was merely accurate. Either way it amused her. Still she couldn't relax enough to smile. His mention of ghosts put her back on her guard. Had the mention been intentional? Pushing the power of suggestion? Mocking? Or was it just coincidence?

"What are you doing up?" she shouted over the noise. Half a dozen generators, each eight feet high at a guess and half again that long, created noise that poured into ears and corners and arches and nostrils like wet concrete filling spaces, then hardening till it was an effort to move or think.

Daniel made a gentlemanly gesture indicating they step out of his office and away from the racket. For half a breath he paused to let her go first. When she didn't, he moved ahead. On the whole Anna approved of good manners and believed "ladies first" was a pleasant perk. It wasn't misplaced feminism that kept her feet rooted to the floor; it was a desire not to have anyone behind her till she figured out what was throwing her world out of balance.

Daniel walked to the underground cistern built where once the foundation of a chapel had been laid. He sat on the edge of the raised flat "roof" used to collect rainwater.

Though the water was filtered and purified, Anna winced inwardly to see what was undoubtedly a hairy butt planted so firmly on the surface from which her drinking water was collected. She followed him, glad to be away from the generators, but did not sit down. Mind and body were tuned to the dark side, and she preferred to remain on her feet. Had he ushered her out first because he was polite or because he was dangerous? Had he left the generators for ease of conversation or because he needed time to think of a lie in answer to her questions? Did he sit because his legs were tired or to put her off guard?

"What did you ask me?" Daniel dug in the pocket of his shorts and fished out a pack of Marlboros so crumpled it looked as if he slept with the things.

Anna's suspicious mind started to question every detail of his language and body language. With an effort she shut the internal inquisition down. Over-vigilance was as blinding as being oblivious and wasted a whole lot more time. She repeated her original question. "What are you doing up?"

Daniel lit his disreputable-looking smoke with an old-style lighter made of silver with a top to click open and shut. The wings of the Harley-Davidson insignia were on one side in raised brass. "Thought I heard something. I figured I'd better check the generators."

"What did you hear?"

Daniel looked up at her, surprised maybe by her tone. "I don't really know. A door slamming, tool dropped. I was asleep."

Anna thought about that. "I was in the office. It could have been me," she said. She had been careful to open and close doors with stealth born of paranoia. She just wanted to give him an easy out and see if he took it.

"When?"

"Fifteen or twenty minutes ago."

"Wasn't that, then. Besides, it was closer. Or sounded like it was."

"If it woke you up and you rushed out to check, why aren't

you in your bathrobe?" The question sounded like what it was: an accusation.

Daniel took a drag on his cigarette that burned a third of it away. "I can go put it on if you'd like," he said. "What's eating you?"

"Weirdness," Anna admitted. "General weirdness. I was up chasing the noise as well." It crossed her mind that the sound that had awakened the maintenance man might have been the sound of her intruder, her moat wader, coming back to roost either in through one of the many gun ports or through the sally port, then shutting his own door behind him.

Daniel looked at a watch nestled in the dark curling hair that covered his wrists. "The sun will be up in a bit. No sense in going back to bed now. I've put coffee on. Want a cup?"

Anna realized she did want coffee. More than that she wanted the normalcy of a kitchen and conversation.

Daniel's rooms were the antithesis of Lanny's, neat and well appointed. Either he'd come to terms with the single life and reveled in it or, beneath all the body hair and tattoos, he was actually or spiritually gay. Having seniority and fulfilling an indispensable job had won him the finest quarters. Two casemates had been taken over to create space for a comfortable kitchen opening onto a graceful living room. Two doors opened off one side. Probably bedrooms. Created before DRTO changed to the prefab boxes inserted into the upper casemates, his apartment retained the natural brick and vaulted ceilings of the fort. Daniel had filled it with tasteful furniture and good rugs. The rooms were tidy, the kitchen counter devoid of clutter.

He poured them each a cup of coffee from a pot in a coffeemaker with numerous buttons and digital readouts. The cups were good quality china, thin enough to be elegant but not so thin one felt in danger of crushing them. The rims were gold and royal blue, the side decorated with four small pink rosebuds. They were of a piece with the rooms and the Japanese kimono and at odds with the burly biker physique of their owner.

Sitting across from one another at a blond wood table with matching chairs, probably Swedish, possibly expensive, they chatted about the noise, the wrecked go-fast boat, the heroics of Bob Shaw.

"The heavy fuel load—smugglers?" Anna said.

"Could be. A lot of it goes on in this part of the world."

Anna had known that: drugs, guns, people, exotic plants and animals, even the tried-and-true classics, Cuban rum and cigars. Neither she nor Daniel had answers, and for a while they sipped excellent coffee from their understatedly elegant cups. Talk soothed Anna. Silence was even better. The fogs of weird were lifting. She could feel the slipped gears of her brain snicking back into their proper grooves and wondered if it indicated a second wind or was engendered by the knowledge that sunrise was near; the dark that frightens children in their beds and is home to hobgoblins was soon to be banished. Sitting, sipping, muscles unclenching, mind clearing, Anna felt the sleepiness that had evaded her for the past twenty-four hours fold around her.

"Two bedrooms?" she asked, just to make conversation.

"I'm one of the lucky few," Daniel acknowledged.

"It must be nice to have a place to put guests besides on the sofa."

"Second bedroom belongs to Mrs. Meyers."

Not knowing Mrs. Meyers, Anna said nothing.

Daniel tilted his head much as a quizzical dog might. "Haven't you ever met Mrs. Meyers?"

His voice changed subtly, triggering Anna's internal alarms. She was being set up for something, she just couldn't figure out what. Moving her coffee away slightly, she gathered her feet under her in case a quick exit was called for. "Can't say as I have," she said neutrally.

"That's right," Daniel said as if remembering something of importance. "Mrs. Meyers hasn't been out since you came onboard. You want to meet her now?"

Grisly images of mummified grandmothers in rocking chairs, corpses in freezers and blood-splashed walls flashed through her mind. The weird was back. She sighed. "Sure. Why not?"

With the excitement of a twelve-year-old showing off his favorite toy, Daniel abandoned his coffee and veritably bounced to the nearer of the two doors. Anna followed, too tired for caution and grown unnaturally accepting of the bizarre.

Daniel moved with a light-footed buoyancy that was unsettling in a man of his heft. Reaching the door, he paused, shot

Anna an elfin look at odds with his troll body and beard, and said: "Shh. She may be sleeping."

He opened the door, then stood back that Anna might enter. "Mrs. Meyers," he said with obvious pride and affection.

In the middle of the otherwise empty room was a vintage 1952 Harley-Davidson motorcycle. No dirt marred her perfect surfaces, no grease besmudged the gleaming exhaust pipes or dulled the black shine of her engine.

"Wow," Anna said, genuinely impressed. "And all this time I thought you lived alone."

"Tank full of gas, key in the ignition," he said delightedly.

For the next fifteen minutes he extolled Mrs. Meyers's finer points, and Anna fought the sandman to a draw in order to stay on her feet. Finally he wound down. She mumbled her thanks for the coffee and compliments to Mrs. Meyers and all but staggered back to her quarters.

As everything had been this longest of nights, the fatigue was sudden and unnatural. It wasn't the simple tiredness after too long without sleep but the bottomless exhaustion left when amphetamines wear off and the user crashes.

Piedmont was curled into an orange ball on her pillow. The bedside clock read four twenty-seven. Anna nudged cat and pillow to one side and crawled in beside them. Because it was a lifetime's habit to read herself to sleep, she'd brought a piece of Aunt Raffia's correspondence with her. The last thing she remembered was the slither of paper as the letters slid from her hands to scatter on the tile.

10

Tilly's doctor was a recent addition to our jolly crew. Dr. Mudd is one of the Lincoln conspirators and very possibly the most hated man at fort. Perhaps because he protests his innocence so loudly when there are those of us who can only find solace in the sincere confession and repentance of those responsible. He is not even well thought of by his own. Many of our confederate soldiers view assassination as a base and cowardly act not befitting what they view as their noble cause.

I promised Tilly I would do my best. To this end I set out to find Joseph.

He was out on the coaling dock organizing a group of men to go to the neighboring keys to dig for eggs and catch turtles for meat. (Did you know that *Tortuga* was Spanish for tortoise? These lonely sand scraps were named for the creatures.) I am awestruck by their ponderous beauty, yet because I am also awestruck by their delicious taste, I am as eager for the hunting of them as any soldier. Turtles have the added benefit of staying fresh—a distinct problem with meats of all kinds in this heat. The hunters simply roll the turtles onto their backs, rendering them immobile till it's time to slaughter them.

As the men moved out to the dinghies, Joseph noticed me waiting. For a moment he seemed glad to see me, but only for a moment. Then it was as if he remembered who I was and some old anger fell between his heart and his eyes.

I have often wondered what I have done that he works so hard at hating me. Sometimes I think it was that day he struck me and I swore if it happened again he would never be safe, not waking, not sleeping. I believe I frightened him. For a man like Joseph to be afraid, even once and for so brief a span of time, is unacceptable. That I caused it or, worse, saw it, must make me unacceptable as well.

Or perhaps it's not hate I see in his face but the countenance of a man eternally disappointed that the endearing kitten he brought home had the bad judgment to grow into an ungainly cat.

As the welcome faded from his eyes he came to where I stood. "What is it now? Has Tilly's pet rebel died?"

"Not yet," I told him and, though he'd deny it, I saw relief in his look.

I took it for kindness till he said: "Good. Sinapp doesn't need many more 'accidents' on his record. He's a good soldier."

"Private Lane needs to be looked after by a doctor," I said. "His hands are badly injured. I'm afraid without more care than Tilly and I can give him he will lose the use of them."

"What a pity. He'll no longer be able to pull the trigger of a gun aimed at our boys," Joseph said.

I waited. There's no responding to Joseph when he is in a sarcastic mood. Twice he ran his fingers through his hair. He wears it longer now, nearly to his shoulders. Here, where there is so much humidity, it curls. Finally he spoke to me and not just to the place in which I stood.

"Look. I've talked with Captain Caulley. He flatly refuses to treat a traitor, a man who approves of Mr. Lincoln's assassination. He might go so far as to refuse a direct order. I'm not going to risk having to put the garrison's doctor behind bars to save the hands of Johnny Reb."

"He may die," I said.

"So be it. Speaking out in favor of the murder of a United States president has consequences. I'll not pity him."

"What did he say?" I asked. I wasn't trying to provoke Joseph, I was genuinely curious. "Was it truly traitorous?"

"Damn you, woman, Sergeant Sinapp says it was, and that's good enough for me."

Since Joseph chooses not to confide in me, I've learned to read him. When he curses it's because he hasn't an answer worthy of voicing but has no intention of admitting defeat or, heaven forfend, that he is wrong. Joseph's cursing is also an indication that the next word I utter will be treated as the straw that broke the camel's back.

Standing quite silent and still, trying to look as inoffensive as possible, I waited for him to either walk away or to be overcome by what I see as his better nature and I'm sure he sees as weakness.

"You have something in mind. God knows you always have something in mind. You are the thinkingest woman ever put on earth."

"Actually this is Tilly's idea," I said in hopes of making it more palatable. "Dr. Mudd."

Raging, belittling, lecturing, laughing—I'd been braced for those. The actual response nearly knocked me to the ground.

"Why not?" he said. "Let 'em patch up their own. I'll have some of the men move him."

I made my thanks quickly and turned to go before I spoiled Private Lane's chance at professional care with an ill-advised word or look.

"Raffia," he called after me. You will think me a fool, Peggy, but I love to hear him say my name. He seldom does, you know.

"Yes?"

"You and Tilly can go with the men. You can stay and help Mudd with whatever he needs within reason. But you go only with a soldier, never alone. I will send someone by quarters."

"Thank you, Joseph."

"Don't you abuse this privilege," he snapped as if I'd already done so by thanking him.

We endured, Tilly and I, until nearly half past three in the afternoon, when the promised soldier tapped lightly on the frame. The door was open to the balcony.

"We'll be moving the confederate to Mudd's cell. The captain said you ladies had some part in it and I was to fetch you along." The soldier asked no questions, and if he had an opinion he kept it to himself. Such are the times I envy my husband's power over men.

Tilly shot me a look that I wouldn't trade for diamonds, or even a long swim in a cool river. I hope this orphaned child raised by five doting sisters never has to lie to save herself. Her emotions shine in her eyes as bright—or dark—as if an actual lamp burned there. Being a tiny baby when Mother and Father died, she suffered the fate of being the light of our lives during those awful times.

With Tilly clutching my arm, we followed the soldier across the parade ground. The men hung in the trees had been taken down before the heat could kill them. Men with small work had carried it to the east side of the fort to take advantage of what little shade there was. The fort had that sleepy summer feel. Tensions I'd not known I harbored baked out in the bright hot light.

Two more soldiers joined us. With only a little grumbling—and that done from habit or sense of obligation—they lifted Joel onto a canvas field stretcher. The three boys, probably of an age with Private Lane, were gentle when they handled him and glad to have an opportunity to laugh when Joel made the old joke about doing anything to avoid work. This has been such a strange war. The soldiers can hate one another in theory, but when brought together without officers to agitate and politicians to tell them what they're fighting for, they tend to like each other. I've seen more kindness here between soldier and prisoner than between officers and men.

Passing the sally port, we were ordered to a halt by a vicious bark from that dog in wolf's clothing, Sergeant Sinapp. He emerged from the shadows with his inimitable swagger. Like the ogre he is, he came from beneath the stone arch to where the soldiers waited dutifully in the hot sun supporting the weight of Private Lane between them. Enjoying himself, Sinapp walked a circle around the men with the stretcher and our Miss Tilly, standing at Joel's side.

"What we got here?" he asked in the most jovial of tones. "Meat for the sharks?"

One of the soldiers, the man at the head of the stretcher holding most of the weight, started to explain Joseph's orders for moving the prisoner, but of course Sinapp had no interest in the answer but only in being horrid. He overrode the man's words, saying to Tilly: "Still playing at Florence Nightingale? You all hell-bent on curing what ails somebody, you can come to me. I need some *relief.*"

He was looking at Tilly as if she'd appeared before him again sans knickers.

"It's downright unpatriotic you giving your ... *attentions* ... to a Johnny Reb when there's good union men going without."

I had said nothing up to this point, not because that man frightens me but because I was shocked into silence by his audacity. Joseph would not put up with this thinly veiled vulgarity aimed at a woman under his protection. In my case he's defending his pride. In Tilly's he might do it simply out of affection.

"Joseph will not be pleased to hear of your rudeness," I said when I found my tongue.

"Who's going to tell him? You?"

The question took me off guard. *Of course me, you stupid stupid man,* I wanted to shout.

"You do that, Mrs. Coleman. You do that," he said before I'd found the presence of mind to respond.

He stepped to the side then and let us pass without further insult. I was livid, but it was undercut by an unsettling feeling that Sergeant Sinapp believed Tilly and I no longer enjoyed Joseph's protection.

It is to my credit that I did not spit at him when we passed.

At the stairs Tilly was forced to abandon her post. Spiral stairs are not ideal for the transporting of the injured, but the soldiers managed it without spilling Joel from the stretcher. To my surprise, once on the second level, they did not turn left toward the cells of the Virginia men Joel had been quartered with but right toward those located over the guardroom and sally port.

"Captain's orders, ma'am," I was told when I asked. "The captain won't have Mudd given free run of the fort. If he's to look after this man he's got to be quartered next to the conspirators."

Since Joseph had given me my way in all else, I did not fuss, though the cells over the guardroom are among the worst at Fort Jefferson, having no windows but only three high gun slits that let in little light or air and one must lift oneself up just to see outside. I expect this is why the conspirators were housed there.

Joel was carried into the casemate adjoining that of our most famous inmates and lifted from the stretcher to the bare floor with less gentleness than when he'd been picked up. Being in close proximity to two of the men guilty of conspiring to kill Mr. Lincoln reawakened the outrage and hatred in the soldiers.

As it did in me. I'd not thought I hated the conspirators, but hated only their acts. Knowing I was close to them, even with a wooden partition between us, a wave of fury swept over me so hot I was surprised my hair didn't catch afire. If it had not been for the innocence of Tilly and the pathos of Private Lane, I believe I would have turned my back on the whole thing.

All but one of the soldiers left us. He walked to the door leading to the adjoining cell and banged it hard. "Mudd. Got a job for you. Try not to kill this one," he shouted, then retreated to the egress from what was now Joel Lane's cell. Like me, I think he feared not Mudd but his own hatred of the man.

Tilly had knelt by Private Lane. Both stared at the door, as did I, preparing to meet the monster who was to serve us.

11

Anna awoke at quarter till eleven feeling rested if not refreshed. She'd not had a drink of anything alcoholic in a long time and deeply resented suffering a hangover when she'd not had the pleasure of earning it.

The greatest delight—when she had burned away enough mental fog in the shower she could take note of it—was that her mind was clear. Or at least relatively so. The crawling sense of urgency that had driven her the previous night had slowed to a creep at the edges of her adrenal system. Sunshine drove the skittering shadows from the outer limits of her vision.

Due on duty at noon, she breakfasted on a Coke and peanut-butter-and-saltine sandwiches. Customarily she drank only coffee or sparkling water in the mornings. This morning she couldn't face carbonated water gone flat and didn't have the time for coffee but needed the caffeine.

As she dressed, she mentally apologized to Bob Shaw for mocking him—if only in her heart—for wearing full battle regalia out to count the fishies. Coral-enraged patches of skin cried out against fabric and leather gear, and Anna's vestigial fashion sense was outraged by the combination of shorts and duty belt. On a woman barely five feet four inches tall, knobby knees below and bristling armament above made her look more like a walking antipersonnel mine than a woman of sense. She wasn't unduly affected. Some days it paid a girl to look like she might go off at any minute and blow a hole in anybody standing too close.

Out of habit, she called in service. Bob was in the hospital in Key West. By now Teddy would be at his bedside to admire how bravely he handled the pain of his broken bone.

"Ten-four. I'll be listening," came back over the airwaves. Daniel. Anna was glad that in Bob and Teddy's absence he would stay by the radio in the event she needed him.

"Mrs. Meyers," Anna said aloud and laughed, startling Piedmont. "Never mind," she told the cat. "Homo sapien humor. Guard the house."

Celebrating a return to normalcy, as proved by a sun-drenched parade ground sparsely populated with tourists reading plaques and wandering through shaded arches, by white sails on graceful boats and by the fact that Anna had no doubt these things she witnessed could be ratified and corroborated, she took the scenic route to her office.

The "Chapel" was near her quarters on the fort's second level, above the rooms that had housed the garrison's bakery. Park historians had more or less intuited The Chapel. No proof existed that this vaulted room in the northwestern bastion had ever contained an altar, pews or baptismal font. Nothing in the architecture was suggestive of narthex, nave or sanctuary. But this one room of the ten outermost rooms on both levels of the five bastions had no gun port in its end wall. Unbroken brick flowed from the beautifully vaulted ceiling to the floor. To sacrifice such a prime gun placement, the builders must have had in mind a room of equal or higher importance in turning the tide of battle as armaments. It was speculated that this room had been dedicated to getting God on one's side.

Anna liked The Chapel. In addition to grace of architecture and masonry, she sensed the spiritual there as well. Not so much a deity as a place where people have poured enough of their belief in a deity that the power of faith soaked into stone and wood, brick and mortar.

At the eastern arch of The Chapel, just outside where the many-arched walkway and casemates chased away in a straight line of forced perspective, was where she had nearly met up with her great-great-aunt Raffia the night before.

By the light of day Anna hoped something more corporeal than faith had been left behind, a sign that might lead her to whoever the prankster—or person intent on gaslighting her—was.

Either the ghost had truly been of ectoplasm—the slime-free variety that leaves no gooey residue—or the ghost-maker was neat as well as effective. She found smudged tracks in the mortar dust, left by someone running with no shoes on. Recognizing her own footprints and no others was mildly disconcerting, but any number of reasons could account for it. On this side of the fort the flooring on the upper tiers had never been completed. Gun casemates were floored in slabs of granite—stone hard enough to take the shock from the guns. Near The Chapel, where Anna looked, the floor was rubble and didn't take tracks well.

Shelving the spectral side of life, she finished her morning commute. The next two hours were spent on the phone.

Before she'd had to deal with it, complaints about the one-to two-second delay before words said on one end trickled into an ear on the other had struck Anna as frivolous. Not so. She was amazed at how seemingly small a thing could cripple conversation. It was nearly impossible for those not accustomed to it—or those accustomed but impatient—not to talk over one another. Half of her calls consisted of the words "what?" and "I'm sorry."

The Florida State Police hadn't been able to trace the John Doe Bob had towed to East Key. The Dry Tortugas were in the Gulf of Mexico sixty miles from Florida's land mass but, as they were part of the state of Florida, the waters fell under the state's jurisdiction. Anna described the military-looking tattoo on the John Doe's calf. Lieutenant Henriquez, the officer with whom she spoke, said they'd made a note of that and were following up. He didn't sound hopeful or even particularly interested.

The police couldn't begin tracing the boat till Anna got a name or registration number off the wreck. Henriquez told her he wasn't going to hold his breath while she looked. If the vessel belonged to a smuggler there would be no number and the name would be meaningless.

Theresa Alvarez posed less of a problem. She'd joined Lanny Wilcox as a VIP—Volunteer in Parks—a designation often given spouses and significant others for reasons of record keeping and insurance should they perform work while on the premises. Andy, the woman in Human Resources at Dry Tortugas and Everglades headquarters in Homestead, pulled up Ms. Alvarez's personnel file.

"Let's see what we've got." She had a trace of a Maine accent that cooled Anna just hearing it. "Ms. Alvarez...here we go. Twenty-three years old, five-foot-three, one hundred and three pounds—must be a size two, I hate her already—Cuban born, naturalized U.S. citizen at the age of six, fluent in Spanish and English. Do you want her last known home address and number?"

Andy read off a Miami address.

Anna wrote it down. "Has anybody else called you guys asking after her?"

"You mean other than poor Lanny?"

"Lanny Wilcox called?"

"Constantly. Since he'd been acting...well...*peculiar,* we were advised not to give out any information on her. Stalking, you know—you can't be too careful."

"What did he want to know?"

"The usual: home address, phone number, parents' names, that sort of thing."

"He lived with this woman and didn't know her home address?"

"Apparently not. I guess Lanny had better things to talk about with Ms. Alvarez than her vital statistics—if you don't count thirty-four, twenty, thirty-four in that category. She was pretty enough to model."

"You knew her." Anna was hoping for more to go on than an outdated address and phone number.

"Only to look at the way a cat can look at the queen," Andy said.

Anna dialed the number from Theresa Alvarez's personnel file. No one answered and no phone machine picked up. She would try again come evening.

Time had come to return to the sea.

Years before, in Lake Superior, when Anna worked as a boat patrol ranger at Isle Royale National Park, she'd learned first-hand the dangers of diving wrecks alone. Daniel didn't dive but was an experienced dive tender. If they had time to donate to law enforcement, she'd see if Daniel could stay topside and Mack dive with her.

She found Mack in the shop between her quarters and the generator rooms. This was where her amphibious intruder had fled into the dark, then, when she wouldn't go away, out the shattered gun port into the moat. The shop was a favorite place of hers when she wanted to hang out and gossip with Daniel. Woodworking shops, with the smell of sawdust and signs of productivity laid out in a pattern of tools, were always warm and welcoming in her mind. As a girl she'd spent hours in her father's shop, listening to his stories and building things, things that always turned out well because at night, after she'd gone to bed, he would go back and make what she'd done beautiful. No wonder she'd believed "The Shoemaker and the Elves" was a documentary till she was in her teens.

Mack was at the lathe, his back to her, safety goggles' strap pushing his brown hair into a rooster's tail. For a peaceful minute, she watched the wood turning under his corded fingers, a sensuous shape being drawn out. Mack was as scrawny and sere as a mountain man. Too long in the sun had melted off the fat and tanned his hide till it wrinkled and cracked.

He wore the green NPS shorts and gray shirt. The shirt was three shades darker at the armpits, wet with sweat. Anna was too well bred to look, but hers would be the same. The air was close to ninety-five degrees, and down on the lower level, the ocean breezes weren't strong. Watching him work, her mind floating free on the noise of the lathe and the hypnotic spin of the wood, she noticed the back of Mack's arms and legs were striped. Thin white lines cut through the browned skin at an angle. Scars. They were barely visible, his downy leg and arm hair grown up around them, but in the hard light of the sun they were unmistakable. Anna would have been surprised if his back was not similarly marked.

Mack had been viciously whipped, maybe with a material harsher even than leather—barbed wire, maybe. From the healing and fading of the scars Anna guessed it had been done a long time ago, probably when Mack was a little boy.

She looked away, staring vacantly at the parched grass of the parade ground, wondering why knowledge of childhood abuse should make her both ache and feel ashamed for him. She must ask Molly about it when next she got to a telephone that didn't drive her half-mad with frustration. Education explained why the abused child felt shame over the abuse, but not why that shame was echoed by the observer. Maybe Anna was ashamed because she belonged to the same species as the perpetrators, and maybe a kernel of that craven evil lay dormant in her own heart.

A shudder took her, violent and sudden the way muscles sometimes spasm just before sleep.

"Don't tell me you're shivering. I've got news for you; it ain't cold."

Anna turned back and smiled at Mack even more warmly than she had intended. It didn't go unnoticed. His blue eyes took on a glitter that makes a woman want to flirt or flee depending on the glitterer.

"To what do I owe this honor?" he asked and moved so he stood a little too close for comfort.

Quashing an urge to reclaim her invaded space, she cloaked herself in business. "With Bob out of commission and Linda and Cliff back in Key West I'm going to need help finishing up the investigation on the wrecks. I was hoping you'd dive and Daniel would tend. Do you guys have any free time?"

Mack wiped the sawdust from the length of wood he'd turned on the lathe, a table leg by the look of it. While his eyes were thus busy, Anna took the opportunity to step back a pace.

The maintenance man looked up, his gaze wandering into the sky above the far rampart. He narrowed his eyes and scratched at his grizzled beard, dislodging a minute blizzard of sawdust. "Lemme think."

It wasn't that hard a question. Anna wondered if he had a problem with the dive per se or if he was playing hard to get.

"Daniel and me got to work on generator five. Been sounding funny. How 'bout maybe four o'clock?"

Sunset wasn't till nine.

"Suits me," Anna said and, belatedly, "Thanks."

Impatience urged her to dive the wrecks without them, but good sense prevailed. Ignoring reports to be written and schedules still to be done, she decided to return to Lanny Wilcox's house and see if anything new presented itself. The decision to revisit the scene of last night's adventure was made more from homage to rationality than because she expected to find anything. After six hours of good sleep the events of the previous night—the ghost, the light in Lanny's window, the wet prints on the moat wall, even Mrs. Meyers—had taken on the ephemeral quality of a dream imperfectly remembered.

Wilcox's quarters weren't improved by daylight. Theresa's art still took Anna's breath away, as did the crowded living room, though for less exalted reasons. Ignoring the niggle and nudge of claustrophobia, she made room for herself on the sofa by pushing aside a stack of magazines and two ratty pillows and settled into the cluttered confines of Lanny's life. Minutes passed as she absorbed the room, waiting for anything added to make itself known, anything taken away to reveal its absence by a sign.

The ailing Supervisory Ranger's housekeeping habits were a petty thief's dream. Amid the choking plethora of goods, she doubted Lanny himself would be able to detect a minor disarrangement. After a time one small anomaly came to her. There were no photographs of Lanny's inamorata. No pictures of Theresa hung from the walls; no framed photos of her joined the clutter on shelves and tabletops. Lanny was there, grinning from mountaintops, monstrous-looking in snorkel and mask. Other women, never alone or particularly featured but with Lanny and friends, lived the half-life of memory in colored snapshots. Unless Theresa was phobic where cameras were concerned, her absence was peculiar.

Glad to have even this teensy weensy thread to follow—anything to stay occupied and out of her tomb of an office—Anna began searching through Wilcox's piles in search of Theresa's likeness. With sunlight and an achievable goal, Anna had better success than she'd had the night before. Two plastic bins, six by fourteen inches, the lids long gone, were stuffed full of snapshots, most of them still in the envelopes from the developers. Both bins had been shoved into the bottom niche of one of those units fashionable in the seventies, the kind made by stack-

ing any number of wooden cubes. The number Lanny had chosen to live with was fifteen, piled into a pyramid shape with five
of the units forming the base. The cubes housed everything
from tattered record albums to beer bottles, each from a different country. In his fifties, Lanny retained the decorating instincts of a college boy.

Finding the photos was moderately satisfying. What Anna
found intensely satisfying was discovering she probably wasn't
the first person to seek them out since Lanny's unpremeditated
departure—unless Lanny himself had pawed through them, sur-
gically removing the images of the woman who had betrayed
him; an explanation too common, too human, to dismiss out of
hand. Anna refused to let the thought rob her of the mild buzz of
discovery.

One of the flimsy envelopes had torn, and half a dozen pictures had fallen out. She'd not noticed them in the general mess
because, shoved between couch and cubes, was an end table
probably from the early fifties, when blond pseudo-cowboy
style was popular. The loose pictures fanned out beneath the
table, two pinned under a leg. The end table had been moved,
the photo bins gone through, then the table put back.

Before leaping to the conclusion she preferred—that she had
seen a light, someone had been in Wilcox's quarters, had poked
about, the intruder's search culminating with the digital camera
upstairs and, ergo, Anna was not nuts—she carefully inspected
the pinned photographs, then the top of the table. The table was
sufficiently dusty, had she been so inclined, she could have
written her initials therein. In a way somebody had. Two prints,
clearly, the heels of ungloved hands, marked the dust where the
table had been picked up and moved. On the scattered pictures
there was no dust at all. The table had been moved recently, the
mess of pictures was newly spilled.

Anna pulled latex gloves from a pouch on her duty belt. She
was a world away from snazzy modern lab equipment. The
NPS hadn't the money to spare on expensive tests when, as far
as she knew, no crime had been committed. Not even breaking
and entering. She'd found Wilcox's door closed but latched.
Who was to say Lanny'd not left it that way when he'd gone?
Or Teddy had, on her mission of mercy cleaning the spoilables

from the refrigerator. Still and all Anna didn't want to add her
prints to the mix and, just for the hell of it, would return later
with a kit to lift the palm prints.

The pictures were a disappointment. They were what one
would expect to find in a ranger's quarters between the Gulf of
Mexico and the Strait of Florida: boats, more boats, blue water,
pale sands, people in swimsuits and, occasionally, people without swimsuits. Three of the envelopes were dedicated to the fort
and were all but indistinguishable from those Anna had taken
her first week to send home to Paul: arches disappearing within
arches, the camera aimed down either the casemate's larger section where the cannon were once housed or the same perspective down the long line of man-sized arches that fronted them,
the parade ground, the lighthouse: the usual.

Social pictures captured the Shaws, Daniel, Mack, Duncan
and his wife and son. There was even a photograph of Mrs.
Meyers.

Again what was interesting was what wasn't there. No photographs of Theresa. Four that Anna had separated out were of
what she thought might be Theresa's backside. And a fine backside it was. Anna could well understand why a man, especially
a man entering his fifties on an island with no single women in
residence, might well choose to follow that backside with all
the ardor with which the three wise men were reported to have
followed the star.

Anna pocketed her find, fetched her kit from the office, and
lifted the prints from the table. Besides the heels of the intruder's hands, she was lucky to get a good-sized partial from
the person's right fore- and middle fingers—given he or she had
lifted the table in a normal way. The prints would probably lan-
guish in a file proving nothing, but it was something to do.

When she finished, she still had a couple hours to kill before
Mack and Danny would be free to lend a hand with the wreck
dive. Rather than return to an office that, without Teddy Shaw
on site, Anna had looked forward to as a place of glorious solitude but which turned out to be merely lonely in a creepy sort of
way, she fired up the *Reef Ranger* and motored over to Loggerhead Key.

The endless expanse of blue water had the same calming ef-

fect as the mountains on a clear day. Being able to let her eyes
stretch for a horizon without stumbling into walls, to see in
every direction for miles, to shout without being heard, gave her
a sense of reckless freedom. The cloying claustrophobia of Fort
Jefferson's substantial ramparts and Lanny Wilcox's packrat's
den was blown away on the hot wind. She steered the boat in
lazy S patterns and belted out several of the cruder verses of
"What Do You Do with a Drunken Sailor."

Midday, mid season, Fort Jefferson's docks, harbor and
beaches were teeming with campers, fishermen and tourists.
The two ferries from the mainland, both enormous catamarans
capable of dumping over two hundred visitors between them,
filled the fort with bodies.

Loggerhead was refreshingly deserted. There was but one
small dock for NPS use only, no camping, no toilets, no drinking water for the public. Neither of the ferries stopped there.
People lucky enough to own their own boats occasionally
brought a dinghy into shore or swam in, but there were none today.

At the landward end of the dock where a sand path started
through the scrub to the lighthouse keepers' quarters and the old
lighthouse, a strange garden had grown up. In the low dunes
swelling to either side of the trail, passersby had planted bits of
flotsam or dead marine animals they'd come across; things too
wonderful not to pick up at the beach and too useless to take
home.

Fishing nets, broken lobster traps, buoys in all sizes and colors, pieces of dead coral, skeletons of horseshoe crabs, sand
dollars, bottles scrubbed clean of their labels, seashells, fishing
lures and other oddments had been arranged in an ongoing
work in progress. Nothing in this ten-by-twenty-foot sculpture
garden appeared to have been tossed. Each piece had been
placed with somebody's idiosyncratic idea of beauty.

The result fascinated Anna. Each time she visited Loggerhead Key she looked for new things. The garden made her feel
good about her species, as if fed, watered and left to peaceful
pursuits, mankind would tend toward making the world a better
place. Today she stopped for a minute and rearranged a horseshoe crab and four sand dollars to make an ersatz turtle. Satisfied with her contribution to the ephemeral world of art, she

walked to the house shared by the women charged with main-
taining the lighthouse.

Lighthouse keepers were volunteers who came to Loggerhead for a month at a time. The post was so isolated and the
duties so specialized and yet mostly undemanding that more
than thirty days drove most people crazy. All there was to do on
the tiny key was to keep the generator in good running order
and the visitors from damaging anything. Besides the light and
the light keepers' cottage, there was a house used by visiting research teams. At the moment it stood empty.

The cottage delighted Anna. As it came into view over a
sand dune she stopped to admire the scene. The building was of
stone, two stories, one small room stacked atop the other; a
haven in which to weather storms. The house and the concept
appealed to Anna. This afternoon the reassuring picture was
completed by Donna and Patrice. Patrice was seated at a picnic
table as gray and warped as driftwood, staring intently at the
guts of a piece of machinery. Donna stood at her shoulder,
pointing and talking, one hand on Patrice's shoulder.

What kept this scene of domestic bliss from being a cliché
were the women themselves. When Neil Simon wrote *The Odd
Couple,* he had no inkling of how very odd couples were to become in the near future. Donna was tall, thick of shoulder and
narrow of hip with arms that she'd probably earned at her
"other job" as a boiler-room engineer. Breasts and shoulder-
length hair framing a distinctly craggy face denied the manly
frame.

Patrice, who had retired from walking a beat for the Boston
police department some years before, switching careers to
teach kindergarten, was slightly less masculine-looking, being
squat rather than tall, but she too had what looked to be signs of
a vestigial X chromosome. Gossip rampant in the close and often closed circles of the National Park Service had thoroughly
chewed over the lighthouse keepers. Anna leaned toward the
theory that one or both women had undergone sex-change operations before which they were heterosexual and after which
they discovered they were lesbians.

Since this was the seventh year Donna and Patrice had come
to Loggerhead during the month of July, fort personnel and
park regulars had grown accustomed to them. Because they did

their job well and proved excellent company, they'd come to be accepted, their odd looks and mysterious origins merely one more wonder of this tiny world.

Anna enjoyed them immensely, particularly Donna, whose wit was so dry and subtle often Anna would only get the joke after she'd put to sea headed home and would find herself laughing all alone on her boat.

"Ranger Pigeon," Donna called in a voice tuned to overcome the noise of a boiler room. "What brings you to our island paradise?"

Anna joined them at the picnic table, was given a glass of sweet tea in return for which she was expected to tell them the news of the previous two days' happenings.

She began with the last dive she and Cliff had taken and ended with the tale of Bob Shaw's heroics. She hesitated to tell her ghost story. People periodically claimed to see ghosts at Fort Jefferson. Daniel, a foursquare chunk of Americana with the tattoos to prove it, insisted he'd felt a spectral hand on his shoulder in the generator room. It wasn't that Anna believed her story would make the two women look at her askance; it was that Donna and Patrice were clever.

Clever and smart with senses of humor honed sharp as razors, probably from years of fending off prying questions and rude remarks. Of the staff at Fort Jefferson, these two struck Anna as the most capable of pulling off a complex hoax. Why on earth they would want her to believe either in ghosts or her own incipient insanity was beyond her.

Instead she asked: "Did either of you guys know Theresa Alvarez?" When dealing with minorities in the oh-so-politically-correct climate of government service, whether they were minorities because of race, infirmity or gender bending, Anna was hyperconscious of her words. She hoped "guys" would not cause offense.

Donna and Patrice were blessedly ignorant of this social gaffe.

"Oh, yes," Patrice said with an enthusiasm that clearly annoyed her partner.

"We didn't know her all that well," Donna said repressively. "She'd come over here now and again. Sometimes to visit, mostly to comb the beaches for things she used to make her picture boxes."

"She is a terrific artist," Patrice said.

Donna raised her eyebrows. "Especially in that tiny little thong bathing suit." Her voice was a seductive growl.

Patrice laughed and punched Donna in the arm, a slug that would have sent Anna ass over teakettle but didn't move Donna at all. "You!" Patrice said playfully. Then: "You've got to admit she showed off that thong to good advantage."

Donna put a beefy arm around Patrice's shoulders and told Anna: "Neither of us knew her in the biblical sense, but we were allowed to admire her from a safe distance."

"Safe from Theresa?" Patrice asked. "Theresa was gentle as a kitten."

"Safe from me, sweetheart."

They both laughed and Anna was glad to see accord restored.

"Tell me about her," Anna suggested. "From the thong upward."

Donna and Patrice were silent for a bit and Anna began to suspect the thong and regions there adjacent pretty much constituted their notice of Ms. Alvarez.

"She didn't talk much," Patrice said finally. "Kept to herself."

"Unless she got on her soapbox," Donna amended. "Then she'd run on till your eyes rolled back in your head."

Patrice nodded. "A liberal."

"Fire-breathing, heart-on-your-sleeve liberal. Major snooze."

"Except for the thong," Patrice said dreamily, hoping to get a rise out of Donna. Donna obliged with a boiler-room snort.

"Anything else?" Anna asked.

Patrice shook her head.

"We didn't see that much of her—" She shot Patrice a look that stopped the obvious rejoinder. "Theresa left not long after we got here."

"That did kind of surprise me," Patrice said. "Teddy'd told us she'd figured Theresa for using Lanny, but I got the feeling she loved the man."

"Using Lanny how?" Anna asked. Lanny Wilcox wasn't going to attract gold diggers on a GS-II's salary, and though there was no accounting for taste, Anna couldn't see a balding man in his fifties with the housekeeping instincts of a frat boy as anybody's idea of a sex toy. "Was she broke enough forty thousand a year would seem like money?"

"Not money, I don't think." Patrice looked to Donna for corroboration.

"No. Teddy didn't make it sound like a money thing. Besides, Theresa had the looks to use a man for a whole lot more than forty thousand a year less taxes. Teddy kind of thought Theresa might be running from something, using Lanny and Fort Jefferson as a place to hide out."

"A lot of people who wash up on islands are running from something," Anna said.

Donna and Patrice exchanged a look that made Anna think she'd hit a nerve.

"Or running to something," Patrice said softly.

"Or running to something," Anna agreed.

"Ask Teddy," Donna suggested. "Teddy is from whence all information worth having around here flows."

Anna would do that as soon as the Shaws returned from the mainland.

"Why the sudden interest in Lanny's love life?" Donna asked.

"I've been seeing ghosts," Anna said and watched them carefully. Donna's face was impassive to the point of frozen, but Anna couldn't tell if she'd solidified her facial muscles to hide a guilty secret or to hide the fact that she thought Anna was an idiot.

Patrice seemed delighted. "Oh, man, I would kill to see a ghost. Even part of one: a spectral hand, a rattling chain. I wouldn't even mind being slimed. Tell us *everything*," she demanded, and propped her chin in her hands expectantly.

The juxtaposition of the girlish pose and the hairy forearms shook Anna's insides, but she didn't laugh; she liked these women too well.

She obliged them with the story of Great-Great-Aunt Raffia's fleeting visit to the casemate near the chapel. She'd meant to keep it bare bones and focus on their reactions, but Patrice was such a good audience and Anna so in need of women confidants with whom there was no one- to two-second delay from mouth to ear, she found herself relating every detail: the turn of the head, the upswept hair, the delicate long fingers pushing in otherworldly hairpins.

"Doesn't sound like Theresa Alvarez," Donna said when she'd done, hearkening back to the non sequitur that she believed had launched this ghost story. "Theresa was dark and, as Patrice has so observantly pointed out, not much given to clothes that covered her from neck to ankles."

"No. Sorry," Anna said. "I never thought it was Lanny's girl-friend. Talking about Theresa just put me in mind of it because she disappeared. Ghostlike. Poof?"

The segue was spotty at best but the lighthouse keepers chose to accept it without question. Anna didn't know what gender the two had been born, but there was no doubt in her mind that they were girls now. It was good to be one of them.

"Do you think she was 'disappeared' against her will?" A funny edge came into Patrice's voice that bothered Anna till she remembered the woman was a retired law-enforcement officer.

"You think old fire horses are bad," Donna said as if reading her mind. "They've got nothing on retired cops."

Patrice was not to be deterred. "Do you suspect felonious play? We heard she'd run off, presumably with a man younger, prettier and richer than Lanny."

Hearing her vague suppositions laid out in words, Anna backed away from the idea. It sounded melodramatic, like a bored ranger making something out of nothing. Or a woman of a certain age having mid-life delusions.

"Just poking around," she said. "Nothing really. What I came over here for—besides to waste your time and drink up your tea—was to see if either of you recognized this boat. Here's what's left of it." She took a printout of an underwater photo of the bottle-green go-fast boat. It was taken before the second explosion, when the bow was still recognizable as such.

"Looks like a Scarab, maybe," Donna said. Anna took note of the fact that the woman knew her boats.

"It is."

"What's that color? Looks almost black in the picture."

"Metallic sparkly dark green."

"Where's the boat out of?" Patrice asked.

"I don't know yet. We're working on it."

"We see a lot of boats come through," Donna said.

"We'll keep an eye out," Patrice said. "What am I talking about? The boat's on the bottom. It's history. I'll see what I got."

"The Dick Tracy File," Donna explained when Anna looked confused. "Patrice videos anything the least bit odd. In *case* . . ." She laughed.

Patrice didn't.

"Not just odd," she defended herself. "Though of course odd is particularly interesting. Just a photographic record of comings and goings." For an instant she looked sheepish.

Donna patted her with a big callused hand, grease from working on the generator ingrained under her round, clipped fingernails. "It's good you keep it, Patrice. It's come in handy. Because of Patrice the Key West cops—"

"Key *Stone* cops," Patrice interjected.

"Your opinion. The Key West police and the coast guard were able to track down a twenty-nine-year-old felon who'd run off with his boss's fishing yacht."

"And his boss's fourteen-year-old daughter."

"She went willingly."

"It was her idea, but that doesn't change anything," Patrice said.

"Nope. He should have been keelhauled."

If the current theory about the lighthouse keepers was correct, neither of them had ever been little girls. Perhaps the undertone of anger Anna heard had nothing to do with chromosomes and everything to do with humanity.

Because she had time to kill and because she was enjoying herself and because her position as Supervisory Ranger in the Dry Tortugas was temporary, Anna decided to indulge in a little gossip—real gossip, not police work disguised—good old-fashioned dishing the dirt with the rest of the girls.

"What do you guys know about Mack?" she asked. "He strikes me as a man with a past."

Donna straddled the bench on the far side of the picnic table and rubbed her jaw. The way she pushed upward on her cheek made Anna wonder if it was a habit left over from years of checking for five o'clock shadow.

"He's an odd duck, that's for sure. He loves to talk, but only about himself."

"He's quite manly in that," Patrice said, and the three of them enjoyed an uncensored laugh.

"I noticed his back and legs are scarred. He ever mention how that came about?"

"I noticed those too, right off," Patrice said.

"She asked him about it right off, too," Donna said.

"I asked nice," Patrice said.

Donna mimicked her partner, batting her eyes like a femme fatale, which clearly tickled Patrice: "Hello, Mack, isn't it a nice day? By the by, how the hell did you get all cut up like that?"

"I did not," Patrice laughed.

"Did he tell you?" Anna asked.

"He told us a story," Patrice said. "Something about falling off an all-terrain vehicle and being dragged across gravel by a pant leg. A load of hooey."

"Child abuse, you think?"

"That's my guess," Patrice said. "If we're right, it's a wonder he didn't grow up to be another Jeffrey Dahmer. It had to've been brutal. I don't blame him for making up a better story."

Anna didn't either. "What does he talk about, then, if the past is out of the picture?"

"Oh it's not out," Donna said. "It's the picture that's a wee bit different than you'd expect after seeing the scars."

"Mack's got a lot of stories about how his folks were these rich aristocratic types. According to him he had his own horse, nannies and the trimmings," Patrice said.

"And he's a lowly government employee now because some evil relative squandered it all away," Anna finished. The fantasy was fairly common among dissatisfied men who thought they deserved better.

"Something like that," Patrice said. "He gets vague about it. Maybe that part of the story's not written yet."

For a while the three of them sat in comforting silence, Anna sipping her tea, Donna fiddling with the chunk of machinery, Patrice seemingly content doing nothing at all.

They made a bit more desultory talk. Anna asked politely about the eviscerated motor on the table and was treated to a list of internal combustion symptoms that meant nothing to her. Finally Patrice took pity on her and summed it up.

"Generator went ker-put."

"Terminally ker-put?" Anna asked.

"Over Donna's dead body."

"I'll have it up and running by dark," Donna promised. "I think we got a mouse problem. They get to building nests in the moving parts of your machinery and it's a nightmare."

It was on the tip of Anna's tongue to offer Piedmont's services as a mouser. He could rid an island of the size of Loggerhead Key of rodents in under a week. What stopped her was selfishness. She liked Piedmont at home.

Unless Donna pulled off her usual miracle, Loggerhead Key would have to swelter in the dark. Anna was keeping her cat.

She looked at her watch. Two forty-seven. Time to meet some men about a wreck. She made her goodbyes and walked away from the snug cottage and into the glare of white sand and a hard-looking sea. It occurred to her that she felt good for having had tea with Patrice and Donna. It also occurred to her that she had come with questions, and had given out a great deal of information and gotten little.

Patrice must've been one hell of a cop.

12

My Dearest Peg,

Five days have passed since I last sat down to write. To turn back the clock: the four of us waited in the casemate next to that shared by Dr. Mudd and a second of the conspirators.

The cell was dim, as they all are once the opening arch onto the parade ground has been boarded up, and this one darker than most, having but a small opening on the sea side. My eyes had adjusted, however, and I could see with that misty clarity one experiences at twilight. Though the cell was stiflingly hot, the sweat prickling my skin had the quality of winter perspiration brought on by exercising in extreme cold.

Joel was still and silent, the effort to be brave and charming during transport having taken what little strength he had. The soldier who was to remain with us as guard and chaperone stood to one side of the door leading to Dr. Mudd's cell, looking agitated and thunderous. Eyes big and mouth pinched, Tilly knelt beside Joel, watching the door where the soldier had rapped, summoning the devil upon whom we had pinned our slim hopes.

The door opened. An urbane-looking man, hairline receding, a lush mustache covering his upper lip above a well-trimmed goatee, said: "May I help you?" for all the world as if he answered the door of his own home and under better circumstances.

I don't know if it was the relief that he did not look like a slavering beast or the surprisingly kind eyes under thin, low brows, or the offer of precisely that which we had come seeking—help—but Tilly started to cry.

"Are you Dr. Mudd?" she asked through tears that flowed prettily—when I cry, my face goes red and blotchy and my nose runs. Perhaps that's why my tears lost their efficacy with Joseph too many years ago to count.

The most hard-hearted of men would have responded with chivalry to the picture of feminine distress Tilly presented.

"I am," he told her and bowed slightly. He was elegant, even—or perhaps I should say especially—given the surroundings, and spoke with a whisper of a southern drawl that served to enhance the image. "How can I be of service?" All this was directed to Tilly, I suppose because it was she who first addressed him.

Whatever the reason, I could see her becoming as grave and mature as befitted a woman addressed on matters of importance. This "honor," if indeed attentions from the likes of him constituted such, coupled with his offer of medical help for Joel Lane, completely won Tilly over. Our little sister and one of the men condemned for the most heinous and cowardly of murders were staunch allies before they'd exchanged a baker's dozen of words.

I did not like it. I very much did not like it. Unfortunately my discomfort came only later. Joel's needs being foremost in my mind at the time, though not so swayed as Tilly, I was glad enough of the doctor's help.

As she had established a rapport with the notorious doctor, Tilly became mistress of the situation. I was content to stand by the soldier against the back wall and act as an observer.

She showed the doctor Joel and told him how he had come to be injured. Dr. Mudd's expression didn't appear to change, but when mouth and chin are completely obscured by hair, the face was unreadable. I wouldn't doubt if a few of the union's famed stoics owe the compliment not to moral fortitude but a plentitude of facial hair. The doctor did not give in to the temptation to comment on the brutality of the union soldiers. He merely nodded, said: "Please?" and, when Tilly made room, knelt to determine the extent of Joel's injuries.

I had been so caught up in Dr. Mudd's examination of Joel, the quick surety of his long fingers, the small helpful movements of Miss Tilly as though she'd spent years in a sickroom, that I forgot there was another soul incarcerated in these rooms until the soldier at my elbow moved suddenly.

Samuel Bland Arnold. You of course remember the name from the trial and the accounts in the newspapers. Words cannot convey the impact that laying eyes on this man has.

Mr. Arnold had taken Dr. Mudd's place in the door leading into their cell. He'd apparently started to enter the casemate where we were. That's what stirred the soldier assigned to Tilly and me. Arnold held both hands up, palms outward, to assure the soldier he would not try to cross the threshold again. This gesture is universal for surrender, acquiescence, yet in a manner I cannot put into words, when done by Mr. Arnold, it was mocking as well.

He leaned against the lintel, ankles crossed, and lit a cheroot. Dark haired, mustache worn clipped above the lip and long at the corners of his mouth, brows level and thick over deep-set eyes, the man is just the sort with whom silly girls ruin their reputations.

Mr. Arnold said nothing, nor did he interfere in any way, yet, to me at least, his presence was as disruptive as a soprano singing off-key. I turned my back on him yet remained so aware of his presence I believe I could have told you the instant it happened had he left that doorway.

My peculiar suffering wasn't to last long. Dr. Mudd was in need of many things for the care of the patient he had taken on with such automatic grace. The guard could not leave either Tilly or me alone with the prisoners, and Tilly would have had to be dragged from Joel's side by a team of wild horses. It fell to me to fetch and carry. I found it a great relief to be freed of that close room with its absence of air and presence of prison smells and the disturbing emanations from Mr. Arnold.

Dr. Caulley is a lean man, but his moon face, glistening summer and winter as if basted for roasting, gives the illusion he was meant to be corpulent but was too stingy to allow his body to attain its predestined shape. The fort's surgeon is unfailingly polite to me but manages by intricate manipulations of eyebrows and narrow mustache to semaphore the message that he doesn't like me and has a low opinion of my intellectual abilities.

When Dr. Caulley found me acting as errand girl for the infamous Dr. Samuel Mudd, his eyebrows surpassed themselves in communicating that which his pursed and niggardly little mouth was too pious to say. With those two scanty lines of reddish hair, he managed to disparage Dr. Mudd's medical abilities, lineage and politics while his mouth murmured only, "*Mister* Mudd. I see."

Joseph must have taken time to speak with him, because he granted my requests. It took several trips, but I brought Dr. Mudd everything he'd requested with the exception of morphine. Using hints and eyebrows, Dr. Caulley conveyed that the confederate doctor and conspirator in murder could not be trusted not to sell the morphine or use it himself. I was afraid Joel would be left to suffer. That he was in great pain was evident even to the untrained eye.

When I'd brought what I'd been given and relayed the information about the morphine—sans the eyebrow signals—Dr. Mudd was silent for a moment, rocking back on his heels where he'd been kneeling by his patient.

He finally stood and pulled what had once been a crease in his trousers straight. "Pain can kill a man," he said simply. "I saw it on the battlefield. The pain takes the strength that could otherwise be used for healing." Then he brushed his hands together, one against the other.

Tilly read the gesture as clearly as I did. "No," she said, but not with the girlish tears she'd shown earlier. In the little time we had been in this dark and sweltering room, Tilly had grown up. "Stay with him, Raffia," she said. "I won't be long."

I was so stunned by the change in her that she'd swept by me and was gone before I had time to protest or even to ask what she intended.

She wasn't gone more than twenty minutes, but it seemed a good deal longer. Tilly was the binding presence, I discovered, not Private Lane. When she left, none of us remaining could find anything to say to one another.

By the time Tilly returned with Joseph, though I'd not spo-

ken a single word to either Dr. Mudd or Mr. Arnold, I felt I had
spent a short lifetime in their midst.

From the moment Tilly stepped off the ship that brought her
over from Key West she has had Joseph eating out of her hand.
It delights me to see it and, I must confess, often makes me
wonder if being barren is quite the blessing I believe it to be. He
responds to her with gentleness I've seen him use only with
horses and dogs. It reassures me the boy I fell in love with still
dwells in the man I am married to.

Dr. Mudd reemerged from his cell when he heard the ring of
Joseph's boots on the brick. Joseph stayed in one doorway and
Mudd, having displaced Arnold—who seemed not so much to
leave but to vanish as a shadow will when exposed to light—
stayed in the other. Between them Joel's "hospital" room was
neutral ground. Across it I could feel the animosity from my
husband and the rebound of it from the doctor.

"Mudd," Joseph said curtly. "Morphine for the boy."

Dr. Mudd started to cross the open space to retrieve it. Point-
edly, Joseph handed it to me.

"My wife will have the keeping of it. She will give you what
you need for the boy and stay to watch until you have administered it."

"Thank you—" Mudd began, but Joseph cut him off.

"This is not a privilege and will get you no special treatment.
Never test me."

An arrogance I'd not seen—or not noticed—before came
over Dr. Mudd, stiffening his back and hardening the muscles
of his face. It made him a different man from the kindly doctor
who tended to Joel. I could easily see how, if he wore this guise
in court, he was condemned. This Mudd could possibly lie and
kill and continue to feel righteous for having done so.

"Sir," Dr. Mudd said icily. "Considering you are willing to
imprison an innocent man, your rudeness does not surprise
me."

There was an awful moment after the doctor spoke. Joseph
said nothing but let Dr. Mudd's words hang in the air. I don't
think the doctor is aware of what a slender thread his continued
well-being at Fort Jefferson depends on.

"Please . . ." Tilly said to no one and everyone.

"Do not test me," Joseph repeated in a tone I have come to

respect. He turned to our soldier-escort. "Private Mason, as soon as the morphine is administered, see Mrs. Coleman and her sister back to the officers' quarters." On his way out he stopped beside Tilly and me. In less frightening but no less serious tones, he said: "Don't you two test me either."

Tilly scarcely heard him, nor, I noted, did she thank him for getting the morphine. I could only hope she had the sense—and the grace—to do it before they had returned to the casemate. She was halfway across the cell, the morphine in her outstretched hand. "Dr. Mudd, I cannot thank you enough. Without you we would be so alone."

Joseph looked back over his shoulder at Tilly clinging to Dr. Mudd's arm as they knelt by Joel. The expression on his face was alien to me; I could not read it, yet it made me afraid. For whom, I don't know. Maybe for myself.

13

Motoring into the harbor, things seemed peaceful enough. It was too early in the day for the shrimpers, and many other boats were out of the park fishing. Passing a sportfishing ban in Dry Tortugas National Park had caused an outcry heard all the way to Mississippi. Not killing animals in a national park was one thing, but *fish?* Surely it's every American boy's birthright to kill fish anywhere they are to be found.

The superintendent of Dry Tortugas and Everglades had stuck to her guns and backed the unpopular ban. The results were much what the NPS had hoped they'd be. Not only were there more and bigger fish within the park boundaries, but significantly more and bigger fish were being caught outside the boundaries as well. By banning fishing in fifty thousand acres of sea, a nursery, a veritable cornucopia of fishes, had been created.

None of this impressed the sportfishermen. Talk still turned ugly when the subject came up, and they still whined piteously over the inconvenience of having to go a mile or two farther from their favorite anchorages to legally drop their lines in the water.

Anna was firmly on the side of the fishes. As far as she was concerned, a less populated harbor was a perk, not a consequence. She turned the Boston Whaler and backed deftly into her slot. Water and boating skills honed as a patrol ranger at Isle Royale National Park in Lake Superior that she'd thought lost in the intervening years had come back with a week's practice, and she gloried in their return.

Maintenance's boat, the *Atlantic Ranger,* was not at the dock. Anna was just as glad. She had a little time to grab a bite to eat, say "hi" to her cat and gather up her gear.

Twenty minutes later, when she came down in suit and flip-flops, the many contusions left by her encounter with the coral complaining about being exposed to the direct rays of the sun, Daniel and Mack were sitting in the shade outside the shop waiting for her.

"Number five up and running?" she asked as she neared them. Daniel shot her a peculiar look, and she wondered if he took it personally when the generators consigned to his care were on the fritz.

"Right as rain," Mack said. He changed the subject as the two men fell into step with her. "What are we diving for?"

"Identification, mostly," Anna replied. "I'm hoping the green boat has a registration number or, failing that, a serial number on the engine that's still readable. So far the Florida police haven't had any luck tracing our John Doe."

"Juan Doe," Mack said. Anna didn't know if he was being racist or clever. She let it pass. Mack wore only orange trunks and sandals, and sneaking a look at his back, she found her guess had been correct. Striping the lean muscles and knotty spine were the same narrow whipping scars she'd noticed on his legs and upper arms.

Dive tanks, buoyancy compensator vests, weights and regulators were kept in a small room behind the ladies' toilets on the visitors' dock. A few minutes were spent loading the heavy gear, then they were motoring out toward the wreck. It crossed Anna's mind that the NPS would want the *Bay Ranger* salvaged and possibly the Scarab brought up and disposed of. Old wrecks had charm. She wasn't so sure about the modern variety. Having no idea what went into salvage work, she made a mental note to call the chief ranger in Homestead at the next opportunity.

The seas were by no means rough, but neither were they at

the dead calm that had facilitated diving the day before. There was a stiffening wind out of the southeast and a definite chop to the water. The rangers' boats in the Dry Tortugas were graced with Global Positioning Systems, but Anna hadn't been a boat patrol ranger since the days of loran—long range navigation— and hadn't yet bothered to learn how to use them. Trusting in the old ways, she'd marked the wrecks with buoys. Despite the chop, they found them easily.

It was decided she and Mack would dive the Scarab first to see if they could find any identifying marks, numbers or papers. Often boats kept important papers in waterproof containers so the idea was not that far-fetched. That done, they'd scavenge Bob's boat and bring up anything useful or even detachable. Once the sport divers or snorkelers found the *Bay Ranger,* she would be picked clean by souvenir hunters. Regardless of laws forbidding the vandalizing of sunken artifacts in protected waters, it was virtually impossible to overcome the allure of taking home a trophy pried from a genuine shipwreck.

Ignoring the uproar from her abused flesh, Anna wriggled into an old dive skin—the nicer one shredded in the explosion—fins, vest, snorkel and mask. Mack, finished before she was, waited till she was ready, and together they rolled off the gunwale.

The pristine clarity of the water was gone, as was the glassy surface above. Particulate matter clouded vision and leached colors from fish and coral. Visibility underwater was an ever-changing thing. Like the weather, it seemed to make its own unpredictable choices. One day clear, cloudy the next and often without the easy logic of groundswell or storm to explain the sudden fluctuations.

Mack vanished in the murk, swimming expertly with an economy of motion. He wore neither dive suit nor skin. Underwater his body hair floated and sunlight refracted, making his scars startlingly apparent. Or perhaps Anna had speculated on them so long and so rudely with the lighthouse keepers she'd sensitized herself. Now they put her in mind, not of an abused child, but a tiger shark. Kicking hard, she caught up and swam beside Mack. The physical exertion was welcome. With the murky water and the fleeting thought of man-as-tiger-shark, she worried her mind might be taking that particular twist it had the night before. Moving, working, relegated the ghoulies and ghosties to a half-remembered dream state.

The hull was scattered in fragments. Between them she and Mack turned over every piece they could find, the largest being the stern portion, without finding any name or numbers. Either the identifying marks had been pulverized in the explosion or the owners of this super-loaded speedboat chose to remain anonymous.

As they worked, it began to dawn on Anna that someone had been stirring in the pile. Though she'd not said it to herself in so many words, the idea germinated when they'd moved the stern. After the initial explosion the orange PFD had been floating like a child's birthday balloon above the transom, tethered by its own strap. Following the second explosion it had been pinned beneath the upended stern. Now it was gone. If there'd been nothing else, she would have assumed it had gotten loose and floated away. The sea is a strange place. Things happen.

But there were other changes. Nothing dramatic, nothing even as noticeable as the removal of the life jacket; it was that objects weren't quite the way she remembered: a little to the right, farther left, turned on its side, shifted farther under or over something else. It reminded her of the way drawers and dressing tables look after being searched and restored to their presearch configuration by most males. Everything is there. Everything is where it was. But better, the carefully tended chaos made slightly more orderly, slightly less random. Anna hadn't come primarily for taking photos, but she took a lot of them, and from the same angles she remembered the last shots having been taken. When she compared the two sets of photographs she would know for sure if someone had been diving here, doing major rifling, in the past twelve hours. *No,* Anna corrected herself as she lined up a shot of the shattered midsection, *I already know for sure. The pictures are to prove it.* Whether to herself or someone else depended on whether she continued to see ghosts or not.

Finally, each and every piece of debris examined, Anna gave up on finding either name or registration number. Their only remaining hope was getting a serial number off one of the Scarab's engines in hopes they could trace it to the manufacturer and from there through the various sales slips to its present owner.

Both engines, imposing chunks of black metal with white plastic tubing, were virtually intact. One was buried in the sand, the top down, the number unreachable. The blast had separated the other from the hull and carried it to a complex, if small, mountain range. Anna chose not to think of the thousands of years of careful creation destroyed on impact or the millions of tiny lives extinguished. The grace and delicacy of the coral cities put Anna in mind of Dr. Seuss's Whoville. She couldn't help picturing the living coral as full of minute Who people going about their little Who lives. The fairy tale—programmed anthropomorphism—made the destruction ridiculously poignant.

To complete the image, the plastic tubing on the engine, ends severed from wherever they'd been designed to take a necessary fluid, floated out like tentacles from the black squatting body of the monster.

Too many horror movies as a kid, Anna thought, and smiled around the plastic plug of her regulator as she pictured Rodan pursuing a Japanese maiden across the sea floor.

Catching Mack's attention, she pointed to herself, then to the engine.

Mack shook his head and pointed to the surface. He tapped his watch, then the pressure gauge that indicated how much air remained in the tank.

Anna looked at her own gauge. She had just under half a tank. Even given the difference in their size, unless Mack had been hyperventilating, it was hard to believe he was out of air. She tapped her own gauge and circled thumb and index finger in the "okay" sign, then began to swim to him to see if there was a problem with his equipment but, after shaking the gauge hard, he gave an exaggerated shrug and the "okay" sign.

Evidently it had fixed itself. She turned and finished the short journey to where the engine lay on uneven peaks of coral. The explosion had flipped it so it landed top downward on the rocky surface. Little fishes had already begun exploring the intricate crevices and caves of metal. Tiny eyes, working mouths and colorful flicks of tails met Anna as she inspected the under-

side for identifying numbers. Mostly she was being thorough.
Serial numbers were meant to be seen and used while the vehicle the engine was housed in was right-side up. Manufacturers
usually put them on a metal part close to the top.

Mack floated nearby; more company than help, a flicker of
color and movement in her peripheral vision much like the shy
visit of a large fish. Having proved to herself there were to be
no easy answers, Anna let her body sink a couple feet deeper.
The nest of coral boulders the engine rested on was not more
than three and four feet high. Fins on the sandy bottom, she was
at eye level with where the metal met the rock in a crush of
once-living coral and plant life. It hadn't fallen on a single boulder but the meeting of several slowly growing together. Beneath
the engine was a miniature canyon eighteen inches or so deep
and three or four feet long. The top of this ravine, capped by
iron and steel, was a couple of feet across, the bottom tapered to
nothing where boulder met boulder. Living walls, now in darkness, housed the delicate and wondrous beings so common in
these waters.

Ignoring the imaginary screams as the Whos of Whoville
rushed about in panic, their fairy cities in ruins, Anna poked one
arm in, flashlight in hand, and followed it with her head. A
skull-shuddering clank stopped her as her air tank rang against
the metal of the engine. Between metal and bone, the noise
sounded inside her head as if her skull were the bell and her
brain the clapper.

She waited till the ringing ceased shaking her gray matter,
then poked about carefully with her little underwater light.
She'd not used it before and, like some of the men she'd dated,
it was cute but dim. After scraping the back of her hand and
murdering several thousand more Whos with her elbow, she
found what she was looking for. Maybe. Cramped in at an odd
angle with bubbles and wee little Who corpses floating before
her eyes, it was hard to be sure.

Pulling head and flashlight out, she stuck her right arm in up
to the shoulder and tried to read the numbers with the tips of her
fingers. Her fingertips were, if anything, too sensitive. Such a
plethora of information was sent back from the wet and rough
and smooth and greasy, one proficient in Braille could possibly

have deduced all of *Hamlet* or prophesied the apocalypse from what her fingers read there.

Anna was merely confused and frustrated. Again she peered into the triangular-shaped tunnel. There was no egress at the far end. The engine capped a miniature box canyon. Backing off, she pondered the feasibility of shifting the engine. A few experimental shoves alone, then with the help of Mack, couldn't budge it. That was probably just as well. From where she hung before the opening of the black box protecting her number, the edge of the engine to her left only overlapped the edge of the coral by an inch or so. Had they succeeded in shifting the engine it would slide into the crack and, short of a hoist from a salvage ship, she'd never get at the serial number.

A minute, maybe more, she stared into the hole trying to ignore the solution to her problem by sending her thoughts chasing down various cheeseless rat holes.

Other avenues exhausted, she was forced back to the obvious. Without her vest and tank she could fit in the crevice. It would take a bit of wriggling to keep her hand up near her eyes so she'd have light when she reached the number, but it wouldn't be that tight a squeeze.

She'd been in tighter.

And hated it, she reminded herself. "Hated" was the word she chose to remember from her last crawl in Lechuguilla Cave some years back. It saved her from admitting to herself how terrified she'd been, how desperately close to coming unglued and running mad through the labyrinths of the underworld, a modern metaphor for Tolkein's Gollum.

Nothing for it, she decided. Mack was hovering and unsettled to the far right edge of her vision. She pointed to herself then to the crevice and began to take off her vest. The regulator hose was long enough; if she held it tight against her chest, she could continue breathing though the tank was not on her back. Anna was much in favor of continuing to breathe.

Mack was shaking his head pointing at his pressure gauge, then toward the surface. Again Anna looked at her own. Just over a quarter full. They were no more than twenty-five feet down—a free dive. It would take but a minute or two to see if she could get in far enough to read the number.

While venturing into worlds unfriendly to human beings, Anna tended to err on the side of caution, but they were not even within shouting distance of the danger zone. Mack had done enough dives that this shallow junket in warm waters could hold no horrors for him. Anna guessed he wasn't playing it safe, he simply had an agenda of his own, probably one that involved beer.

She shook her head, pointed to the crevice, then turned her back on him. Without the vest she was less buoyant and took a weight from her belt so she could move easily in the water, having neither to fight to stay submerged nor struggle to move toward the surface.

In an unusual synchronicity with the needs of the human world, Mother Nature had created, with the help of many soon-to-be-abused creatures, a shelf near Anna's crevice. There Anna put vest and tank, arranging them so the least amount of disturbance would be caused when she moved into the hole. That done, she lay on her back in the water, her hands on the edge of the engine where it hung over the edge of the coral. Resting a moment, she made sure everything was in order, light clipped in the neck of her dive skin, underwater pad and pencil stuffed under the zipper between her breasts, breathing hose smooth, no kinks. Satisfied, she began pulling herself gently into the crack beneath the Scarab's motor.

The fit was not tight, but she had to leave her left arm at her side, the hand sticking out of the hole near her left thigh, and use her right hand to pinch and pull herself along. Her face was about six inches below the engine, leaving plenty of room for regulator and goggles. The air hose trailed across her chest and down her left side, where it was held reassuringly in the fingers of her left hand before it snaked away to the tank on the shelf.

Five seconds, maybe less, and her head bumped gently on the end of the tunnel. Her right elbow was trapped against her ribs, but she had enough space to maneuver hand and wrist easily enough. With a minimum of fumbling, she unclipped the flashlight and turned it on.

Serial numbers. Bright and clear and nearly new. A feeling of great personal resourcefulness and the joy in a prize won pushed claustrophobia—still an infant at barely ten seconds old—back into the womb. Having clipped the light to the strap on her mask, she wedged her notebook against the engine with the heel of her hand and, using the underwater pen cleverly tethered to the pad, began copying down the numerals.

Grinding so loud she thought the plates of her skull were coming apart and the number shifted to the right, the heel of her hand carried with it, then weight, crushing weight. Air pushed from her lungs. The flashlight was shoved to the right. The butt of it banged against her teeth, then metal and light were gone.

That was it. The whole thing. Over in a heartbeat.

It had happened so quickly it took her a moment to believe she was trapped under an internal combustion engine on the bottom of the ocean. The next thing she noticed was that she was still breathing. Her lungs had to work a little harder. The hose must have been constricted but not pinched closed. Either that or she was hyperventilating. The grinding noise had triggered a shot of adrenaline into her system so substantial her insides felt jellied.

Over the years, tales had filtered in about people imbued with superhuman strength in time of crises; usually a mother, a child and an overturned tractor were featured. Unfortunately this was not the case with her. Her right arm, pressed tight across her chest, couldn't move itself let alone the tonnage of the engine. Fleetingly she wondered if she were to be entombed beneath the sea, laid out in an eternal flag salute. The thought brought on a twinge of hysteria followed by terror so great it took more willpower than she would have believed she had not to fight herself into an early death.

Breathe, breathe, breathe. Slow. A breath. Slow. Anna forced herself into a semblance of calm. It was not utterly dark in her crevice. The flashlight was somewhere beside her head, still emitting its feeble beam. The water was a colloidal suspension of Who bodies and Who buildings and Who villages under a black corrugated sky.

The fantasy, delightful earlier, scared her now. For reasons she hadn't the time or the inclination to pursue, going insane, even in an insane situation, was scary as hell.

A breath. A count. A breath.

Panic momentarily at bay, it occurred to her that not only was she not dead, as she had every right to be, and breathing, which she had no right to be, but, near as she could tell, miraculously unhurt. The engine had slipped down only far enough to press her tightly but not to squash anything.

To Mack it must look as if she'd been killed.

Another wave of panic swept over her. Living people were rescued as quickly as possible. Americans, especially Americans in the National Park Service, would move mountains, would not rest, would not stop and would spare no expense as long as there was even a slim hope life still burned.

They took their own sweet time about body recoveries.

Frantically, she began kicking her feet, waggling the fingers of her left hand. The image of half her body swallowed by a black and craggy mouth, neon-green flippered feet and white fingers flipping out of the metal and coral lips, struck her as unbelievably funny. Before she could control herself laughter borne on absurdity and hysteria bubbled out of her mouth. The regulator's mouthpiece was loosed from her lips and teeth and floated upward following the bubbles.

The regulator stopped against the engine an inch or so above her mouth, air gently leaking out. Oxygen hunger welled in her lungs and with it desperate panic.

Pushing with all her strength, she managed to move her right hand up from her heart to her collarbone. With the tips of her fingers she could tickle her chin. There it wedged so tightly she could feel the blood being cut off and numbness creeping into her fingers.

Metal pressed across the top of her mask, immobilizing her head and neck. Forcing her tongue out till the root ached, she managed to lick the bottom of the mouthpiece, but no more.

Her lungs wanted to break open, force her to breathe in the water. *Not yet,* Anna thought. Seconds only had elapsed. Though she'd lost air on the ill-fated laughter, she could last another minute, maybe more.

There was one more thing she could try but, should it fail, she'd die. *Like you're not dying now, for Chrissake?* a rude voice in her head mocked. *Chrissake. Christ's sake. Whoever or whatever really is God, if you exist, I'm sorry I never got in touch.*

Having covered the eternal bases, Anna blew every bit of air from her lungs, collapsing them down till the final bubbles were squeezed out.

14

Dear Peg,

At last I have some good news to relate. First and foremost: rain! We have so desperately needed it and have been teased by seemingly endless storms that brought nothing but high seas and drying winds.

For four days it rained. The lighthouse keeper (who keeps records of all things meteorological for the army) said we got seven and three quarters inches. The cisterns are filled and we've bathed, washed our hair and laundered our clothing. Till coming to live on Garden Key I had not known what a blessing it is to be clean. Out here one begins to think constant itching and irritation in areas both public and private are simply how God ordered the world.

The only ones not put in a happier disposition by this recent deluge are Dr. Mudd, our benefactor, Joel Lane and the unsettling Mr. Arnold. Rain was driven in their high narrow windows and, though one would not believe it possible seeing the thickness of the ramparts, seeped in through walls and ceiling. The brick and mortar became so saturated, for a day and a half after the skies cleared it continued to "rain" in their casemate. The cells became ankle-deep in water. We had to raise Joel's bedding on a pallet of loose brick to keep it dry.

Joel has regained partial use of his right thumb. He was

cheerful enough to make jokes about surviving the war only to drown in bed. When last I was at the cells, both Mr. Arnold and Dr. Mudd were busying themselves by chiseling drainage ditches in the cement of the flooring so they'll not again be flooded.

Unlike other prisons, it is not unusual for the men incarcerated here to be given tools. Indeed many have complete freedom of the island. Without a boat, escape is impossible.

The discomfort of the conspirators aside, the rain brought the feel of a new beginning and, so, hopes to the garrison. Thirty-seven of the confederate soldiers were released and given passage to Key West. Seeing the exodus begin put the others in high spirits. A lessening of the hostility and the burden of overseeing so many men passed these good feelings on to the guards.

Colonel Battersea—remember me telling you of him? He's the confederate officer who befriended Joseph at West Point and became a prisoner here. His wife was ailing and he wished an early release. Though he tried, Joseph was unable to get it for him. Well, not a week ago he managed to escape. How, I don't know. It is suspected he stowed away on one of the ships that docked during the confusion when the conspirators were brought. Joseph did all the things duty required, but I could tell he was glad the colonel was never found.

Into this holiday mood came the *Quinterra* under Captain Johns. Captain Johns and his crew come to the island twice each year, and he and Joseph have formed a fast friendship. As captains, they have few outlets for conversation among equals. To make him welcome, Joseph suggested a dance with the garrison band making the music. Captain Johns kindly offered the use of the *Quinterra* for the festivities.

Oh, Peggy, you cannot imagine how we looked forward to getting off this teeming pile of brick and sand! I didn't know how much I longed to escape until the opportunity was presented. You would have thought I'd been chained in the dungeon itself, away from light and air for a hundred years. Tilly, at sixteen, couldn't have been any more excited than I. We would go out to sea only a mile or more—not even out of the sight of the battlements—but the women of the fort—including old Mrs. Farrow, the lighthouse keeper's mother-in-law—decided we were going to make the evening as fine as we could. Our officers needed a return to civility as much as we did, and while we pestered the laundresses with our skirts and fancy sleeves, they tried to bribe them away with money, rum or promises of love to get them to attend to their dress uniforms.

Molly, ever proper, saw to it Tilly was sent to Fort Jefferson with one good gown. It had lain in Tilly's trunk, folded in the tissue she'd used to pack it, there being no need for anything finer than ordinary day dresses. My gown was sadly out of fashion but, if noticed, it will be forgiven. Most of the women here are in the same situation as I, and a couple have been here longer.

My blue taffeta is cut well and drapes beautifully off the shoulder, and even at my advanced age I can customarily turn a head or two of the older—or more myopic—men, but once we'd completed our lengthy toilette I knew I could have gone in a pair of Joseph's old work trousers for all the attention I might expect.

Tilly was stunning. The dress, a rich bronze that carried light with it, exposed her shoulders and as much of her bosom as was decent. The browning of her skin, unavoidable in this climate, rather than making her look coarse as it would any mortal woman, coupled with the coppery tint of the dress, turned her to gold. Even I, who had witnessed the curling rags, the pins and the petticoats in need of repair, had my breath snatched away when she turned from admiring herself and curtseyed to me.

Knowing myself to have been effectively rendered invisible, I took those gold and lapis combs you gave me on my eighteenth birthday out of my hair and put them in hers and handed over my good fan. She was so lovely, even knowing it was Tilly with all her pouts and pets and passions underneath, one was moved to make offerings.

"Let's go show Joel and Dr. Mudd," Tilly said.

That, of course, was an exceedingly bad idea, but she'd asked it while I was still in thrall to her startlingly new and totally womanly elegance, and I simply followed her like lady-in-waiting to the queen.

My wits returned as I trailed her up the spiral stairs leading from the ground floor to the second, then the third tiers. The rustle of the taffeta as her skirts swept over the steps put me back twenty years—twenty-two—to my first grand ball. I doubt you'll remember, but I have forgotten nothing. My gown was of scarlet silk, and I met Joseph. Stumbled over him nearly. He was shooting dice with two other bored lieutenants in a dark corner of the upstairs veranda.

"Tilly," I called up to her. "Stop at the top of the stairs. I need to speak with you before we go any farther." The light rhythmic shush of her soft-soled slippers on the stairs increased. For a moment I thought she meant to run away from me—not in wickedness or disobedience but just in the playful way of girls giddy with the sudden knowledge that they are grown, gowned and gloriously pretty.

To my relief she did as she was bid. The climb was not long, but both of us were corseted as tightly as whalebone and Lu-anne's strong hands could make us, and we were in need of a moment to catch our breath.

I had recovered sufficiently to explain to Tilly why we must go back, meet the others at the dock, when I heard footsteps approaching. Though the usual ring of heels reinforced with iron was replaced with the gentle tap of leather-soled dancing pumps, the military stride gave his identity away.

"Joseph." I turned and, Tilly behind me, watched him come. The sun was near the horizon, the light burnished and saturated with color as though it passed through honey. Each of the brick arches separating the casemates threw its own shadow. Joseph passed from shadow to light, back straight, hair as shining and black as the day we married, the brass of his sword scabbard, buckle and buttons polished and gleaming; he looked very much a hero from one of the old books. Had he been on horseback, I believe I might have swooned.

As is his wont, he brought me back from my dreaming posthaste.

"And just what in hell do you think you are doing up here dressed like that? Where do you think you are, woman? I'll not have you—"

I believe he was sufficiently wound up with the excitement of the dance and his responsibilities for seeing that all came off in a way that would bring honor to both Captain Johns and Fort Jefferson that he might have gone on berating me for some

time. Knowing full well I was every bit the idiot he took me for,
I would have stood and taken it, too. Fortunately Tilly saved us
from having to play out the entire scene.

"Uncle Joseph, it was my fault," she insisted and stepped out
from behind me into the light of the setting sun.

Joseph abruptly fell silent. It wasn't her assumption of responsibility. Joseph knows better than I that ultimate responsibility falls at the feet of the man—or in this case, woman—left
in charge. Seeing Tilly in her evening splendor and drenched in
the fairy light that had my heart spinning when I saw him approach had struck him dumb.

You would have laughed to see his face. Years fell away. His
lips, often a bit cruel these last years, softened to the sensuous
line that so captivated me as a girl, and his eyes widened like a
child's. The transformation was so quick as to be comical. It
made me want to cry rather than laugh, though I cannot tell
you why.

"My lady?" he said and held out his arm. Tilly took it and he
escorted her back to the stairs.

My lapse in judgment had brought us to no harm, and Tilly's
new gown saved me from having to withstand a tongue-lashing,
however deserved. I told myself to be grateful; count my bless-
ings.

Despite the inauspicious start, the evening was everything
our joint wishes and those of the officers and crew of the *Quinterra* could have wished. We dined in the crew's mess (the captain's being too small to seat us all). The ship had been cleaned
and buffed till the fine old wood of the hall looked rich rather
than tired, and the tables had white linens. The food was good
enough, and by fort standards, excellent. Captain Johns provided the wine. It was from New York State but surprisingly
good.

We danced on deck. The crew had hung lanterns from the
rigging. The night was clear and full of stars, and the band in
excellent form, making our makeshift ballroom more romantic
than any well-appointed hall lit with candles. As she deserved
to be, Tilly was the belle of the ball. I watched her carefully but
I needn't have. She was having far too good a time being admired and fawned upon by thirty adoring swains to sneak off

with any one of them. And, too, Joseph never took his eyes off
of her and cut in a time or two when a partner held her too
closely.

The men outnumbering the women five to one, none of the
rest of us had reason to begrudge Tilly her conquests. We were
all danced off of our feet, and, near three in the morning when
time came to go back to the fort, all but the youngest and
strongest among us were ready to do so.

Night had grown so still it was decided that rather than raise
sail and bring the ship back into harbor, the party from the fort
was to be rowed back in the *Quinterra*'s dinghies. There were
but twenty-two of us in all, and we fit snugly in three boats
along with crew to row us home.

But for Tilly's misguided enthusiasms the trip would have
been a lovely and peaceful end to a wonderful evening. I was
sandwiched between Mrs. Dicks, the lighthouse keeper's wife,
and her mother, Mrs. Farrow. Mrs. Farrow is a trial at the best of
times. This night she'd stayed out late and drunk too much of
the captain's good wine. One might have hoped this combination would have sedated her and the most we'd be called upon
to do would be to keep the old harridan from falling asleep and
tumbling into the sea. Unfortunately being tipsy and overtired
only served to agitate her nerves. She fidgeted so the boat
rocked, and actually pinched me twice to make me move over
as though her derrière hadn't already claimed a good half of the
seat we three shared.

Tilly and Joseph sat on the bench in front of us. The moon
was very low—near to setting—but there was still much light
from stars and sea. The moon had the effect of turning Tilly
from the shimmering golden girl of sunset into a lovely silver
statue. Well, not a statue. Miss Tilly was as vivacious and lively
as she had been when the evening began.

At first her chatter was of the ball and the sailors with whom
she danced, the clever things said and witty rejoinders made. As
she was the youngest in our lifeboat by a good twenty years, all
but Mrs. Farrow seemed to enjoy the girlish babble. Tilly was
already well on her way to being a pet of the officers and their
wives. Even Joseph, usually stony faced, was looking at her
now and again. In profile I read an indulgent smile on his lips,

and he kept his arm protectively about her waist lest her excessive reenacting of the waltzes hurl her over the gunwale.

I thought it a pretty picture of avuncular devotion, but Mrs. Farrow, not satisfied with merely savaging my upper arm with her bony pinches, leaned close and whispered: "I'd watch out if I were you. In some societies it's considered the man's duty to marry the sister if his wife dies."

I was so furious, wondering if anyone would really mind if I pushed the old witch overboard, that I didn't notice the turn Tilly's prattle had taken till it was too late to stop it with a few well-placed pinches of my own.

It was the cold that brought me around. Joseph's voice had gone from honey to ice, and it penetrated the fog of my self-absorption. "The man conspired to murder our president," he said softly. Tilly, unaccustomed to reading my husband, must have heard only quiet reasonableness in the words and not felt the crippling chill underlying them. Either that or her youth and innocence led her to believe there is such a thing as a friendly argument when discussing politics.

Whatever the delusion, the little fool went on: "But he *didn't*," she insisted. "Dr. Mudd had nothing to do with Mr. Lincoln's death. Oh Joseph, if only you'd talk to him." Tilly turned sideways the better to clutch Joseph's arm and make her plea. He turned as well, and I could see the warm and doting look was gone; the glitter was that of rain turned suddenly to ice.

Tilly did not notice.

"Dr. Mudd was only following his Hippocratic oath to help people, like he's helping Joel. He is really the most wonderful man. If only you would—"

Joseph started working his jaw the way he does just before he chews someone up into tiny pieces. "Oh, Tilly, look! A flying fish!" I said. I know it was silly. I don't even know if they fly at night, but it was what came into my mind. She didn't even hear me.

"—get to know him. I know you would come to love him as I do."

At this I resorted to Mrs. Farrow's tactics and gave Tilly's shoulder a good hard pinch.

"Ouch. What *is* it, Raffie?"

"A flying fish," I repeated, my poor wine-sodden brain able to come up with nothing new. It succeeded in distracting her. She's been wanting to see one of these wondrous creatures since she arrived. We spent a few minutes gazing out at the calm surface of the sea where I had pretended to see the phenomenon.

Joseph's jaw stopped clenching, but I knew the disaster had not been averted but merely postponed. I had seen the flash in his eye when Tilly said she loved Samuel Mudd and knew my husband well enough to know this was not over.

15

Anna had seen cavers use the exhalation trick in tight places. They'd expel all the air to shrink their lung cavity in hopes of squeaking through. She'd believed them insane. Now she hoped there was at least a grain of method in their madness.

The last of her air dribbled out. Her lungs, mind, every cell in her body was screaming. With all the power she possessed, she shoved her right arm toward her face. Three inches were gained. It was enough. Fingers scrabbled on the smooth rubber, grabbed and the regulator was shoved back into her mouth. Air rushed in, and for that moment life was good. Closing her eyes, she sucked on the regulator like a kitten at its mother's teat, at peace to feel the stuff of life flowing in.

Joy was intense but short-lived. An odd memory of her husband playing Rosenkrantz—or was it Guildenstern?—in *Rosencrantz and Guildenstern Are Dead.* "Life in a box is better than no life at all," the character had said. Anna didn't agree.

Again she waggled the fingers of her left hand and her neon-flippered feet to let Mack know she was alive. This time she was not even tempted to laugh.

An ugly thought bloomed in her brain—given her situation, she'd believed it couldn't get uglier. She was wrong. The engine had not been precariously balanced. Had that been the case, wild sea horses could not have dragged her underneath it.

The instant before she'd become entombed in coral and cast iron she'd been shaken by a harsh grating sound, sharp, metal on rock; a pry bar, maybe, levering the engine from its seating, causing it to shift and fall on her. Who but Mack? Surely there were not marauding aquamen with crowbars stalking the ocean floors in hopes of finding idiot women in compromising positions.

She stopped kicking. Perhaps it was unwise to let Mack know she lived. Her lifeline, the air hose, was a fragile thing, easily pinched or cut.

A tapping on her thigh broke her from this miserable reverie, and she kicked. Maybe Mack was a murderer—if he was she was a dead woman—but he was the only game in town.

The tap turned to a pat probably meant to be reassuring. Pretending it worked, Anna lay still, letting the bubbles she breathed out rise through the maze of internal combustion parts to signify her continuing life. In some peculiar way it was a relief to realize she was completely and utterly helpless. There was nothing she could do: no trick, no act, no cleverness of mind. If she was to die, no fault could be laid at her door. It could not be said she had not been quick enough or strong enough or smart enough to save herself.

To her surprise, she relaxed. She enjoyed each breath wondering if it was to be her last, if Mack even now reached for his knife to cut the air hose. Death, so close, was seductive, welcoming. Perhaps Death was the true possessor of the phenomena attributed to vampires: if one looked into its eyes one became entranced, eager for union with darkness.

She was still breathing.

It seemed she lay in this otherworldy peace for an infinity. When she was jerked back to awareness by the clamor of metal stakes pounding on her iron coffin lid, she woke with something very like anger. It faded, quickly to be replaced by a more corrosive and dangerous emotion: hope.

Someone—presumably Mack—was banging about. Working, maybe, with his pry bar to finish the job, lever the engine off whatever small ledge had saved her life, so she would be crushed.

That made no sense. Thumb and finger on the air hose for a few minutes would do the trick, take less energy and leave no clues. Mack was trying to save her.

That made no sense either. Why try kill to her, then try to save her? So he could look the hero?

Don't worry about it, she told herself. *The rescue attempt will probably kill you just as dead.* Lifting a massive weight wasn't easy, even underwater. Should the load shift or slip, she would be pâté for the fishes. The hypnotic pull of death had been broken, and now Anna was afraid. Her body pressed and cramping, the engine cutting where it mashed against the back of her hand, immobility, the small half-lighted space before her eyes, all this crawled into mind and bone till she wanted to fight, to scream and flail. She could do none of these and watched inwardly as panic turned to acid and tried to melt her resolve not to fight.

Clanking near her head grew louder. Sound coming through iron and skull to join with the shriek of soul and cells. Above her face motes in the water moved. The cast-iron ceiling of her world began to shift, lift ever so slightly. Before she could move or breathe, strong hands clamped around her ankles. Grind changed to a shriek. Her claustrophobic world kaleidoscoped. Anna had an instant to wonder if she was dying or going mad. Black sky moved. Her back and sides scraped over the coral canyon forming her shroud. The regulator was ripped from her mouth. Vision swam in bubbles and particles of once-living plants and animals. Caught in this vortex, she didn't fight to keep the scrap of rubber that fed life to her one lungful at a time but let the world change, watching it with a timeless fascination.

Then light. She was out. The engine rolled, teetered, then crashed back down on the place from which she'd been so abruptly delivered. A hand was on her arm, Mack's face close, his thumb jerking upward.

Newborn and free, Anna came back into herself and kicked for the surface to erupt into sun and air. Ripping off mask and snorkel, she let them sink away from her. Though it was foolish, she could no longer bear to have anything covering her face. She kicked off her fins, and they, too, fell away. Then her weight belt, unbuckled, sank like a stone.

Hands were grasping, pushing, pulling her up. Scrabbling, she tumbled over the gunwale and onto the boat's deck. No longer could she bear anything against her skin; she clawed at her zipper and fought to free herself of her dive skin. The nylon suit caught and tangled over the booties and she kicked and cried out. Daniel and Mack moved to strip the suit and booties off. Twice she kicked the men helping her, but she couldn't stop herself.

At last she wore nothing but her swimsuit and still it was too much. Ripping it off, she pushed away the hands that would have steadied her, lashed out at the legs standing between her and the sun. Like a panic-stricken cat, she hissed and clawed till she was alone on one side of boat, Mack and Daniel cowering on the other.

Space around her, she stopped the struggle. She breathed. She began to shake so badly she had to sink to the deck to keep from tumbling overboard. Snot ran from her nose. Naked and gasping and crying and swearing, she sat in a wet heap until the fit passed.

As she quieted, so did the world. Only the lap of waves against the hull gentled the silence. She let her head drop back against the side of the boat.

"Whoo, boy," she said to no one in particular. "Not my idea of a good time."

The men said nothing. Anna focused her eyes on them and smiled at their horror-stricken faces.

Her brain had broken. Never would she admit that. Too scary. Too alien. Panic would come back. "Sorry," she said. "I guess I needed some space."

Another silence was lapped away by the sea. Mack was the first to break it.

"Are you hurt?" He asked like he genuinely cared, like her hurt was his hurt. "I saw your hand wiggling and your feet kicking and I was afraid you were hurting. Are you hurting? Did it hurt you?"

His very real, white-lipped anguish at the thought she'd suffered pain took away any residual suspicion she harbored that he was the cause of her recent incarceration.

"I'm not hurt," she said.

"Good. Good. That's good."

Mack's relief was evident. And exaggerated, unless he had loved her pure and chaste from afar all these weeks. She doubted that, but was grateful for the concern.

"You okay?" Daniel asked warily.

"I guess." Anna leaned her head back but didn't close her eyes. The harsh glare of the sun, the impossible blue of the sky, the infinite miles and years of *space* above and around her were heaven.

"You maybe want to put something on?" Daniel asked.

"Sure." Anna didn't move.

He took off his shirt and tossed it to her. Anna did not slip her arms into the sleeves or button it but used it like a blanket to cover her nakedness. She was not being coy. Any form of confinement, however benign, was too much to contemplate. The freaky sense of doom licked at her brain again. *What the fuck is wrong with me?* she screamed, but only in her mind.

"What happened?" she asked.

"The engine shifted," Mack said.

"Why?"

"I don't know." He looked at her when he said it, voice and face way too earnest, eye contact too firm. He knew. Or he knew something. Could there have been a third party with them, one she'd not seen? Had Mack done something careless or stupid that he did not wish to take responsibility for?

Anna decided to let it pass. There would be time enough later to worry at the details.

"Then what?"

"You were wiggling. I thought you were hurting. I came up and told Daniel."

Mack wasn't one for edifying detail or embroidering a story.

"We didn't know what you were suffering," Daniel took over. "Didn't know if we had time to get equipment for a safer lift. Mack hooked the anchor to the engine and I pulled with the boat."

"When it lifted a little I yanked you out," Mack finished.

Stripped of emotion and "what ifs," it sounded absurdly simple.

"I'm glad you did," Anna said. "Thanks."

Mack just looked away, embarrassed, maybe. "Don't mention it," Daniel said politcly.

Twice now Anna'd been rescued on this same wreck. She hated being the victim, hated being beholden and was fast coming to hate water sports.

"I'll get your stuff," Mack said. "Fins, mask—you dropped them."

Before Anna could protest, he was over the side. It was in her mind that she would never again venture into water deeper than that in a bathtub, but she knew she would, and soon. A horror left untreated had a nasty habit of becoming a phobia.

He was gone for what seemed like a very long time, but Anna didn't mind. Above water, breathing, she worked to settle her mind. Put on clothes. Stop acting crazy—crazy like Lanny. Daniel respected her silence and busied himself organizing equipment till Mack returned with her BC, tank, mask, fins and weight belt. Having dumped the stuff on deck, he sat on the gunwale staring at her.

"You're scarred," he blurted out apropos of nothing. The compassion in his face and voice robbed the declaration of rudeness.

Anna did not need a moment to figure out what he meant. For nearly ten years she'd borne the jagged, shiny, pink line across her chest from above her left nipple to her right armpit, but she'd never grown so accustomed to the disfigurement that she forgot she had it. It was the deciding factor in the purchase of all bathing suits and some tops: was the neckline high enough to cover the scar? It took an effort, but she did not reach up, trace the mark with her fingers, nor did she give in to the need to tug Daniel's uniform shirt up to cover it.

"I'm scarred," she agreed.

"How did you get it?"

Anna searched Mack's face, looking for the avid curiosity, the touch of the vicarious ghoul that usually accompanied the question. What she found was an old pain and what looked to be a genuine concern, perhaps even fondness, for her. Maybe saving someone's life did that. The Chinese said once you saved a life you became responsible for it. Or perhaps the vicious scar on her chest made her a member of the club, a victim brutally marked as Mack had been marked by the whip.

Resentment and revulsion boiled up in Anna, and she looked away for fear he would see it in her eyes. The feelings were base, unworthy, unfair, but she couldn't help feeling angry that she, too, might be considered a victim, a helpless child once tortured. For a fleeting moment she tasted the shame Mack had carried all of his life. It shook her enough she could banish the most uncharitable of her illogical thoughts.

"A fish gaff," she said and was able to refrain from adding that she'd gotten it in a fight, a fight she'd won. "Where'd you get yours?" Tit for tat. I'll show you mine if you'll show me yours.

His face, till now uncharacteristically open, his emotions as easy to read as those of a child, slammed shut. "Prison," he said. Then: "Are we about finished here? I've been off the clock for thirty minutes."

Anna wasn't going to get any more out of him, and she didn't want to try, not really. She'd felt enough of his shame not to want to stir it up again in either one of them. Floggings in prison had gone the way of the passenger pigeon, and the fine cut marks on his back and legs had faded as only scars received before one comes into their growth can. If it took a fantasy for Mack to hold his head up, Anna wasn't going to be the one to dismantle it. Ripping open old wounds was best left to sociopathic relatives and psychiatrists.

"I'm done here," she said. "Salvage can do the rest."

The men politely busied their eyes elsewhere as she wriggled back into her swimsuit lest she frighten the tourists or the fishes.

Back at the dock on Garden Key, equipment stowed in the room behind the ladies' lavatory, Mack offered to take care of Anna's dive skin and snorkel equipment. The concern was again in his face, but it had gone flat, like a smile held too long for the camera.

Anna declined and was surprised at the look of disappointment, disappointment so intense it bordered on annoyance.

"C'mon," he said, and it was dangerously near a whine. "You've got to be about wore out. Let me help you." If being hounded by Mack's good intentions was the price of having her life saved, Anna figured she'd gotten the good end of the deal, but maybe not by much. This new eagerness to be nursemaid was already wearing on her nerves.

Gratitude and kindness urged her to hand over her suit and

gear if he needed to be of service for some unfathomable reason. She rose above them. "Nope. I'll do it. But thanks," she added. After all, she did owe him her life.

It was nearly six by the time she let herself into her quarters. Piedmont met her at the door, complaining of abandonment and starvation. Not for the first time she marveled at how one small cat can so fill a place with life. Despite the loneliness of this posting, the unexpected addition of a cat made it home; a single furry welcome let her know she belonged.

Along with her salt-soaked dive skin and snorkel gear, Anna dropped the stiff upper lip and macho façade. Scooping up Piedmont, she began to cry, not the crazed sobs that had shaken her after her narrow escape but warm tears, the kind that release tensions too long buried. Holding the old yellow tomcat in her arms as one might cradle a baby, Anna buried her face in the soft pale fur of his belly and wept.

Piedmont, to his credit, let her do so for most of a minute. After that he squirmed till she ceased and desisted. A cat has his pride.

Refreshed by the tears, Anna thanked him and apologized for dampening his fur. For half a can of Kitty Gourmet Seafood Delight, Piedmont was willing to overlook the transgression.

Dehydrated and so tired simply remaining upright was an unpleasant chore, Anna grabbed a fizzy water from the refrigerator and gulped it while leaning over the sink. Again the stuff was flat. This time she didn't mind too much. Quantity not quality was what she craved. She could get it down faster unencumbered by carbonation. Salt water seemed not only to leach moisture from the skin but to pull it from deeper tissues. She drank till her belly was full and still felt thirsty.

The water was amazingly rejuvenating. After she'd let it soak in for a few minutes, she felt energy returning. Thus strengthened, she believed she might shower without risk. In her previous depleted and deflated state it was possible she might have drowned like the apocryphal turkey in a rain shower.

As was her habit, she dragged her dive gear into the shower with her and rinsed it there. Mack was easier to thank from a distance, and as she rinsed mask and fins she thanked him heartily. These accoutrements weren't terribly expensive—cer-

tainly not by sporting goods standards—but she'd found stuff
that fit, that worked, that she genuinely liked and so would have
been hard to replace. Momentarily she entertained herself by
starring in an imaginary commercial. "Not only does this mask
not leak under water, it won't leak under an eight-cylinder engine."

She laughed, partly at her image and partly because she was
alive and could create it.

The dive skin was wadded and knotted with a vengeance—
Anna's as she'd fought free of life's unnecessary restrictions.
The booties were halfway up the legs, which had been turned
outside in. Both arms were partly inside out, the zipper half
down and the torso stuffed into the seat of the suit.

For a short and silly while, in the confines of the tiny shower
stall, wet and naked, she danced an odd *pas de deux* with a neon
shadow of herself. At length she got it back into its proper
shape and began rinsing the salt water out. The right sleeve had
a lump in it. Wondering what on earth she could have shoved
there during her frenzied striptease, she reached into the
springy sleeve. Her underwater notebook and pen were lodged
partway up. Like most underwater tools, they were worn attached to the body. Anna kept hers tethered to her wrist with a
rubber loop.

"Hurray," she muttered as she pulled it free. Her ordeal by
water and iron hadn't been for naught; she had the engine's serial number. She pulled the notebook free and looked at the pad.
A fairly neat line of figures was written there. Light had grown
dim, but there was still plenty to read by. She stared at the numbers. At least she remembered writing numbers. The scratch-
ings on the pad made no sense. It was as if they were ancient
hieroglyphs or musings of a Japanese calligraphist. As she
stared, she could feel confusion rising in her mind, a cold
graveyard fog that robbed meaning from her thoughts. The acid
bite of fear followed it, and the confines of the shower began to
shrink, the beat of the water on her skull to reverberate, deafen-
ing her.

With a cry she flung the sodden dive skin and note pad
through the curtain, fumbled the water off and half fell, half
stumbled out into the small bath, crowded with toilet, sink and
shower stall. Drying off was out of the question. Dripping, she

fled the closing in of the walls. The bedroom gave no respite. Walls, ceiling, floor pressed close, squeezing the breath from her lungs.

Dragging a long tee shirt over her wet body, she pushed on into the living area, stepped into the lemon-yellow flip-flops that lived by the door and fled.

Briefly she leaned against the picnic table, but a sudden terror she'd be found there, forced to interact with another human being, drove her through the wooden gate bearing the sign, Employees Only, and into the converging brick archways leading to The Chapel. No window created by brick tumbling from the edges of a gun port perforated the end of this bastion, but there was a large break in the southwestern wall. An alcove in the thick rampart formed a bench seat before a picture-window-sized break in the brick with a view of Loggerhead Key and miles of ocean and sky. On hands and knees Anna scrambled onto it, hung her head over the opening, moat below, sky above, and breathed in the open spaces.

Post-traumatic stress syndrome, she heard Molly say in her head and was comforted. From one class or another she remembered that flashbacks, sudden overwhelming reliving of the seminal event, were one of the symptoms. "Post-traumatic stress," she said aloud to see how it sounded. It sounded good, sane, reasonable. But she didn't feel much better. The nightmare was back, the sense of parallel universes, or this universe turned evil, she'd had the night before—surely it wasn't just the night before? Part of her felt as if it had been years ago—when reality and visions that sprang from dreams became difficult to separate, burglars and ghosts intruding upon her peace without differentiation. It was the same crawling sense of insanity that had left her naked and sobbing in front of the maintenance men.

Creepiness, not quite yet anxiety but headed in that direction, prickled up her back and over the top of her head. To normalize it, she scratched her scalp with all ten fingers, shaking water from her hair.

The scraping of a foot over mortar dust and brick injected an icy needleful of terror into her gut. Had she made the noise? Moved inadvertently? Anna's head was still in her hands and she was afraid to take it out, afraid to look up. She knew an apparition watched her from the shadows where the brick-on-brick vaults folded into total darkness before opening into the casemates along the northern side of the fort.

Surely if she didn't look, didn't see, whatever it was would not exist. Like a tree falling in the forest, if a ghost went unseen did it really exist?

"Nothing is there, for fuck's sake," Anna shouted into the bend of her elbows. "Okay. On three. One. Two. Three." Letting her hands slide down the sides of her face, still holding on lest her head begin to rotate and spit green bile or something equally alarming, she looked into the premature night beneath the knit of ceiling arches.

Nothing but darkness. Nice quiet friendly darkness. No boogeymen, no dead relatives.

"See?" she said. Having conversations with herself didn't make her question her sanity. She'd lived in New York City too many years for that. Many of the finest people in Manhattan talked to themselves.

At some point during this fit of weirdness, she had folded herself up as small as possible, knees under her chin, heels up against her butt, elbows tucked in. With a conscious effort, she unfolded and stood up. Insanity didn't run in her family. She needed to talk to Lanny Wilcox. Now.

Determination vanished as she stood in the growing shadows and realized she hadn't the faintest idea how to get out of this maze of black arches and blind passages. "Of course you do," she said to bolster her courage. "The fort just isn't that complex." Hearing it, Anna could not remember if "complex" was a word or if she'd simply uttered a jumble of sounds. The fear, momentarily at bay, rushed back.

In a science fiction book she'd read once, a man had recited "rented a tent, rented a tent" over and over in his head, creating white noise to keep the Thought Police from getting through to his deeper knowledge. Hoping it would serve as well to keep insane thoughts from clouding her mind with terror and confusion, Anna mentally chanted the words and began to walk.

The direction was irrelevant. Fort Jefferson was roughly circular. No matter which way she went, she would eventually reach an open casemate, a spiral stairway, and she would be back in the real world. Choosing not to think about what she might meet on her way, Anna walked straight-backed and resolute into the inky darkness of the northwestern bastion.

When she reached the darkest center, the place where many arches knit together overhead, a place she knew from memory, the ceiling lost now in darkness, Anna left off trailing her fingers along the brick for guidance.

Back to the wall, she sat down and waited for them to come.

16

My Dearest Peg—

At long last I received your letter. The mail, slow always, reaches Fort Jefferson only when weather and the capriciousness of the Union Army permits. Had not Mrs. Teller taken it upon herself to (yet again) interfere in family affairs, I expect Molly would have kept her illness from all of us. This once I am grateful to the old biddy. I only wish I could come home. It is clear now why Tilly was sent to me; not "hoydenish ways" but Molly looking ahead as she always has. I'm glad she is being cared for by the Sisters of Mercy. The convent is where she is most at peace.

Peace is something I think of a great deal of late because there is so little of it to be had here. The constant clamor of construction, drill, the testing of the munitions, the coarse clatter and shout of a thousand men squeezed into a tiny space, the endless high-pitched fussing of the sooty terns on Bush Key next door: I have grown so accustomed to it it is as the roar of the sea on the Massachusetts shore, underlying my days and informing my dreams.

Tilly's clamorous passion rises above this cacophony. Despite much effort and the occasional cross word, I cannot ignore it and she cannot forbear speaking of it. Dr. Samuel Mudd and his "innocence" have become an obsession with her. An unhealthy hobby in this political climate. I finally convinced her to refrain from bringing up the subject in Joseph's hearing, but now and again she cannot resist slipping in a plea for her cause. Then I must live with my husband's icy looks and stony silence for half a day.

Joel is much better. He walks now and will recover complete use of his right hand, Dr. Mudd tells us, and possibly his left, though the thumb was more severely damaged. His nose was twice broken—or more—and, having been left so long untreated, heals crookedly. This and a scar beneath his right eye will commemorate this beating for the remainder of his life. With his spirits returning, he is still an attractive man, though no longer as handsome as he was.

Tilly's affection for him has settled from that of a lovesick girl to that of a friend, sister and nurse. Whether this is a maturing of genuine love or a cooling of ardor I cannot tell. I would rather she returned to making calf-eyes at her soldier. It was less alarming than her new quest.

Her fixation on Dr. Samuel Mudd does not appear to be romantic in nature, and the doctor seems devoted to and speaks warmly of his wife back home. Hero worship might be nearer the mark. The doctor has a forceful personality and an inner strength that is compelling. He spends much of our time together speaking quietly and convincingly of his innocence. Tilly, wide-eyed and innocent, drinks in his words as if they were the stuff of life and has become enamored with the idea of winning his freedom.

Over these last days most of her sentences begin with: "Dr. Mudd said..." or "Dr. Mudd told me..." or "Dr. Mudd didn't..." I have had to deliver more than one hard kick under the table to distract her as any mention of Samuel Mudd from her sends Joseph into an arctic mood.

If these northern tempests were confined to our quarters I think I might be able to calm the waters, but Tilly has not been circumspect even when out of doors. So full is she with her youthful love affair with truth and justice and the belief that a pure heart will win over evil (oh how I rue the days we spent reading this child fairy tales!) that she has carried her quest on her sleeve, prattling earnestly to all and sundry.

Before the advent of the much-vaunted Dr. Mudd—whom I

am coming to detest simply because Tilly so clearly does not—
Tilly was very much the pet of everyone here. Now I see people
turn away when she approaches. I suppose I could live with social ostracism, but I'm worried that the repercussions of Tilly's
wild talk could cost more dearly.

Oh yes, talk. I forgot to tell you. We finally found out the
horrific and treasonous outburst of Private Lane's that got him
in trouble. You would laugh had not the words gotten the boy
beaten very nearly to death. What Joel said was: "I wish Lincoln had been shot in the street. I've always wanted to play at
Ford's. Now I suppose it will be shut down." Callous perhaps,
but he is a boy and an actor. For this Sergeant Sinapp almost
killed him.

There is something going on with the sergeant, and it worries me. His natural hatefulness—and it must be natural, it goes
too deep to be learned; it would surprise me not in the least
were I to find his mother was a black widow spider who de-
voured Sinapp Senior moments after Sinapp Junior was conceived—*anyway* his natural hatefulness has changed into
something more menacing. Before he was much like a vicious
dog on a strong chain. He would leap and snarl but the chain
(firmly held by Joseph, his commanding officer) kept him from
harming most people.

Now it is as if that chain is gone. He stalks and snaps as if
devilishly gladdened by the knowledge that when he chooses to
strike, nothing will stop him.

The day before yesterday Tilly and I were taking food and
fresh water to Joel. To regain his health Joel needs to have all
we can provide in the way of fresh vegetables, meat and fruit.
Joseph would have our heads if he knew we pilfered from his
larder to fatten a Johnny Reb.

The sergeant was standing guard over a group of prisoners—mostly union deserters from Pennsylvania and New
York—who were working on the new shot oven as Tilly and I
crossed the parade ground with our little basket of purloined
tomatoes.

Sinapp saw us and left his post, swaggering in our direction.
I know it was just a fancy, but I swear I could *smell* his smile,
feel it like whiskery horse lips on the back of my neck. Tilly
and I walked faster, and I'm sure it gave him pleasure to think

we were afraid of him. Had he known it had more to do with revulsion than fear, he would not have smirked so.

He caught up with us just as a soldier was unlocking the
door to Joel's cell for us. He followed us inside and told the soldier assigned to chaperone our visit to leave. Sinapp closed the
wooden door, then stood with his back to it, letting us know that
we were trapped, as imprisoned and helpless as the three confederates who shared the cells.

After the brilliant fog of dust and sunlight, the casemate was
so dim it took a minute before I could see properly. When I
could, I longed for the sun-blindness I'd enjoyed moments before. In all his thickness, Sinapp leaned against our only avenue
of escape. "I thought I'd come by and have a piece of that nursing you ladies been giving Jeff Davis's boys." The way he said
"nursing" would have made any woman cringe. Lest we miss
his filthy point, he began stroking himself. Truly, Peggy, the
man stood before us, his sticky eyes on Tilly, and petted the
front of his trousers as though a small dog lay there. Which,
perhaps, is exactly the case. In all the years I have spent living
in a world populated by men—and many of the roughest sort
imaginable—I have never seen such a display. Had I been told
of it, I would not have believed. Oddly I was not alarmed immediately, just paralyzed by that horrible embarrassment one
gets when one has the preacher over to afternoon tea and the
dog mistakes the vicar's leg for a bitch in heat.

"Good God, man, have a care!" Mr. Arnold said. He had
come to the doorway connecting the cells while I stood trans-
fixed.

Sinapp heard Mr. Arnold, I could tell by the change in his
face—a slight shifting of the sides of beef that pass for cheeks.
If someone spoke to me as Mr. Arnold spoke to the sergeant
(and for such reprehensible behavior) I should have sunk into
the brick for shame. Sinapp did not. Apparently the man has no
higher instincts with which to compare his baseness. Indeed
this very baseness seems to be a matter of pride with him,
coarseness being a skill he has honed to a fine point. Using it to
skewer others gives him a tremendous sense of accomplish-
ment.

He laughed, a warm rumbling sound that in another man I
might find pleasing, and, to the immense relief of those of us

trapped in this theater of his making, ceased rubbing his trouser front. It is not my custom to stare at men below the waist, but because Sinapp had so purposefully called our attention to this part of his anatomy, I couldn't but notice his lewd thoughts and clumsy manipulations had caused a like erection beneath his trousers.

Retelling this story in the safety of my own bedroom, knowing Tilly is snug and sleeping and Joseph working at the desk in the hall adjacent, I cannot but see it for the absurd incident it was, with Sergeant Sinapp as the leading character, a clown; a dark clown but a clown with buffoonery and exaggerated features all the same. In Joel Lane's cell I was not amused, nor were my "companions." I was frightened, as I believe were Dr. Mudd and even the cynical and unflappable Mr. Arnold. Joel was terrified, his body and mind knowing the depth of Sergeant Sinapp's power and cruelty. Tilly alone was unafraid. Angered by his manner, even if not completely aware of his meaning, she set her basket down with a thump. "We have every right to be here," she declared before I could stop her.

Joel stepped between Tilly and Sinapp. A small thing this one step, but it spoke of such courage even in that airless room with the reek of Sinapp clogging my thoughts, I felt my heart swell.

This one good and decent moment was not allowed to stand.

The sergeant leapt forward. After his posing and posturing, the speed of his movement startled. It was as if he'd become more than human, vanishing from his place by the door and reappearing, his face but inches from Joel's. Fist closed, he backhanded Joel, a blow from his knuckles and wrist striking the boy from ear to chin. Joel fell as one dead.

Tilly screamed and hovered, undecided whether she should drop down beside her patient or fly at his attacker. None of us had time to so much as breathe before Sinapp decided for her. Arms struck snakelike, fingers biting into her upper arms. I do not know what he meant to do. Kiss her perhaps, though that seems a gentle thing compared to the violence in his face and body. Even he could not have intended to ravage her there and then on the floor of the casemate with the three of us in witness.

"That's quite enough," I said and moved to Tilly's side. He didn't loose her, so I slapped him hard enough it stung my

palm. Violence begets violence. He let go of Tilly with one
hand and drew back to strike me. Tilly and I had backed up till
our shoulders were nearly touching the brick of the archway
separating Joel from Dr. Mudd and Sam Arnold. I could not
run, nor could I duck.

The blow, which I believe would have felled me as surely as
it had Private Lane—who had neither stirred nor made a sound
since he went down—didn't come. Mr. Arnold caught the sergeant by the wrist.

In that moment it came to me that the rules of honor were
written by men. I took this opportunity to punch Sinapp in the
eye with all the force I could muster. I hit him so hard I cried
out as loudly as he when the bones of my hand met those of his
face. In shock or blind fury he let loose of Tilly's other arm.

"Go now," came a soft voice so close to my ear I felt the hair
stirred by his breath. Mr. Arnold's dark eyes were fixed on
mine, and I think he was smiling. It happened so quickly I cannot be sure of anything.

His advice was sound. I grabbed Tilly and ran for the door.

"Bitch." Sinapp hurled that at my back. After his bestial behavior, being called names by such as he was harder for me to
take than his physical threat had been.

"My husband shall hear of this," I told Sinapp.

He shook off Mr. Arnold's grip. He said nothing but he
smiled at me. I turned and ran after Tilly, not knowing if he followed or not, not knowing if Joel Lane had died or still lived.
The only thing I did know was that Tilly's hero, Dr. Samuel
Mudd, had made no move to help his patient or to protect Tilly
or me. He'd stood back in the corner where the arch met the
outer wall and watched in such a way I wondered if he were a
coward or if things were unfolding as he had hoped and he was
calculating the advantage this show of choler, lust and ill discipline might afford him.

Once Tilly and I regained the sane light of the parade ground
with its homely smells and familiar sounds of men at work,
what ragtag remnants of the fear I'd felt in the casemate turned
to anger, then settled into disgust and, I must admit, a desire to
see Sinapp hanging from one of the trees he was so fond of decorating with the persons and misery of other men.

That evening, when Joseph returned to quarters, I told him

of what his sergeant had said and done, then settled back to watch the build of the cold fury he displays when his authority is knowingly thwarted by a subordinate.

I do believe it began to blossom, but within moments a new emotion withered it. Often enough I've boasted of how well I know my husband, how easily I can read his moods. This time I could not. Or read too much. A flood of feeling poured into his face: anger, remembrance, shock, fear, sorrow and—I can scarcely credit this and would say it only to you—that implosion of thought and soul behind the eyes that speaks of cowardice. Mind you, I could be wrong. I must be wrong. These things I speak of seeing with such confidence were all a jumble and over in the space of two heartbeats. Joseph's face went blank then, the way it looks when he's been several days without sleep. The way it looked when he knew he would sit out the war on this island.

"Don't put yourself in the sergeant's way again," he said as if Tilly and I had caused Sinapp to act as he had.

I started to remonstrate—never wise, I know, but a habit I cannot break—but Joseph stood so abruptly the small table beside his chair rocked on its feet. "Do as I say," he snapped. "Or I will not be responsible for what happens to you." He left me, left our quarters. I heard the door onto the veranda slam shut.

Knowing Joseph, for reasons I do not understand, has withdrawn his protection from Tilly and me, that we are very much alone on this too-crowded island, makes me truly and deeply afraid.

17

The silence that is unique to the sea out where the tides are nonexistent settled around Anna with the darkness. Beneath, and at her back, the warmth that never left the brick throughout the long summer soothed her aching muscles. She waited and she breathed and she relaxed. Once before she had been in a like situation, and it had ended badly with a screaming fear that stayed in her mind for years afterward. She wouldn't think of that. She was older now. Her horrors were known. She would not invite them in.

The first change was in the light. A last ray of dying sun skipped across the Gulf of Mexico like a molten stone, piercing the tangle of arches to paint a single golden stripe no more than an inch wide across the brick of the far wall. As she watched it grew brighter, pulsed with the rhythm of the sea, the rhythm of her heart. Light broke away from the stripe in tiny showers, each spark leaving a contrail as if it were a minute jet airplane flaming out.

At length the light show shimmered into the darkness and was gone. To see if it worked, if she had any control over what was to happen next, Anna called softly: "Aunt Raffia?" and waited. Where the last spark had died, a pale shape began to pool on the floor. Luminosity poured into it from an invisible

pitcher, the form of a woman being filled with light from the
boots up the skirt to shirtwaist, arms, and finally the head, face
averted, the hand raised as before, fingers poking nervously at
escaping hairpins.

"Be a nice aunt," Anna whispered to the apparition. "No
turning scaley with long lickety tongues or anything." The figure dissolved and Anna wondered if she'd taken the fun out of
its spectral life by ruling out reptilian metamorphoses.

Anna was tripping. Days before it would have terrified her.
Her memories of the bad old days during the early seventies
were not of Lucy in the sky with diamonds but of the mind-
crippling terror of losing her reason. Because she feared that
same thing so recently, it was a relief to know that she was not
going mad. She'd been drugged. It would turn out to be in the
plastic bottles of carbonated water she'd been drinking, introduced, no doubt, by a hypodermic needle. That was why the
water was flat, why there was water on the bottom shelf of her
refrigerator and Lanny's. Whoever was doing the poisoning
must have gotten careless, been rushed and pierced the containers below water line. Tomorrow, when she'd regained domi-
nance over what gray cells remained to her, she'd call Wilcox
with the good news. If he'd been a straight arrow during his
formative years he would have no way of recognizing this drug-
induced insanity. Anna might not have caught on if she hadn't
guzzled nearly a quart of the doctored water on an empty stomach.

When the dark began to fill with monsters of the id, Anna
moved on to a casemate open both to the sea and the parade
ground. Briefly she considered climbing the spiral stairs to the
third level where cannons were still in evidence and the view
rolled away, unfettered by a frame of brick. High places were
not a good idea when one might take it into one's head to fly
with the magnificent frigate birds. She remained where she
was.

With air and moonlight and strength of will, she passed the
night seeing strange things. Raffia never reappeared, but as the
monsters stayed tucked away in her subconscious, Anna was
satisfied. By sunrise the world ceased to warp and weave, stars
and planets stayed in their orbits. Anna could wave her fingers
through the air and not see ghosts trailing behind them.

Her body told her sleep was now a possibility. Her mind suggested it was not a good idea. The wall between waking and dreaming, the real and the fantastic, was still weak. Allowing consciousness to slip away might breach it. She returned to her quarters to take another shower, staying to rinse the soap from her hair and body this time. For breakfast she had a coke and half a can of vegetable soup. What she didn't eat she threw away. Till this thing was over she had no intention of consuming anything that could have been tampered with.

Clean, fed and in uniform, she felt shaky but ready to face the day. Her first task was to sort out which bits of the past seventy-two hours were real and which were drug-induced. When she left her quarters, she locked her door behind her.

The first order of business was getting the engine's serial number tracked down. To that end she called the Key West Police Department and the coast guard. But for a short time on Isle Royale in Lake Superior, Anna had little experience dealing with boats. That, and being denied easy communication with the rest of the world, decided her to leave the police work to the police. Lieutenant George Henriquez, her contact on Key West, a man who might have been squat, balding and pockmarked but who was blessed with the telephone voice of an Adonis, told her they'd had no luck as yet identifying the John Doe Ranger Shaw had towed to East Key. They had, however, identified the tattoo on his leg with the help of a local DEA agent who worked, if not closely then amicably, with the local police force. He had seen it before on the leg of a Cuban, an illegal alien arrested for smuggling drugs from Central America across the Gulf of Florida.

"More than that we don't know," Henriquez said. "Could be some kind of gang ID. A lot of these guys—the low rungs on the totem pole—have that adolescent mentality. The higher-ups, the brains, know better than to intentionally brand themselves as criminals."

Anna asked him if he would find out the whereabouts of Theresa Alvarez for her. He grumbled at having his already considerable workload increased but promised to try. Enduring another two minutes of conversation aborted then accelerated, then made simultaneous by the phone delay, Anna gave him

what she had gathered about Lanny Wilcox's erstwhile inamorata.

She did not tell the lieutenant of being drugged, nor would
she tell anyone, not for a while. The only way to be absolutely
assured of keeping a secret was to tell no one. No suspicion attached itself to the Key West police—because of the repeated
and hands-on nature of the poisoning it had to be someone at
the fort or one of the boating regulars who'd learned enough of
the ranger's living situation to take advantage of it. Anna leaned
strongly toward the idea that it was an NPS employee. Who else
could move unseen and unremarked upon in a society as closed
as that at Fort Jefferson? She just didn't want a chance remark
or careful question to reveal to someone that she was onto the
drugging. As long as whoever was behind it believed her to be
partaking of the contaminated waters, it was less likely a new
approach would be devised.

These thoughts trickling through her mind, she knew she
would have to let Lanny Wilcox suffer the fears of the newly
demented a while longer. Should she tell him he had purposely
been made delusional, odds were good he'd begin asking questions, upsetting her precarious applecart.

And he might be returned to duty and she sent home. Much
as she wanted to go, she had no intention of leaving till she
found out who was messing with her mind.

That done, she settled in to find out who had chosen to drive
the Dry Tortugas' Supervisory Rangers mad, and why.

The computer had the most reliable link to the real world,
and Anna logged on.

For starters, she ran everyone working on Garden and Loggerhead Keys for wants and warrants. Mack, the man who'd
said he'd earned his stripes in prison, came up clean, not even
an outstanding parking ticket.

Daniel had been arrested twice, once for assault and once for
drunk and disorderly. He'd served three months in the Dade
County Jail and been given two years' probation. Both arrests
and convictions were seventeen years old; a misspent youth.
Since then, nothing.

Bob, as Anna expected, was clean. Should she take it into
her head to do an illegal search of his quarters as she had done

of Lanny's—though she did have probable cause unless the will-o'-the-wisp lights and nocturnal moat creature were drug-born and not of this world—she had little doubt she would find under a bed or high on a closet shelf a box of merit badges. Probably covering his years from cub to eagle.

By regulation National Park Service law-enforcement officers were given background checks. The execution of this had been haphazard at best until it was revealed in a series of short-lived but unpleasant public-relations nightmares that there were quite a few gun-toting felons stalking the woods in flat-brimmed Stetsons and gold buffalo badges. Since then, the various offices of personnel management in the parks had been more thorough. Most felons in the green and gray would be those hired way back, probably genuinely gone straight or getting too old to bother with violent crime. If by some fluke Anna had uncovered a felony in Bob Shaw's past, unless it had a direct bearing on why she and Lanny were drugged, what the go-fast boat was up to when it blew up, or why Theresa Alvarez took a powder, she might not have said a word.

She'd spent much of her adult life catching criminals. Not once had she been accused of being too soft on them. But, unlike some others in the field of law, she never quite lost her need for fairness. When a debt to society was paid, all rights and privileges should be restored: the right to vote, carry arms, protect and serve.

The surprise was Bob's wife, Teddy Shaw or, as her rap sheet would have it, Theodora Placer alias Teddy Andrews, Teddy Lee and Lily Lee. Wanting the woman's history, Anna had run her under her maiden name as it appeared on her VIP application papers: Theodora Lily Placer. Teddy was thirty-two years old, her last arrest had been when she was twenty-seven, only months before she became Teddy Shaw and left her past on the mainland. Or moved her business to the Keys.

Anna printed out what there was and leaned back, deck shoes on Teddy's desk, to read it. The sudden tilt of the chair startled her. Whatever ball bearing in her head served to reorient the brain had not fully recovered from the hallucinogen. Either that or her body cried out for sleep.

Throwing caution to the winds, she put down the printouts and made a pot of coffee. Surely the water supply for the entire fort hadn't been contaminated. As the coffee began to percolate, it occurred to her how easy it would be to do just that, drop acid, ketamine, PCP, Ecstacy, rat poison, kerosene or a dead cat into the cistern. Easy as pie. Access wasn't difficult; trapdoors big enough to climb through were set in the cistern's top. The traps weren't hidden and they weren't locked.

Anna clicked the coffee machine off before the pot was half full. She sat back down at Teddy's desk and rested her forehead on the pages. For poisoning her, she wanted to catch the jerk. For denying her morning coffee, she wanted to kill him.

Or her. Reminded of Teddy Shaw's checkered past, she sat up and once again began to read. Teddy had been a busy woman. She'd not given up a job as head nurse in the ER; she'd been fired for stealing prescription painkillers. The judge had sentenced her to rehab and five years' probation. The second arrest had been for forging doctors' signatures on hospital prescription pads, stolen from the clinic at the rehab center. For that she'd served three months. Two and a half years later she'd broken probation again. This time she was arrested in Philadelphia for trying to buy Percodan from an undercover narcotics officer. She'd been sent back into the state jails to serve out the remaining six months of the original nine-month sentence. Shortly after being released she'd again broken parole by leaving Pennsylvania for parts unknown. There was a warrant out for her arrest.

After her release she must have left Pennsylvania for Florida, where she met and married Robert Shaw and fled as far in the U.S. of A. as she could without having to tread water. It was a good bet Bob didn't know. The man was such a boy scout he would have wanted to make things right with the law before he endangered his career by becoming an accomplice. Then again they seemed very much in love. Love was a great leveler. Maybe it had enticed Bob to look the other way. Just this once.

Anna set the papers down and stared longingly at the coffeepot. Not the entire water supply. Not yet. Why bother when the perpetrator knew Anna was swilling down doctored fizzy water?

She walked over and punched the "on" button again. Some things were worth the risk. Watching the coffee drip into the pot, comforted by the gurgles and clicks of the machine, Anna thought about Teddy. From her long association with the medical profession by way of her psychiatrist sister, Molly, Anna knew the terrible flaws in the myth of its superiority. Drug addiction was one of them. Rehab centers were one of the best places to have a heart attack. A large percentage of the clients were doctors and nurses. Psychologists were next, then the usual scattering of strippers, rock musicians and regular citizens.

Medical professionals often worked under great pressure. They were called upon to go without sleep or to remain alert more hours than the body or psyche could realistically maintain without help. They had access to drugs, both to buy and to steal. A good many of them also had the arrogance to believe they could handle it, would never become dependent.

The coffee was done. Anna mixed in a chunk of Cremora to take the edge off and carried the mug back to the desk. Her first sip brought that tight sensation to the back of her neck, fear that she was condemning herself to another few hours where pigs could fly and beggars ride. Putting the creeps firmly out of mind, she took another sip to commit herself and returned to her cogitations. If she were doomed to be a drug-crazed lunatic, at least she would be a wide-awake drug-crazed lunatic.

Teddy had the knowledge to drug somebody. Chances were good she still had contacts or a prescription pad she'd squirreled away against future emergencies before she'd been packed off to jail. If the doctor they worked with on the mainland hadn't bothered to check too carefully, he wouldn't know her nursing license was revoked—if it was. There was a possibility the various institutions hadn't communicated with one another and Teddy could still practice legally.

Why would Teddy want to poison her? Make her believe she was going nuts? Teddy had saved her life when she'd been knocked unconscious by the second explosion.

Not poison just me, Anna reminded herself. There was Lanny Wilcox. Was it that simple? Did Teddy think once Lanny was deemed incompetent, her very own hero, Bob Shaw, would be elevated to the position of Supervisory Ranger? When Anna came on scene instead had Teddy seen her as merely another obstacle to be removed from her husband's career path?

Though simple and—given the negligible hike in money and

power such a promotion would bring with it—to Anna's mind petty, as a motive it was not bad. Women ambitious for the man they loved had done worse for less.

The phone rang. Nearly upsetting her coffee, Anna squawked and flapped in the tradition of Chicken Little. By the second ring she'd recovered.

"Dry Tortugas National Park."

"Anna?"

The sound of her name spoken with the honeyed warmth of a Mississippi drawl brought tears to her eyes.

"Paul," she said, not because she was unsure who the caller was but for the sheer pleasure of feeling his name on her tongue. A thousand years had passed since she'd thought of him. Mountains had crumbled to dust, seas dried up, civilizations fallen to ruin, and yet just to hear his voice and say his name took her back to the good safe times on his living room couch before a fire. Life ceased to be made of ghosts, iron and salt and became once again a thing of flesh and blood.

"I've been worried about you, Anna. It's been—"

"Listen to me, Paul. Oh. What? Days since—"

"You haven't answered the phone, no—"

"No—Listen—"

"What?"

"Wait." Anna stopped talking, letting the line clear of the overlaid clogging of words, delays and spaces. During the break she soothed herself by saying goddammotherfucking-phone three times.

"I'll marry you," she said when silence was established. "The sooner the better. Meet me at the airport with a priest."

Another silence, this one organically grown, filled the line after she'd spoken her piece. Two seconds, three. Maybe this, too, was a hallucination. The phone hadn't rung at all. Lost in the wherever of the mind, she'd dreamed the noise, grabbed at the phone, pressed it to her ear.

"Oh, Jesus," she whispered and threw the coffee into the wastebasket, splashing her leg and the first two desk drawers. Carefully, she moved the handset away from her ear.

"Anna?" A tiny voice pushed through the terrible darkness of a thousand miles of telephone wire and abyss of the microwave. Her hand stopped. She did not hang up. Neither did she put the phone back to her ear. Time and reality had been suspended and she was afraid to move, to believe.

"Anna, are you there?"

The voice sounded so lost and alone. Even if Paul had become one more symptom of impending disaster, she could not leave him unanswered. "I'm here," she whispered, realized the receiver was still halfway to the phone, brought it back to her ear and said again, "I'm here."

"I hate this phone. Did you say you'd marry me?"

"I did."

"You sound funny."

"I am funny."

"Anna, this phone makes me crazy. I'm going to be quiet now and listen. You tell me what's going on, okay?"

"Does the offer still stand?" Anna asked.

"What offer?"

"You asked me to marry you."

"It still stands. It will stand forever. Maybe lean a little after eight hundred years like the tower of Pisa, but it will still be standing."

"I want to do it. I want to marry you. Right away. As soon as I get back."

Another silence threatened Anna, but this one was blessedly short-lived.

"I would like that," Paul said carefully. "Right now I need to hear what is happening to you."

Anna told him everything. Words poured out haphazardly, the plots of her various tales interweaving, pronouns dropped, sentences with subjects and no predicates. Chronological order was abused and misused and her emotions colored fact and fiction alike. She was not a law-enforcement officer making a report, she was a tired, shaken woman talking to her lover.

The drugs with which she'd been washing down her peanut butter sandwiches had eaten away a wall she'd not known was still standing. Though only vaguely, she was aware that she had never talked this way to anyone—or not for so many years she'd lost count. Not even to her sister.

Retaining control, a degree of professionalism, appearing to be always master of herself, if not the situation, had been so much a part of her she'd not been aware of it till it was gone.

Never—at least not since the death of her husband Zach and possibly not before—had she allowed herself to be so vulnerable.

This scrap of knowledge flittered through her mind as she babbled. She tucked it away for further investigation. Ecstacy, a designer drug that had hit the world running in the eighties, was said to have an opening effect on the heart and mind. Ecstacy had come long after Anna's days of seeking recreation and/or enlightenment with various toxic substances. She had no personal experience to draw upon.

At length she had, in her uncalculated and fragmented way, told Paul Davidson of the adventures both physical and metaphysical which had befallen her. He left a moment's silence and she resisted the temptation to blurt: "Are you still there?" while the last of her words surmounted whatever delaying obstacle lay between Fort Jefferson and the rest of the world.

"Have you told me everything?" Paul's voice returned after the expected seconds had ticked away.

From anyone else—anyone besides her sister, Molly—Anna would have fielded that question with care; responding to the accusation often cloaked in the words, the suggestion she was hiding something.

In Paul's kind tones, coming from a mind she was learning was subtly complex but never devious, she believed the question was only what it seemed. "Everything I can think of," she told him.

"Do you want me to come out there?"

Did she ever. She'd not thought of it, but when he asked, she knew how desperately she had been needing exactly that. Someone she could trust. Warm arms to hold her at night. A fine mind with which to share her great-great-aunt Raffia's letters. A hard-nosed southern sheriff to keep her from harm. A wise and loving priest to whom she could confess her sins. The thought of Paul Davidson stepping onto the dock in front of Fort Jefferson engendered a sensation behind her rib cage that lent credence to the bard's allusion to hearts taking wing.

"No. No thanks," she said. Supervisory Rangers did not call in their boyfriends to help out when things got sticky. There would be no faster way to feed her career to the sharks and her credibility to the endless gossip mill run by the boys.

"You're sure?"

Anna didn't trust herself to answer. As she'd hoped, he took her silence for an affirmative. "If you change your mind—"

"I won't." A lie. She'd already done so fifty times in the brief pause between the asking and the answering.

The call went on as calls between sweethearts do, with professions of love and mutual "I miss you's," but Anna kept it short lest she weaken and take the White Knight option. Being a damsel in distress had a dark fascination for her; the idea of being without responsibility, merely enduring and hoping and—if the scenario happened to be in a fairy tale—ultimately rescued not only from the situation but from the specter of loneliness. In real life she'd never had the guts to try it. Even had she found the courage to wait, to have faith, she knew she would never have the patience. When things went wrong she couldn't rest till she'd righted them, or tried to. And, too, self-respecting damsels were not allowed to kick, spit, shout or swear at their respective dragons. "Got any guesses as to who might be doctoring my water?" she asked to get the conversation back on safer ground.

"My money is on Ms. Timothy Leary, R.N.," Paul said. "Poisoning is a woman's crime traditionally, and the fact that this was not poisoning with intent to kill or even harm permanently strikes me as additionally female from a statistics point of view. A way she could safely remove you and what's-his-name—"

"Wilcox."

"Wilcox from her husband's way without feeling guilty about it. It fits in with the nursing, too. Unless she's got that Angel of Death thing going on, she probably views herself as a healer, a caretaker. Using a nonlethal drug might tie into that."

"Works for me," Anna said. Hearing his rationale given in deep, strong tones with roots deep in the Mississippi clay made her feel calmer, saner. The thoughts he expressed dovetailed with those she had had in her skittery drug-paranoid fashion. It was infinitely comforting to know her mind not only worked but had done so under duress.

"Do you dive? How about that engine on the coral moving?" Asking the question, it occurred to her that, though she'd known Paul for a year or so, there was a great deal about him she was not yet privy to. They'd met and courted under unusual circumstances, what with dead men and living wives underfoot. Even realizing this, she did not change her mind about matrimony. "Do you know anything about scuba diving?" she amended her question.

"Not as much as you do," he replied. "But I've had a whiff of high school physics and I've lifted more than my share of engines in and out of secondhand pickup trucks. If that motor was seated as solidly as you say it was then it didn't shift because you put your tiny little self underneath and wriggled about a bit."

"I braced the heel of my hand on it when I was copying down the serial number," Anna confessed.

Paul laughed. "Even given the strength of your good right arm, I don't think you could have shifted that thing. Either it was already unseated or somebody moved it."

Anna had known that. Of the various neuroses, the one she most lusted after was the one she could never quite attain: denial. Always, just when she thought she had a handle on it, a pesky fact or puzzling anomaly would punch a hole in the dike and reality would pour in.

Of course she'd checked the seating of the motor on its coral bed. Having no desire to be trapped—or crushed—beneath the engine, she had pushed and shoved and peeked at its edges to confirm it had reached its final resting place. Without that reassurance, she could never have tricked her claustrophobic self into slithering into the crevice beneath it.

Then it had shifted and caught her, nearly killed her.

Ergo someone or something or some event had caused it to move.

It was at this point that logic ceased to work and the practice of denial would have come in handy. Who or what could have moved the engine? The obvious choice was Mack. As the only other creature with opposable thumbs within a hundred-foot radius, he was at the top of the suspect list. With a pry bar and a working knowledge of levers and fulcrums, he could have managed it. Why he would want to was an open question, but Anna had always considered herself a pleasant enough person and relatively harmless. Still, Mack might have his reasons. It was possible he'd been behind the light in Lanny Wilcox's bedroom window, had known she'd followed and didn't want her poking her nose into whatever business he'd had there. Could be he loved her and felt rejected, hated her and felt seduced or didn't like the fact that she never parted her hair.

Why he may have tried to crush her could be any of a hundred things the human psyche finds irresistible or intolerable. Given that he had means, motive and opportunity, if he did it, why not finish the job? Mack had gone to great lengths to rescue her. There were no witnesses but the fishes. Had he wanted her dead, it could have been done with thumb and forefinger: no muss, no fuss and no evidence left behind. Instead he'd worked feverishly to get her out and, once she was safe and topside, showed a concern for her welfare that Anna did not believe was feigned.

Unless he'd suffered a brief psychotic and homicidal episode, then repented and saved her, Mack was not her man. There'd been no seismic disturbances, not tsunamis, no ground swells shifting the sands. According to Daniel, no torpedoes had been fired, and the only anchor dragged was his when he and Mack had engineered her release.

The tried and possibly true Sherlockian assertion that once everything possible has been ruled out, whatever remains, however improbable, is the truth, suggested an answer.

There was another diver.

Anna returned to her quarters. There was much to think about: the second diver, the whereabouts of Theresa Alvarez, Teddy Shaw's proclivity for drugs, two sunken vessels and one accepted proposal for marriage. The first four she would attend to in due time. The fifth she was oddly content with, pleased, excited even. Marrying Paul Davidson felt as warm and light and supportive as this southern sea when first tumbled into. If like dangers to life and limb lurked in the connubial depths, so be it.

Tired as she was, she sat down with her great-great-aunt Raffia's letters. In a way she hoped the affects of the hallucinogen had not completely worn off. The drug had given her a heightened connection to Raffia: reading the letters was as poignant as speaking to the dead.

18

Dear Peg—

I was in the downstairs parlor—it's quite a gracious room and used by all the officers and their wives on occasion— restuffing the pillows with moss some of the soldiers gather and sell to their fellows to make mattresses. The moss is not so comfortable as a feather bed, but it has the advantage of being cheap and easily available. In a place where one's bedding mildews and is subject to becoming a home for creatures that bite, being able to stuff pillows anew is almost a necessity. I was called from this mindless task by a shrieking as of fish-wives.

I ran upstairs to see who was murdering whom and found Tilly and Luanne in a tug-of-war over a skirt. Luanne was in one of her stubborn moods. They come upon her when she is doing her duty as she declares, "In a right and God-fearing way," and one of us has the temerity to interfere with her. Tilly, who has been raised properly and ought to know better, had worked herself into a tear-streaked state of shouting and pulling. With some difficulty and a bit of fishwifery of my own, I managed to wrestle the garment from them before they tore it into pieces.

Because Luanne is older and has not had the advantages that Tilly has, I let her tell her side first. "I gathered up the laundry like I done every Tuesday since I started doing for you," she told me. Despite the odd use of language the slaves have adopted, her indignation gave her dignity. Tilly began to behave less like a wild animal and have the decency to look a little ashamed of herself. "I got this dirty old skirt out from under Miss Tilly's bed where it's got no business being. It got foods on it and now she got it crumbled and all over with dust. I was taking it with the rest to see to it, and out she comes screaming I was stealing. I never stole nothing in my life."

Stealing, in the life that Luanne was given, the life of a slave, was a serious accusation. Where she had come from she would have been beaten or worse for theft.

"Matilda, what have you got to say for yourself?" I demanded. I sounded so much like Molly at that moment you would have laughed or cried to hear me. Tilly had the grace (or the very sensible fear of my wrath) to apologize to Luanne.

"There's something in the pocket I need to have back," she said as if this explained her outrageous exhibition.

"Why didn't you simply ask Luanne to take it out of the pocket and give it to you?" I asked reasonably. I added the "reasonably" because I am inordinately proud that, given the embarrassment I was suffering because of our sister, reason did not come easily at that moment.

"It's mine," Tilly stated.

Well, that was no sort of an answer at all. I waited for the rest of the explanation but it was not forthcoming. Luanne, her blood still up from the unwarranted attack on her character, started in again with "I never took" etc. etc. Not wishing to be drawn back into it, I cut her off.

"Why didn't you just ask?" I repeated to Tilly.

Tilly lost her prettiness in that moment. I have never seen a child so changed. Her face grew sullen, her eyes hot and dull and she would not look at me. It struck me as a blow. Our Tilly has always carried such a light within her. Foolish she can be, and rash most certainly, but I had never seen her secretive and sly. The ugliness with which it clouded her delicate features made me want to cry. At this point I had sovereignty over the disputed skirt. It was clear that whatever was in the pocket was not only of utmost importance to Tilly, but was something she believed would cause others a great deal of displeasure.

"We'll see about this," I said, once again using Molly's voice and, though I disliked myself for doing so, could no more have stopped than I could carry one of the great cannons to the third level of this fort.

I fumbled through the wad of fabric in my arms till I found the pockets. Inside one of them I felt the crinkle of folded papers and pulled them out. I shook them open to see what dreadful words could change Tilly from child to cornered fox. Before I could read a word, she snatched them from my hand, shouting, "They're no concern of yours!" and ran down the hall, through our rooms and, by the slamming of doors, I surmised out on the veranda and down the stairs.

For a moment I thought to give chase but chose not to humiliate her or myself in such a way. I was angry, but mostly I was worried. This was so unlike Tilly. After apologizing again to Luanne, I went not back to the parlor but to our rooms, where I could be assured of being alone. There I sat and thought.

Peggy, do you think it could be a love letter? Maybe from Joel Lane? That was my first thought, but surely the discovery of a love letter would bring on blushes, stammers and giggles, not the desperation and wretchedness I saw. Unless it was a profession of love (or, God forbid, some baser emotion) that was not appropriate. Perhaps from Dr. Mudd or Samuel Arnold? I mention them because, other than Joseph and Joel, they are the men she sees, speaks of and I know full well Dr. Mudd has gotten too much influence over her. Lord knows Joseph has made note of it as well. The mere mention of the doctor is enough to put him in a pet.

I assumed Tilly would be back within the hour. On this bit of earth there simply is no place to run to. In the heat and the dust, the ever-shifting sea of men on land and water from horizon to horizon, I was sure discomfort would hound her home without my having to dangle after her.

Two hours passed. Then three. Many times I cycled through anger to worry and back again. Worry won out in the end, and I decided to search for our errant sister—not to reprimand her but to see her safe and well for my own peace of mind.

I went first to the top tier of the fort. After that last cannon was lifted into place, the building and arming was stopped. Since we are no longer at war, an order came through that the arming of the fort was to cease, though the construction continues as Jefferson will be used as a prison for some time to come. Within six months Joseph estimates that our confederate soldiers will all have been released, but those sent here for other crimes, the deserters, thieves, murderers and, of course, the Lincoln conspirators, will remain to serve out their sentences.

The third tier, blessedly devoid of humanity, was manned only by sentries and a few knots of off-duty men up catching sea breezes and smoking and gambling. Not wanting to air our domestic concerns before this rough gathering, I did not ask any of the men if they had seen Tilly.

A circumnavigation of the fort revealed no truant girl. It is close to a mile walk to complete the circumference of these walls. By the time I had done so I was sweating, and worry had once again come round to anger. I returned to quarters expecting to find her there. She was not, and my anxiousness for her safety again pushed out my anxiousness to slap her.

I debated whether or not to tell Joseph. In telling him I would have marshaled the forces of the Union Army to search for Tilly. I was not yet sufficiently concerned for her welfare to subject her—and us—to the ensuing gossip. That is the good reason I did not tell my husband but not the only reason. The other is not so easily articulated even to myself. I shall try to tell it to you, but you must burn this letter should I die unexpectedly. I would not like a distant relative to read it and know what a small person I was.

I did not tell Joseph partly because I was afraid, not of his anger at Tilly or of his anger at me for failing to run our home in such a way that its inner workings did not interfere with him. On reflection I believe I did not tell him because I was afraid to see the concern in his face, afraid it would be greater, deeper than any concern he has ever shown me. Peggy, I was jealous of our sister, jealous of my husband's affection for her. May God forgive me. You, my dear sister, I know will understand. Though it is undoubtedly a sacrilege, to be understood is far more comforting than the cold release of forgiveness.

In this unpleasant state of the heart it came to me that possibly Tilly had been so madly protective of her letter because her brother-in-law had written it. I cannot tell you what sudden sickness this thought engendered in me. The instant it came into my mind I was doubled over with it as if I had received a blow to my midsection and could not draw breath.

Fortunately this miserable and unworthy state was short-lived. The letter could not have been written by Joseph. It simply could not. Joseph is not given to writing letters of any sort and least of all love letters. Even when he was courting me with such purpose, he never wrote me. And, though I only glimpsed the papers, I am sure I would have recognized his handwriting.

Once I recovered myself, I set off to look in the only other place I could think that Tilly might have run to. Both Joseph and myself have expressly forbid her to visit Joel Lane's cell unaccompanied, but given her newly acquired insolence, I thought that's where she might have gone.

It took only a moment to bully one of the sentries at the sally port into escorting me to the cells above and unlocking the door. By now they were not only accustomed to my going there but had become used to the Lincoln conspirators and, though they are still much reviled, Arnold and Mudd are no longer feared as they once were. The sentry was an older man, nearly fifty—much too old to be an infantryman, but it is the life he's used to. As we ascended the spiral stairs adjacent to the guard-room, he said: "First the young miss and now you. Those rebs must be pouring some mighty fine tea to attract the prettiest ladies at the fort."

I did not thank him for the compliment. He took my silence as a rebuff and didn't say another word. I had not intentionally snubbed him. It was his testimony that Tilly had visited the cells that caught up my attention. I wanted to ask when she'd come, if she was still there, but that would have been to admit I did not know the whereabouts of the child entrusted to my care. Soon enough I would find these things out.

He unlocked Joel's cell door, then said: "I'll be waiting just out here. You call out if you need me." It wasn't concern for my privacy that motivated this act. As he turned away he was already fumbling for his tobacco pouch. Men are not allowed to smoke on duty. They can be beaten for it or made to carry a heavy cannonball in circles hour upon hour or even be cruelly strung up from one of the trees. Though I believe the regulation

to be just and necessary, it is hard on those men who have come
to depend on tobacco. Behind these enclosed casemates was an
ideal place to enjoy a smoke undetected.

Joel was lying on his mattress, his back propped against the
wall, doing nothing. The forced inactivity of our prisoners must
be the most difficult cross they bear, worse even than bad food
and poor living conditions. Those who can work are able to
earn money for the small luxuries available at Sentler's store by
the docks. Joel was healing quickly but was not yet fit enough
to join the crews building or recoaling the ships.

"Good afternoon, Private Lane," I said, attempting to sound
cheerful. There was no need to add the weight of my concerns
to his.

"Is it?" His sullenness so matched Tilly's I began to wonder
if poor manners were contagious.

I chose to ignore his tone. "Has Tilly been here?"

He glanced at the door that communicated between his casemate and that of Dr. Mudd and Mr. Arnold.

"Is she here?" I amended my question with some alarm. The
thought of her behind closed doors with two men—any two
men—was not something I would have condoned.

"She was. She's gone," he said.

There was some comfort in that at least.

"Do you know where she went?"

"Why don't you ask my glorious physician? It was him, not
me, she came to see." At this moment Joel Lane was no longer
a soldier, a man recuperating from a beating or a carefree actor
and balladeer. He was a peevish boy looking and sounding as
young as our little sister.

Clearly I was not the only one bitten by the green-eyed monster this day. I was beginning to understand why women are often banned from military postings. It is not our behavior that is
an endangerment but that of the men made foolish and rash by
the presence of a skirt in their midst.

"Is Dr. Mudd in?" I asked, then realized the stupidity of my
question and crossed to the adjoining door without awaiting
a reply.

I felt a bit silly knocking on the door to a prison cell as if I'd
come calling of a Saturday afternoon, but simply flinging it

open like an invading army was unthinkable. I tapped and called out: "Dr. Mudd? It's Mrs. Coleman. May I speak with you a moment?"

Rustling came from within and went on much longer than I would have expected. In the heat they may have been resting in a state of undress, so I did not hurry them. At another time it might have crossed my wicked mind to see Mr. Arnold in shirt-sleeves or singlet. My mind was so full of Tilly at this moment that I was saved such evil thoughts.

It was Samuel Arnold and not the doctor who finally opened the door. "Raphaella," he said. "How can I be of assistance?" It took me aback both that he knew my Christian name and that he had the audacity to use it. Since he seemed genuinely pleased to see me—and a man has not looked at me in that way or said my name with such gentleness in a good while—I'm afraid I did not reprimand him as I should have. We all have an unlocked window through which the devil can creep, as Molly was fond of telling us. It's a pity that mine is dangerous-looking men. (Oh. Dear. Peggy, when you are burning up pages of this letter would you expunge that bit as well?)

This foolishness passed in the blink of an eye, and I do not think I let any of it show on my face. "I'm looking for my sister," I said. "We had an upset over a letter and she ran from me. She's been gone several hours and I've become concerned." Why I decided at this moment to tell the truth and to this man who both frightens and attracts me I cannot say. Certainly not because I trust him above all people—or above any people for that matter. Maybe I told Mr. Arnold because the weight of the situation had been building within me and I needed to shift some of the burden. By shifting it onto one even more helpless than I, I was assured there would be no outcry, no search and no recriminations. Rather like talking to the cat.

"Miss Tilly was here an hour ago, maybe two," Arnold said. "She didn't stay long."

"Did she mention where she might go?"

Arnold laughed a pleasant sound, but I resented it given the state of my nerves. "I well know there is not anywhere to go," I said tartly. "But she is indeed gone, and in a brick box of a thousand men I believe I have cause to be concerned."

"I'm sorry," he said at once. "I was laughing at my own prospects, not your sister's."

With the heat and the dashing about, a strand of hair had come loose from the pins and fell in my face. This man actually tucked it back. Of all the schoolboy tricks, that has to be the first one learned. I'd not thought any man over twenty would still be using this crude form of seduction. If indeed it was seduction and not merely an attempt to improve the aesthetics of the cell. To my credit I neither melted nor swooned, but neither did I put him in his place as he most richly deserved.

"Tilly didn't talk to me; she came to see Mudd," Mr. Arnold said.

I couldn't but notice he had dropped the honorable title of "doctor" and wondered if they had quarreled. Mr. Arnold did not move from the doorway as I'd expected, and I was forced to ask: "May I speak with him?"

He stepped aside and, holding the door wide, gestured me through with mock gallantry. Dr. Mudd had fashioned himself a desk of sorts from a wooden cask begged off one of the guards and fitted it with a stool of piled brick. The "desk" had been set to catch what shards of morning sun came through the three deep gun slits high above the floor. At the time of day I was there the sun had moved into the western sky and the cell was uniformly gloomy. Regardless of this, Dr. Mudd was writing, paper and pen sent to him regularly by his wife, along with other items to make his life bearable.

I stood inside the door, Mr. Arnold to my left, close enough I could sense him without turning to look. The doctor kept right on scratching away. It was bizarre to be kept waiting like a tradesman come looking for work by a man one's husband keeps under lock and key. Another time I might have allowed him this fleeting and petty exercise of power. That day I had no patience for it. "I need to speak with you," I said.

He looked up, sighed to signify his annoyance and forbearance, and said: "Very well. One moment," and went back to his correspondence. The world was topsy-turvy. Tilly turning from bright to dull, Mr. Arnold from sulking to seduction, Joel from man to boy, Sergeant Sinapp from Joseph's lapdog to cur and now Dr. Mudd from prisoner to potentate.

"My sister came to see you," I said, ignoring his attempt to ignore me. "Mr. Arnold and Private Lane say she met only with you. She has since disappeared. I need to know of what you spoke."

Dr. Mudd finally rose, perhaps remembering his manners, perhaps merely stretching his legs. "It was a personal matter," he said.

All at once Sergeant Sinapp's proclivity for stringing traitors up by their thumbs did not seem so incomprehensible.

"My sister is not yet seventeen years old," I said. "She is under my protection and that of my husband, the captain of this garrison. Until such a time as she comes of age or marries, she has no *personal* matters. You will tell me what transpired." I didn't add any threat about thumbs and trees, but it was in my voice and my mind, and I could tell he made no mistake about my intentions.

"Your sister is concerned only with justice, Mrs. Coleman. Have no fears for her moral rectitude."

The way he stressed "your sister" it was evident he meant to suggest that I, and the rest of the union supporters, were not concerned with justice. I was not in a mood to be challenged on my political beliefs or to second-guess our nation's legal system. Mudd was, of course, referring obliquely to his own innocence, a theme of which he never tires.

"I am not concerned with her morals," I snapped. "Only with her whereabouts."

He shrugged and gestured at the limited confines of his cell, and said, "As you can see . . ."

Rather than remain and bandy words with a man who had nothing to lose but time, and of that he had a plentitude, I simply said: "Good day, then," and left. It would have been right and good to leave with an especially cutting remark, but I'm afraid Molly raised us too well for that. I did not even slam the door on my way out. He shut it firmly behind me before my skirt had cleared the lintel. Having never been snubbed by a convicted murderer before and having no clear idea where to go next other than to inform Joseph and begin an all-too-public search, I stood a moment inside Joel Lane's casemate.

Mr. Arnold leaned against the wall beside the door I'd just

come through. As seldom as that man stands without support of one structure or another, one cannot but wonder his back has not atrophied.

"Mrs. Coleman?" Joel had gotten up from his bed, his manners and his maturity evidently relearned while I sparred with his neighbor. "I didn't know Tilly was missing. You told us but it didn't come home to me till you were talking to Samuel. I wouldn't for the world have anything happen to Tilly."

For an awful moment I thought he was going to cry. There is that about a brutal beating that breaks more than men's bodies. Joel recovered himself and said: "After she left me—us—Dr. Mudd, I heard voices raised outside. I think some of the guards were taunting her. The sentry was with her and there was nothing I could do anyway."

This last was said with a self-loathing that cut to the heart. For a man to be utterly helpless to defend the woman he loves—or thinks he does—must be a debilitating thing. And I do believe Joel is in love with Tilly. It's Tilly who has cooled toward him, transferring her youthful passion to the supercilious Dr. Mudd. How far that has gone, I cannot say. It occurs to me as I write that today might not have been the first time Tilly visited the conspirators' cell without me.

"Did you recognize the voices?" I asked.

"Only Tilly's. I'm sorry."

Again tears threatened. Maternal urges are rare with me, but I suffered one then, wanting to rush over and hold this sad and battered boy-man. I quashed it. "Which sentry came with her?" I demanded.

"Private Munson." Joel named the boyish-looking soldier who'd been on duty with the vile Sinapp the night Tilly and I found Joel hanging by his thumbs in the sally port.

"Thank you."

Sam Arnold walked me to the door. It was only two steps but I appreciated the civility of the gesture. At the threshold he stopped, knowing he could not pass. I rapped loudly to let my smoking escort know I wished to come out. Mr. Arnold leaned close. He is a tall man and, since coming to Fort Jefferson, has worn his hair long. It fell over his face and I could smell the mix of man, salt and tobacco. "Mudd does not mean well by your sister, Mrs. Coleman. He is using her to his own ends. He is not a man to be trusted, especially with the affections of an innocent."

The door opened and I was allowed to escape.

Joel's assertion that Tilly had been accosted by, and had heated words with, our own troops and Mr. Arnold's cryptic warning heightened my alarm for her safety. Till then I'd worried only that in her girlish huff over a love letter revealed she'd done something foolish, perhaps injuring or embarrassing herself in the doing. Now I became concerned that either through the natural roughness of our soldiers or the machinations of Dr. Mudd she'd involved herself in something far more dangerous.

What that could be I had no inkling.

My chaperone, looking relaxed and reeking of tobacco, locked the door behind me.

"Are you aware of an altercation of any kind between my sister and the guards an hour or more earlier?" I asked.

"I am not, ma'am. I have been in the guardroom since two o'clock and nothing's happened. Just hot and more hot and dust and noise like every other day."

Customarily I can spare a word of sympathy for the plight of the soldiers garrisoned here. This day I could not. "There is a soldier named Munson," I said. "Where is he now?"

"That'd be Charley Munson, ma'am. I relieved him when I came on duty. He'll be in quarters I expect."

"Take me to him."

"He'll be sleeping, ma'am. He was on most of the night."

"I don't care if he's bathing. I would see him now." I suppose I shocked this old soldier. The prudishness of the old-timers is almost comical.

Munson was abed. While he was ousted and made ready to receive the captain's wife (a pronouncement I am sure put the fear of God into him), I waited outside near where the new armory is being constructed. These are buildings most fascinating in nature. Of brick, as is the rest of the fort, but with domed ceilings within so the explosives stored there will not be set off even by a direct hit should the fort be attacked.

Within a short time Mr. Charley Munson, bleary-eyed and stinking of the gin he'd used to put himself to sleep, came blinking out from the barracks set up in the casemates behind the unfinished armory.

"You were with my sister Tilly when she called upon Joel Lane and Dr. Mudd. Shortly thereafter she had words with some of the men. I need to know what was said and by whom," I said without preamble. Whether he was reluctant to tell me or simply needed time to marshal his muddled thoughts I do not know. For half a minute he shuffled and rubbed at the stubble on his chin.

"Do I need to fetch my husband?" I threatened. That straightened his spine and cleared his mind. After Sergeant Sinapp's insubordination I was relieved to see this man still respected Joseph's authority enough to be afraid.

"Now Mrs. Coleman you don't have to go doing that. No, ma'am. I took Miss Tilly up to the rebs' cell, but only like I been told to should you ask. It's captain's orders."

"To take Miss Tilly up there without a chaperone, Mr. Munson?"

This breach concerned him, and I felt a moment's pity knowing how Tilly can wrap men around her girlish fingers, but only a moment's.

"She said you'd be along directly," he defended himself. "She said Lane had taken a turn and needed his pain medicine and it couldn't wait."

"So you took her to his cell."

"Yes, ma'am, I did. To tell you the truth, ma'am, I never did go inside with her. She said I was to wait outside. As you'd been in and out so much I never saw any harm in it. I can't tell you what they got up to but it wasn't long. She was out quick as you please and looking like the cat that got at the cream, if you know what I mean."

"I need to know what occurred once she left the cells."

"Well, whilst she'd been in there some of the boys kinda got together. You know how it is. Anyway out she comes and so pleased with herself and I'm locking up the door like I'm supposed to and she up and says: 'There won't be nobody to lock up much longer, Mr. Munson.'

"Of course I got to ask why so I do, and she says: 'You can't keep an innocent man under lock and key.' So I says, don't worry none 'cause her Johnny Reb'll be shipping out with the rest of 'em quick as never-mind. And she says she's not talking about Joel Lane but the other one."

"Dr. Mudd or Mr. Arnold?" I asked for clarification. Use of the King's English is not one of Mr. Munson's strong suits.

"She didn't say, but I'm thinking it was the doctor."

I didn't press him on the point because that was what I was thinking as well. "And the soldiers heard this?"

"Yes, ma'am, they did and the sergeant took up about it."

Sergeant Sinapp's involvement in any unpleasant encounter did not surprise me. What did was that Joseph's authority over the man had been undermined to the point he would openly condone—and no doubt participate in—the insubordination of smoking while on duty, a serious offense.

"What did the sergeant say," I prodded.

"I can't tell word for word like. Things got kinda fast and snippety."

I will not put you through any more of the agonizing process of conversing with Mr. Munson than I already have. Suffice to say the vile Sinapp, who you will recall actually put his hands on Tilly when last we suffered his company, spoke to her roughly regarding her unchaperoned visit to the cells, and she responded by baiting him with supposed proof of Dr. Mudd's innocence, coupled with unflattering comparisons of Sinapp to Mudd. The sergeant became angry. He demanded her "proof" and apparently threatened to strip and beat her as a traitor to the union. Tilly, finally showing some tiny semblance of wisdom, fled, "skirts all a-dither" according to Mr. Munson.

The recital chilled me. Sergeant Sinapp, like any dog of war, cannot be masterless without becoming dangerous to the very people for whom he was trained to fight. I would give a great deal to know what gave Sinapp the upper hand or led him to believe he has the upper hand. Joseph, never the most communicative of men, has become like the Spartan in the old tale. He seems to have a purloined fox under his coat and will let it devour his entrails before he will admit to stealing it.

Mr. Munson, being unable to tell me anything else of value but that Tilly had run toward the northeastern bastion and not toward the spiral stairs closer by, I returned to the second level of the fort above the guardroom and began making my way around it. Many of the casemates along that side of the fort have been boarded up on the parade ground side to fashion cells. This is not true of those first in line. These have remained open

and have been used for various things during my time here: barracks, sick ward and prisoners' mess. Currently they are used as
a catchall for brick, board, armament and machinery.

Because that was the direction Tilly was said to have run after her altercation with "the boys," I picked my way through the
piles looking for some sign of her. I found two of the fort's cats,
essential in a place as frequented by rodents as a port of call for
ships. Neither was pursuing its avocation. One slept in the sun,
a long and leggy pattern in tiger stripes. The other I found by
following small helpless cries. Thinking to find a repentant girl
I found instead a mama cat and four kittens hidden behind a
rampart of board ends and broken brick.

Several casemates down, just before the cells began in
earnest with heavy timbers and locked doors for our less-
trustworthy clientele, I again heard the mewling of a small
frightened creature.

"Tilly?" I called and was answered by a furtive scuffling
noise. This part of the fort has a peculiarity that caused me a
moment's confusion. Then I found my way down a narrow
brick passage. To my right lay one even narrower and shaped
like an L, where no light could penetrate. I remembered from
our first tour of Fort Jefferson three years ago that this was one
of several secure chambers built for the storage of gunpowder.
Since that time I'd not had any cause to visit.

"Tilly?" I called again, and feeling along the wall for guidance, I went in.

19

Three hours' sleep, which served to whet her appetite for bed rather than refresh her, and Anna went in search of Daniel. Shops, quarters and generator rooms were empty of bipeds. She found him by the docks, head and shoulders buried in the engine box of the *Curious*.

"Hundred-hour check?" she said for openers.

Daniel withdrew from the engine compartment, wiping his hands on a red oil rag. For an instant Anna was put in mind of her father. He, too, had been a stocky man of endless strength, scarred knuckles permanently blackened by years of working on airplane engines.

"Burned her out," Daniel said. "Shifting that motor off you I had to gun her. When she hit the end of the anchor chain she stood up on her tail."

His tone was mildly accusing. Accustomed to the feelings of those who husband internal combustion engines, Anna was not offended.

"My life for hers," she said easily. "If she dies it's a hero's death."

Tribute given and accepted, Daniel said: "What's up?"

Anna did not choose to share her theory about a second diver and the engine being shifted intentionally, so she just

asked if he had noticed any other boats near the dive site. He
hadn't, but couldn't swear there hadn't been any. "My attention
was focused down pretty much," he said. "Anything short of a
Spanish galleon under full sail could have gone unnoticed."

Mack, the only other witness, was her last recourse. She'd
not yet spoken with him on the assumption that, had he seen
anyone—and how could he not if a second diver had been in evidence—and had any intention of volunteering the information,
he would have done so already. Mack may have saved her life
for reasons of his own, but the mere fact he had been there
when the "accident" occurred made him suspect of collusion or
criminal negligence at least.

This line of inquiry was to be aborted. Mack, Daniel told
her, was on his lieu days and had hitched a ride to Key West on
the early seaplane. He'd be out of pocket for five days. The
"good" news was the Shaws had returned on the first ferry of
the day. Anna'd slept through the hero's welcome Bob had been
given on the docks. All the fort's personnel had been there,
partly out of respect for Bob, mostly because everyone but a
skeleton crew were leaving the island for a three-day session
regarding health and benefits at headquarters in Homestead.

Bob and his wife were tucked away in their house.

Not anxious to interview them with an eye to the poisoning,
Anna took a leisurely route back to the west side of the fort.
Tourists off the huge catamaran, one of two that ferried visitors
from the mainland each day, wandered the parade ground and
drifted from casemate to casemate. Anna could see them
through the brick arches, small and dressed in bright colors like
dolls in a dollhouse viewed from the back. People made places
mundane, robbed them of mystery and romance. Crazy, delusional, absurd as the human animal could be, it carried homely
reality around its neck like the mariner's albatross. Religion,
the fantasy of the occult, the paranormal, close encounters of
the third kind, served to indicate how burdensome life without
magic had become to some.

Moving slowly, taking the steps one at a time in deference to
her hard-won aches and scrapes and her desire to put off meeting with the Shaws a little longer, Anna climbed the spiral stairs
beside the Visitors Center, the room that had housed the guards
when Raffia Coleman was in residence.

On the second level she turned right, instead of left toward the Shaws and home. When she'd first come to the fort, Duncan had taken her on a tour. One of the stops was in Dr. Samuel Mudd and Mr. Sam Arnold's cell, they being the two most famous—or infamous—of the inmates when Fort Jefferson had been a prison.

Duncan adhered to the theory that the doctor was guilty as charged. Despite the fact that a couple of presidents had written letters amounting to an apology to the doctor's descendants, the court's ruling had never been overturned and the doctor's name was still Mudd. The information available from the highly public legal proceeding gave rise to reams of paper on the subject, and Duncan preached his gospel of Mudd's guilt in learned terms and soon, he hoped, from the *New York Times* bestseller list.

As Anna understood it, Samuel Mudd's contention was that he had not known John Wilkes Booth when, hours after Lincoln's assassination, he set the man's leg, broken in the jump from the balcony to the stage of Ford's Theatre. This was why he had given treatment and, upon learning of the assassination, had not turned Booth in. Mudd's poor-country-doctor-living-up-to-the-Hippocratic-oath defense was, according to Duncan, undone by the fact that several witnesses had seen Mudd in the company of John Wilkes Booth on two occasions prior to the shooting of the president, making it extremely unlikely that Booth, who remained overnight in the doctor's house, was unrecognized by Mudd.

Till reading Raffia Coleman's letters, Anna had little interest in the guilt or innocence of a man so long dead. Drugs and family ties having dragged history through time and dumped it in her living room, she looked on the cell with new eyes. The channels so painstakingly chipped in the floor to carry away standing water were as Raffia had described them. In running her fingers over the fissures Anna could feel the anger and desperation it had taken to carve them. Imagining the casemate, now open to the sunlight with a pleasant view of the parade ground, boarded over, the three high, narrow slits on the east wall must have crushed the life from what little light they allowed through.

Regardless of the deeds of the men condemned to serve time

in the cell, Anna felt pity for them. She sided with those op-
posed to the death penalty because it did not deter crime, was
not cost effective and those on death row seemed anxious to
live. She was not against it because it was deemed cruel or unusual. Had she been sentenced to such a room as this without
light, without hope of release, the death penalty would have
been a great kindness.

Still, keeping company with her aunts Raffia and Tilly, Anna
took her time walking the northern bastion and casemates. Partway down she veered from the dramatic drench of sun and
shadow in the great arched spaces and slipped into the brick
passage Raffia had described outside the black powder storage
room.

Built within the walls, closer to the parade ground than the
sea, these small rooms were designed for security, a place safe
from the guns of an attacking force yet convenient to the gun
ports they served. The tight doglegged passage to gain entrance
reminded Anna of the way into Injun Joe's Cave on Tom
Sawyer Island in Disneyland. Time warped briefly—a sensation
she was beginning to get used to—and she suffered the same
pinch of panic going in as she had at nineteen in southern Cali-
fornia.

Inside, the room was lined—floor, walls and ceiling—with
wood. She'd have to ask Duncan why. Maybe, in this humid climate, it helped to keep the powder dry. The timber-lined, many-
angled internal ceiling going up to a point, it felt like the inside
of the grain silos she'd played in as a girl. Three weeks before
her eleventh birthday a kid had suffocated, drowned in grain,
and her father never let her or Molly play in one again. Looking
around this confined space, protected from the elements, graffiti
from the eighteen hundreds still legible on the boards, she felt
again that unsettling mix of excitement and dread silos had engendered in her since the neighbor boy had died.

For several minutes she let the centuries shift and listened
for the weeping of Tilly, the calls of her older sister, the clatter
of men and hammers. Before she could conjure up the past, two
teenaged boys wearing shorts so large the crotches hobbled
their knees burst in with sweating exuberance and Anna was
driven back into the new millennia where boys Joel Lane's age

were still children and had the tee shirts and the manners to
prove it.

Hounded from her hiding place, she gave up procrastinating
and finished the journey to the Shaws'. Their home was just below her apartment and mirrored Lanny Wilcox's quarters. On
the southernmost end of the house was a screened-in porch.
Anna always paid attention to this on her way past because the
Shaws kept two fine fat cats who often lounged on the porch.

Thinking life would be grand if she dealt exclusively with
felines, she knocked on the door. Teddy let her in with what appeared to be genuine pleasure. Wondering if this woman regularly poisoned people to further her husband's career, Anna
experienced no reciprocal emotions but believed she'd faked
them adequately enough to pass muster.

The two houses, the Shaws' and Wilcox's, were structurally
alike, but there ended the similarity. Where Lanny's was made
smaller by the encroachment of his collected interests, memen-
tos, incarnations and necessary junk, the Shaws' home was
made larger by white paint, mirrors, clean, polished wood-and-
canvas furniture and an absence of any trappings of the past.
Though she traveled light, Anna had not been this unencumbered since college, when a bookcase of bricks and boards and
a couple of thumbtacks were all she needed in the way of interior décor.

Not that the Shaws' tastes ran to plastic milk crates and
beanbag chairs; what there was was classy and probably expensive. It was just that there was so little. What there was appeared planned, cautious, devoid of knickknacks, personal
photos, souvenirs, toys, dog-eared books or anything else to
play with. The room could have been designed for a magazine
cover.

Given what Anna had learned of Teddy's past, it wasn't surprising she had no wish to be reminded of it on a daily basis.
Why Bob would have so little of his history on the walls Anna
had no idea. Regardless of pathologies, she much preferred the
Shaws' living space to that of Lanny Wilcox. In the Shaws'
quarters she could breathe.

Having ushered Anna over the stairway landing and down
into the living room, Teddy left her to find her own seat. Anna

chose the one with the white cat named Joey, as Teddy fluttered around her husband. Bob was ensconced on the sofa, a cream canvas sling supported by blond wood that had to be more attractive than comfortable. Had Anna been the one with her leg in a cast, she would have been forced to crawl to the closet, get a gun and shoot Teddy. The amount of fussing and plumping and cooing would have driven her around the bend.

Bob thrived on it. A warrior carried from the field of battle, he accepted the attention with gracious humility that only just dimmed the glow of pure contentment on his face. Probably this idyll would be short-lived. Having tasted what he'd thirsted after for so long, odds were good he'd be craving another adventure before the scars of this one had time to fade.

Following an offer of drinks, which Anna almost forgot to decline, the domestic Teddy, exhibiting none of the Borgia characteristics Anna'd envisioned once she'd seen her as a suspect, left Anna and Bob alone and went into the kitchen.

The life of the party gone, there didn't seem much to say. Anna would have busied herself playing with Joey, but the cat was having none of it and jumped down at the first tentative pat.

"You're looking good," Anna said to keep the silence from getting embarrassing.

"I'm a fast healer," Bob said.

He probably was. So far his other inflated opinions about his worth had been proved out. Still, Anna had to make a point not to smile. Bob must even outdo other men in the superior functioning of his cells.

"Bring me up to speed. What's been happening on the boat thing?" Bob plucked two brightly colored pillows from where Teddy tucked them and tossed them to the floor. Basking in the glow of past deeds had lasted an even shorter time than Anna'd given it. The adrenaline junkie was back.

Teddy returned with drinks on a tray, a Coke for Bob and iced tea for her. Seeing the Coke can was unopened and meant for Bob Anna quickly changed her mind and asked if she could have that drink after all. Nosing around the haunts of Civil War dead was thirsty work. Teddy gave Anna Bob's soda without so much as blinking and fetched another. Had she been planning on drugging her guest she was unperturbed at being foiled.

"So," Teddy said, flopping down on the only empty chair.

"Who was Bob's dead guy? Anything on that?" She was as anxious to return to the glory days as her husband.

The delay Anna had instigated with the Coke business had given her time to think, something she should have done before making the call.

She told them everything, leaving out only that she and Lanny had been drugged and that she knew there was a warrant out for Teddy's arrest.

Both Shaws listened with the rapt attention of children being told a favorite bedtime story. As carefully as she watched, Anna could detect no flickers of fear or guilt.

"Teddy," Anna said as the younger woman saw her to the door. "Do you think Bob could spare you for a little while? There's something I'd like to discuss."

"Can't we do it here? I have no secrets from—" Teddy jerked the way a small dog does when it runs headlong into the end of its leash. For the time it takes to breathe, she met Anna's eyes. Other than maybe Matt Damon, Anna had never seen an actor who could match the sudden and overwhelming vulnerability of Teddy's face. Emotion was clearly written there. Anna watched it come and go. Dismay, that almost laughable look a toddler gets when its first balloon pops in his hand, the sudden shock before the shrieking, robbed Teddy of her years. An adult's realization of consequences brought them back with another ten she'd not yet earned. The baby face hardened then sagged, lips thinning.

"Let me tell him I'm going out," Teddy said softly.

As she crossed the kitchen and climbed the three stairs over the hump into the living room, Anna wondered if Teddy would face her monsters with the courage she'd so lauded in her husband. Hard to tell. Fessing up to sleaze and paying the sordid price took a different kind of courage than taking a bullet for the president or rescuing a child from a burning building. No adrenaline helped one through the terror; no promise of reward in status or simply goodwill pulled one through the hard marches. It wasn't even as good as the biblical sort of bravery, the willingness to suffer degradation and abuse for the good of another.

It was pure payback. Scraping it up for the bookie when the bet was lost.

A murmured conversation later Teddy came again into the kitchen. Anna'd seen people go pale beneath a suntan before. Teddy's skin had the unpleasant grayish cast skim milk lends to coffee.

"Let's walk," Anna said. The day was impossibly hot and windy, but being in public would be safer. Besides, Anna wanted to conduct an experiment.

They walked in silence across the parade ground and out the sally port beneath the sweep and cry of the frigate birds. Teddy had guessed what the conversation was to be about, and silence would do more to soften her up than questions.

As Anna turned right to walk around the moat wall, Teddy couldn't take it any longer. "You ran background checks," she said.

"I did."

They reached the southeast corner of the fort, and Anna turned right again, following the wide walkway that topped the moat's wall. Between them and the fort lay the water, shallow at this end, maybe three feet deep and twice that from the top of the wall to the surface of the water. To their left was the ocean, sparkling where the wind roughed its surface.

"I've been clean since I married Bob," Teddy said. "All that was another lifetime. I was another person."

"Does Bob know?" Anna asked.

"He knows."

That was a lie. Anna'd read the truth in Teddy's face back in her kitchen. She let it alone. Beneath the crystal waters of the moat a nurse shark, not yet two feet long, hung motionless, strands of brown seaweed trailing over its tail.

"I never told him," Teddy confessed at last. "Bob is so . . . *good*. It was too late for me. I already loved him. I was afraid he wouldn't see me the same way anymore."

"What was it?" Anna asked.

Teddy understood the question. Like any lover or addict, the name of the necessary object stays close in mind. "Percodan," Teddy said. "Prescription painkillers."

"You stole them from the hospitals where you worked."

"For a while. Then I knew I was taking too many so I started stealing prescription pads and signing the doctors' names to them."

Again a right turn. They walked now along the western wall where Anna believed she had seen the wet prints of whoever had run from her the night she'd seen the light in Lanny Wilcox's quarters. She stopped midway down the wall and looked out toward Loggerhead Key. Three miles away, it looked ghostly in the mist the wind teased from the ocean. Out of the corner of her eye Anna studied Teddy Shaw. Black snakes of hair whipped her cheeks, stuck to her lips. Color had returned and she no longer looked as if she might pass out.

If she had indeed splashed across the moat that night and slithered over the wall, she didn't seem to be thinking about it now. Her attention was directed inward.

"Will you tell him?"

"Yeah," Anna said. "You can have a few days to tell him yourself if you like. Then we'll go on in to Key West and you can turn yourself in. I doubt you'll get more than a couple months' jail time. Maybe not even that, maybe just more probation."

"Can't you just pretend you don't know?"

Teddy knew she couldn't, so Anna didn't bother to answer.

"Two months, probation or whatever and it'll be over. You can come home," Anna said. "Over forever unless you screw up again. I'd think that'd be a relief."

"If I have a home to come to."

"You will." Anna didn't doubt for a minute the truth of her words. Bob and Teddy had such a rich dream life they'd be able to romanticize even jail time into their story. "Tell you what I can do," Anna said as the story they might write unfolded in her brain. "You don't have to tell Bob I found out. I won't. Then you just tell him you have to come clean, square yourself with the law."

Teddy thought about that. If it were possible to see someone mentally embroider a tale, Anna would have sworn that was what she witnessed in Teddy's eyes.

"That would be good," she said at last.

They walked on, circumnavigating the fort. Anna felt no need to talk, and Teddy was busy with her own thoughts, perhaps scripting her confession scene with her husband. The sun baked sweat from their bodies, the wind sucked it away. Anna's throat grew dry. Across the narrow isthmus on Bush Key the

sooty terns wheeled in a gray cloud crying their endless cries.
Tourists dotted the old coaling docks and sat on beaches enjoying their day in the sun. They reached the sally port and went
into the fort. The grass on the parade ground was so dry it
crackled underfoot, putting Anna in mind of crispy Chinese
noodles.

When they reached Teddy's back door and the wooden stairs
to Anna's second-tier apartment, Anna spoke again. "Would
you mind coming up for a minute? There's something I'd like
your opinion on."

The pull to escape into her house, to be with Bob, was so
great Teddy's body actually leaned in that direction. For a second Anna thought she'd refuse. Evidently she decided keeping
on Anna's good side was worth extending her stay away from
her wifely duties.

"For a minute," Teddy said.

"Sit down," Anna said when they'd gone inside. Teddy
perched on the edge of the couch. At the far end Piedmont
opened his eyes the merest of slits. Apparently the idea of sharing his bed with a stranger appalled him. He jumped to the
chair, curled up, and resumed his nap.

"I'm thirsty," Anna said. She opened the refrigerator and
took out a bottle of sparkling water.

"Can I pour you a glass of water?"

"That'd be great," Teddy said. No hesitation. No flicker of
alarm.

Anna put the bottle back and took out two Cokes. "The water's gone flat," she said. "I'd forgotten."

Teddy pulled the tab. Anna sat by Piedmont.

"What did you want my opinion on?"

"Drugs. If somebody wanted to induce mild psychosis, hallucinations, paranoia, what would be the best way to do it? You
know, tasteless, easy to get a hold of, easy to administer in liquid."

Teddy liked story problems. She leaned forward, elbows on
knees, can of pop in both hands. "Legal or illegal?"

"Doesn't matter."

"Lysergic acid diethylamide."

LSD. The old classics were always best.

"Any way to control the dosage?"

"In a lab, sure, but with street stuff who knows?"

That fit with Anna's experience. One of the tainted bottles had agitated her only a little. The other had taken the top of her head off.

"Thanks."

"Why? You planning on taking a trip?"

"Just curious," Anna said.

Another time Teddy might have stayed and tried to wheedle the truth out of Anna. Today the need to be with her crippled husband took precedence.

Anna walked her home.

She stood for a minute in the sun. Air-conditioning could be counted on to provide two wonderful moments: the first blast of cool air when coming in from a sweltering summer and the relief of being enveloped in heat when one stepped out again. While standing in the Shaws' tiny courtyard feeling her skin expand and grow supple after the dry arctic winds of General Electric's winter, Anna's radio crackled to life. The noise startled her. With Bob gone the radio waves had been uncharacteristically empty.

It was Donna the lighthouse keeper on Loggerhead. "Dick Tracy hit pay dirt," she said.

"I'll be there shortly," Anna replied. Glad to have direction, she set out for the docks.

With no discernable change in the weather, the sea had entered another season and rose gray and choppy, the low short swells guaranteed to unsettle the stomachs of the uninitiated. To her shame, Anna was not a particularly good sailor and had been known to run for the rail with the best of them. When she was piloting the boat, this was changed; she had a stomach of iron. In these warm seas where the spray was a blessing and not a curse, she enjoyed the ride.

Patrice was at the house. Donna, Anna was told, was at the top of the seventy-five-foot-tall lighthouse inspecting the railings. The lighthouse had been built in 1886. The railings around the walkway at the top were rusting away. It wouldn't be good for the park service's image to have a visitor plunge to her death while on holiday.

As Patrice ushered Anna into the tiny and wonderful old house, pots and pans, tiny stove, sink, and two-person dining table lining the stone walls, Donna joined them. Come for no other reason, Anna guessed, than to bask in the cleverness of her beloved. In a serendipitous aping of Daniel, Donna was wiping her blunt square hands on a red grease rag. With the two broad-shouldered rough-voiced women in it, the ground floor room with its pint-sized appliances was further reduced until Anna felt she'd entered a dollhouse.

"Upstairs," Patrice said and led the way. The open staircase was made to scale with the house. For Anna it was just narrow enough to feel cozy. With a big woman in front of her and another behind, she was suddenly aware of the structure's great age. Treads creaked in protest, and Anna could feel challenged wood thrumming through the soles of her deck shoes. She took comfort in the fact that, should the stairs collapse, Donna's substantial self would break her fall. Then it occurred to her Patrice would fall on top of them both.

The bedroom was reached without incident. Anna and Donna sat on the bed that took up most of the space. Patrice loaded one of an impressive stack of videotapes into the VCR set beside a television with a thirteen-inch screen.

"I knew it was here somewhere," Patrice said. "My clerical skills being on a par with Donna's cooking, it took me a while to find it."

Donna snorted but seemed unoffended.

"That boat you found—or one like you described to us, might not be the same banana—has been out here a bunch of times in the last couple of months. We get a lot of regulars and I don't videotape them, but these guys were acting fishy."

"No pun intended," Donna interjected.

"I never paid much attention to them till they beached on the west shore under the lighthouse." The tape was in. Patrice joined Anna and Donna on the bed and the three of them stared intently at the small screen as a video of white sand and blue water began to play.

"There's no beaching here—"

"As you know," Donna interrupted.

"But that doesn't mean boats don't land. Donna or I just politely shoo 'em away or, if there's a problem, call you guys. So, this guy beaches." Patrice let the tape lay for fifteen seconds or so in silence. A sleek green missile of a boat thrust into frame and she paused the tape. The picture held but twitched and jerked as if the power of the boat would pull it back into play.

"This guy," Patrice continued, pointing at the captured image, "beaches that thing. He and another guy jump out. Both Hispanic: Mexican, Puerto Rican, Panamanian—something. So Donna here goes down to shoo them away."

"It was my turn," Donna explained, apparently needing Anna to know nobody wore the pants in this particular family. "I'd just done my hale-fellow-well-met wave and smile preparatory to chucking them nicely back into the sea. They saw me and got themselves launched, back in the boat and were leaving a wake wide as a three-lane highway before I had time to get my arm down."

"Donna told me about it and I kept an eye out. Next time they showed, I taped them."

"You can take the woman out of the policeman . . ." Donna said.

"But you can't take the policeman out of the woman," Patrice finished. This was an old joke, the best kind, and the two of them enjoyed themselves.

"They never beached again. Never even came close. That's why this shot's not all that great. But it's the same boat."

For a long minute the three of them stared at the tape. Patrice had zoomed in on it but it still was a good ways away and, on the thirteen-inch screen, no more than three inches long. It was a Scarab. Anna had looked up go-fast boats on the Internet and familiarized herself with the various silhouettes. The differences were small, but each designer left his or her mark on the product. The boat Patrice had caught on film was the same metallic green as the one wrecked off East Key. There was no way to prove to a jury the two were the same boat, but Anna didn't need to. At present she needed only to satisfy herself.

"It's the same boat," she said.

Patrice leaned forward and clicked off the television, ejected the tape and gave it to Anna without being asked. "I'd like it back when you're done."

"No problem." The three of them continued to sit, each alone with her thoughts, blissfully unaware they painted a picture of the "see no evil" monkeys as middle-aged white ladies.

"Why do you figure they beached here, then took off?" Anna

asked at last. She had her own theory but respected Patrice's police skills enough to entertain others.

"My guess is they thought the Key was unoccupied," Patrice said. "You'd think a great phallic black-and-white tower with a light on top would have tipped them off, but there's a few Keys out here with buildings that are abandoned."

"You said you'd seen the boat before."

"Right. It's been out here—or we've seen it—maybe five or six times. Five or six, Donna?"

"About that but not before it beached and ran. That was the first time."

Patrice thought about that. "Right," she said. "I had my brain calendar screwed up. Because it beached I got interested, not the other way around."

"You said it the other way," Donna pushed.

"I'm old and I'm fat and I lie, but you adore me." Patrice said and smiled at her partner.

Donna threw up her big grease-stained hands. "What can I say? I like to walk on the wild side."

The three of them gnawed over the question of the green boat till it was frayed and sodden, stretching the possible from the probable to the fantastical to see if anything shook loose. In the end they returned to earth not that much wiser. The go-fast was not fishing or camping, yet it frequented the park. The go-fast boat was owned or captained by males of a Hispanic cast, two of whom were now dead. The boat had probably beached on Loggerhead mistakenly, either believing it to be uninhabited or believing it to be a different landfall entirely. These paltry facts, put together with the fuel containers that had obliterated the sunken hull and the operator's strong desire to remain unnoticed by anyone in authority, seemed to point to drug smuggling. Smugglers drove powerboats to outrun the coast guard cutters, carried extra fuel, and used isolated and uninhabited places for caches of illegal goods. The drawback to this theory was that if the men killed on the Scarab were drug smugglers, they had to be among the stupidest criminals ever to cross the law. This was a grave insult, given criminals are not known for their cleverness, education, long-term planning or impulse control.

There were thousands of square miles of Caribbean and

Gulf waters. To choose the fifty thousand or so acres of that vastness guaranteed to be crawling with tourists, flown over by seaplanes and patrolled by federal law-enforcement officers in the persons of park rangers, made no sense. A vampire in the Vatican would have a greater chance of going unnoticed.

Anna took the videotape and went home. There were three things on her To Do list today that couldn't in good conscience be put off. She needed to call Lanny Wilcox and let him know he was not insane. She needed to revisit the Theresa Alvarez abdication/vanishing. And it behooved her to dive the green Scarab one more time. With Bob laid up and Mack on the mainland, she'd be diving alone. Teddy Shaw was an accomplished diver and had come to her aid after the fuel tanks blew up, but Anna couldn't help seeing her in B-movie guise: the angel of death in starched white uniform, cap and squeaky shoes, slipping into a hospital room, dripping syringe in hand.

As she'd taught herself to do over the years, thus earning an undeserved reputation for never procrastinating, Anna chose to do the most revolting chore first. It was the adult equivalent of holding the nose and gulping the brussel sprouts without having to taste them.

She docked at Garden Key, got her gear from her quarters then, quickly—surreptitiously, if that was possible in the light of day amid a cloud of tourists and pelicans—took tank, vest and regulator from the storage room behind the ladies' toilets. She had no fears of diving alone in this warm shallow place of coral reefs and sand, particularly since she had no intention of getting within forty yards of anything that looked as if it could roll, fall, shift, explode, scrape or bite. The concern that prompted the desire for stealth was that, were her intentions to become known, she might *not* be diving alone.

The water remained choppy but in no way dangerous to anything but digestion. Over a sandy spot near the wrecks she dropped anchor. Having tucked a garbage bag in her vest, she pulled on latex gloves and went over the side. The garbage bag seemed a bit callous, but she figured she would not find any parts of the Scarab's captain too big to fit. In a perfect world— that is to say a world without people—she would have left the puréed remains to feed the fishes. However, when and if the man was identified, it would behoove the National Park Service

to have retrieved the body—or what there was left of it—and
stored it with proper respect.

Whatever forces of nature conspired to make the surface waters rough had also stirred up the bottom. Visibility was not
great. Anna could only see a hundred feet or so. Because she
valued her own skin more than that of the fragmented boatman,
she first inspected the engine that had nearly marked her final
resting place. There were shiny scrapes and scars that could
have indicated the thing was levered up by someone intending
to squash her. They could also have been made by the metal
prongs of the anchor when it moved the engine so Mack could
pull her to safety.

No epiphanies in the iron, she moved on to her gruesome
harvest. The accidental chumming of the man Anna'd known
only as a finger and a half had attracted scavenger fish. The only
ones Anna was concerned with were two largish sharks. One
swam close as if to assure its tiny prehistoric brain that she was
not shark food but a largish fish in her own right. Other than
that they showed no interest in her. She was careful to do nothing that might offend them.

Thirty minutes searching and she had gathered all she could
of what had once been a man. That it was a man was left in no
doubt. Trapped beneath a metal sink, blown intact from the gal-
ley, was half a penis. With a nod to John Wayne Bobbit, Anna
put it in her garbage bag. A line from an old Uncle Bonsai song
robbed the moment of its gruesomeness. *If I had a penis, I'd
still be a girl.* Anna bagged the evidence and wondered if the
song's prophecy would come true. If she'd make much more
money and conquer the world. Had ill-timed merriment not so
recently gotten her in trouble, Anna would have laughed.

Scavengers had carried away or eaten what the explosion
had not obliterated. She did not find the head—a failure for
which she was grateful—or much in the way of edible meat.
The right hand was recovered. It had been immersed in salt water for a while, and smaller fishes had been snacking on it, but
there was a good chance prints could still be lifted. Oddly
enough she found both feet together and relatively intact. One
was still wearing a bright blue flip-flop. Because of their humanity it was these and not the coarser discoveries of a shoulder and clavicle or a part of a ribcage that got to Anna. Before

she'd had time to do more than rip out her mouthpiece, she
vomited. Immediately schools of tiny fish rushed over to par-
take of the unexpected bounty.

Life goes on.

Topside, the bits and pieces in the garbage bag disturbed her
more than the actual handling of them underwater. Flopped on
deck they became somehow more real. Feeling a little silly but
doing it just the same, she covered the black plastic sack with a
yellow tarp so she wouldn't have to see it on the trip back.

Not stopping to put tank and vest away, she gathered up the
four corners of the yellow tarp, the black plastic shroud tucked
inside, and walked toward the fort as quickly as she could without drawing attention to herself.

It was three o'clock. Tourists crowded beach and dock, gathering to get back onto the catamaran for the two-hour trip back
to Key West. Three giggling girls, the littlest not more than
eight or ten years old, caught up in a windstorm of their own
making, tumbled into her as she stepped from the sand onto the
planks of the drawbridge. One collided with the yellow tarp. In-
voluntarily Anna cried, "Oh, God!" as if she carried fine china
or nitroglycerin.

The child was unharmed, her spirits undimmed by this colli-
sion with death in the least attractive of its myriad forms.
Breathing out her relief, Anna became aware she was too
tightly strung. Consciously getting a grip on herself she hurried
toward the researchers' dorm and the chest freezer.

"Hey, what did you bring me?" Daniel called as she passed
the shop.

"Takeout," was her first thought and "seafood" her second,
but to hold the thoughts more than a nanosecond would have
brought on a second attack of nausea.

"Don't ask," she hollered back.

Alone in the researchers' dorm, she tied an apron she found
in one of the drawers over her swimsuit and donned a fresh pair
of latex gloves. Feeling more like Dr. Frankenstein than
Quincy, she sorted through the bits of bone and flesh, bagging
each separately. Forensic pathology was an alien science to her.
It grew and changed on a monthly basis as brains and technol-
ogy raced each other into an unknowable future. Bagging the
hand, she wondered if freezing it would further destroy the

whorls and ridges making identification harder—or impossible. Till she could ask someone, she decided to put it in the refrigerator. The rest went into the freezer like so much venison to await its ride to Key West on the *Activa*.

After a shower, longer and hotter than necessary for rudimentary hygiene, Anna chose to cleanse her mind of the contents of the black garbage bag by being the bearer of glad tidings. Sequestered in her tomblike office against the east rampart, the undersized door closed for privacy, she called the number where Lanny Wilcox was staying in Miami.

A woman with a lilting Spanish accent answered the phone, then went to see if "Mr. Wilcox is taking calls." Not an auspicious beginning. Anna wondered if Lanny was under the care of a nurse. There had been those unfortunates during her college years who had slid over the line while on LSD and were marooned in that place where monsters manifest.

"He's coming," the woman's voice promised after a while. Anna waited so long she thought she'd been forgotten or disconnected. She was debating whether or not to hang up and dial again when Wilcox finally came on the line.

"This is Lanny Wilcox."

At least that's what Anna assumed "iss iss anny Wilks" translated to. The man sounded drugged to the gills. Anna pictured him in a cheap tatty robe in a room full of droolers of whom he was one.

"Lanny, this is Anna Pigeon. I took over as Supervisory Ranger when you got sick." A long silence followed. Faint as a drunken memory, Anna heard clicking over the line or the microwaves or whatever. She imagined it to be the clogged gears of Lanny's brain beginning to move. Finally he managed a word.

"Yeah?"

"Yeah. I called to tell you you are not crazy. While you were out here somebody spiked your water with a hallucinogen. What kind I don't know yet but I will. They did the same thing to me. I was seeing all kinds of strange shit for a while."

Another silence, longer this time, then: "Not crazy?"

He didn't sound exactly thrilled by the prospect of incipient sanity. In fact, he didn't sound sane. "What meds have they got you on, Lanny?"

"Uh," a pause perhaps to drool or think or both, "Lithium I think and other stuff. Since I got it I haven't had ... you know ... visions."

"Quit taking it," Anna said. Then, thinking better of this over-the-phone prescribing and ever-mindful of the litigiousness of the American spirit, she amended it. "Talk to your shrink. Tell him what I told you—"

"Her. It's a her."

"Her then. Tell her what I told you."

Lanny said nothing. "What did I tell you?" Anna asked.

"Uh. Not crazy."

"That's right, Lanny. You are not crazy. What else?"

"Somebody was poisoning me."

Hearing her words repeated by a man on heavy antipsychotics, Anna realized the revelation sounded exactly like what Lanny would say if he was a paranoid schizophrenic or suffered any of a number of other mental illnesses.

"What's your psychiatrist's name?"

"Dr. Kelly. I'm not crazy?"

He was beginning to warm to the idea. "That's right, Lanny. Does she live in Miami? Have a practice there? What's the name of the practice? Do you have her number?"

The rapid-fire questioning was too much for him. "I got to give you to Anita," he said, and Anna heard the receiver crash against the table or maybe the floor.

"Anita speaking," was the next sign of life. Anna'd never much liked the name Anita, but the way this woman pronounced it made it pretty.

"Anita, could you give me Dr. Kelly's phone number please?"

"I have two. One for emergencies and one for regular. Which do you like?"

"Give them both to me." Anna copied down the numbers, then repeated them back. Anita seemed proud of her for getting them both right. Chore accomplished, Anna asked if she could speak with Lanny again. Anita didn't think this was such a good idea. Apparently the news he'd been first drugged into insanity by the criminal element and then drugged into another form of the same malady by the medical community had agitated him.

After Anna twice promised to keep it short and "nice" Lanny was again put on the phone.

"One question before I let you go, Lanny. I had cause to go into your quarters. There are no pictures of Theresa. Did you get rid of them?"

"Theresa left me."

"Right. And did you get mad and get rid of any pictures you had of her?"

"I want to keep the pictures. She left me but I love her."

Anna decided to be "nice" and take that as a "no" he did not get rid of the pictures. "I'll talk to you again when you're feeling better."

"Okay," he said obediently but didn't hang up.

Anna did. She could picture him standing at the phone table with the receiver to his ear till somebody thought to come and lead him away.

Much as she hated to talk to doctors who weren't related to her by blood, she felt she owed it to Wilcox not to put off the call to his psychiatrist. Using the emergency number, she got the doctor after less than twenty minutes of holding. Having briefly explained who she was and the annoying delay on the phone line, Anna told her about the drugging of the water.

Anna didn't know what she'd expected. Maybe a "Yippee" or "I'll get right on that" or a least a "Thank you." None of these transpired. The doctor's voice, warm and solicitous when she'd first come to the phone, had cooled significantly.

"Miss . . . ?"

"Pigeon," Anna filled in for her.

"Yes. Miss Pigeon. As you are not a physician or a family member I can't discuss his case with you. Suffice to say I have spent time with Mr. Wilcox and his symptoms indicated the course of medications I prescribed."

Anna wasn't the only one scared to death of being sued. "He would have," Anna said in what she hoped were comforting tones. "The guy was being fed some kind of hallucinogen. He's been off of them for what, three weeks? He should have come down by now."

"I've been practicing a good while, Miss Pigeon. I think you had better let me judge the medical needs of my patients. Good day."

Boom. Silence. "The bitch hung up on me," Anna announced to the empty office. Dr. Kelly hadn't been afraid of getting sued; she'd been affronted at being told she was wrong. Who knew how long she'd keep Lanny on antipsychotics just to prove to herself she wasn't. Calling back would only make matters worse. Anna couldn't bring herself to leave a fellow ranger trapped in a bad production of *One Flew Over the Cuckoo's Nest*. Much as she hated to make public the news that there was a vicious prankster in the fort—or a perpetrator whose motives were as unknown as his identity—before she'd had a chance to work it out, she culled through Lanny's Rolodex and called half a dozen of the most pertinent names: a sister in Philadelphia, a son who worked for Goldman Sachs in Vero Beach, Lanny's general practitioner in Key West and the Chief Ranger of Everglades and Dry Tortugas National Parks in Homestead, Florida. Surely one of them would be better able to rescue Lanny than she was.

The Chief Ranger, Arnie Flescher, kept her on the phone for three-quarters of an hour. She was given a much-deserved earful for not calling him immediately on the accident with the motor shifting and her realization of the drugging. Fortunately she had been Johnny-on-the-spot with her phone reports on the sinking of the two boats and the injury of Bob Shaw.

Once she had been reprimanded and showed herself properly contrite, he got down to park business. Because of the difficulty of communication with Garden Key, coupled with the fact that as an acting Supervisory Ranger Anna didn't have a working relationship with the various Florida law-enforcement agencies, Arnie himself would take over tracing the identity of the two dead men and the green Scarab. He also promised to follow up on Theresa Alvarez's whereabouts and to question her about Lanny's drugging if they found her. If they didn't find her, he'd file a missing person's report.

"If we don't track down this girl, it doesn't necessarily mean she's met with foul play," Chief Ranger Flescher warned. "The Cuban community looks after their own. That doesn't always coincide with the needs of law enforcement."

Anna thanked him for the help and the warning and hung up

feeling a good deal better than she had. Asking for help: what a concept. She made a mental note to do it more often. Though she was only "acting"—a stranger to the park and the environment—she'd gotten in over her head both literally and figuratively and never once had it occurred to her to call for help.

"It's called teamwork, you idiot," she said to the ghostly reflection of her face in the computer screen.

Vaguely she remembered she'd wanted to accomplish three things before she called it a day. The third escaped her, and for a while she sat in the office chair, swinging back and forth, staring mindlessly at the blank computer screen.

Pictures. It had finally floated into the accessible part of her brain. Lanny hadn't been the one to weed out those of his departed girlfriend. With that information, the few bad snapshots of Theresa that had been overlooked became more interesting. Since the pictures had not been banished by a brokenhearted lover there had to be another reason they were gone. Either the picture abductor had a serious passion for Theresa and stole pictures rather than panties to sate it or they'd been removed because they might show something that would harm the thief.

The few snaps Anna'd gotten from Lanny's box were in her desk drawer. She took them out and turned her chair to better catch the slice of light leaking through the firing slit. A beautiful woman without much in the way of clothing. None of the shots caught her face. Why steal the face pictures? Identification? Surely a woman as good-looking as Theresa Alvarez had photos scattered behind her like breadcrumbs. She could probably follow them back to the first boyfriend she ever had.

Pawing through the desk, Anna unearthed a Sherlock Holmes–style magnifying glass and amused herself looking at the pictures in extreme close-up. Even high-powered magnification didn't reveal a single blemish on Miss Alvarez's behind. Pity. Anna moved the glass over to one of the dark-haired men—both with their backs to the camera—who stood with Theresa on the startling white sand of the beach between the northwestern bastion and the old coaling docks.

"Eureka," she said, and, "Hah!" At last she'd found a connection.

20

My eyes adjusted quickly to the dim interior of the powder room. To my knowledge there has never been gunpowder stored in these strange little rooms. With the war over and the fort, though unfinished, already obsolete, there may never come a time when gunpowder will be warehoused here.

So, but for Tilly and a pile of board ends left from the unfinished walls lining the chamber, it was empty, airless and stiflingly hot. That Tilly was alone at first relieved me of some of my worry. Then I saw what sorry shape the poor thing was in. She lay crumpled on the far side of the scrap lumber. Her hair had come down and was pasted in sweaty strands across flushed cheeks. Dress, hands and face were streaked with dust and sawdust. So much had adhered to her face, even in the questionable light I could see the cleaner tracks where tears had cut through the grime. Her eyes were closed and her left hand pressed, palm on her nose, fingers on her forehead, as if she kept her face from falling off her skull. The back of her hand was bloody and her knuckles scraped.

With the worry and embarrassment she'd caused me I'd thought when I found her I would shake her till her little pea brain rattled in her head. The moment I laid eyes on her that thought was as if it had never been.

Because she was alive, I could not be angry anymore. Because she was so clearly hurt my heart broke for her. My first thought was of the worst. The rough soldiers, Sinapp with his hot eyes, the chase—one might think in a place so overcrowded as this there would be nowhere away from prying eyes or helping hands to assault a young girl. Such is not the case. There are a few such corners isolated amidst the clamor. The powder storage rooms would serve very well. A cry might not be heard over the sound of building and men's voices.

"Tilly," I said and was surprised to hear my voice break with tears. She lowered her hand and I was glad to see her face was unmarked with anything more damaging than dirt. When she saw me she did not stand but held her arms out the way she used to when she was a little thing and wanted one of us to lift her up.

Risking a rusty nail through the soles of my soft slippers, I went to her and held her. Safe or repentant or just emotionally strained, she began crying in earnest. After she'd wept the dust off of her face and onto the front of my white pin-tucked bodice, she settled down. I got her to sit up so I could have a look at her.

I was comforted by the fact that her buttons were buttoned, her laces laced and no part of her attire that I could see was torn. After she calmed somewhat I asked if she was hurt.

"No . . ." The word trailed off as if she wasn't sure or struggled to remember.

"Did anybody . . . did the men—"

"No!" She was sure this time and vehement. Pulling a little away from me she tried pushing her hair back into the bun she wore high on her head, a sign of womanhood I doubt she could have gotten away with at her age if she still lived with Molly.

"No," she repeated, looking ready to burst into a second flood of tears.

She acted at odds with herself—with me—the way she does when she's lying.

"I would never tell anyone, Tilly," I promised. "Not a word, not to Joseph, not to our sisters—" (This last part was a lie. I would have told you the first opportunity I had to get my hands on a pen.)

I truly meant it about not telling Joseph. Had the old Joseph found out she'd been assaulted, the men involved would be hanged. This new Joseph who has chosen to let a sergeant show disrespect might not mete out punishment. Besides, I didn't need Joseph. At that moment I sincerely believed that I would find someway to kill any man who hurt Tilly in that way myself. I still believe it but am deeply grateful I was not called upon to test it.

"I've not been touched," Tilly said. This was spoken in a rational tone and I believed her.

"Tell me what happened." This is a question that becomes all too common when one lives with our sister.

"I had . . . I went . . . I needed . . ."

The silly creature was trying to think of a way to get around the fact she'd been to the conspirators' cell alone. Saving her the effort and me the time, I said: "Went to Dr. Mudd's cell without me."

"Yes," she admitted.

"And not for the first time." She looked at me with such surprise, had my generosity not been taxed by the day she'd forced upon me I might have laughed.

Not ready to confess yet, she went on without addressing it. "Dr. Mudd wanted to see me about something important, he said."

"How did he say?" I demanded. "Did he send a message?"

Tilly realized the thin ice she walked on only when she heard it cracking. Not only Mudd but any soldier or inmate who assisted him could be whipped for carrying messages to a child of an officer without the express permission of that officer.

Rather than lie, she said nothing. I say that to her credit. On looking back, I do not believe Tilly to have told a single falsehood—at least not in words and at her tender age the nuances of deceit, omission, allowing presumption, half truths and misleading statements still seem to dwell on the side of godliness if only just barely. Sam Arnold's warning came back to me then. He'd said Dr. Mudd was taking advantage of Tilly's admiration of him, using her for his own ends.

"Go on," I said when it was clear my ominous silence and baleful stare were not going to coerce any more out of her on the subject of Dr. Mudd's summons.

"I went there—to Dr. Mudd—and we talked."

"What about?" At first I thought she wasn't going to tell me but would add it to the list of secrets that were aging us both far more efficiently than the passage of time ever could. A light came into her eyes and she leaned in toward me, lips parted. She wanted to tell me—tell someone. The secret was positively dancing a jig on the tip of her tongue. Still she hesitated. My guess was she'd been told by our illustrious prisoner not to.

This time my hopeful silence worked.

"You must promise not to tell," she insisted.

Of course I promised, but with every intention of breaking it, and so endangering my immortal soul, should keeping Tilly's secret place her in harm's way.

"Dr. Mudd is innocent," she whispered triumphantly.

I didn't respond to that. It was not much of a secret. He'd been insisting on it since the beginning, and Tilly had been saying much the same thing, thus earning the ill will of union soldiers and sympathizers at the fort. She seemed to take my silence as ignorance because she leaned ever closer, till our foreheads were nearly touching.

"He didn't do it, he didn't have anything to do with the assassination of poor Mr. Lincoln."

"I know what you meant," I said with some asperity. "You told the soldiers as much after you left his cell, did you not?"

Again she gave me that look of foolish astonishment, amazed that an adult might have done homework of her own.

"Yes. But I now have the proof of it."

"Do you have it with you?" I asked.

I must take back what I said about her never having lied outright. She did so twice. This was the first.

"No," she told me and had the decency to turn her head away to save me the disrespect of lying to my face.

There was little I could do short of wrestling her down in the dust and searching her pockets and person, so I let it pass.

I changed the subject. "How did you scrape the back of your hand? It's bleeding."

This was the second lie: "I fell."

I waited in hopes she would see the error of her ways and tell me the truth, but she didn't.

"I came out of the cell and Sergeant Sinapp and some of his men were loitering there," she volunteered, as if this late and little bit of honesty would wipe away the other. "I don't know if they were waiting for me or if they'd gathered in that particular place by chance. That sergeant—I hate him, Raffia. I know Molly says it's wrong to hate and I don't think I've ever hated anyone before, not truly, but I hate Sergeant Sinapp."

She looked at me, waiting for a reprimand I expect, but as that would have been the pot calling the kettle black, I said nothing.

"Anyway, he started saying things about my being in with the prisoners, awful things that just aren't true but are no less hurtful and hateful because they're lies." Tears filled her eyes again.

I ignored it. "So you told him why you'd really been there," I said.

"Yes."

"To gather evidence—proof—that the man condemned by the highest court in the union after weeks of testimony and evidence was actually and against all odds innocent."

"Yes."

"And that you had this proof."

"Oh, Raffia," she burst out. "He was so awful and so smug and superior."

"Tilly, if Dr. Mudd really did have proof of his innocence, don't you think he would have brought it up at the trial rather than wait till he was incarcerated a million miles from home and then entrust it to a sixteen-year-old Yankee girl?"

"But he didn't have it then. Don't you see?" she pleaded.

"So here on a key made of sand in a fort he's never been to before he found something that exonerates him. That makes no sense, Tilly."

"No. No," she said. "He didn't find it, it came."

"In the mail?"

Tilly seemed to think she'd told me too much. Her face, open with enthusiasm moments before, grew still and closed.

I tried a different argument. "If he'd gotten something that could win him his freedom, don't you think he would have called Joseph immediately? Why the secrecy? Why give it to you?"

"He didn't want it destroyed."

"By whom?" I asked, but Tilly wouldn't tell me any more. Clearly any and all persons but for herself were cast as the destroyers. I gave up. "When you came out of the cell, what did he do, Sergeant Sinapp?"

"I hate him," she repeated with even more vehemence than the first few times. "He said, 'Let me see it.' I started to leave and he grabbed at me. Then they were all grabbing at me and I got away and ran. The others stayed but he came after me. I heard a crash and some cursing but I didn't look back. I kept running. I think he tripped over one of the cats that likes to sun itself on the stored lumber." She was quiet for a moment, then she added: "I've always liked cats. Do you think we might feed them?"

I laughed then, and she knew she'd won me over for the time being. "I like cats too," I told her. "Let's get you home." With spit and spanking I managed to get enough of the dust and the mud her tears had made of it off of her face and clothes that we would not invite comments when we crossed the parade ground.

Back in our rooms I put Luanne in a foul humor by ordering a tub filled though it was Wednesday. The bath was partly because I do love our troublesome sibling and partly because I wished to search her dress. I did not let her out of my sight between leaving the powder room and seeing her naked in the bath. I did search her pockets but, by the willingness with which she turned the garments over to me, I knew I would find nothing.

Because she'd lied to me and because she had something she didn't want me to find, she watched me as closely as I watched her. I'd hoped to leave her alone in the tub so I might slip back to the powder room and see if I could find this spurious "proof" she'd been given.

Tilly kept me at her side, first washing her back then brushing her hair dry. She insisted we have tea. I don't think she knew what was in my mind and hoped to keep me away from the powder room where I'm convinced she hid this "proof." (Why else would her hands be scraped raw? I believe she shoved whatever it was beneath the scrap lumber when she heard me calling.) No, for all her practicing at deceit, I believe she kept me beside her because she is young and afraid and her older sisters are the only parents she has known.

It was bedtime and full dark before she would let me out of her sight.

Before she awoke the following morning I was up and dressed and wending my way back to the middle of the northern rampart on the second tier. With me I had fish scraps to reward the pussycats that had brought down Sergeant Sinapp. The kittens are so adorable, one nearly all white but for a gray mark in the shape of a thumbprint on its head. I was tempted to bring it home, but I know Joseph would fly into a rage. I don't think I told you, but I tried it once before with a little gray-and-white tabby I'd named Pandora. Joseph raged and I let him and kept my cat for two days. She was gone on the third morning. Joseph had drowned her.

Joseph's hatred of cats stems, he says, from the fact that they are secretive beasts. Personally I cannot conceive of a creature with a brain the size of a walnut being that much cleverer than I, but to each his own. Perhaps it is a territorial thing. If cats are secretive then Joseph is the greatest tom of them all. He has never been forthcoming but of late he has been hiding things, I know it. Though never open with me, he's not deemed his activities—or my feelings—worthy of keeping things hidden before. This has changed. The other day, after a ship from the mainland came with mail, the fort went quiet while we all ran to pore over news from outside. I was sequestered in the bedroom, delighting in all your news from home, when I remembered I'd not given Luanne instructions for dinner. Lest I forget completely I decided to do it at once so I might enjoy my afternoon with you in clear conscience.

Joseph was at his desk in a widening of the hallway between our room and Tilly's, reading the letters he had received. When I came out of the bedroom—burst out, rather, as I was keen to execute my duty and get back to you—he shoved the letter he was holding inside his vest and snatched up another which he then pretended (rather badly) to be engrossed in.

Knowing it would avail me nothing but cold stares and colder silences, I did not confront him about it. I cannot but think he has taken a lover. Why else would he hide a letter from me? If she is from Key West, or the mainland proper, he must have met her some time ago, yet this is the first evidence of it I've had.

Though you most kindly pretend otherwise, I know you think little of my husband. This is my fault. I've used your shoulder to cry on when we had the usual peccadilloes of the professional soldier. Still, I have deep feelings for him, and the thought that one of these dalliances has survived, grown into a true relationship, hurt me. Probably it was something else entirely. Orders that cannot be shared or some such. Regardless, with Joseph hiding letters and Tilly secreting "proofs," I am beginning to feel I live in a house of secrets. That there is another life than the one I know flowing silently below the surface and, at any time, the barrier between the two could weaken and I could suddenly find myself plunged into events for which I am not prepared frightens me.

Other than a lovely few minutes watching the kittens devour my offerings, the journey was a disappointment. The previous evening the powder room had been filled with cannon barrels, wheels, pins and other pieces of ordnance. A worker, one of the colored boys used by the builder, said they'd no use for them now and the powder room was the only place they wouldn't be eaten up by rust right off. The lumber pile had not been moved. The iron parts had been dumped atop of it higgledy-piggledy. Without enlisting the help of half a dozen strong men I could not shift it to look beneath the pile.

My curiosity was not fated to be satisfied. It is my hope that this will be the end of the matter. If I cannot move the pieces of machinery then Tilly surely cannot. Should the mysterious "proof" be buried beneath it she will either have to tell Joseph so he can have it exhumed or she will have to leave it alone. Either would be acceptable to me.

As I was returning from this fruitless visit, picking my way through the lumber and unused brick where the kittens make their home, I heard a disturbance from the direction of Joel and the conspirators' cells. Curious, I hurried through the bastion to see what was causing the noise. With the powder room, Joseph's letter and the cats, I could not but think of the old saw about curiosity killing, but it didn't slow my steps.

The door to Joel's casemate cell stood open, moving slightly as if it had just been passed through in haste. From within came the sound of men fighting in close quarters. It occurs to me as I write this that over the years I have grown able to tell the different sorts of altercations by their sounds. This did not sound lethal, merely the thumps and grunts expected at the tail end of a fight between unequal adversaries.

Unbecoming as I'm sure it was, I went to the door and looked in. Joel leaned against the windowless wooden wall covering the arch overlooking the parade ground. The door in the small arch to his left, the one leading into the cell of Sam Arnold and Dr. Mudd, was open. Two soldiers pushed Mr. Arnold against the brick of the archway surrounding the communicating door. From the blood pouring out of his nose and the split in his lower lip it appeared they had been none too gentle.

"If it were up to me I'd just as soon let you bastards kill each other," said the soldier, whom I recognized as my overweight secret smoker of the other day. He was no longer the amiable lifer but was taut and alive with a fierceness I never would have expected. He had his forearm across Mr. Arnold's throat and held the man's right wrist pinned against the wall. A young soldier, smaller in stature—not much taller than I—struggled to hold Mr. Arnold's left arm.

Dr. Mudd was in the far corner beneath the three high, narrow slits on the harbor side, one hand held over his left ear as though it was injured. With the other he held the wrist of the ear-clutching hand. Very melodramatic. I thought that of his pose and expression as well: a picture of wounded innocence.

"You bunch are a goddamn fu—" the old soldier began.

"Mrs. Coleman," Mr. Arnold said quickly and loudly, saving the soldier from committing an offense—or imagined offense. I have heard the rough language of army men for so many years I have to remember to look appalled in order they not lose respect for their captain's wife.

The fight, what little of it remained, went out of soldiers and conspirator alike—and to think I once scoffed at the much-touted civilizing powers of the gentler sex. "Mrs. Coleman." My old fat friend acknowledged me with a nod of the head.

Not for a moment did he loose his hold on Mr. Arnold. The

younger soldier dropped Mr. Arnold's arm to pay his respects. A difference in experience, I expect. Fortunately for the young man, Mr. Arnold did not intend him harm.

"You gonna behave now?" the older soldier asked. Mr. Arnold nodded and, still watching and alert, the soldier lowered his arm from his throat, let loose his wrist, and backed away.

For the oddest moment we all simply looked at one another. What behavior we expected in that stuffy cell in the midst of the sea I cannot say. Dr. Mudd ended our peculiar paralysis.

"I request you take me to your surgeon. I fear my ear has been seriously injured," he said in his formal and overblown way.

My old smoking soldier jumped. I believe until that moment he had completely forgotten about Mudd, he had kept himself so still and deep in the shadows of a shadowy room.

"It would serve you right if you got hydrophobia and died," he growled at Dr. Mudd. "Next time you two decide to kill each other, unless you go an' do it quiet like, I'll personally kill you both for making me come up here."

"Death would be preferable to serving a life sentence with a whiner and a thief," Sam Arnold snarled.

You might laugh at me, Peggy, for using "snarled" and "growled" and "snapped" when describing the conversations of men, but being in that cell was so like being in a pen with dogs standing one another off over a bone that I cannot think of another way to describe how they spoke to one another.

After the brief exchange, the old soldier blew out a prodigious sigh. The hackles he'd raised in his role as vicious fighting man fell away, age and humanity took their place.

"And what was it was took from you?" he asked of Mr. Arnold. I had the sense it was not the first time the question had been put.

Mr. Arnold said nothing for a moment. The first time in my memory of him he stood straight and strong, shoulders back, not slouching or leaning. Just when I thought he was not going to answer, he said:

"He stole a personal item of mine."

"And just what might that 'personal item' be?" the soldier asked.

Mr. Arnold ground his teeth. Not only could I see the muscles of his jaw working, I could hear the awful grating sound. Perhaps this is what is meant by "gnashing." "He took it from my mail," Mr. Arnold said. "Tampering with the mails is a serious offense."

Mudd laughed. The humor was bitter but his laughter wasn't unkind so much as sad. "What would you have them do, Sam? Add twenty years to my life sentence? Were that true you would have discovered the secret to eternal life."

"We'll search him," the old soldier said wearily. "Will that keep you from cuttin' up and throwing the furniture, such as it is?"

"Search him," Mr. Arnold said.

"We got to search him for something. We ain't gonna just turn out his pockets so's you can pick and choose. What're we looking for? A ring, a pork chop, eyeglasses—what?"

Mr. Arnold refused to speak.

"Suit yourself. Come on, doctor, we'll get your ear looked at though I'm of half a mind to rip it clear off just to work off the irritation you two caused me."

On impulse I asked if I might stay a minute to look after Joel. The slight young private was left to see to me, and the others left, closing the door behind them.

"What did he take from you, Mr. Arnold?" Why I thought he would tell me what he had withheld from the soldiers I do not know, but I did. In this I was wrong.

"Please excuse me, Mrs. Coleman," he said and retired to his own cell, shutting the communicating door.

I turned to where Private Lane cowered against the wall. "Cower" is too strong a word and sounds as if I think of him unkindly. That is not the case. Since his terrible beating he is a very different boy. Before Sinapp nearly killed him, he was a joyous boy on his way to becoming a strong man. Now he seems only and always a boy, and the joyousness is replaced by watchfulness and too great a dependence on those he feels to be his friends: Dr. Mudd, Tilly and me. "Joel?" I said. "Are you all right?"

"Yes, ma'am. It was nothing to do with me."

"Come over here; sit in the light where I can look at you," I said. Obediently he came to where I waited in the dull light from high openings. I'd spoken before I'd thought. The cell contained but a single stool made of scrap lumber. A gift from one of the guards.

He fetched it for me then knelt so I needn't look up at him.

"What was this about?"

"I don't really know. Sam and the doctor been at odds since I got here. Lately the doctor's been hectoring Sam about him being innocent. You'd think Sam would know whether he was or not, wouldn't you?"

I nodded to keep him talking.

"Today Sam went wild over something. I heard him screaming and breaking the little bits of furniture, calling the doctor a thief and the doctor calling him names and saying, 'You would have me die with scum like you' and other things. Then the guards came."

"You don't know what was stolen?" I asked.

He shifted uncomfortably. The brick was beginning to hurt his knees. I wanted to keep his attention for a while longer so I didn't give him leave to rise. "I don't even know that a thing was stolen," he told me.

"You mean Mr. Arnold lied? To what end?" I did not believe for a minute Mr. Arnold lied. His face was too full of emotion for that.

"No. Not lied," Joel said. "Dr. Mudd took something but maybe not a *thing*. Maybe information or an idea or a secret. I say that because Sam tore the room up and pretty much handled Dr. Mudd till the soldiers came. I think he'd have found a *thing*. Where could anybody hide anything here?" He shrugged at the unforgiving brick and board around, above and below us.

I said nothing but it struck me that Sam Arnold's property might have been stolen earlier and he'd only just this morning noticed it missing. Were that the case, I knew well where this *thing* could have been hidden. In my little sister's pocket.

21

Anna indulged herself in an early and quiet evening. She read Raffia's letters, then went to bed before dark. The following morning she woke, feeling more clearheaded than she had in days.

For the first time since she'd come to the Keys, the morning wasn't bright and sunny. A stiff breeze blew out of the southeast. The sky was heavy with dark clouds and, where they broke open, she could see paler gray clouds above, long, stretched, mare's tails that told of winds at high altitudes.

In the office she turned the radio on and tuned it to the marine weather frequency. Rain and winds to thirty knots. Small craft warnings were out. No hurricane. Anna was disappointed. Had she been a shore-bound homeowner she'd have been relieved. Out on Garden Key the fort had withstood a hundred and fifty years of storms with little damage. The rangers liked hurricanes; they blew the tourists away.

Feeling snug behind fifteen feet of brick wall, she took out the photograph she'd studied the day before.

Just to be sure residual drugs in her bloodstream weren't making her see things, she downloaded the pictures she had taken of the corpse Bob Shaw kept company with on East Key.

Sure enough, on the dead man's calf was the same tattoo as

in the snapshot of Theresa and two Hispanic men she'd pilfered
from Lanny's house. Given this tattoo was the mark of a broth-
erhood of smugglers, as Florida law enforcement said, it was
safe to assume more than one man had it. The height, weight,
hair length and coloring of the corpse and Ms. Alvarez's companion also matched.

It was the same guy.

Anna turned from the photos to let her mind clear. The run-
away girlfriend had spoken with the man on the Scarab hauling
fuel. Theresa was Cuban. It was a good bet in this part of the
country the two Hispanic men with her were Cuban as well.
The second man might very well be the fellow whose penis and
hand rested in cold storage in the researchers' dorm. Garden
Key was a small place. The three of them might have met by
chance, gathered together in birds-of-a-feather mode to speak
their native language or exchange recipes.

Anna doubted it. The men killed in the Scarab's explosion
were here for reasons other than socializing. It was their knee-
jerk reaction to run from the law in the person of Ranger Shaw,
which brought about the original blast. They must have had a
pressing reason to come to the docks and beaches where
rangers lurked, a pressing need to talk with Theresa.

Anna flipped over the photograph of Ms. Alvarez and the
men to check the date. The picture had been printed in Key
West a week or so after Theresa left Lanny. Anna called up the
prior month's duty roster. Lanny had his days off the week the
photo was printed. The timing was right but what mattered was
when the photo was taken.

Again she dialed Lanny's number. Anita answered, and after
a minute of cajoling went to fetch her patient or master—Anna
still wasn't sure what sort of place Lanny was living in.

At length his voice came over the phone. Anna thought he
sounded marginally sharper, but sufficient time had not passed
for the antipsychotics to wear off even if he remembered not to
keep taking them.

No other avenue open, she asked her questions, couching
each in simple descriptive language to help him remember.
Since he was in a particularly suggestible state, she had to con-
centrate on her words lest she create a false memory for him.

The talk, though mumbling, often slurred and beset by me-

anderings, was not completely a waste of time. Lanny might remember the picture. He might have taken it himself. He must
have had it developed on his lieu days if that's what the date
was. If all that could be so, then it might have been the roll he
finished up the day before Theresa left.

Not exactly testimony Anna would want to put before a jury.

The radio crackling snatched her out of this morass of
thoughts.

"Hey Anna, it's Patrice, are you there?" the lighthouse
keeper said. Though Patrice and Donna had been coming to
Loggerhead one month a summer for many years, and Patrice
had once been a police officer, they refused to use proper radio
protocol. It was a point of pride with them.

"I'm here," Anna said and smiled. The rebel women made
the male-created radio protocol seem foolish: boys playing at
being soldiers.

"While Donna was up in the lighthouse fiddling with something greasy she spotted another one of your go-fast boats.
Thought you might want to know."

Go-fast boats weren't a rarity in the Dry Tortugas but neither
were they the usual fare. Recent events made this sighting of interest. Anna jotted down the color of the boat and the direction
it had been heading, thanked Patrice and went back to her tele-
phoning, this time tracking down the owner of the green boat.
Since she'd turned this particular task over to Lieutenant
George Henriquez in Key West, she was relegated to the job of
nag. Accepting the new role, she dialed his number.

Luck was on her side; George was in and answering his
phone. It might have been her imagination or her inborn cynicism, but it seemed with each new invention developed to make
communication easier—call waiting, forwarding, voice mail,
fax, pagers, cell phones—the more difficult it became to get in
touch with anyone.

"Hey George, Anna Pigeon out at Dry Tortugas." She heard
a sigh and a shuffle and knew her projects had not been on the
top of Lieutenant Henriquez's undoubtedly daunting To Do list.

He was kind enough to be apologetic instead of peevish.
He'd faxed the registration number she'd gotten off the engine
to Manny Silva in the coast guard office. He gave her Mr.
Silva's direct number and the extension. On the Theresa Al-

varez thing he'd gotten a few numbers, which he passed on to her.

The boat registration could wait. Theresa's connection to the men on the boat would not. Anna dialed the first of the numbers Lieutenant Henriquez had given her, a Mrs. Alvarez, Theresa's aunt on her father's side.

Mrs. Alvarez was home. No number menu to punch, no machine; a human voice. The woman's English was not the best and Anna's Spanish was rudimentary, but they managed.

Anna introduced herself and said why she was calling. Through a patient sifting of words in two languages and the aggravating delays on the line, Anna pieced together a short and unenlightening story. Theresa was happy with Lanny. She'd never mentioned leaving him. She'd never come home. According to the aunt, Theresa was a good girl, "never in no trouble," and had strong ties with her community. "Everybody love our Theresa. She always doing for people."

Theresa was not an American citizen but was in Florida legally. When Anna asked after Theresa's mother, father and Mrs. Alvarez herself regarding the immigration issues, the aunt suddenly lost what English she had.

Out of questions and Mrs. Alvarez frightened into *"Sí"* and *"No comprendo,"* Anna was about to begin her thank-yous when Theresa's aunt had a sudden attack of confidences.

"Something bad happened. Theresa don't just not come home. And she don't walk out on Lanny. When Willy he introduces them, Theresa seemed not to care, like she's pretending. But Theresa loved that Lanny even he's an old man for her and not rich. Something bad happened."

Anna tended to agree that something bad had happened to Theresa. "I'll look into it," she promised and put the receiver back in its cradle, not much wiser than before she'd made the translingual call. Before she'd had time to let go of the receiver, her mind clicked back to Mrs. Alvarez's last remarks. "When Willy introduced them." Willy, William.

"Shit," Anna said, picked the receiver back up, and hit redial.

"This is Ranger Pigeon again, Mrs. Alvarez," Anna said as soon as the other woman picked up.

"Hallo?"

Realizing she'd rattled her words so quickly Mrs. Alvarez

probably wouldn't have understood even if English had been her first language, Anna repeated herself at a more genteel pace.

"Yes?" During the second Anna'd needed to reach epiphany Mrs. Alvarez had thought better of talking openly with government authorities.

"Who did you say introduced Lanny and Theresa?" Anna asked.

"Willy, he introduce them," she said guardedly.

Anna wanted Willy's last name but had a hunch her calling back so abruptly had scared Mrs. Alvarez more than a little. "Is Willy American?" Anna asked. "I'm not from immigration, Mrs. Alvarez, and I don't want to cause anybody trouble. I just want to find Theresa. I think this Willy may know something. Is he an American?"

"Oh yes. He is an American now," Mrs. Alvarez replied.

Anna felt a pang of disappointment strong enough it was physical. She had been so sure she was onto something, she was tempted to think Theresa's aunt was lying, but she'd answered with such enthusiasm Anna believed her. Basically decent people preferred to tell the truth and often grew angry when backed into a corner they had to lie their way out of. It was exactly the opposite with those who were not basically decent. Willy was not born in America. He was originally a citizen of Cuba. To finish up the charade Anna would ask another couple of questions and move on. "So Willy came here when he was little? With his folks?"

"No. No. His parents they got killed. This lady—nice lady, she been dead a long time now—he call *Tia Blanche*—Auntie Blanche—she raised him up. Such a sad little boy. You would cry to see him. Marks of those *chingalas* still on his body."

Anna sat up from the slump her disappointment had lured her into. "What marks?"

"This was a long time ago when Castro he throw out all the Americans and snatch lands. Some of his men they tortured this little boy. Willy never said but Blanche tell me they whip him over and over with barbed wire to try and make a baby tell them where his mama and papa hide. Then they kill them."

Without realizing she did so, Anna put her free hand over her eyes as if it would help to block out the image in her mind. To torture a child with a brutal beating that would leave scars in body and mind was evil. To force that child to betray his parents to their deaths was unspeakable. It would almost have been kinder to kill him.

Barbed wire. Her hunch about Willy was correct. "The little boy was born in Cuba?" Anna asked.

"Yes, but his papa was American so Willy is an American, too, without taking no tests."

"Willy—William—Macintyre."

"Sí. Macintyre. His papa's name."

William Macintyre, Mack, the man who said he'd been born into land and money but had it stripped from him. The man with old scars on his back and legs, scars he'd said he'd gotten in prison when he had no felony record, the boy who'd been whipped with barbed wire by guards in a Cuban prison before he was six years old.

"Gracias, Señora Alvarez," Anna said politely and returned the earpiece to its cradle.

Mack had more depth to him than she had suspected. He was born in Cuba and raised in a Cuban neighborhood in Miami. The same neighborhood as Theresa Alvarez. Anna'd thought she'd met Theresa here at the fort. He'd never said otherwise—apparently not to anyone. Surely if he had, with all the talk there'd been of Theresa's absconding with the Supervisory Ranger's heart, somebody would have mentioned it.

Theresa was photographed talking with two men, one bearing a smuggler's tattoo Anna'd later seen on a dead man. Odds were good that Theresa had known these men prior to moving to Garden Key. Had Mack known them as well?

Anna considered calling Lanny Wilcox again to see if she could get the details out of him: where and when he'd met Theresa, if he knew she was more than a chance acquaintance of Mack's, whether or not the course of true love had run smooth, and, possibly most important, whose idea had it been that Theresa come to live with him on Garden Key. The state of Wilcox's brain dissuaded her. He wouldn't be able to tell her much, and what he did divulge would be highly suspect.

Anna put in a call to the Chief Ranger in Homestead. This time she did have to push menu buttons, speak with a secretary and sit on hold for a while. When Flescher came on the line

Anna told him what she needed. "You're bound to have more clout than I do," she said. "Can you work it out?"

"I'll call you back."

He hung up before Anna had finished the bye in goodbye. She didn't know whether he was in a rush to get right on it or whether he needed time to decide whether or not to waste his credit with the local FBI on the say-so of some lady ranger out of Mississippi who had a reputation for stirring up trouble.

For forty-five minutes Anna waited by the phone. She didn't dare make any calls to follow up on the engine serial number lest she tie up the line. She couldn't leave the office for fear she would miss the call. Her mind was too scrambled to focus on anything else. To keep herself from pacing and rehearsing the four-letter words she'd learned after hours at Mercy High School, she clipped her nails, ordered Lanny's desk drawer and worked three crossword puzzles gleaned from a stack of old newspapers piled beside the coffee machine.

When the phone finally rang, she pounced upon it with such alacrity she knocked the receiver to the floor and had to drag it up by the cord.

"Dry Tortugas National Park."

"What are you doing? Playing hockey using the phone as a puck?"

It was Chief Ranger Arnie Flescher.

"Can you do it?"

"Let's slow down," he said.

Those words, spoken by a superior, usually segued into "No."

Anna made a point to say nothing, not the teensiest little peep that would give away the fact she was not really a team player.

"Cliff and the *Activa* will be out in a couple days. Why don't you hold off till then? Send the dead boatman's hand in and ID can be done in proper order at the lab. Finding out who these guys were has got to be attempted, but there's no rush on it that I can see."

Anna ran a quick check to make sure no snide words or sarcastic edges tainted words or tone, then said: "I think they may have had something to do with the disappearance of Theresa

Alvarez. I found a picture of her and the man Bob tried to rescue."

"Disappearance? I thought she ran off. Is this the guy she ran off with? We don't want to get a thick finger stirring in the domestic pot."

"Maybe she didn't run off."

"I don't want to hear this."

"How was it decided she'd run out on Lanny? Who said that? Lanny?"

There was a jumble of words as the chief and she talked over one another, forgetting the one-second wait the phone system levied.

"I don't know," the chief said at last. "It was just sort of known the way those things are."

"If she ran off she didn't take much with her and, according to her aunt, never showed up anywhere."

"Nope. Didn't want to hear that. Check it out."

"That's what I need your help with."

Several ticks of the big wall clock went by, the red second hand seeming to pause to gather its courage before each jump. "This is news," the chief said. His voice was sufficiently neutral Anna guessed he was pissed off. Chief Rangers—the good ones—do not like being kept in the dark.

"I just saw the picture," Anna said. "And I talked to Mrs. Alvarez only a few minutes before I called you. I mean, I'd seen the photo before, but I didn't recognize the guy till just now."

Probably because he wanted results, he didn't question her story. "Okay," he said after a bit of thought that came at Anna in edged silences. "Here's what you do. No guarantees. It depends on how good the prints you lift are. The submersion in water may be a help. It sort of puffs things up."

Though the instructions were short and simple, Anna wrote them down. She had no intention of screwing this up.

Finally free of the phone, she collected her fingerprinting kit and returned to the researchers' dorm. As she turned the key to let herself in, she had the sudden and horrible thought that the hand, her only way of finding out the identity of the man blown to smithereens on the green Scarab, would be gone. In her naiveté she'd not secured the body parts, not even thought of them as evidence and had made no effort to lock them up. Anyone at the fort could easily get the key to the dorm if they didn't already have one.

Her fears were unfounded. Sitting in the refrigerator, palm up in lonely supplication, was the most important remaining part of what had once been a human being. Having had his penis severed, the victim might not have agreed with her assessment on the varying levels of importance, but there were no national data banks for finding matches to penis prints.

From the rough and disengaged life these five fingers had suffered, the skin was perilously loose, and Anna handled the thing with extreme care. Using black ink, she would print only the thumb. Her knowledge of how printing worked after death and submersion was sketchy at best. Should her method somehow destroy the skin of the thumb, she wanted to leave the other four fingers for a technician more schooled than she.

Had the hand been newly dead, firm of flesh, she might have lifted the print on sticky tape. As it was she feared the tape would pull away flesh as well as ink. When she gripped the back of the hand to roll the thumb, she had a bad moment. Till then the hand had been merely an object of study. Feeling the give of the flesh, the familiar bone structure beneath, it reverted to a macabre chunk of a once-living person. Revulsion would have had her throw it away with a girlish shriek. Closing her eyes, she let the impulse pass, then carefully rolled out three prints. The first two were smudged. She'd used too much ink. The last was good.

Because it seemed wrong not to do so, disrespectful or at least untidy, she gently wiped the digit free of ink before restoring it to its temperature-controlled sarcophagus.

Following the Chief Ranger's instructions, she scanned the print into the computer and e-mailed it to the man he'd recommended at the FBI office in Miami. Chief Ranger Flescher had worked with the agent a time or two and knew the man to be an avid diver. Anything that helped keep the park pristine he was glad to do.

Anna also faxed him a copy, though the final printout probably wouldn't be clear enough to read.

Mission accomplished, she returned to her station at the phone. Ironically, never a big fan of telephones, she had spent a good bit of her life on them. Molly, whom she saw once a year if she was lucky, stayed close in mind and heart over the phone. The last semiserious relationship she'd had with a man—an FBI agent now married to her sister—had been conducted largely over the telephone. Still, she hated it as a woman on life support might come to detest the tubes and pumps that kept her among the living.

Knowing herself destined to live with this love/hate relationship for many more years, Anna dialed Manny Silva, Lieutenant Henriquez's contact in the coast guard. Her run of luck was at an end. Silva was out. She left a message on his voice mail and went home. Fortified with an egg-salad sandwich and a Coke, she hurried back toward the office.

It surprised her that the day was still gray, that the wind still blew. Crossing the parade ground, a few spatters of rain hit her face. Anna loved wild weather and threw her arms out as if to catch it. Wind made her crazy, like a cat in autumn leaves. An exhilarating sense of expectation. A hurricane would have been grand. The thought engendered a stab of guilt. Not all that many years ago Hurricane Andrew had devastated the town of Homestead. Park employees living there lost everything. Most didn't stay to rebuild but scattered to parks across the country. The demoralizing effect had been felt by the entire service.

Still and all . . . a hurricane would have been grand.

Having checked the answering machine to satisfy herself that she hadn't missed Manny Silva's call, she settled down with the old crossword puzzles.

Puzzles were done. Anna knew way more than she'd ever wanted to concerning what the paper in Key West considered news. Finally, the phone deigned to ring.

It wasn't Manny. It was Agent Tad Bronson of the FBI office in Miami. Before he would give Anna any information, she was forced to pay for it by talking dives and fishes and wrecks for a quarter of an hour. By bringing to bear what rudiments of southern hospitality she'd picked up in Mississippi, she managed not to snap, "Cut to the chase" even once.

Finally her patience was rewarded. "But I guess we've frittered away enough of the taxpayers' money on blue water. You'll be wanting to know about your fingerprints. Where'd you find this guy anyway?"

Anna paid another installment on the coveted information by telling Tad of the explosion, dives and body parts recovery.

"Well, we got a match on your boy," he said when she'd answered half a dozen questions on gear, water clarity and scavenger fishes.

'Bout goddamn time. "What did you turn up?"

"Guy's name is Ramon Diego, born in Cuba, came to the U.S. at the age of twelve with his mother. Became a citizen at twenty-two. No wants, no warrants. His prints were on file because he and his mom entered the U.S. illegally. Mother and son were kept in a holding area by immigration for a couple of months. That's where his prints got into the system."

"Anything else on him?" Anna asked.

"Nope, he lived a good clean life since coming to the promised land. No trouble. He hasn't gotten so much as a DUI, according to the records. I do have the DOB. According to his birth date, your guy would have been forty-three day before yesterday."

"I hope the fishes blew out the candles before they ate him," Anna said.

"What do you want this guy for?"

"I don't know yet," she said truthfully. "But he was up to something." Anna promised him the rest of the story next time he came to the park to dive, and he allowed her to disconnect.

Leaning back till two chair legs left the floor, Anna put her feet on Lanny Wilcox's desk. Thought came more easily when the body was disconnected from the earth. Two guys on a go-fast boat. One probably knew Theresa Alvarez. No ID on him yet. Prints probably not in the system. A tattoo supposedly favored by smugglers. The other guy on the boat was a Cuban refugee-become-U.S.-citizen. Given his age, he would have lived in Cuba around the time Castro threw out the landowning Americans, including William Macintyre's parents. Anna didn't know Mack's age. His skin was so sun-damaged it was impossible to tell. If he were younger than he looked, it was possible he'd met Diego either in Cuba when he was a little boy or in the refugee holding area in Florida.

She put her feet back on the floor. Too much speculation with too few facts. Nothing suggested Mack knew the men killed on the green boat, only that he knew Theresa and that she knew one of them.

Picking up the phone, she began punching in Manny Silva's number at the coast guard office. The receiver hadn't even cooled off completely from her last call. Thinking she'd probably end up with some bizarre fungus caused by holding damp plastic against her ear for too many hours, she settled in to listen to the rings, leave another message if need be.

"Manny Silva."

"Hallelujah."

"I beg your pardon?"

Manny Silva sounded like a parody of the generic Midwestern radio announcer. His voice held none of the salsa or music implied by the name. Anna missed it, while being glad communication would be facilitated.

Explaining her outburst would be a waste of time and she couldn't think of any way to do so that wouldn't carry the insult of implying he should have gotten back to her sooner.

She let it pass, introduced herself and reminded him that she was the lady who'd sent him the boat engine registration number by way of Lieutenant Henriquez.

"Yes. Yes. We did get something on that. Hold, please."

Anna would have given up coffee for a week to see this man. He didn't say "yeah" it was "yes" and his voice was so neutral and careful she pictured him looking more like a Bob Johnson and suffering mild embarrassment that a warmer-blooded ancestor had saddled him with a name he couldn't live up to.

"Here. I was going to call George with this. I didn't know there was a rush on it." He left a short silence for Anna to apologize and tell him there was no rush.

She'd taken against his voice and said nothing.

"The boat was bought from the manufacturer by Enrico's Marine Supply in Miami. It was purchased new in May of this year."

"Anything on who Enrico's sold it to?"

"Inquiries were made, but Enrico's was not forthcoming."

Manny Silva was not particularly forthcoming himself.

"Could you run it from the other end? If I gave you a name could you see if he had a boat registered anywhere in Florida?"

"Not everyone registers, licenses or even names their boats

for a variety of reasons, not all of them criminal, but yes, I can do that."

"Ramon Diego," Anna said and waited. The faint clicking of fingers on a keyboard passed the time. Manny evidently was not one to give out progress reports or make small talk.

"Nothing. Many Diegos. No Ramon Diego."

"How about boats reported stolen?"

"No. We ran that automatically. Only one Scarab was reported. It was last year's model and cherry-red in color. I suppose it could have been repainted and the year written down wrong."

"I'll check into it," Anna said but she wouldn't. She'd pawed through enough smithereens of the blasted boat, she was certain she would have noticed if there'd been a coat of red paint beneath the green.

She appreciated he'd wasted none of her time with chitchat and thanked him with a degree of genuine sincerity.

Her investigation had reached a dead end. On her lieu days she could rent a car and drive up to Miami to question the people at Enrico's, but it would be a waste of time. If they weren't telling the coast guard, they certainly weren't going to tell her. With no crime but dying in a boat not your own, she was nowhere near getting a subpoena.

For a while she sat like a lump, thinking of nothing at all. There were things she could do: check out the boat Patrice had reported, start writing the reports on Bob's injury and the loss of the *Bay Ranger.* None of the options struck her as entertaining. Sitting in a dim air-conditioned room with the phone to her ear had sapped her of motivation. A nap sounded good.

Three fifteen. The day was about shot anyway.

There was another call she could make, Anna realized. It was based on a hunch, but an informed hunch. The pieces she'd collected came together. Mack—William "Mack" Macintyre—and Theresa met in the Cuban neighborhood in Miami where they had grown up.

Once again she dialed the number of Theresa's aunt.

"Mrs. Alvarez, it's Anna Pigeon with the National Park Service again." Anna expected the woman to be irritated—as well she had a right to be. It was bad practice to call a source over and over. An officer should have her ducks in their assigned places in the row before making contact. Anna had started out with only a couple ducks and no row.

Fortunately Mrs. Alvarez was not only cooperative but sounded glad to get a third call. This welcome was fueled, Anna guessed, by the hope that finally the authorities were going to find her wayward niece. Anna suffered a momentary stab of guilt or sadness—the two had become so linked over the years she wasn't sure where one stopped and the other began. Theresa would probably never be found. If she were, it would be washed ashore on some lonely key, her body munched upon by crabs.

"One last question," Anna promised. "Do you know if Theresa knew a man named Ramon Diego?"

"He was a neighborhood boy." Mrs. Alvarez answered without hesitation. Anna wondered how many long-established white residents had such a working knowledge of who they lived and raised their children next door to.

"Does he still live there?"

"No. Old Mrs. Diego did till she died, but Ramon got a good job and I guess he travel all the time. We didn't see him for long times."

"Where did he get the job?" Anna asked.

"Some big boat place. I think he sells boats but I don't know for sure."

Again Anna thanked her and rang off. A big boat place. The Scarab was originally sold to Enrico's, which Anna had heard was a Cuban-owned and -operated marine supply in Miami. Enrico's had been investigated for harboring and/or employing illegal aliens.

One more call, Anna promised herself and reached for the phone. She didn't pick it up right away. Given Enrico's checkered past with authority figures, particularly those investigating the whereabouts and origins of Cuban immigrants, honesty would probably not be the most productive policy. The employees might be laboring under a double need for secrecy. Maybe they had something to hide and maybe, where they came from, the police weren't nice people who were trained not to hurt you if you didn't hurt them first.

She toyed with the idea of affecting a Spanish accent. From her years in Texas she was actually quite good at it. The idea was quickly abandoned. If the accent wasn't believed whoever answered would be put on guard. If it was they'd let loose in rapid-fire Spanish and Anna'd be lost.

She switched personas, picked up the phone and dialed.

"Enrico's Marina. *Buenos días.*" The voice was heavily and unapologetically Hispanic.

"Hey. This is Anna Putnam. I need to talk to Ramon Diego. Can you get him for me?"

"I'm sorry we do not know no Ramon Diego."

The woman said this quickly and with the pat disinterest of someone uttering a standard response. Anna doubted it was the truth. Or if it was, it was purely coincidental.

"Oh pooh," Anna said. "It's his goddaughter. She's been asking for him. This was the only place I knew to call. Shoot. She's only seven, and since the accident..." Anna let that hang there, hoping Cuban Hispanics had the same cultural love of family and children she'd noticed in Mexican-American women.

For a moment the woman said nothing, then she chose for the fictional child. "Give me your number. He comes in, I have him call."

Anna rattled off a Miami area code and the first seven numbers that came to mind. Nobody would be bothered; Ramon was through making telephone calls for this lifetime.

The office had grown dark. Living in the strange tunnels of telephone communications, Anna'd not noticed the light going. She glanced at the wall clock expecting to find half a day gone, but it was just after four. She walked to the window at the parade-ground side of the walled-in casemate and raised the blind. The sky was low and fast and dark. The trees, usually so serene in their brick-walled sanctuary, tossed their branches in wild celebration of the storm.

Anna turned on the office radio. It was already tuned to the weather frequency. Gale warnings. Gusts to fifty knots, seas six to ten feet. The hurricane Anna'd hoped for was not to be. She turned the radio off and sat down without bothering to turn on the lights. Darkness at midday called on the ancient in her bones, filled her with a sense of portents and omens. With the wild race of clouds and the trees in jubilation, the foreboding swelled to a strange expectation—of what, she didn't know.

Placing both hands palm down on Teddy's desk, she stared out the small window and let her mind race with the wind.

Theresa, Ramon Diego, Mack, all from the same neighborhood.
Diego and Mack both born in Cuba, both spending their first
months on American soil in immigration's custody. Diego em-
ployed by Enrico's, a marine supply known for its connection
with illegal aliens. Mack scarred at the hands of the Cuban military. Theresa, always supportive "of her people," introduced to
Lanny by Mack. Theresa who seemed uninterested in the older
man but moved out to Fort Jefferson to live with him. Theresa
who fell in love with Lanny later on.

Her first mistake. Very probably her last.

Then the go-fast boat exploding twice, once from the haste
of the pilot in his desire to avoid law enforcement, the second
time because the boat carried fuel. The boat from Enrico's, piloted by a boyhood friend of Mack and Theresa. Theresa who
was photographed with a man wearing the tattoo alleged to be
the mark of a smuggler's gang.

Patrice, on the radio, telling Anna she'd seen a red go-fast
boat headed east from Loggerhead. The only Scarab reported
stolen a red model. Had Anna been paying attention to what
was going on around her instead of keeping her ear and brain
affixed to the telephone, the obvious anomaly would have stuck
her.

The go-fast was headed east, out to sea. A tropical storm
watch had been on the radio since morning. Small craft would
have been fleeing for the coast.

"Jesus Christ," Anna muttered. "Not drugs."

She headed for the dock.

22

Following the quarrel and the removal of Dr. Mudd, Mr. Arnold retired to his cell and closed the door. When I'd done questioning Joel six ways from Sunday and learning nothing more than that the row between Mssrs. Mudd and Arnold had been the latter calling the former a thief and the former accusing the latter of being responsible for his prison woes, I determined to take the matter to Mr. Arnold, closed door or no. My rapping and calling "Mr. Arnold" was made somewhat easier by the fact that the cells at Fort Jefferson may very well end up being a man's home but by no stretch of the imagination can they be considered his castle.

Mr. Arnold opened the door and bowed ever so slightly but said nothing.

I told him about Tilly's experience with the union soldiers, how she'd boasted of having proof of Mudd's innocence. Despite Molly's constant reminders about airing our dirty linen in public, I told him that Tilly had been hiding papers or letters from me—or that I believed she had—and that I believed she had carried something away from his cell earlier and hidden it.

Several times he asked where I thought she might have hidden these supposed papers. Human nature is a peculiar thing. The moment I came to believe the whereabouts of an item or items regarding which he'd not yet confided in me were important to him was the moment I decided not to tell him. This once I was determined to keep my secrets, such as they were, till I found an honest person.

After too much cat's play, each of us batting at the crumpled bit of honesty we'd allowed ourselves, Mr. Arnold told me the following.

The mail had come several days before. Both he and Dr. Mudd had received letters and packages.

This much I know to be true—Tilly collected our mail then, from the guardroom where we asked to be brought to Joel that day; she'd taken the conspirators' mail to them. From here on I cannot say whether Mr. Arnold was telling me the truth or not. I expect he was but only so much as he wanted me to know.

Mr. Arnold went on to say that he had received an important communiqué regarding personal business. He'd left the *document*—he wouldn't trust me even to know if it were letter, deed, last will and testament or an old bar bill—in what he believed to be safekeeping. In his straightened circumstances this would be beneath the moss-filled mattress and the ropes of the beds they were recently provided with.

Tilly had come, ignored Joel, given Mr. Arnold cold looks, and spent her visit in whispered consultation with Samuel Mudd. Shortly thereafter Mr. Arnold had discovered his "document" was missing. He confronted Dr. Mudd. The doctor denied it. Arnold searched. There was a fight. Nothing was found.

He did give me one bit of useful information. Tilly had been to the cell half a dozen times by herself—the soldier escort remaining outside to smoke, undoubtedly. Each time she spent less time with Joel and more with Dr. Mudd, speaking earnestly in tones too low to make out the conversation.

In leaving, going most gratefully back out into the sunlight and ocean breezes, it occurred to me that the passing back and forth of secret notes—whether they be summons, sonnets or, as Tilly would have it, "proof"—might not be the whole of it; might not be the least of it.

Since Dr. Mudd was seen with John Wilkes Booth by a number of credible witnesses before the assassination, I doubt there can be any real proof that he did not know the man, as he claimed at trial. Given this, and accepting that Dr. Mudd is ad-

mittedly an intelligent man and has shown no other signs of being irrational, it does not follow that he is using our sister to
keep, save or transmit this hypothetical truth.

Romance was my second thought, but you know how it is
with the very young, Peggy. If Tilly were in love she wouldn't
be able to hide it for an instant.

All that remains that one might use a sixteen-year-old girl
for is a means to escape. I believe Dr. Mudd intends to try to escape from Garden Key and means for our sister to help him.

This is truly a dangerous game and one I cannot tell Joseph
of. Not yet. Not until I know how deeply involved Tilly has become.

These thoughts stinging behind my eyes and in my throat, I
hurried back to our quarters with every intention of confronting
Tilly, getting the truth out of the little beast if I had to hold her
head in the washtub till she told me or drowned.

I believe I would have—and would have been successful as
well. Tilly was not the only one of us girls to inherit grandmother's legendary stubbornness—but our quarters were as
tense and bitter and loud as the prison cells I had just quitted.

Apparently Sergeant Sinapp had run to Joseph with the tale
of Tilly's misbehavior. *Tilly's.* Joseph was in a rage. Neither the
white silent nor the red and shouting to which I've grown accustomed. This was unlike any I've seen. Joseph would not listen to my side. He would not listen to Tilly. Indeed he had
reduced her to a gray-faced ghost curled in my rocking chair.
He would not allow us to speak. "Not a word. Not one damn
word," he shouted every time I dared to so much as draw breath.

Joseph has always listened to my side when it comes to the
behavior of a soldier. Not (as I once thought) out of respect for
me, but out of a need to discipline, guide and improve the men
given into his care.

This lack of parity was not the only thing that showed him
so changed. Joseph's rages are much like those of the sea, full
of wind and crashing with a clean sense of righteous wrath.
This was different: hulking somehow, small and sneaking. I
cannot put my finger on the difference but I felt it was so.

Tilly was confined to her room for an unspecified sentence.
Both Tilly and I were forbidden any intercourse with Joel Lane,
Samuel Arnold, Dr. Mudd or any other confederate prisoners

residing at the fort. Joseph forbade me to speak with our sister then, knowing the ban would not stick, chose to keep me under his eye for the rest of the day.

While he worked at his desk between Tilly's room and ours, I was ordered to "work on my infernal correspondence" and so, of course, I am writing to you. Though Joseph's new and sulking ways alarm me, I must say that I find myself relieved at the edict that we are to stay away from the casemates over the guardhouse and that, to this end, the soldiers under Joseph's command have been ordered not to take us to the conspirators' cells or give us the key to go by ourselves.

What started out as an act of Christian charity—caring for poor Private Lane—has become perverted. I feel the influence Dr. Mudd has over Tilly is unhealthy for her spirit as well as making her a target for those at the fort who are still reeling from the assassination of Mr. Lincoln.

She is not the only one changed since the arrival of the Lincoln conspirators. If I am remembering correctly, Joseph's alteration commenced at about the same time. Or, rather, I should say I began noticing it then. Our lives here were cheerful and productive before they came—if one can say that of a life led on a prison island. Now it feels the very sunlight has soured and strikes like a fist and not its customary wet welcome, like the tongue of a large and gleeful dog.

I've not yet decided whether or not to tell Joseph of Tilly's fleeing to the powder room with her "proof." As long as it is buried under a ton of cast iron it is safe from Tilly and she from it. Perhaps for the time being it is best to let sleeping secrets lie.

I'm hoping this will all be a moot point after I get your next letter. What I am asking is that you take Tilly for a while if you can. Her life here has become entangled with forces from which I can't protect her.

Oh dear. I must go now. Joseph just put his head into the room to inform me he requires my presence. I expect he wishes to leave our quarters and knows the instant he's gone I will go and talk to his pathetic prisoner down the hall and undermine her corrective punishment. Joseph is a great believer in the restorative powers of solitary confinement. I should know. He has discovered ways to isolate me even when in the company of others. Forgive me the self-pity. It has been a trying day. I will finish this tomorrow. A boat with the mail is expected and I can send this off to you.

Tilly is gone.

Joseph kept me with him for the remainder of the day yesterday but, before bed, I crept down the hall to wish Tilly good night. She was in her room then and told me to sleep well as she always does. This morning she was gone. Her bed was mussed as if she had slept there, and all that was missing were her shoes and the clothes she had worn the day before.

At first I thought she'd defied Joseph and was walking about the fort, possibly just enjoying the breeze on the moat wall after so long cooped up in her room. I searched the island and the fort, hoping to find her before Joseph did. There was an unsettling sameness to my seeking her as before, and it lured me back to the powder magazine, but this time she wasn't there.

Finally I grew afraid for her—not of Joseph's wrath, but for her very person. I told my husband, and a search was begun in earnest. With everyone engaged, soldier, prisoner and even the work crews, it was but a half to three-quarters of an hour before every nook and cranny of this small key had been looked at.

It was discovered that Joel Lane was gone from his cell and Sergeant Sinapp was missing the small sailing skiff the *Merry Cay* he uses to go fishing and turtleing.

Everyone thinks Joel and Tilly have run off together and it must be so. Joseph has sent soldiers out to all the keys within half a day's sailing from the fort to see if the two runaways have landed. A handful of the men keep small pleasure boats, most just big enough for two or three passengers. As far as I know Joel has no skill as a sailor and, till she came here, Tilly had never been on anything but the canoe in the pond behind our old house.

Forced inactivity has worn me down to tears more than once today. Joseph blames me for Tilly's running away and the escape of Private Lane. He has condemned me to sit out the search when it would be a relief to me to be with one of the sailing parties. I cannot speak to Mr. Arnold, Mudd or anyone else with the exception of Luanne.

That chafes more than restricting my movements. As Sam Arnold and the doctor live in such close quarters with Joel, it is

my hope that they might have heard or seen something that
would help us. Joseph will, of course, speak with them, but I
hold to the belief that they—or at least Mr. Arnold—would tell
me things they might not tell one of the soldiers. There is also
the possibility that Dr. Mudd had a hand in this. Should he have
other "proofs" of his innocence that he felt he could not trust to
the hands of Mr. Lincoln's army, I do not now think he would
hesitate to use an innocent girl as the vessel for getting them to
his supporters. What keeps me from really believing this to be
the case is, though he might risk an innocent's life, surely he
would not risk his precious *documents*. He must know as well
as I the near impossibility of two unskilled sailors surviving a
sixty-mile sail in a tiny skiff.

   Joseph's condemnation of me as the author of this tragedy
would cut me had not my own already cut to the quick. What
possessed me to allow—no, not merely to allow, but to join in
with—Tilly's fascination with these men? Pride? Did I see myself, as Tilly did in the beginning, as ministering angel? Christian saint? Saving the tormented boy from the evils of war and
Sinapp?

   I am coming to question myself; in pretending to do a kindness was I merely seeking excitement or entertainment?

   And when Tilly began to lose interest in Joel (an interest that
was obviously rekindled when I was not doing my duty and
watching over her) and fall under the sway of the persuasive Dr.
Mudd, why didn't I tell Joseph? Had he truly become unap-
proachable, changed? Or was it that I was changed, changed by,
if not welcoming then certainly not rebuffing, the current of interest I sensed from Mr. Arnold?

Peggy, two hours have passed since the above sentence
was written. I return to this interminable letter because I've no
other channel for the chaos that has become my thoughts and
feelings. I took time out from that fruitless and indulgent self-
castigation and did something unthinkable. Do you remember
how deeply offended we were when we were girls and Molly
would search through our things to make sure we were not involved in improper behavior? I swore then, should I have

daughters, I would never submit them to this invasion. Molly was right. Young girls need guidance more than privacy.

Today I searched Tilly's room in hopes of finding an indication of where she'd planned to go. To that end I was frustrated. What I did find has deepened the mystery of her elopement (at least we must hope it is an elopement and young Mr. Lane doesn't intend to ruin her). In a wooden cigar box beneath her underthings—why is it as girls we believe that is a viable hiding place?—I found several notes I can only presume were written by Dr. Mudd. Who delivered them I don't know. I suspect the doctor, with his gentle demeanor and air of injured innocence, managed to turn one of the soldiers to his purpose.

Two were simple summons: "Please come alone, S." And: "Could you find time today? S." The third was rather more interesting. "I have found something. S." They weren't dated, so I have no way of knowing when they were sent, but it serves to ratify Tilly's practice of sneaking to their casemate without me attending her.

Other than that, her room was as always: untidy and girlish. She'd carried Joseph's dictionary in and left it in a heap by the dressing table. I rescued it lest he discover its absence and the rude indignity with which it had been treated. A place was marked with a black feather. I doubt there's any significance to this. With the constant circling of magnificent frigate birds, we have an abundance of these. Before returning it to Joseph's desk I turned to the page she had marked.

She'd underlined one of the words and put three exclamation marks next to it in the margin. The word was *doppelgänger*. Whether it means anything as pertains to her elopement, I have no idea. There was nothing missing from her closet or dressing table that I noticed, and it was not till afterward, when I'd had time to think, this began to bother me.

Till then I'd accepted the obvious; Tilly and Joel had run away together in the stolen skiff, the *Merry Cay*.

I'd convinced myself Tilly's ardor for Joel Lane had rekindled during her solitary visits to his cell. Now it would seem those visits were instigated by Dr. Mudd. The last two times I visited, Joel was not behaving like a man who has regained his lady love but as a sulky and jealous boy. These things could be explained away easily enough by the gaps in my knowledge of what transpired in my absence. It's Tilly's wardrobe that is so wrong. I know our sister. She had run to this presumed assignation wearing the skirt, blouse and stockings she'd worn yesterday—the day she fled the soldiers and I found her in the powder room. She'd worn them again though they were dirty, dust-streaked and stained with sweat.

Would a girl eloping with the man she loved intentionally wear such disreputable garments? Wouldn't she rather dress as if she would soon be standing before a minister? Especially Tilly, who is so fastidious about her appearance?

I had not thought I could feel more frightened for her, but I do. If she did not elope, what then? Is she carrying Dr. Mudd's messages to the mainland? Were that the case, one would think she would wait till next we sailed to Key West to shop or visit and take it then. That would be the safer way both for her and for Dr. Mudd's supposed documents. Were Mudd foolish enough to wish this ill-conceived flight, would he not go himself? Joel Lane will be released in the next few months, perhaps even weeks. It is the Lincoln conspirators who must serve out their lives on Garden Key. Escape for them must be paramount, and for Joel absurd.

This logic, if logic it is and not the imaginings of a febrile mind, applies to the elopement. Tilly, though passionate, has ever been a practical girl. Why risk possibly dying at sea to run away with a prisoner, when in a very short time he would be free and all she'd need do is book passage on one of the many ships that pass through here to meet him?

If this is so, where are these children and what has become of the missing boat, the *Merry Cay*?

23

The enormity of the skies was as dark as the small square Anna'd watched through the office window. Wind blew hard from the south with gusts from the southwest. Swells were six to ten feet. She had boated in rougher water when she was a ranger on Isle Royale in Lake Superior. There the water had been deadly, the summer temperatures of the lake ranging between thirty-nine and forty-two degrees. Here wind, rain, water and preternatural darkness were all warm; a phenomenon Anna found hard to get used to despite her time in Mississippi.

The warmth was comforting, offering a false promise of safety. Lake Superior had learned its cold treachery from the Atlantic Ocean; warm water would drown one as quickly as cold and without the anesthetic of numbing its victims first.

She didn't bother with rain gear. In twisting wind and waves, she'd be soaked to the skin in minutes even if she pitched a tent on the deck of the *Reef Ranger* and piloted the little craft through its window. As the Boston Whaler's engine idled, she buckled on one of the standard-issue, full-sized personal flotation devices, easing the bottom strap so the vest would fit over her sidearm and Kevlar vest. The days when one strove to keep one's powder dry were long gone. Modern weaponry would fire when wet. Chances were good the SIG

Sauer would work on the bottom of the ocean, though Anna had no desire to conduct that experiment in the near future.

Her handheld radio was another matter. Maybe it would work wet, maybe it would work over the disturbance of the storm, but not likely. Fortunately the boats were equipped with more powerful communications equipment. She could raise the mainland from the *Reef Ranger*'s radio if she had to.

Given her druthers, she would use neither. Before she'd come to the dock, she'd taken the precaution of asking Bob to stand by on the radio. She'd forgotten this was Bob Shaw she was talking to. Ensconced in pillows, a cat on his lap, iced tea and magazines within easy reach, he still had his radio at his elbow and turned on, monitoring his realm. With his leg in a cast from toe to mid-thigh there was little he could do physically, but he could alert Daniel or, should the need arise, the coast guard. Teddy was good with a boat as well, so there would be plenty of people to come fish her out if she was washed overboard.

For the next little while, she wanted to stay off the airwaves. The bits and pieces of information she'd been poring over all day suggested Ranger Shaw wasn't the only one monitoring the National Park Service's law-enforcement frequency.

Safe as she was going to get, Anna cast off the mooring lines and opened throttle, powering up quickly before the elements could smash her boat into the pilings.

There was no danger of colliding with much else above the water. Not a single boat remained at the fort to weather the storm. The harbor was empty, as was what she could see of the ragged slate-colored sea.

Pushing the throttle to full, she headed south, out of the harbor. There were no park visitors to rock with her wake and, in water this high, power was necessary to hold a course and keep the bow into the wind so a wave wouldn't broadside her and roll the boat.

Out past the markers she noted not everyone had run for shore. Half a dozen shrimp boats, nets furled and rigging sticking out the sides like whiskers on an ungainly catfish, had fled for shelter in this harbor in the midst of the sea as commercial ships had since Cortez began sending gold back to Spain.

Before she reached the shrimpers, Anna took advantage of a smooth high swell; riding to its crest then letting the wind help her spin the *Reef Ranger* shortly before it would have crashed into the trough. Her vulnerable side was exposed no more than a few seconds, then, wind at the stern, she was turned, heading north between Garden and Loggerhead.

In alignment with wind and waves, boating was not so much dangerous as battering. Sailing around the world in a one-woman boat, never high on Anna's list, was dropped from adventures she would like to have before she died. The bow broke through the uppermost part of oncoming waves, then fell to the trough and again began to climb. Anna didn't sit, bent her knees and every other trick she could remember from years back. Still she was jarred to the marrow. She'd once met a ranger from St. John National Park in the Virgin Islands who'd broken vertebrae in his neck in just such water as this. The bones had cracked from the pressure of being jammed repeatedly.

What with other matters clogging her mind, a piece of key information had gotten by her. Or she hadn't had a context in which it would show as important.

Patrice had radioed. A red go-fast boat had passed Loggerhead heading east.

East Key was Anna's bet.

In the Dry Tortugas nothing that wasn't man-made stuck up much above sea level. Even the few trees tended to be stunted, low to the ground, evolved to withstand the hurricanes that blew each summer and autumn. East Key had no trees, just a courageous collection of salt scrub bushes circled between the dunes like a wagon train in Indian Territory. The waves were higher than the sand dunes on the tiny key, and Anna watched from the crest of each as she breached, looking for the small island. Possibly the key was underwater in storms. She'd not served at this posting long enough to know. The park was mostly shallow water. In rough weather, when the water was scraped into mountains and the valleys were bare, some of the coral reefs were too close to the surface to pass over in a boat.

When she knew she was almost upon it, East Key chose to reveal itself. The *Reef Ranger* rose on a crest and ahead less than fifty yards was a wave of another color. Not awash, Anna noted and wondered if her hoped-for hurricane would have drowned it.

Wind shifted from south to southeast. It was safer to land on the windward side in the natural sandy scoop of beach. Not only was the wind direction right but Anna had beached in this spot before. Today was not the day to learn new terrain. She waited for a lull, then powered the Boston Whaler in, letting the wave she'd ridden lift her onto the sand. Having pulled anchor and chain out of its nest in the bow, she threw it as far up on the sand as she could. Not far. Anchors were not made for small women to use as projectile weapons.

When she jumped the few feet from the deck to the beach, she fell on hands and knees. The ride over had altered her perception of fixed. A part of her reptilian brain expected the beach to rush up to meet her as the deck had for the past twenty minutes. She dragged the anchor to high ground—high ground on East Key being about three feet above low ground—dug it deep into the sand and hoped for the best. What she needed to do wouldn't take long.

Rain pelted her in dime-sized drops. Wind pushed and snatched at her till she felt as beleaguered as if a pack of children attacked her. The lee side of the key behind the largest dune, running the length of East Key—sixty or so feet—was the most likely place. That shore was almost on the park's boundary. Beyond it the bottom of the ocean fell away abruptly into the deeps of the Atlantic. Using hands and feet, a low profile to the prevailing wind, she scooted crablike over the ridge and slid down the other side where the courageous shrubs dwelt.

There she began pawing about, a dog in a field of bones. It wasn't long before she found what she knew must be there. She wasn't exactly searching for a needle in a haystack.

Bright blue fuel containers had been buried up under the dune. Not buried precisely, but shoved with a camouflage netting and sand thrown over them.

East Key, then, was where the first go-fast boat, the Scarab piloted by Ramon Diego, had been headed when Bob had happened upon it. After it, along with its cargo, exploded, a new fuel cache had to be put in place. Fuel caches discovered on remote keys weren't unheard of. Smugglers using the fast boats with their powerful engines and tremendous fuel consumption would often leave diesel or gasoline to refuel after a run so they could get back to their homeport in Cuba, Mexico or Central America, where the coast guard couldn't reach them.

East Key, though not often visited, could in no way be considered abandoned. In the summer the pleasure boats frequenting the park occasionally beached there to picnic and swim. At least once every couple of days a ranger came by on patrol. Unless they noticed something untoward, she and Bob never landed. There was no need. The entire key could be seen from the deck of the boats. A fuel cache would probably be safe enough for a few days or a week. By the hasty and slipshod nature of the sand-and-camo hiding place, Anna guessed the people who put it there planned on using it soon. The amount of fuel suggested a much bigger operation than Anna had envisioned from the piecemeal information she'd waded through.

Rocking back on her heels, she turned her face into the wind, hoping the rain would clear her vision. Bad idea. There was simply too much water in the world. Anna wished she had swim goggles or a wide-brimmed hat.

Weather permitting, Mack was due back to the fort on the morning ferry. The fuel cache, Theresa, Lanny's mental collapse, fort personnel in conference in Homestead, Mack's timely departure and return: the event was probably planned for tonight or tomorrow night. Tonight the weather would be on their side.

For once crime in the park was not Anna's problem. This fell under the coast guard's jurisdiction first. Immigration and Naturalization was the second line of defense. Anna's only job was to holler for help.

She scrambled back up the side of the dune. "Shit," she whispered and flung herself backward, landing hard on the wet sand. Air flew from her lungs and she suffered that horrific moment when it feels as if they will never remember how to breathe again. Breath returned. She rolled onto her belly and crept back up to peek over the low crest.

Beached beside the *Reef Ranger* was a sleek torpedo of a machine, the red go-fast boat Donna had seen; the one that brought and cached the fuel.

There were two men onboard. Two more stood on the beach, their backs to her. Mack was on the *Reef Ranger*. For a moment the men shouted at each other, trying to be heard over the wind. Then the two on the beach turned. Anna slipped down but not before she saw that both carried automatic weapons. Uzis, maybe. Something small and evil looking.

They'd killed Theresa. God knew why. Maybe love had turned her and she'd threatened to tell Lanny. Men who carried automatic weapons weren't famous for their mercy. Chances are they'd chosen a less violent alternative with Lanny because a dead ranger would cause an investigation. A crazy one wouldn't.

Me they'll kill, Anna thought and wondered what the hell she was going to do about it. Rain pounded her face and chest making it hard to see, to think. The sand spit had no cover, no hiding places. For an instant she considered burying herself but knew there wasn't time.

A shoot-out was doomed from the start. She would probably kill the two walking in her direction. As satisfying as it might be at the moment, it would only add to the death toll. The other three, undoubtedly armed as well, would kill her sure as hell.

As if to ratify her worst fears, the rattle of automatic weapons fire raked the dune just above her, the force exploding sand out and down. Shouting followed. Ears ringing and blood pounding, Anna couldn't make out the words. She chose not to hang around and try.

Belly down on the sand, she crawled for the sea. What she would do there wasn't clear in her mind. Only that it's warm embrace and the company of sharks was suddenly the lesser of evils.

The surf met her in a smothering crash. She pushed on, her vest and gear keeping her belly to the sandy bottom, waves breaking over her back. Shouting followed but not gunfire. Taking a last breath she dove under. The water was but two or three feet deep. Blind with sandstorm winds churned into the water, she swam till her lungs felt close to bursting. When she could stand it no longer, she came up. The water was still no more than three feet deep. Poking her head out, she let the air explode from her lungs, sucked in fresh breath laced with salt water and fought not to cough. No way could she survive in the open sea unless she dumped her gear. Using all her strength and an aching lungful of air, she'd traveled less than the length of a standard gym pool.

The two men with the automatic weapons had followed. One was on shore, the other, waist-deep in the waves, was less than forty feet away. His face was turned from her, searching the place where she'd gone under.

"There." The man on the beach had spotted her.

He raised his weapon but didn't shoot; afraid he'd hit his companion as well as his prey. The Uzi—or whatever it was—he held at his hip like a movie gangster. Evidently he'd never learned to aim but only to spray bullets. Anna took little comfort in that. Close as she was, even in an undifferentiated hail of bullets, one or two would probably hit her.

Anger so hot it surprised her the ocean didn't begin to boil and so intense it burned away fear rose from the depths of her soul. For a year after her husband Zach was killed, Anna had wanted to die. For a time after that she'd chosen to live only to keep Molly happy. Then she'd chosen to stay alive out of sheer spite. Now, when she'd finally realized she didn't want to die because life was so damn good, some son-of-a-bitch was going to shoot her.

The gunman in the water was turning. Anna fought to unsnap the keeper on her holster. Rain and salt water had swelled the leather. The automatic rifle was coming up. She threw herself back, felt the water close over her, her feet rising off the bottom. Her SIG Sauer broke free. Without waiting to surface she fired two shots, hoping she wouldn't blow off her own foot. Underwater, unable to see or breathe, her belt pulling her down, her legs rising buoyantly, she felt thrust back into the insane grip of the acid trip. In seconds she found the bottom, pushed off and rose out of the waves, still firing, *Venus on a shell casing,* she thought idiotically.

The man in the water was screaming, bent over. He yelled: "Don't shoot! Don't shoot!" not at Anna but at the man on the beach who'd gone into panic mode, spraying bullets perilously near the wounded man.

Anna neither dodged nor dove. Feet planted against the waves slamming at her back, she took careful aim at the gunman on the shore. Before she could squeeze off a round she heard the crack of gunfire. It was as if she'd been hit between the shoulder blades with a baseball bat.

Helplessly she watched as her service weapon flew out of her hands, watched it disappear beneath the sea taking its own sweet time obeying gravity's laws. She was following it, pitching forward. The man on the shore quit firing. The gunman in the ocean stopped screaming. Weather roared ever so discreetly and there was a moment of utmost peace in the world. Water engulfed her. Again the baseball bat smashed into her. Hands filled with sand; the bottom.

Anna's life retreated into the confines of her skull. The light of her mind was shrinking to a pinpoint. She was blacking out. *Pass out and you die.* The tiniest part of her welcomed that darkness. It seemed comforting somehow. That which has kept the human race procreating for two million years overrode it.

She concentrated on that pinpoint, willed it to grow brighter.

The light dimmed. Heavy with gear, Anna was sinking. In a last effort she tried to remember where her legs were, tried to get them beneath her, but up and down had become meaningless. With a suddenness that increased the disorientation, she felt herself being pulled. God or the devil seemed in an inordinate hurry to claim her soul.

24

It has been three days and I have begun to despair. Regardless of why Tilly was taken or left, three days on the open sea in that small boat and they would be dead of thirst unless they'd thought to bring water. Joseph has forbidden me to run out on the quay and question sailors. "Unseemly," he calls it, but I feel somehow that he is afraid for me and so I obey. What else can I do? If I continued in the face of his orders he'd simply have me confined to quarters.

Since Tilly disappeared, Joseph's metamorphosis has become complete. What he has changed into I cannot say. The fire that has always been such a part of him has gone out. Where he once raged he is now querulous. The energy that permeated him, flowed from him to ignite men's passions (and, once, mine) has failed. He sits for long periods of time doing nothing. Sometimes it's hard to rouse him.

I spend my days on the third tier of the fort. Construction on that level has stopped. The engineer says this patch of sand cannot bear any more weight. Should they continue piling brick and cannon on it the fort will sink into the sea.

I wish it would.

Sergeant Sinapp, apparently on Joseph's orders, continues to forbid me seeing Sam Arnold or Dr. Mudd. I don't even know where they've been moved, though I suspect they are separated and one is probably condemned to wait out his time in the dungeon.

Joseph promises me that each boat that docks is questioned. None have seen a small sailing skiff either afloat or wrecked.

My thoughts keep turning on Dr. Samuel Mudd and the "proof" of his innocence that Tilly—in genuine innocence—boasted of in front of the soldiers. Whether Tilly could have proved anything is no matter—except, of course, to Dr. Mudd and possibly the other conspirators. Mudd seems to have held himself aloof from them. I believe he finally severed connections entirely when he fought with Mr. Arnold the day before Tilly disappeared. What matters perhaps is only that someone believed her.

I pray to all of the saints who owe Molly a small fortune in candles that if Tilly and Joel left not of their own will but were taken, they were taken by southern sympathizers, men who believe the conspirators should be released. If this is so, Tilly will be guarded, taken care of, treated—one could hope and expect—as a heroine of the confederacy.

Because Joel was taken (or escaped) at the same time, I allow myself hope. Why take Private Lane as well unless one's sympathies were with the south? The hope is small. Too many questions assail it. Why not take Mudd/Arnold? Why take Tilly and not merely the documents—if documents exist? Perhaps because they remain buried in the magazine and Tilly will be needed to testify to their existence?

Was Tilly taken from the fort for her own safety?

I'm sorry, Peg. It is as if I had a skull full of stinging hornets. I can neither eat nor sleep from the pain and the buzzing of questions.

More has happened here than Tilly and Joel's disappearance, though my worry over them was such I didn't notice for the first days. I've told you of Joseph but not of Sinapp. It's as if he has stepped into the captaincy and allows Joseph only the title while he wields the power. It's not just I who have noticed this. There's been grumbling among the men who have been put to extra tasks: cleaning the parade ground, bricking up the ruined cisterns and clearing out the powder magazine. Once I went to

the magazine in hopes of having a chance to look for the mysterious documents, but he ordered me away as if I were his laundress and not the captain's wife. I said nothing to Joseph. There
would be no point as he continues to ghost about as if his soul
was taken along with the children.

I cannot but feel this topsy-turvy situation is in some way
connected with Tilly's disappearance. Since I have been banned
from the powder magazine and forbidden to speak with Arnold
or Mudd, I turned my attention to what I might discover in my
own house. Again I searched Tilly's room, looking this time for
less obvious things. On her windowsill I found a broken bit of
brick. There is certainly no shortage of this commodity on the
island, but it has none of the charm of the pretty stones and
shells she was in the habit of carrying up to her room. The only
reason I can think that she might have such a bit of masonry is
that it was thrown through her window, no doubt with the note
wrapped around it that enticed her to put on her soiled dress of
the day before and sneak out of quarters. The only message that
could have induced her to do such a thing would have been
from Joel or Dr. Mudd. As the latter is the only one remaining,
I am ever more determined to speak with him.

Joseph keeps his desk locked. This is not new. I believe he
locks it not because the correspondence of a prison warden—
and that is what he has become though it shames me to say it in
so many words—pertains to matters of such delicacy it must be
secured, but because, having been left out of the war, he needs
to pretend to himself, and, perhaps, to me, that his work is of
national importance.

A month ago I would not have dared it—indeed it would
have been unthinkable—but I put a letter opener under the top
and pried until the lock popped free of its latch. Joseph will see
it is broken and will no doubt know that it was I who broke it. In
this strange mood that's taken him, I don't think he will say
anything. Among his letters I found one that was of interest
though of no relevance to my present worries. Joseph has put in
for a transfer to a small post in the west, in the Nevada territory.
With the war over and the army letting men go, closing forts or
leaving them with a skeleton garrison to man them, this is not a
good time for a move. Should Joseph get this transfer, he will

keep his captaincy but the pay will be that of a second lieutenant.

Joseph is running from something. From Sinapp, I think, though I cannot guess why. I believe Sinapp has found a weapon with which to threaten Joseph.

Reading the transfer papers, the in-all-but-name demotion, the remoteness of the post, the small number of soldiers stationed there, I knew that, should Joseph flee to this place that—surely not forsaken by God, but forsaken by water, green plant life and human beings not well-armed—I will not go with him.

This is not the first time I've ever thought of leaving Joseph, but it is the first time I knew I would really do it; knew it would be forever. How long I sat at my husband's desk, more stunned by than thinking about the ramifications of this, I do not know. I'd not gotten through all the letters when I heard Joseph downstairs.

More accurately, I heard Luanne speaking to "Master Coleman"—she's not yet accustomed herself to "mister." Joseph customarily enters like a stallion chased by the wind, much clatter and fuss. Now he creeps about like the cats he so detests.

Joseph mightn't say anything about my trespass, but once he found the broken lock, anything of interest would be removed. I put the unread letters in my pocket and returned to my bedroom window and my sewing before he reached the top of the stairs. I've become a sneak and a spy. I've planned to abandon my marriage and taken up thieving. If Tilly were here we would laugh at my fall from grace. As it is no one seems to laugh now. Least of all me.

For what remained of the afternoon Joseph sat at his desk in the hall. He must have known I was in our room, but he neither came in nor spoke to me. So still was he several times I went to the door and checked to see if he'd gone. He was just sitting there. If he was working I couldn't tell at what. I pretended to sew until it grew too dark to see, then lit the lamps and pretended to read, waiting till it was late enough I could go to bed and pretend to sleep.

Recent events and the unease in our rooms have infected even Luanne. Just before eight she tiptoed up to see if we wanted a cold supper since I had made no plans with her earlier.

With the burden of pretense I'd already taken on, I couldn't bear to pretend to eat, and I sent her away. It occurred to me to ask her to bring something up to Joseph, but at that moment I cared so little for him even this small kindness—or, rather, duty—was beyond me.

After nine I deemed it late enough to go to bed and took the lamp to Tilly's room. Joseph was no longer at his desk. I've taken to sleeping in Tilly's room these last nights. Joseph says nothing and it comforts me to be among her things. I suppose I hope she'll come climbing back through the window one night, flushed and laughing from her adventure.

I didn't undress or lie down but sat in the dark by the window, watching the parade ground empty and go dark. Around midnight I heard Joseph come in and go to our room. Again he never sought me out and I didn't go to him. The longer I sat there the more I knew I couldn't go on doing nothing. Finally I gave up trying. Downstairs I took britches and a shirt belonging to Joseph from Luanne's laundry bag and, back in Tilly's room, put them on.

Melodramatic and absurd as I felt disguising myself, it was necessary. In our tiny world, populated almost exclusively by men, if I were to go outdoors in the middle of the night except to visit the privy I would be noticed. I would not have passed muster for a man if anyone were to study me. I cannot say what it was. As you know I am not made as womanly as you are, and my face has been coarsened by wind and weather over the years, but it was abundantly clear I was a sheep in wolf's clothing. Two thoughts bolstered my courage. One was that in the hive of men, no one would notice one more, however peculiar, and in the middle of the night, I might well never even be seen. The other thought was, should I be found out and returned to Joseph either in person or by report, the sheer effrontery and outlandishness of my crime might shake him into a semblance of his former self.

My years here were not wasted. I've seen the watches change nearly a thousand times, heard the hours called. I know where the soldiers sleep and hide, gamble and drink. Having sneaked successfully out of the officers' quarters, I crossed to the unfinished casemates behind the half-built enlisted men's quarters. No one is housed there, prisoner or soldier. There is also no hope of light at night, the new barracks having now grown high enough to block out what the stars provide.

Feeling my way by inches, I came around the parade ground to the sally port and guardroom. I didn't like to risk passing this one place where I could be assured men were on duty and, in all probability, awake—though the country is no longer at war, sleeping on guard duty is still punishable by death. I have noticed officers stomping and whistling when they approach a sentry station at an unexpected hour simply to avoid the possibility of finding the man asleep.

My only other alternative had been to follow the southern side of the parade ground and so avoid the guardhouse altogether. But that is where a bulk of the men and prisoners are housed.

Feeling patently absurd and frightened nearly half to death, I chose to cross the parade ground beneath the hanging trees. Since Sergeant Sinapp's "coming to power" those trees have not stood fallow but are always full of their dreadful harvest. The men tied, their wrists bound behind their backs and ropes thrown over the branches, would be too stupefied by a day without sufficient water and more than sufficient suffering to pay much attention to me and, should they call out, their cries would go unanswered by the guards.

Seven men dangled in the night branches. Joseph is a proponent of corporal punishment—it's necessary to retain order with men—but always ends the punishment at sunset. Twelve hours a day is not adequate for the cruelties Sinapp feels compelled to commit.

As I passed, several men roused themselves to call out for water, but I kept my face turned away and only walked faster. Fear kept me from feeling the guilt that assails me now for refusing this small service. At the time I was so terrified their pathetic croaks did little more than make me hurry on.

It's odd that I was so much more afraid than I had been the night Tilly and I went out before our theatrical evening to see who screamed so achingly. Partly it was that I was alone this time—I have been horribly alone since Tilly disappeared. Partly I think it was that Fort Jefferson no longer feels safe. With Joseph's protection removed and Sergeant Sinapp having his way in everything, I believe I could come to harm. Mostly, though, it was fear of the humiliation I would suffer were I discovered out adventuring at night in my husband's soiled clothing. One might think it would be a little thing, but it was not.

Safely (if cravenly) past the sally port I slipped back into the darkness beneath the casemates and made my way toward the southeastern bastion and the dungeon. In the absolute darkness behind these thick walls I had to make my way by touch. With light to see by the trip is short. Without it, I believed I might go on forever, feeling the ends of my fingers growing raw from trailing over rough walls.

So much time seemed to pass I thought I'd surely missed the dungeon. When I finally came into the vaulted area where it is located, I knew it by the change in the sounds my feet made shuffling across the brick. What had been close, furtive noises became amplified and scared me before I realized I was still the only one making them. And there was the smell of fresh mortar and brick dust where the men had been sealing up the entrance to the cisterns beneath this section of the battlements.

There is a small barred window in the dungeon's door—the kind in the ink drawings that used to give us delicious shudders when we were children, the kind through which the hero sees the ogre. By standing on tiptoe I could get my mouth to the opening. At first I could make no sound. Fear and silence and a day where I spoke to no one but those few words to Luanne robbed me of my voice. When I finally managed to whisper Dr. Mudd's name it sounded like a shout in my sensitized ears and frightened me into a few more moments of speechlessness. After that, not knowing what to expect, I kept repeating his name.

No response came for the longest time and I began to fear this whole masquerade had been for nothing, that Dr. Mudd had been moved again and the dungeon stood empty. I suppose I would have given up and gone away, but I had no other plan so I stayed whispering and calling far longer than a sane woman might have.

My persistence was rewarded. From inside the cell a light was struck, just a flint then a candle, to my wide eyes it was a conflagration. For a minute lights swam and starred. The candle was held up and I saw I had indeed found Dr. Mudd.

Despite his straitened circumstances—if being reduced from

a cell with little light to one with no light and a bed of wooden planks to a stone floor can be dignified with the term "circumstances"—the doctor slept in nightshirt and cap. With his one blanket thrown around his shoulders for modesty he managed, but for the cap, to look almost dignified.

I introduced myself. The look of disapproval that screwed up his lips—or so I imagined, all I saw of it was the twitching of his overlong mustache—made me glad he couldn't see the rest of me. Once he'd grasped I was a woman in flesh and not a dream or ghost, he asked me to look away. When I looked back he was dressed even to his coat and shoes.

Having nothing to lose, as there are few at the fort more powerless and ignorant than I, and nothing to fear from him as a bolted door stood between us, I told him I'd found the notes he'd sent summoning Tilly.

"You sent her a note the night she disappeared, Dr. Mudd. It was wrapped around a bit of broken brick and thrown through her open window. She has been gone for more than three days. You must tell me why you asked her to your cell in the night and where you have sent her."

He turned from me like a man gazing out of a window but he had only brick and more brick to look at. I was close to a screaming fit. I could see myself shaking the bars, shrieking like a madwoman, as guards with torches pounded down the passages to find me. Had I been able to unlock the prison door I believe I would have, just to feel my fists strike Dr. Mudd's face.

Fortunately he turned back before I lost my wits. "Where is she?" I demanded.

"I don't know."

"You sent her the notes," I said.

"Some of them, yes. Not the last one."

He sounded reasonable, tired and sad and reasonable. It made me even angrier because I didn't want to believe him. For a minute—a very long time in the night—I said nothing. Were I to speak, I should have frothed at the mouth like a rabid dog. When I'd regained a modicum of control, I asked him who sent the last note.

"I don't know."

My temper frayed to snapping. "Tell me what you do know, Dr. Mudd, or may God damn you to hell!" Not only was I taking the Lord's name in vain but I was spitting. I could see flecks of my saliva where they caught in the candlelight beyond the bars separating us.

"Very well, Mrs. Coleman. With your sister gone, I doubt it much matters now. Though I believe your being here tonight endangers both of us. I shall tell you what I know, then you must leave. If you return I will not speak to you. If you repeat what I have told you I will deny it."

Much as I hated this cold dictation of what I must and must not do, I held my tongue. I believed him when he said he would never again speak with me. I would not call Dr. Mudd a man of honor, but he seems to be possessed of an iron will.

"Your sister believed in my cause," Mudd began, and I knew I was to be forced to hear again of his innocence. "Do you know what a doppelgänger is, Mrs. Coleman?"

"I know." Either he didn't believe me or he was enjoying the condescension. I didn't interrupt. A man behind bars must wield power however he can.

"A doppelgänger is a look-alike, someone who looks exactly like you in every aspect. Some theorize that each man has, somewhere in this world, his own doppelgänger. I know I have mine. It was this man and not myself who was seen meeting in Washington with Sam Arnold and with John Booth. It was this man and not I who conspired to assassinate or kidnap the president."

Dr. Mudd had gone as mad as I felt I was at that moment.

He spoke as if he addressed a court of law and not one angry woman dressed in her husband's britches.

"What has this to do with my sister?" I asked and none too politely.

"I was getting to your sister, Mrs. Coleman. Your sister was kind enough or perspicacious enough to believe me. When I came into possession of proof of this, I felt she was the only person at this prison whom I could trust to carry this proof outside to my lawyer. Anyone else within these walls would possibly destroy it, preferring to punish an innocent man than to admit their blessed union had been duped."

The document, the letter, the secret proof. I had come to be sick to death of this game of hints and possibilities. "What did you give my sister?"

"A photograph of this man who looks like me. He is standing with Samuel Arnold and members of Mr. Arnold's family. A photographer who travels to events where people gather took the picture. The place and date as well as the name of the photographer are on the back of the picture, put there with the man's own stamp. It was taken at a cattle sale held in Richmond, Virginia, several months before John Booth killed Mr. Lincoln. The cattle sale was three days long, days I can prove that I was with a very ill patient more than a hundred miles from where that photograph was taken."

This news staggered me. If it were the truth, then Dr. Mudd was an innocent man and he had put the rest of his life into the hands of a sixteen-year-old girl because none of us could be trusted. Strength left me. Where I had been clinging to the prison bars in anger I now clung to keep from falling. The weariness of the past days caught up to me. If I'd let myself slide to the floor, the guard bringing Mudd's breakfast would have found me still there.

25

Only when air hit her lungs was Anna sure she'd been
taken up and not down by the god of her understanding,
as AA would have it. Bits of spray entered with the first breath
and a fit of coughing alternately racked her then paralyzed her.
The upward journey continued. Her arms and legs dangled
down; water poured from her. She was flipped over and the
powers that be—not gods as she would have pictured them but
two heavily armed white guys with the power of life and
death—landed her like a witless fish. Goggle-eyed and breath-
less she stared up at them without even a fish's ability to flop or
flounder.

"She's not dead," one of them said. He bent down to peer
into her face. Along with his disappointed utterance came a
poke in her side from the barrel of his weapon.

Anna'd never seen him before. He was maybe thirty, dark
brown hair, chin-length and plastered unbecomingly over a
high forehead and sunken cheeks. His flesh had the worn, pa-
pery look of a longtime drug user, but his eyes were normal. Either he'd straightened up for the job or was "in recovery" at the
moment.

"She sure as hell got José," the second white guy said and
laughed. He was heftier than the one passing judgment on

Anna's lamentable survival, and a good ten years older. He, too, wore his hair long, but it had grown thin. What might once have held a certain piratical charm was now sad and stringy.

"His name is Rick. For Christ's sake help me. There was to be no killing. This is a goddamn mess."

Anna rolled her eyes. The speaker was William Macintyre, Mack, lean as a whippet, voice angry. The white guys were hired help. Mack leaned over the gunwale, his skinny butt and scarred legs all she could see of him.

"Help me, damn it," he shouted.

The man scrutinizing and prodding Anna straightened up. "Watch her, Butch. She's not dead," he said.

Butch. Maybe thug number one was named Lefty or Spike. Anna felt herself smile. She'd realized a great truth. Life did mirror art. These two had surely patterned themselves after movie bad guys. Probably John Travolta in *Pulp Fiction.* It made them no less deadly. She thought better about the smile.

Behind Butch, Mack and Thug Number One were hauling in another human catch. The Cuban man Anna had shot at. Rick.

Control was returning to her torso. She was breathing more or less regularly, and the paralyzing blows to her back had morphed from numb to an ache so deep she worried for her spine.

"Butch, I'd like to sit up, if I may," she said. Unarmed in the enemy's camp, it was good to be polite whenever possible.

"I hit you," he said. He sounded annoyed.

"You did," Anna assured him kindly. "Kevlar vest."

He knelt and reached toward her. At first she thought it was to help her to her feet and was about to decide this Miss Manners approach wasn't half bad. Butch, however, wasn't cut of gentlemanly cloth. He punched at her chest, a professional's interest in her vest.

"These things are a lot lighter 'n I remember. Handy. You'll be sore as hell."

He seemed to want that, and it was true so Anna gave it to him: "I already am. Feels like my back's busted in two places. Mind if I sit up?"

He held his firearm in his left hand. Up close Anna could see it was indeed an Uzi, an old one manufactured in the late eighties and not kept in mint condition. Probably a hand-me-down or a piece lifted in another job. Across the knuckles of Butch's right hand a crude H and an A had been tattooed. Undoubtedly meant to be "Hate" but would forever read "HA."

"Get paroled before they finished the job?" She nodded toward the aborted chuckle in flesh and ink.

"Yeah. Well..."

"Butch is scared of needles." The younger man said from where he pulled a bleeding Cuban gunman over the side.

"Shut the fuck up, Perry."

Perry. So much for the movies.

" 'Ha' is nice," Anna said, but their moment of blossoming rapport had been nipped in the bud.

"You shut the fuck up." This time Butch was talking to her. He backed up a foot or two and allowed the muzzle of his gun to veer away from her chest to a more benign position.

Anna took this as permission to sit up. It was harder than she'd expected and hurt a lot worse. She got her back against the hull and her knees pulled up just in time to avoid being landed on by Rick. Perry and Mack flopped him onto the deck with the same lack of gentleness with which they'd managed her landing.

Rick had lost his weapon. Blood trickled from a neat round hole a couple of inches above his kneecap. Salt water had washed it clean. It was seeping not spurting. He would live. Anna wasn't sure how she felt about that.

He wasn't much more than a boy, and when he talked he sounded just enough like Ricky Ricardo that Anna wondered if his name wasn't a cruel joke laid upon him by uncaring parents. His hair was a perfect black with water but would have reddish hues when dry. The face was square and boyish, innocence only marred by a bad case of acne and the fact that he'd tried to kill her. He was dressed in khaki shorts and a white polo shirt complete with tiny alligator and web belt. Anna guessed he'd had Weejuns but lost them while floundering around in the water.

"You didn't have to shoot me," he said to her in a lilt millions of Americans would find comedic.

"You were going to shoot me," she said reasonably.

Butch, Perry and Mack crowded back to the gunwale to help the last gunman onboard. Anna looked around for something that might better her odds but saw nothing. Going over the side wouldn't do her much good, and at the moment her back was a plank of stiff hard-core pain. She doubted she could move very fast.

"I was not," Rick said. "Nobody's supposed to get shot."

"You play with guns, accidents happen," Anna said unsympathetically.

The gunman from shore was brought aboard, cursing—or so it sounded to Anna—in rapid-fire Spanish. He, too, was young and Cuban and as clean-cut as a fellow could be dragged from the surf carrying an automatic weapon. He held it by the barrel the way a drunk might hold a bottle of Johnnie Walker. Once he had both feet in the boat he threw it down.

"Hey! Watch it, José."

That was from Butch. A chill shivered through the two Cuban boys and Mack. "Paulo," the boy said, then spoke angrily in Spanish while the boat rocked, Rick bled and Anna watched.

Mack cut him off with a few words Anna didn't understand—her Spanish running a short gamut from *hola* to *cerveza*. Then Mack turned to Butch. "Leave it alone," he said.

"Sí, señor," Butch said.

In her mind Anna was chanting *fight! fight!* but they didn't.

Mack expressed his anger mechanically. He shoved the cigarette boat's throttles ahead, and the powerful engines all but stood the narrow boat on its stern. Anna and the Cubans were sitting on the deck and only slid. Butch grabbed onto Perry and both fell, landing on young Rick's wounded leg.

The engines roared. Rick screamed. Perry lost his gun. It and Paulo's discarded weapon slid down the deck. The pain in her back anesthetized by hope and adrenaline, Anna pounced on the first one that came her way, rolled and, still lying on her side, hugged the butt close to her ribs, muzzle pointed at the tangle of blood, water and men.

"Shit."

"Fuck."

"My leg."

"Watch it, José."

"Jesus."

Anna waited as this intellectual exchange sorted itself out. Over the sound of engine, wind and waves, any shouted commands would be lost.

Perry was the first to extricate and right himself and the first to notice the balance of power had slid into Anna's court during the impromptu skirmish.

"Holy fuck, she's got a gun," he announced.

The men stopped mid-scramble. Had Anna been in a cheerier frame of mind she would have found it funny.

"Stop the goddamn boat," Butch yelled.

Mack looked back for the first time. He cut power and the boat's bow fell into the ocean with a jar that sent a numbing pain up Anna's arm from where her elbow connected with the deck. She didn't drop the Uzi, nor would she. She and Charlton Heston. They would have to pry the thing from her cold dead hands.

Before the others could recover, she snatched the second weapon and threw it over the side, then sat up. Two automatic weapons remained with her kidnappers. Rick was all but sitting on one. Butch's Uzi was still in his hands.

"Put it down, Butch," Anna said into the relative quiet of the engine's idle. Without forward drive, the boat pitched and heaved sickeningly. Anna had her elbows braced on her knees, butt and feet firmly on the deck so it bothered her not at all. Rick looked as if he was about to be sick. Given pain, shock and rough seas, Anna wasn't surprised. Butch, Perry and Mack were clearly used to the water. They rode the deck without effort.

"See what you've done with your stupid fucking around," Perry yelled at Mack. "If you'd driven the boat like a goddamn white man she wouldn't've gotten it."

"Leave it alone," Butch said. He never looked away from Anna. Perry was dangerous but Butch was the powerbase. Kidnap, killing: Anna guessed he'd done it before. Unlike his young protégé, when things went bad he became calm.

Butch twitched the gun.

"Down," Anna said sharply, and he stopped but he didn't let go of it. "I haven't the patience to screw around with you. Throw it over the side." The ache in her back, near drowning, maybe shock, came over her in a palpable wave. She was too wired up to feel afraid, but shaking started behind her breastbone and began spreading outward. Before it reached her hands, she needed compliance.

Mack watched her, an odd mixture of admiration and stunned disappointment on his weathered face.

"The gun," Anna said quietly, and she moved the barrel of hers till it pointed at the middle of Butch.

"Oh, wait," Rick said, his voice light and young all of a sudden. "That gun's got no bullets."

"Shall I test out Rick's assertion on you?" Anna asked Butch. "Throw it over the side."

Careful not to turn the automatic in such a way Anna might mistake it for aggression, Butch held the Uzi out over the gunwale.

"No. Really," Rick insisted. "She got my gun. I used all the ammo. See, it's got my initials on the barrel. I used my sister's fingernail polish because it won't come off."

Anna didn't look but the ring of truth and the childish detail of the name shook her.

"Drop it," she yelled at Butch, but he'd believed Rick. He swung the gun toward her. Anna pulled the trigger.

"See?" Rick said.

Before it could be retrieved and reloaded Anna threw it overboard to join its fellow. Diving around East Key was going to be exciting for somebody.

"No!" and the rattle of machine gun fire so close it hurt the eardrums. Anna flattened into the bottom of the boat. At this range a bullet would go through her body and the boat's hull. If they shot her, at least they'd sink their own damn boat. Nobody shot her, though it had been a genuine attempt. Mack had hit Butch's arm and the shots had gone high.

"No killing," Mack said.

"She's a pain in the ass. You get rid of her or she's going to be trouble."

"No I won't," said Anna. "I'll be good. I promise."

"See?" said Rick again. Rick and Paulo believed her. They really were very young.

Butch ignored her. "We don't need trouble," he said.

"You shoot a federal law-enforcement officer and all of a sudden it gets personal. They won't give up," Mack told him.

"They don't find the body so nobody got shot so they're short one pain-in-the-ass bitch. Nobody's going to look too hard."

"No killing."

"Yeah. Right," Perry said and smirked.

Butch shut him up with a look. "You got it, Mack. But the vest goes. I don't want any supergirl shit."

"Sure," Mack said.

"Lose the vest," Butch said.

"I can't," Anna said. "I don't have anything on under it." Butch was unmoved by the argument, but Anna figured anything was worth a try.

The shakes that threatened earlier had migrated and her fingers trembled and fumbled with the buttons of her shirt and the Velcro tabs on the Kevlar vest underneath. For the first time in a while she wished she were in the habit of wearing a bra. The rain had let up to a gentle, wind-born drizzle, but when Anna removed the heavy vest she felt cold. Colder. Fear, consciously admitted or not, had shut down much of the blood flow to her extremities.

Because she needed to know them, Anna watched the men watching her. Rick and Paulo averted their eyes. Perry saw the vest come off with a leer in his eye, looking for a cheap thrill. Butch looked on only for treachery and concealed weapons. Mack's face registered something very like pain or maybe hatred.

"Toss it," Butch said.

Anna did as she was told, but as the hot, miserable, uncomfortable thing had saved her life, she hated to see it go. She put her shirt back on. The back of it was in shreds. Both bullets had struck her at an angle. Without the vest the lead would have cut tunnels the width of her body.

"Are we set?" Mack asked.

Butch was still focused on Anna. "Cuff yourself."

Anna took the cuffs from her pouch on her duty belt and put one loosely around her left wrist. It was funny how much louder the ratcheting was to the one being cuffed. In various law-enforcement training sessions Anna and countless others in the field had been warned of how deadly a weapon unsecured cuffs can be, or cuffs secured only on one side. Properly used, the metal, the hook, the chain, the teeth on the locking mechanism, could maim and kill. Fleetingly, Anna wished she'd paid more attention in class. Probably when she was drawing cartoons or writing her sister under the guise of note-taking, one small middle-aged woman armed with half a pair of handcuffs facing five grown men, two armed with automatic weapons, had been covered.

"Other side."

Fantasies of morphing into Jean Claude Van Damme evaporated. Anna closed the cuff over her right wrist. Secure enough to come closer, Butch leaned down and squeezed the cuffs, tightening them to where she wouldn't be able to wriggle out.

"Where's the key?"

"It's on the key chain in the *Reef Ranger*'s ignition," she told him.

Butch gave her a few seconds to recant her lie, and Anna fought the urge to say *Honest, really, go look* and settled for sullenness. One cuff key was on her key ring. Like many law-enforcement people, she kept a spare key—they were tiny things, like the key to a girl's jewelry box—in the watch pocket of her trousers. As women's uniform shorts lacked this amenity, she carried it in the breast pocket of her shirt. Had Butch cuffed her hands behind her back she'd have been out of luck.

Mack watched the exchange with growing impatience. Anna wondered if he regretted his decision not to let Butch shoot her. Cuffed, she sat timidly back in the stern by the wounded Rick.

"We're set," Butch said.

Before Mack could power up, Anna said: "Hey, Mack, could you put one of these goons on the *Reef Ranger*? Drive it back? I lose another boat here and I'll be writing reports till you guys get out of the penitentiary."

For a bleak while he stared at her. Then he smiled, a mere cracking of the wrinkles on his cheeks. "Sure."

Perry started to say something rude, but Butch cut him off. "Anybody sees an NPS boat adrift's going to raise an alarm."

They'd intended to rescue the boat all along. The strength

Anna's tiny victory afforded her soaked into the ache in her back and was absorbed. Mack circled the little key. Perry jumped ship to pilot the *Reef Ranger* back to the fort. Butch watched Anna. When Mack got the go-fast boat up to speed and the howl of the engine and pounding of the hull on the waves created a solid wall of noise between the stern and where Butch leaned near the pilot's console, Anna spoke to Rick.

"I'm an emergency medical technician," she said over the racket. "I've seen a lot of wounds. That's a bad one. It could have nicked the femoral artery."

Rick looked up, his ashen face growing perhaps a shade paler. "Butch said it wasn't spurting. I was okay if it wasn't spurting. It's hardly bleeding at all."

Anna studied the red-black hole for a moment. "I hate to say it but the placement's bad. You could be bleeding to death inside. Never know it, then bang. Lights out."

The pupils of Rick's eyes grew larger, blacker. "No," he said. "That's crap. It's not spurting."

"Easy enough to tell," Anna said, then leaned back and pretended to lose interest.

The Cuban boy stood it as long as he could—about forty-five seconds—before he blurted out "How can you tell?"

The boy was too easy. Looking at the pale and sweating face, the too-wide eyes, Anna knew she ran the risk of putting him into deeper shock. People died of shock. Guilt prodded her insides. Handcuffed and aching, she found it fairly easy to ignore.

Starting with questions to which the answers had to be yes, she asked: "Are you feeling lightheaded?" Then she went through the litany of shock: "Dizzy, sweating, nauseous, anxious?"

Rick, growing more panicked by the moment, answered yes to them all.

"Internal bleeding," Anna said matter-of-factly. "If we don't get you to a doctor soon . . . Maybe I should call for the medevac helicopter when we get back to a phone."

"Oh Jesus. Oh Jesus. Mary Mother of God."

Anna didn't know if the boy prayed or swore. She just knew she needed help. To justify the caching of fuel, the kidnapping of a ranger and probably at least one murder, Mack and his cronies must be planning on importing a whole hell of a lot of "product."

Mack cut power so he wouldn't cause a wake. He was too clever to call attention to himself by rude or illegal boating practices. A shrimper had arrived and rocked at anchor.

Butch left his place by the helm and stepped back to where Anna sat terrifying Rick. The moment the roar of the engines died, the wounded man began babbling. "Look you guys, you got to get me to a doctor. This lady says I got bleeding inside. Please. I don't maybe have long. Oh God. Oh Jesus."

"Shut up, you'll live," Butch snapped. "What she been telling you?" he demanded. The boy repeated the dire forecast Anna had outlined.

"It's crap. She's lying. No calls." He leaned down and back-handed Anna hard across the face, moving so quickly she scarcely saw it coming and had no time to duck. The blow caught her ear and the pain made tears start. Before her head cleared she was aware of a rough voice near her ringing ear and hot breath on her cheek. "You're a sneaky bitch, I'll give you that, but I ain't got time for your shit. You talk to anybody and I kill you. Got that?"

"Got it," Anna said. This time she saw it coming but could do nothing about it. The back of Butch's hand smashed into her temple with such force it loosed the pains in her back. If she hadn't been so pissed off, she would have screamed.

"You got that?" he asked again.

Anna nodded, no sound.

"You may stay alive, but don't count on it."

He took a blue plastic tarp from storage beneath a bench seat, shook it out and threw it over her. "You move and I crush your skull."

Anna didn't nod. The first time had been enough to loose her neck hinges, again and her head might topple off into her lap. Being smuggled into her own harbor beneath an old tarpaulin as if she were a shipment of something so vile the public mustn't be affronted by having to look upon it wasn't the indignity it could have been. Hidden in the tent made by head and knees, she was free to fish the tiny handcuff key out of her shirt pocket.

Blinded, the leap and crash of the cigarette boat was more disconcerting than when she could brace herself, but in the harbor,
the water was considerably flatter and she managed her task.
Having unlocked both cuffs, she didn't remove them but loos-
ened them to the point where, with a little effort, she could
wriggle her hands free. That done, she put the key back in her
pocket and waited.

On shipboard, with men intent on keeping her in their control apparently at any price, was not the time to flaunt her
freedom or attempt escape or coup. Maybe later when the
odds were better. If there was to be a later. If the odds got better.

Bumping that caused Anna to fall into Rick, and Rick to cry
out in pain, announced their arrival at the dock. The tarp was
jerked off and rough hands hauled her to her feet.

Mack had taken the slip at the visitors' dock. Butch leaped
offboard and began tying the boat to the cleats. The wind had
slacked off but rain came down steadily, and low, thick skies
brought an early dusk. Visibility was down to nearly nothing,
and the beach was deserted. Two tents, campers huddled inside,
remained in the small campground.

Butch grabbed a towel and threw it over Anna's cuffed
wrists, then took her by the elbows. "Keep those handcuffs covered as if your life depended on nobody seeing them," he hissed
in her ear.

Anna nodded, gently this time, keeping her head balanced
on top of her spine. Butch half lifted her out of the boat. She
stumbled on the dock and he hauled her upright. "None of your
crap." His grip tightened above her elbow, squeezing till she
could feel her fingers growing numb from lack of blood.

"No crap," Anna said. "Just clumsy. Loosen up before I get
gangrene, for Pete's sake. You afraid I'm going to get the better
of you in hand-to-hand combat?" Butch outweighed Anna by a
hundred pounds and was a good ten inches taller.

"Shut the fuck up," he said, but he did loosen his grip somewhat.

Rick was next. Mack and Paulo helped him out of the boat
and over to one of the pilings so he could support himself.

"You gotta walk, José," Perry said. He'd docked the *Reef* behind the red boat. "We aren't calling attention to ourselves because you got yourself shot by a girl ranger."

Rick looked to be fighting back tears. "I can't," he said. "You got to get me a doctor."

"You'll walk and you don't limp, neither," Perry growled. Anna'd not seen him pull it but Perry had a knife in his hands, a wicked-looking little number with a blade about three inches long and nearly that wide, both edges honed for cutting.

"Hey!" Mack yelled when he saw the blade. Both Perry and Butch turned dull, flat eyes on him. *Eyes like carp*, Anna thought. *Or shark.* Eyes in which the windows to the soul were blacked out from within.

Mack looked from one to the other. His blue eyes, once too light and cold for Anna's taste, by comparison looked reassuringly human. There was an exchange between the three men, thug number one, thug number two and Mack, but Anna wasn't sure exactly what transpired. An understanding was reached, a balance of power shifted, a new card turned up on the table.

This moment of dark epiphany was over before Anna could swear it happened. "I'll get one of the carts," Mack said. "It'll be easier than herding her and holding up Rick."

"Give him a hand, Perry," Butch ordered. The two men walked off over the sand to be swallowed by the black maw of the sally port. Under hostile skies, brick dark with rain, the fort was a forbidding place. Anna found herself thinking not of the gunman at her elbow, the wounded Cuban boy or Mack's treachery, but of her ancestors, Raffia and Tilly, of the pressing company of warring men, innocence preyed upon and innocence lost. Though Anna would kill him if she had to—and if she got half a chance—William Macintyre had started out the innocent here. Maybe. Maybe it didn't matter, but she'd watch, ready to shove her fingers into any small crack that might appear in this little crime family.

"You got to get me to a doctor," Rick began again. Movement had started his leg bleeding. It was no more than a seep, but mixed with the rain, and the only true color in a gray landscape, it made a good show. The sight of it was renewing the boy's panic, pushing him deeper into shock. Anna wondered if she'd killed him with her lies.

"You keep crying and I'll give you something to cry about," Butch said.

The statement was so incongruous Anna said: "You got kids?" before she remembered the cuff her last spontaneous outburst had earned her.

"Shut the fuck up," Butch said. A man of few words.

Rick turned panicked eyes on Paulo. White showed around the dark irises. His skin was the color of the sky. "You'll be okay," Paulo said. "We'll get you to a doctor tomorrow."

Anna's plan to divide and conquer was probably doomed to failure. She might have literally scared Rick to death for nothing. She took pity on the boy.

"Rick, listen to me," she said.

"Shut the—" Butch began.

Anna stopped him, both hands up, palms out, "No. Let me." For some reason he did.

"Look at me, Rick."

He did.

"You're not going to die. You're not bleeding internally. You've got a little bitty piece of lead in your leg about the size of the tip of my little finger. I said all that stuff so these bozos would let me call the mainland. You're not going to die. Are you hearing me?"

"You lied about me bleeding to death?" The look of shocked disbelief made her want to laugh. Knowing it would verge on the hysterical, she didn't give in to it. "Yes. I lied. A bald-faced lie. There's a nurse here, she'll tell you the same."

"No nurse," Butch said.

"Okay. No problem. We'll get you some hot tea, get that leg up, and you'll be right as rain." Anna's decent impulse earned her the reward of seeing a hint of color return to the boy's lips.

"You can do that, okay?" she asked Butch. "Let me get him some tea, bandage the leg?"

"Maybe."

Paulo got a bit of his spine back. He stood up straight, balled his fists. He was a big guy, almost as big as Butch. The older man took in his situation and did some rapid mental calculations. "Sure," he said. "Why not?" He even managed to force a semblance of affability into his voice, if not his eyes.

Mack, driving the electric cart, materialized out of the rain. The absolute silence of the machine continued to amaze Anna. On occasion she pictured cities running in blissful quiet, the streets and avenues of New York whispering through rush hour.

"Is everything quiet?" Butch asked.

"It'll take a few minutes to kick in," Mack replied.

An image of poisoned corpses strewn about sprang to Anna's mind. For a panicked moment she fought the urge to slip off her cuffs and take her chances in the sea.

26

I stayed with Dr. Mudd another quarter of an hour. I tried all the tricks—bluster, threat, innuendo, pleading—I have learned over a lifetime of watching Molly and Joseph get the truth from wayward girls and soldiers. Mudd never changed his story: he had not summoned Tilly the night she disappeared, he had asked neither her nor Joel to carry his proof to the mainland in any but a safe and usual channel, he knew nothing of the children's whereabouts or destination.

Dr. Mudd theorized—and it sounded as if he believed what he was saying, but I am a woman easily fooled by liars—the plan to remove both Tilly and Joel was hatched by Samuel Arnold. According to Mudd, Mr. Arnold knew the doctor was innocent of conspiracy but would do all he could to keep that information from getting out and, thus, starting a hunt for the real conspirator, this doppelgänger in the purloined photograph. Knowing Mudd to have had a falling-out with his cellmate, I found his theory self-serving. It too neatly fitted facts only Dr. Mudd was privy to and told a story he was desperate for others to believe. I did not take it on faith. Still, it was sufficiently sensical, I knew I must speak with Mr. Arnold despite the strictures laid upon me.

After much cajoling on my part, Mudd told me the name of

the soldier he had suborned into carrying messages to Tilly:
Charley Munson. At first I couldn't place the name in the roster
of near a thousand boys and men at Fort Jefferson. Once Mudd
described him it came back. Charley Munson was the boy-
faced soldier Tilly and I briefly glimpsed the night of the theatrical, when we'd been drawn into this prolonged insanity by
Joel's screams. Private Munson had been on duty at the sally
port when Sergeant Sinapp hung Joel by the thumbs. I remember how white-faced and stricken he looked. Sympathy for a
fellow recruit, even if an enemy in name, must have made him
vulnerable to Dr. Mudd's winning ways.

Shortly thereafter I left Dr. Mudd to his dungeon, feeling my
way out like one of the blind mice and sharing the same terror
that a carving knife was poised above my tail. The watch was
calling three A.M. when I slipped out of the stifling darkness of
our man-made cavern and into the shadows at the edge of the
parade ground. Less than an hour had passed. I'd thought I'd
been so long whispering through the bars of the dungeon I
would emerge to a full dawn and have to run a gauntlet of curious and mocking eyes as I scurried home in my husband's
trousers.

Knowing I had at least two more hours of darkness decided
me. Trying to keep to the shadows, call no attention to myself,
yet not appear furtive should a sentry catch sight of me, I made
my way through casemates housing cannon and shot till I
reached the small opening into the south side of the sally port.
This is a mere slot in the brick, narrow and shaped in an el for
easy defense. There in the black of the shadows I watched the
guardroom across the entryway.

It was too much to hope that Charley Munson would be on
duty. Neither of the sentries were men I knew. They were passing the time in the forbidden but common practice of one keeping watch while the other napped.

From my many visits to Joel I knew where the key to the
casemates was kept. All the keys were stored in a heavy
wooden box bolted into the brick to the left of the guardroom
door. The box was padlocked but the key to the lock was
stashed in a niche carved out of the mortar a couple of feet
above and to the right of the box.

There was a good deal of coming and going in the cells:

food, water, men going to and returning from work, laundresses, mail when the ship brought it, so I suppose this weakness in the system was considered less problematic than having sentries lose the key periodically or have half a dozen keys in as many pockets.

The guard whose turn it was to sleep was doing so most profoundly. From where I stood in my niche in the shadows I could not see him, but I could hear the snoring. The sentry on watch paced back and forth. Four times he walked through the sally port, stopping for a moment to gaze out over the harbor, then back to stop again to do the same with the parade ground. Each time, he passed within six feet of where I stood and never sensed or saw me. I was frightened and anxious about my ability to carry out my plan—if you will allow me the conceit of calling anything so crude a plan—but being thus secret and watching gave me a heady sense of power, as though I could go where I wished, do what I wished and there would be no consequences. Perhaps I am cut out for a life of stealth and deceit. If not for the accompanying feeling that I should vomit at any moment, I would be tempted.

Under his breath the sentry was whistling a lively tune brought to the fort by the confederate soldiers. We have won the battle but it is their battle hymns our children will sing.

Whether this pacing out and in and out was what was required of the night sentry or whether this whistler merely stretched his legs to stay awake I couldn't know. Nor could I foresee how much longer the pattern might continue. Before the utter stupidity of my so-called plan could dissuade me, I acted. As the sentry reached his farthest-most point from the guardroom door in his pendulum swing, I slipped out of my crevice, across the sally port and into the guardroom. There I flattened myself against the wall as he turned and paced back.

Hearing sharpened by fear, I was aware of every scuff of his boots, every fragment of gravel set in motion by his passage. He slowed as if he stopped or turned to come back to his roost. My stomach grew tighter till I had to swallow back the bile in my throat. Across from where I stood was the sleeping guard. I watched with terror each time an explosive spasm of snorts and gurgles threatened such violence that I thought he must surely wake himself.

Hearing the outside soldier's boots stop, this time for real, at the parade ground end of his short patrol, I slipped the key from its niche and unlocked the cabinet. A person perennially terrified would miss nothing of life. Each movement, each second that passed, I was acutely aware of: small snicks of the key in the lock, the faint creak of the hinges as I opened the cabinet. These were magnified till it seemed I passed half a lifetime in the doing. The clatter the key I took from the third peg made as it bumped the one below rang so loudly in my ears I thought the whole garrison must wake.

Lest the guards have cause to look in the cabinet anytime soon, I took a key from another peg and used it to replace the one I'd stolen, in hopes immediate suspicion would take them some other place than where I intended to go. This done, I relocked the cabinet and slipped the key to the padlock back between the bricks. The key to the casemate I put in my trouser—or, rather, Joseph's trouser—pocket.

Footsteps began again. The eternity I'd spent fumbling with locks and keys, with snorts and snores and the sound of my own heart beating in my ears, had passed in that brief moment while the sentry surveyed the parade ground.

Once again, back against the wall, face to face with the man dreaming in his chair, I prayed to each and every saint Molly ever made us light candles to but especially to St. Dismas, the patron saint of thieves. It was he whom I thought might be most sympathetic with my spiritual needs at that moment.

Either my prayers were heard or heaven was closed to me, leaving me free to do the devil's work. The sentry passed. I slipped out of the guardroom and around the corner. In moments I was in the inky darkness within the spiral stairwell. Courage and strength deserted me and I sat till the shaking in my legs and the staggering faintness of my heart passed and I could walk again. Sitting in the dark hugging my knees, gasping for breath and trying to keep my insides from vibrating so hard they rattled my teeth, I thought of the soldiers asleep around me. How did they go into battle? How could they make their legs work as cannon banged and their fellows bled and died or fell screaming? Once I fancied myself a courageous woman and had fantasies of stanching wounds with my petticoats or daring enemy lines to carry messages to turn the tide of war.

No more. Hiding in that twisting round of slate and stone I was acutely aware that life is the only gift God gives us that we cannot earn, find, build or bake for ourselves.

When I had recovered—a matter of minutes really, though they passed a thousand times faster than in the guardroom—I felt my way to the second tier. Whereas the utter dark of the passage to the dungeon had unnerved me, this darkness was my friend, indicating I was alone. I was sorry to leave it when I reached the top of the stairs and had to walk in the open for half a dozen yards before I could again hide myself, this time in the passageway behind the enclosed casemates.

I had stolen the key, I had reached my destination, yet I stood before the door and did nothing. It wasn't fear of Sam Arnold that held me there. Foolish as it looks in retrospect, I had no fear that Mr. Arnold would do me harm. My fear was for whom I would become in the eyes of my neighbor, of my husband, when it was known I had gone alone in the middle of the night to call on a man. As I stood feeling terrible shame, as if every woman in the fort already gossiped about me and every man made bawdy jokes when my name came up, I couldn't but think of the times Tilly had come without me. Young and foolish and wrong as she was, Tilly had not hesitated to do what she believed was just. She was taught, as are all girls, what involving herself in scandal could do to her reputation and her future, yet she did it anyway.

Could I do less?

I unlocked the door and stepped inside. The darkness here was different. Little air came into the casemate. Without the cooling ocean breeze to clear away the heat and the inevitable stink of occupation, it was a darkness that not only lay heavy on my eyelids but thick and choking in my throat.

Mr. Arnold had shared the back casemate with Dr. Mudd, Joel using the first one inside the door. I hoped, though Joel and the doctor were gone, Mr. Arnold would have kept to the same bed out of habit. If Mr. Arnold was still in residence. It had not occurred to me until that moment that Sam Arnold might have been moved as well; that new tenants might be sleeping around my feet at that very moment. The quaking fear that had beset me in the stairwell threatened to return. Before it could cripple me or send me crashing blindly for the door, I began speaking.

"Mr. Arnold? Mr. Arnold. It's Mrs. Coleman. I'm sorry to call so late." Calling indeed. It has been years since I have used calling cards, and this was not a place with a silver salver in the entrance hall to receive them.

At last a light was struck in the far room and I fairly rushed toward it. Mr. Arnold, candle in hand, was propped up on his bed of bricks and boards wearing nothing but the corner of a thin blanket. Stopping in the doorway to the room he now had to himself, I wanted to explain myself but no words came.

For the longest time he stared at me and I felt myself growing smaller by the moment. Finally he spoke: "What do you want, boy?"

The success of my disguise reassured me for some reason, and my vocabulary returned. "It's Mrs. Coleman. I need to speak with you."

"Does anybody know you are here?"

Before I could think better of it, I told him no.

27

The storm brought darkness early. As the electric cart slipped noiselessly through the sally port, Anna could see welcoming gold light in the windows of the Shaws' house across the parade ground and the window of Daniel's casemate apartment to the left. Mack stopped the cart in front of the administrative offices. With the switching off of the electric motor there came a metallic crunching sound as if a giant spoon had fallen into a monster garbage disposal. As one, every light in the compound went dark.

"That's it then," Mack said.

Perry and Butch leapt from the cart and, automatic rifles under their arms, ran across the parade ground, one toward Daniel's apartment and one toward the Shaws'.

"The generators," Anna said. "You sabotaged them."

"Nobody's to radio out," Mack said.

Without at least one of the six generators up and running the fort was dead: no lights, no water pumped, no radio or phone contact with the mainland.

"It's not going to work, Mack. You don't have enough men. You don't have enough men with Rick wounded. The Shaws, Daniel, somebody will radio a boat in the harbor, and they'll call the coast guard."

"We've got enough," Mack said. "All we need is a couple of hours."

"The storm will have held your boats up," Anna predicted. Mack said nothing. Paulo was holding a pistol he'd been given by Butch in place of the Uzi Anna'd thrown overboard. It was a .44 Magnum, a huge gun and one Anna hadn't seen since Clint Eastwood quit making the Dirty Harry movies. Paulo stood aside as Mack opened the office door, then returned to the cart to help Rick. Paulo followed Anna inside.

She started to sit at Teddy's desk by phone, computer and Mrs. Shaw's radio sitting in its charger. "There," Paulo said, indicating a lonely chair in the corner by the coffeepot.

"They won't work without the generators," she said. "Why not let me be comfortable?"

Paulo took the portable radio and stuck it in the hip pocket of his shorts. Mack came in and settled Rick in the chair Anna'd been denied. "Keep her away from the radios. She could raise a shrimp boat from one," he said and left.

He would be going to the third tier to destroy the microwave dish, Anna guessed. It alone had the power to function without the generators, to contact the mainland. Mack was a maintenance man. He knew how the fort worked.

"Let me help Rick," Anna said. The two young men were easy with each other. Willing to stand close to each other, willing to let a shoulder brush or an elbow touch. Rick and Paulo were friends, maybe even related. "I lied about Rick dying of internal bleeding," she said. "But I didn't lie about the danger of shock. Let me help him."

Fear still pinched and grayed Rick's face. He wanted to be helped, comforted. He didn't speak for himself but looked to Paulo. Older men, in their thirties and forties, had been out in the world long enough to realize they were truly alone. For young men not long from home there was no person more reassuring than a woman their mothers' age; a safe middle-aged lady, the traditional bringer of soup and kisser of skinned knees.

"Maybe you're lying now," Paulo said.

"I'm not. I swear on the Virgin Mary and all the saints, I'm not lying," Anna said. Cuban boys, raised in Miami, Anna was banking on the fact that they were Catholic and her oath would not only mean something to them but suggest in some part of their minds that she was like them, one of them.

"Okay," Paulo said. "But no funny stuff."

"The red nose and fright wig will say in my pocket," Anna promised.

"Whatever. But you don't try anything."

"I'd work better with the handcuffs off," she said.

"No."

Anna took that calmly. She'd not wanted Paulo to mess with the cuffs and notice they were loose, but it would have been out of character not to ask.

Her life might depend on whether or not these men took a liking to her and because Rick, despite being a kidnapper, a pirate and possibly a murderer, seemed like a good kid, Anna treated him as best she knew how. Half a pot of water for tea, not yet grown cold without electricity, remained on the warming plate.

"How many are coming?" she asked when she'd established as homey an atmosphere as possible given a man held a gun on her.

"Three hundred, about," Rick said proudly.

"Don't talk to her about that," Paulo said, but there was no force behind the words, so Rick ignored them. They both wanted to talk, and Anna was just the woman to listen.

"That's a lot of souls," she said without looking up from cleaning the blood away from the wound. It had almost stopped bleeding, and she had no intention of opening it up again with overzealous washing. She just wanted to get a better picture of the damage.

"Why here?" Anna knew why here, but she wanted to keep the words flowing.

"All they gotta do is put one foot on American soil and you can't turn 'em back. One foot. Out here is still America. By the time anybody gets word, all our boats will be long gone. Nobody goes to jail." Rick was sipping the tea Anna poured for him. The warm liquid and the sugar were putting color back in his face and confidence back in his voice.

"Three hundred," Paulo said. "I don't think anybody's ever done it so big."

They were so clearly pleased with their work, Anna decided

to push. "So. You two guys will get rich off the problems of your Cuban brothers and sisters." She uttered this condemnation as if it were a compliment, as if she admired their entrepreneurial spirit. "What will you rake in, two, three thousand a head? Split five ways. Let's see...nine hundred grand.... That's close to two hundred thousand a piece. Not bad for a couple days' work."

"No!" Rick said. The cry was so full of pain Anna wasn't sure whether it had arisen from the poke at his intentions or the wound on his leg.

"It's not for the money," Paulo said simultaneously. "You Americans, you sit over here rich and fat and you got everything when ninety miles away people got nothing and they're getting hurt and killed for what they believe, and you turn the boats back like they were garbage scows not good enough to dirty up your pretty white beaches. Money, that's all you think of."

"Pretty much," Anna said agreeably. "We've got all this terrific stuff. You guys want some of our great stuff. You come over here and we have to share and there's less stuff for us. Capitalism, free enterprise, it's all about stuff."

They seemed nonplussed that she neither argued nor acted offended. Quiet prevailed for a bit; the only sound, now that the ubiquitous hum of six generators had been silenced, was the tap of rain on the windows and the spastic tick of the battery-operated wall clock.

"So," Anna said. "You guys are carrying three hundred people to American soil for free, out of the kindness of your hearts?"

More rain. More ticking. "We had costs," Rick said.

"Ah."

"We did it for what it cost us," Paulo said.

"What's water-taxi fare to the free world these days?"

"This isn't any of your business," Paulo snapped as dear young Rick blurted: "A thousand dollars."

"Nice round number," Anna said. "Stand up. Let me see the back of your leg."

Rick stood obediently and turned around. The fist-sized hole in the back of Rick's leg was about half full of bloody hamburger.

"Holy Mary—" Paulo started to whisper. Anna shot him a

filthy look and he had sense enough to keep the rest of his horrors to himself.

"What? What?" Rick was demanding, his voice sliding higher with each word.

"Nothing I didn't expect," Anna said reassuringly. "Most bullets these days are fired with such force they go right through a human body and out the other side. That is if you're lucky and a bone doesn't get in the way. This is just the exit wound. You're in good shape. Not much bleeding. I'll dress it and put a pressure bandage on. You'll be fine."

She stopped comforting Rick and turned to Paulo. "I want you to see something. Come here."

"Show me from here."

How quickly they learn to mistrust, Anna thought. And she was such a good teacher.

"Sure." The light had grown so dim she'd been studying the wound with her nose almost on the back of Rick's knee. "I'm going to need a flashlight. There's one in the right-hand drawer of my desk. My office is straight back. The right door."

Paulo was torn. The night that poured in under the storm wouldn't let her see his face, but Anna could see decisions fighting in the turn of his head and the twitch of his chin.

"You get it," he said finally. Anna started to move and he yelled. "No. Stay there. I'll get it." Then, "Shit."

"Paulo, why don't you give the gun to Rick, he can hold it on me while you get the light," Anna suggested. "I'll just sit over here in this chair." She sat back in the chair by the coffee machine. "Okay. Here I am."

"I don't need to see anything," Paulo said.

"You need to see this," Anna told him. "Trust me."

"Shit," he said again, but he gave the gun to Rick and headed for the back office.

Anna sat very still, face pleasantly neutral. Rick was still standing, the gun held in front of him at waist level. He'd been upright too long. Anna could see the growing unsteadiness, the way he blinked his eyes too often trying to clear away a fog that was not on his eyes but inside his brain. There came a moment when she might have been able to take him down, gotten the gun away from him. Instead she said gently: "Sit down, Rick. You're about to pass out."

"The light." Paulo handed it to her and took the pistol from Rick.

Anna asked Rick to stand again for a minute and trained the flashlight's beam on the exit wound.

"Look at the size of that. Okay Rick, turn around and sit." She pointed the light at the bullet hole above his knee. It was closer to the size of a quarter than a dime. "Now look at the size of the entry wound."

The boys looked but without any sudden enlightenment dawning on their faces.

"I fired two shots blind, underwater with a nine millimeter. It's powerful but small—nine millimeters to be exact. Turns out I didn't shoot you, Rick. I tried, mind you, but today isn't my lucky day. A bigger gun with bigger bullets shot you. An Uzi maybe. Or that forty-four Paulo's been pointing at me."

"What're you saying?" Paulo demanded. "Are you saying I shot Rick? Fuck—"

"No," Anna cut him off before he could work himself into a righteous rage. "I'm saying I didn't. If you didn't and I didn't . . ."

Rick took the flashlight from her and shined it on his leg. "Paulo, she's right. This is one damn big hole."

"She's lying. We don't know how big bullet holes are."

"Shit we don't. How many rabbits you figure you've shot? Ducks? Squirrels? Deer? Alligators? I bet we've seen more bullet holes than most people. None of 'em were big like this, big hole out the back like I got."

"She's lying," Paulo said again, but he didn't sound so convinced this time.

"I'm not," Anna said. "I swear by the blood Christ shed on the cross I'm telling the truth." It was entirely possible she was, too. She had a feeling that these credulous, misguided heroes might not be expected to live through their adventure; that their role, as written by the other men, was to be fall guys or corpses.

"Perry or Butch shot you," Anna said.

"By accident. They were shooting at you," Rick said.

"You were forty feet away from me, Rick, and not in the line of fire. You were off to the left between Paulo on the beach and me in the water."

Rick started to laugh. "You think Butch or Perry shot me on purpose?"

"That's what I think."

Rick stopped laughing.

"Maybe three hundred grand, less whatever you're paying the boat crews, bribes to Cuban officials and Mack's cut, isn't enough for them."

"Mack isn't taking a cut—"

"Shut up," Paulo shouted suddenly. "We don't talk about this anymore. We don't talk to *you* anymore. Shut up, Rick, she's playing us."

"It's not me who's playing you," Anna said.

"Shut the fuck up," Paulo screamed, echoing his criminal mentor.

The office door banged open. Anna didn't say another word.

28

Samuel Arnold, covered only by the blanket, and that rucked up to where little was left to the imagination, was completely collected. He surveyed my strange attire with such cool insolence that it was I who ended up blushing and stammering.

"Out alone at night, disguised as a boy, in a prisoner's cell; do you think that's wise?" he asked me.

"Wise doesn't enter into it," I said.

"Apparently not."

His clear intention to keep me off balance had the effect of settling my nerves. There's nothing like spite to give one false courage. False or not, I welcomed it. "I need to ask you some questions, Mr. Arnold. Please cover yourself." I used Molly's no-nonsense school voice, but he was impervious even to the tones that had us quaking in our seats as children.

"You forget, Mrs. Coleman, that it is you who've forced yourself into my bedroom. I shall receive you as I am." His customary dark humor had returned. As I had come begging, I could not be choosing.

"Very well," I said and seated myself on the neatly piled brick that served as the casemate's only chair. A mouse scuttled from behind it and scurried along the wall and into the shadows away from the candlelight.

"My cellmate," Mr. Arnold said and smiled. Threat, to mockery, to charm in under a minute; he was a man of many faces. The attraction I'd occasionally felt for him turned to something else. Perhaps fear. I didn't wish to linger any longer than I had to.

"I've spoken to Dr. Mudd," I began without preliminaries. "He says he took a photograph from you proving his innocence of conspiring to kill Mr. Lincoln. He says he gave this picture into the safekeeping of my sister and suggested that you, in your eagerness to suppress it, might have been involved in her disappearance." Dr. Mudd had not said precisely those words, but I was beyond niceties and hoped to shock, startle or shame Mr. Arnold into telling me something useful. He was proof against it.

"Dr. Mudd used Tilly and now he's using you. I cannot condemn the man. I think he has gone mad," he said calmly, still lounging on one elbow with lower limbs exposed. He set the candle down on the bricks that served as his nightstand and pulled himself into a sitting position. "Dr. Mudd did steal from me. My sister sent me a photograph of a friend and myself in better days to cheer me. Mudd got it in his head that this photograph was somehow meaningful. He took it from my things and gave it to your sister. I have no idea what she did with it."

"Dr. Mudd said the picture was of you and a man who looks very like Dr. Mudd. He told me there was a date on the picture proving it was taken when he was elsewhere. That the man with you was the true conspirator." When I said these things Mr. Arnold's face underwent a change. By the light of the single candle it seemed as if the bones beneath his skin shifted and reconfigured into a harder form. Whether this was because he recognized the truth of my words or was confirmed in his belief of the doctor's madness I couldn't say.

"Mudd would say anything to free himself," he said.

"Would you say anything to keep him imprisoned?" I asked.

"Why would I do that?" He smiled as if he mocked his own words.

There was little else I could do. I had asked and had my questions answered. Mr. Arnold was quite comfortable with his story. Even if it were untrue, I was not going to shake him loose from it.

"You were here the night Tilly and Joel disappeared," I said.

"I was. I've been told they ran away together. An elopement."

"Did you hear or see anything?" I asked.

He didn't answer me right away but sat thinking so long I began to be afraid he wouldn't. When he finally spoke he seemed to be speaking honestly, as if, during the long silence, he had weighed the consequences and decided the truth would serve as well as a lie.

"Yes," he said. "But I don't know if it will help. I heard voices in the middle of the night. When you are a prisoner, voices in the dark engender strong emotions. Part of you knows the enemy has come to shove a knife between your ribs. Part of you hopes friends have come to set you free. I opened the door between the casemates a crack, but no light had been struck. Men, probably more than one but it was too dark to see anything, had come in. I heard grunts and Joel saying, 'What is it?' and scuffling and another man's voice saying, 'Come on.' That was it. The door closed and the lock turned. I'm sorry I can't tell you more."

He did seem genuinely sorry, and his story had the simplicity of truth. It was not what I wanted to hear. If a man had come for Joel, there was hope it was Charley, Dr. Mudd's messenger boy, either acting on Mudd's behalf or, perhaps persuaded by sympathy or bribes, acting as a go-between for Joel and Tilly. As it had been *men* plural who'd come and taken Joel away, I couldn't but believe it was a conspiracy of another sort, one too large and well-planned to have been put together by a prisoner or a mere girl. And Mr. Arnold said he heard Joel say, "What is it?" Had Joel sent the note or been planning to elope or escape with our sister, he would have been awake and waiting, he would have known what "it" was.

The removal of Tilly would be of no use to Dr. Mudd unless she had been sent to sea carrying his ticket to freedom. When I'd spoken to him, Dr. Mudd did not strike me as a man full of hope. Rather the opposite; a man whose hope has been dashed.

If Tilly had, or was at least believed to have had, proof of the doctor's innocence, there were only two people I could think of who might want her silenced. The first was Sergeant Sinapp. He was a man full of hatred. He would not want Mudd freed. And he lusted after Tilly and hated Joel not only for surviving but for capturing Tilly's heart—at least for a while. The other was sitting across from me. If he were protecting this doppelgänger, the true guilty party in the murder of President Lincoln, he would probably not flinch at a second conspiracy aimed at much less dangerous and important individuals.

"I like Tilly very much," Mr. Arnold said, and I realized I was staring at him. "We all do. She is a spark of all that is bright in the grim place we've been sent to die."

"I have to go." I left immediately. Mr. Arnold did not follow. I relocked the cell's door behind me. I believed Mr. Arnold was innocent at least of Tilly's disappearance. His kind words about our sister, though seemingly genuine, were not what convinced me. It was his powerlessness. A prisoner as hated as himself could not turn enough of our soldiers to carry out the abduction of two people.

That left Sergeant Sinapp. Something had made him powerful, snapped the short leash Joseph had kept him on, freeing him to indulge his appetites and act out his cruelty in the guise of discipline and patriotism. It was well within his abilities to put Tilly and Joel on a ship out of here, maybe even sell Tilly to the sailors or pay them to maroon her and Joel on some out-of-the-way island.

Halfway down the stairs, groping in the dark like a blind woman, tapping in search of the next step, the despicable nature of the human race overcame me, rising like a tide of the worst sort of filth. I cannot describe how unclean I felt, how loathsome to be a member of this species. Despite the original goodness (or so I hope) of my intentions in starting out on this adventure, I despised myself for the absurdity and grotesquerie of dressing in a man's britches and shirt, of creeping about in the dark, cornering men in cell and dungeon, men who conspired to kill one of the greatest men of our time and, one of whom might have had a hand in harming a beautiful and precious child. I recoiled from my own flesh, from the stone around me, from the very smell of this place where men were incarcerated, some tortured, beaten, here to die of fevers and accidents and, the least fortunate, of old age.

Once in the relative light and space of the night parade ground I began to run. I couldn't bear to walk past Sinapp's godforsaken trees and the godforsaken men who dangled there crying out for water, water I hadn't the courage to stop and give them. Had I been thinking clearly I wouldn't have done something so rash. At that moment it was beyond me to stay still and quiet within my insane costume and crawling skin.

"You there!" someone shouted, and I realized my ill-chosen movement had caught the eye of the sentry on the north wall. For an instant I faltered, thinking I would call back. I am, after all, the captain's wife. There are few good reasons I might be out at that hour, but surely I could have come up with something a soldier would choose to believe rather than face the consequences of humiliating himself should he confront Joseph and find out I had not lied. Then I remembered the clothing I wore and ran faster. The clothing could not be explained away.

The distance from the stairwell to the side door in the officers' quarters is not great, but my heart was pounding so I could hear little else, and my lungs were burning when I reached the deep shade of the building's end.

In the fifteen or so seconds it had taken me to cross the parade ground, the sentry had continued to shout: "Halt!" And, "You on the parade ground!" And "Halt," again. Now that I'd stopped, over the thudding in my ears, I could hear crunching on gravel and more shouting as the sally port guards, alerted by the cries from ramparts, had begun to run after me or perhaps merely in the direction the guard above had pointed. There was a chance I'd not been seen by them.

"East end of the quarters," the sentry shouted from what sounded like directly above my head. "There or in the barracks construction. You there. In the shadows. Identify yourself or be shot."

The terrors of the night had come home to roost. I felt I'd been stripped naked and now must show myself to the men of the garrison to be hooted and jeered and used. I looked at the unfinished third tier where the voice was coming from. The sentry had moved with me and was poised three stories up, his rifle squeezed to his shoulder.

The gun wasn't pointing at me but at the deeper shadows across from me in a pile of lumber and brick. He could not see me but only guessed my whereabouts. As quietly as I could, hugging my protective shadow, I crept along the end of the building. The fort's surgeon and his family share the apartments on this end of the quarters. The next rooms house the engineer and his serving man. Then Joseph's and mine. There is no egress from the back of the building to our quarters, but the downstairs windows have not been closed since late April but for the one night we got that blowing rain.

Noise would call the guards down upon me, but time was short. The sentries would soon come from all points to join the search, and I must be in my bed by then, in my matronly night-gown with my matronly virtue wrapped around me.

I reached the window that let into the downstairs hall adjacent to Luanne's room and began pulling myself over the sill. Giddy with relief, had I not needed to keep quiet and to rid myself of Joseph's clothes before the shouting and running brought him out of his bed, I would have laughed.

Then a hand closed in the loose fabric at the seat of Joseph's trousers and I was jerked roughly backwards. Not daring to cry out for help, I caught at the frame and the sill but couldn't win my way free. Kicking, I connected with some part of someone and was rewarded by a grunt and a loosening of the grip. Before I regained even half the inches I'd won, my legs were grabbed and I was hauled outward so quickly my chin banged the sill. It was all I could do to throw my arms down before my face crashed into the ground. My shoulder was clutched so hard it hurt. I was rolled to my back and a fist struck me above the temple.

The shock of the fall and the blow disoriented me. My brain felt as if it had been jarred loose and slipped within my skull. The thick bone of my head must have hurt the sentry's hand because he cursed and didn't strike me again immediately. Into the brief respite I said: "No. It's me. Mrs. Coleman. Don't hit. Don't hit." To my own ears I sounded like a grammar school teacher talking to a small and very bad boy, but as he didn't hit me again, and as I could not feel more foolish, frightened or horrified than I did already, I didn't judge myself too harshly.

"Mrs. Coleman?" the voice said stupidly, and I felt myself being hauled unceremoniously to my feet by the collar of Joseph's shirt. The key to Mr. Arnold's cell slipped from the pocket of the baggy trousers and fell with an odd sound. I believe it must have hit the sentry's boot. Had it been just a key it might have gone unnoticed, but to mark them and keep them from being inadvertently carried away, each key was attached to a small block of wood by a leather thong. On the wooden block the cell number for the key was printed in white paint. It had been my intention to get rid of the thing, drop it on the parade ground where it would be conceivable some soldier could have lost it the day before. In my mental distress I had forgotten to do so.

Quick as a cat he bent down, dragging me with him, to retrieve it. I lost my balance and fell against him. "None of that," he snapped and shook me till my poor brain slipped again.

While he studied the key, I studied him. Even in the shadows there was enough light to see his face. It was Charley Munson, the boy-faced sentry whom Dr. Mudd had suborned into carrying his messages to Tilly.

I heard his breath hiss in as he recognized the cell number on the wooden block. "Quick," he whispered. Before I knew what it was I was to do, he quickly clamped his hand over my mouth and dragged me away from the wall and into the deeper shadows of the casemate opposite.

Once there he hissed, "Shhh," into my ear. I nodded and he transferred his hand from my mouth to my upper arm in that crushing pinch Aunt Margaret used to propel us from one place to another when we were girls. He hustled me into the darker recesses of the casemate. By the smell, I knew we were making our way to the bakery.

Because all other avenues seemed closed, I followed him willingly.

29

Cloaked in wind and rain and darkness, Perry slammed into the office with the violence of the hurricane that never happened. The Uzi was in one hand, in the other a fistful of long dark hair. A shove and Teddy Shaw was sent sprawling to the floor weeping.

Having closed the door so hard the panes in the window rattled, Perry threw himself laughing into the single chair by the coffeemaker. The Uzi swung between his splayed knees in a frightening parody of modern manhood.

"Whooee," he crowed. "Fought like a wildcat but the Shaws are secured." He was obviously high, and Anna doubted it was drugs. Perry just loved his job.

She knelt by Teddy, who remained crumpled on the floor in the position she'd landed in. None of the three men made any move to stop her. Down the right side of Teddy's face was a cut oozing blood and beginning to darken into a bruise at the edges. Other than that she seemed unharmed.

"Lock them in one of the back offices," Perry said. "They'll be safe enough there. This place is built like a fort." Anna waited for him to laugh at his own witticism but he wasn't being funny, just trite.

She helped Teddy to her feet, not wanting to give Perry an

excuse for the violence he so clearly fed on. Paulo and Rick remained in the exact same positions as they'd been in before Perry made his dramatic entrance. Both looked dismayed. The rules of the game had changed and they weren't sure how. Or why.

Teddy was up, still weeping but more quietly now that Anna held her hand in both hers, cuffed together as they were. Anna started toward the back offices without further prompting. An Uzi-toting thug was not her idea of a dream escort. Perry levered himself out of the chair and sauntered behind them. Teddy left a fog of terror and grief in her wake, and Perry apparently loved swimming in it.

Having reached the dwarf-sized door to her office, Anna ushered Teddy inside, then turned to the gunman. Daylight was about gone. Just enough gray showed at the windows fronting the casemate to see him in silhouette.

The self-satisfied smirk on his face came more from imagination than observation, but still she wanted to wipe it off with an axe. "I can't believe what a patsy you are," she said, filling her voice with as much acid amusement as she could. "*A thousand bucks.* Coyotes out of Tijuana get more than that. Haven't been smuggling long, I take it." She laughed. In her ears it sounded hollow, fake, but Perry seemed properly challenged.

"We're getting a hell of a lot more than . . ." He stopped and shook his head as if awakening from a daydream. Though she couldn't see his face, Anna guessed he was shaking off the euphoria of drinking in Teddy's tears and remembered who he was, what he was supposed to be accomplishing. Perry and Butch had an agenda of their own, and neither nationalism nor altruism formed a part of it.

Perry raised his automatic and she thought he was going to shoot her where she stood. Instead he put his right palm in the middle of her chest and shoved. She fell backward into Teddy, and they both tumbled to the floor. The office door slammed and Perry yelled, "Come out and you die."

Short and to the point, Anna thought as she extricated herself from the other woman. From the inner office she could hear the murmur of voices and hoped she'd caused at least a small rift in the solidarity of the conspirators. Her office was dark, only the feeblest of grainy light weeping in through the firing slit and the narrow dirty window the NPS had cemented within. Working by feel, Anna fished the key from her pocket and removed the handcuffs, then helped Teddy to her feet and seated her in the one chair.

Teddy said nothing and was as compliant as a puppet while Anna arranged her arms and legs. In the top left drawer of the desk was a bottle of Tylenol. Anna fumbled it out and swallowed two dry. Swallowing pills was ever an ordeal, and she gagged and gulped, hoping it would be worth it, that the drug would alleviate some of the crippling ache in her back. Throughout this peculiar and unpleasantly noisy undertaking, Teddy maintained her silence. At least she wasn't keening anymore. That high-pitched despair unnerved Anna. It was too like the sound a dying animal makes.

Bracing her rump on the edge of the desk to give some support to her back, her knees only inches from Teddy's in the tiny office, Anna said: "Tell me what happened. Where's Bob?"

A thin moan began to build in the younger woman's throat at the mention of her husband.

"Stop that," Anna said sharply. "Suck it up, Teddy. Tell me what happened."

The John Wayne part of the Shaws' shared vision reasserted. The moan was cut off. Teddy took a couple of shaky breaths.

"We were in the living room watching 'Animal Planet,' a show about baby tigers. Bob's leg was hurting him and he was fretting because Donna had radioed to report the generator had gone down on Loggerhead, and he couldn't raise you on the radio. The power went off and Bob knew the generators here had been shut down and something wasn't right. Then this man comes in. We didn't hear him. Suddenly Joey ran under the couch, her tail puffed out, and we look up and this man with a rifle or machine gun or something is standing on the landing.

"Bob keeps his service weapon secured with his cuffs in the bedroom like he's been told to. The bedroom might as well have been Czechoslovakia. This guy—Perry?"

Anna nodded. Teddy was reporting chronologically and in detail as befitted the wife of Mr. Law Enforcement. Usually Anna appreciated it. This day, incarcerated in her tiny fortress of an office with the world as she knew it being rearranged by armed men, she wanted Teddy to get to the crux of the issue.

"Did he kill Bob?" Anna asked bluntly.

Teddy started to cry again. Anna couldn't see the tears, but she could make out the crunching up of Teddy's face and hear the change in her breathing.

"He smashed Bob's cast and smashed it and smashed it. Bob was screaming. I swung a chair at his head to get him to stop, but he jerked it away from me and hit me so hard I went unconscious for a minute or so. Not clear out, just sort of brownout, you know. Next thing he's got both our radios in his hip pockets and he's dragging me out. Bob wasn't screaming anymore. I don't know if he killed him or if Bob passed out from the pain."

For a second or two Anna said nothing, just winced under the cover of darkness. Why rebreaking a broken limb should set her sympathetic aches to echoing Bob Shaw's screams when the original break didn't, she didn't know, but there was something particularly brutal about it.

"My guess is he didn't kill Bob," Anna said when the involuntary shudder had passed. "Smashing up his cast looks to me like he wanted to immobilize him. Since he succeeded in that, why kill him?" *Because he is a sadistic son-of-a-bitch,* was the obvious answer, but Teddy didn't know Perry's idiosyncratic charms as well as Anna. Maybe it wouldn't occur to her.

"What are they doing?" Teddy asked, her voice spiraling up alarmingly.

"Stop it," Anna said again. "Don't go useless on me."

"Right." Teddy took a couple more deep breaths in through her nose, quelling the incipient hysteria. "Okay."

"Did you see those two Cubans when Perry brought you in?"

"I guess. I saw two men. One sitting."

"I think those two guys, Mack and Theresa Alvarez masterminded this thing. They're bringing over three hundred plus Cuban refugees. They had to disable the fort to make sure we didn't get hold of the mainland in time to get the coast guard out here, stop the Cubans from landing and send them back to Castro. Besides, they had to give themselves and the boat captains bringing the people time to get away."

"Mack and Theresa?"

"I think so. Mack was born in Cuba."

"Where did Theresa go then? Cuba, to plan things?" Teddy asked.

"I don't know."

"Who's this Perry? He's not Cuban."

"There's two of them," Anna said. "Another guy, Butch, is a bigger meaner, uglier Perry. I think they're hired guns. Maybe they've developed plans of their own. They're not following Mack's game plan. They got something else going."

A ruckus from the outer office silenced them. Neither moved. Anna listened with every ounce of her will. *Like bunnies,* she thought, *trapped in their burrow, hoping to hear the danger has passed.*

A saying of her father's came to mind. He'd been dead for twenty years, but occasionally Anna heard his voice in her head as warm and clear as if he stood in the room next to her. "There's wolves and there's rabbits," he used to say. "And there's no percentage in being a rabbit."

"God damn but I hate this," Anna whispered.

The noise moved toward their end of the office. The foreshortened door was jerked open and a body pushed through. Again the door slammed, and a terrific pounding began.

"They're nailing us in."

"Daniel?"

"Who'd you think it was, Tinkerbell?" The maintenance man turned his back on the door to face them. "This baboon shows up on my doorstep with an Uzi. He says Mack sabotaged the generators. He smashes my radio and prods me in the ribs with a gun barrel. What the hell is going on here?"

Daniel made the office almost unbearably claustrophobic for Anna. His bulk crowded the cramped space. His energy vibrated back from the walls. Though he spoke in the hushed tones of the confused, the hunted, as far as the impact on Anna's brain was concerned he might as well have been bellowing.

"I've got to get out of here," she said. Then, realizing how self-centered she sounded, amended her statement: "We've got to get out of here."

From without there came the sounds of another banging door and again the murmuring of voices. None held the sharpness or edge of before. Anna feared the seeds of distrust and dissention she'd sewn had fallen on rocky ground.

She and Teddy quickly told Daniel what had brought them

to this sorry state of affairs. Anna went on to share suspicions and speculations, then Daniel, his thick self hulking into the space Anna'd been using to breathe, joined them in their rabbit-eared listening. Nothing could be discerned. The door had been nailed shut and probably the filing cabinets shoved against it for good measure. Because he couldn't resist, Daniel hurled himself against it several times. There was no give.

"What are they doing?" Teddy asked after a bit.

No one had heard anything she hadn't. Anna knew she asked from frustration and the need to connect, to *do* something. She answered for the same reason. "Waiting, I expect. The refugees should be here soon. They've shut us down. Now all they've got to do is sit on us, make sure we don't get word out and that none of the boaters or campers get in contact with us. They couldn't have wished for better weather. The campground is deserted. The boaters are tucked in. We could scream ourselves hoarse and never raise anybody. Once they've unloaded their cargo, they'll leave. And we'll be found nailed in my office like three chickens in a coop by the first tourist who hears us hollering in the morning." That image was almost as terrifying as the other entertainments the body smugglers had been kind enough to arrange for her.

"I'm getting out of here," Anna said.

"Not through that door you're not," Daniel said, ever practical. "These aren't hollow-core doors. They're solid oak nailed into solid oak frames. And if we did have a wrecking ball and got out, what do you suggest we do? Charge five armed men with paper clips and Post-it notes?"

"There's my letter opener," Anna said.

"Jesus, woman."

Daniel was right: there was no possibility of getting out the door and no wisdom in attempting it even if it were possible. Anna turned to the only other way out of the room. "Move," she said to her fellow prisoners. Any motion in such close quarters was a cooperative effort.

She shoved her desk over beneath the firing slit and climbed up on all fours, the better to inspect the thing by feel, memory and intuition.

"Anna, that window's no more than seven inches wide. I should know. I installed them," Daniel said.

"Can you get it out? The glass and the frame?" Anna asked.

"Maybe. Then it would be almost eight inches wide. Nobody can squeeze through that."

Not so many years ago Anna would have believed him. Since then she'd been a reluctant party to a cave rescue in one of the world's greatest caves, Lechuguilla in Carlsbad Caverns National Park. Claustrophobia and a clear and rational mind kept her from intentionally putting herself in squashy little places. She'd never forgotten for a moment what one of the Bureau of Land Management's premier cavers told her: "You get wedged, you die." A sentiment seldom shared with the public during cave search-and-rescue operations.

But she had seen some remarkable passages. A man who'd become her friend on that hellish expedition, a big Minnesotan named Curt Schatz, had been able to squeeze through alarmingly narrow crevices. "Mouse bones," he'd told her. Mice had sliding skeletons that allowed them to collapse down even smaller than customary mouse size.

"Mouse bones," Anna told Daniel. "Eight inches?"

"Tops."

Turning from the window, she opened the shallow drawer in the center of the desk and felt around for the ruler that everyone, even an acid-befogged, heartbroken Supervisory Ranger, kept there. "Measure my head," she commanded Teddy.

"Width or circumference?"

Anna was pleased to hear the controlled, efficient Teddy was back.

"Width."

Without light it took several minutes. Teddy had to read the ruler by the Braille method, clicking her long nails from groove to groove till she was sure her count was right.

"Six and a half inches," she announced.

"Anna, are you nuts? That's an old wives' tale that wherever your head'll fit you can get through. It's bull. Look at me. My head is nowhere near the biggest part of me. You're gonna get yourself hurt."

"Get the frame out, Daniel." Anna slid off the desk and they shuffled in a tight circle till Daniel could take her place.

The only tools he had access to were Anna's letter opener and Swiss army knife. They were all he needed. Anna and

Teddy sat in the dark, listening to his scraping and muttering, and when he was ready, they pounded on the door and shouted to be let out while he completed the noisy business of wrenching the window frame out.

"Seven inches," he said as he handed Anna the window.

Anna said nothing. Maybe it was an old wives' tale.

"Move," she said.

"Keep your knickers on," Daniel replied. "Let me get what I can of the grouting out. This stuff's sharp as can be. It'd tear you up proper."

Anna bowed to his greater wisdom in the area of grout and appreciated the skin he'd thought to save.

The low-grade grumble of voices from the outer offices quieted, but they'd not heard the door open and close. Probably the smugglers left during the time Anna and Teddy were pounding on the door to cover Daniel's demolition duties.

Anna looked at the slot, a rectangle a shade lighter than the surrounding brick. Eight inches. It looked so narrow. Maybe she'd get stuck part way and be found come morning half out half in, dangling like a breech calf. She didn't want to think about it. She wanted to get out. Stopping the Cuban refugees from landing wasn't important. America could absorb three hundred more souls. Stopping what she suspected could turn into a bloodbath was.

30

Charley Munson and I hid in the back of the bakery behind the wall housing the great ovens. The rich smell of bread was comforting. The knowledge that the fort's bakers must come on duty soon was not. From without, on the parade ground, we heard the sound of men coalesce, disperse, coalesce again then go silent, giving up the hunt. There was no way the sentry who'd seen me could know I was not just a rank-and-file soldier caught out on an illicit tryst with a laundress or engaged in petty theft or drunkenness. When they didn't find me, it was practical to assume I had made it back to the anonymity of my barracks.

When all was quiet, Charley grabbed my arm again. "Bakers will be here soon," he said.

"Let me go," I told him. Now that the terror of nearly being discovered had passed, the sickness I'd felt earlier for myself, for the entire race of humans, returned. It was as if a great fire had burned out my insides, leaving a black and stinking ruin. I wanted to get home, get into a clean nightdress and let sleep erase thought for however long it would.

He hesitated a moment but whether from indecision or something else I couldn't tell. The hiding place he'd chosen

was unnatural in its total lightlessness. The grip on my arm
tightened, and he pulled me after him. I hadn't the strength to
break free or the moral authority to scream for help. Once again
I followed, stumbling after in the darkness. The night had been
so rife with terrors, it seemed I had exhausted my ability to experience the sensation. I was numb, too low in spirit even to feel
curiosity about our destination or what was to be done with me
when we reached it. Me bumbling, Private Munson muttering,
"Oh my Aunt Fanny" and "God's teeth"—curses that triggered
what might have been hysteria, a need to laugh that I was fortunately too numb to give in to—led me up the spiraling stairs to
the second tier, past the Virginia regiment's cells and finally to
the powder magazine where I'd found Tilly.

In the airless confines of that place he let loose of me. His
grip had been so hard my hand tingled as blood began flowing
back into my fingers. Again we were in a place without light.
Since I had not barked my shins or tripped over anything, I assumed Sergeant Sinapp had finished clearing out the items
cached there. The sweet sharp smell of new-cut wood suggested the walls had been completed as well. Massive walls and
mazelike entrance kept out sound as well as light. There was a
sense of being suspended in time and space.

My legs would no longer support me, and I sank to the floor.
My captor—or rescuer, his role in my life yet to be determined—sat near me. His breathing, heavy as though he had carried rather than led me, was the only sound I could hear.

"Why did you have that key?" he asked. The question didn't
surprise me but his tone did. He sounded afraid. As absurd as it
sounds, his fear angered me. I was the one who had been
chased, dragged out of a window, struck in the face, silenced
and brought to a place where, should I cry out, no one would
hear me. How dare he be the frightened one? That I had gone
past fear and was not scared anymore was not the point. Fear
was my inalienable right and it outraged me that he had usurped
it.

Even at the time I knew how ridiculous I was being but it
failed to temper my emotions.

"You carried messages from the conspirators to my sister,
did you not?" I demanded. The position I was in suggested I

should not *demand* anything, but I had grown heartily sick of not only those things I listed previously, but of men, all men and because Private Munson was nearest, of him particularly. "I know you did."

He didn't say anything. The sound of his breathing was joined by the small furtive noises of a man fidgeting on a stone floor.

"Dr. Mudd told me of your complicity, as did Mr. Arnold. Please tell me yourself." Hostility is expensive to maintain, and I hadn't the physical reserves to sustain it. This last came out as a plea.

Private Munson, who had withstood my browbeating, was not proof against my beseeching.

"I felt sorry for Joel," he said. "He was so bad hurt. I couldn't let that go. I mean, prisoners can't be mouthing off, sowing seeds of contention and the like. But I couldn't let that go."

This "sowing seeds" was clearly a quote learned from his superiors. I'd heard Joseph use it many times.

"What couldn't you let go?" I asked.

"The sergeant had crippled the boy. His hands. You oughtn't cripple a person. Not like that."

Joel, "the boy," was only a year or two younger than Charley Munson. The war changed our sons, if not into men, then into half men, half children; children without innocence, men without dreams.

"So you carried messages for Joel?" I had to prod; in this lightless silence he would drift away between words if I did not. There was that out-of-world quality I mentioned earlier and I, too, was having trouble focusing.

"At first," he replied. "Then I carried notes for the doctor. I liked them. Tilly was such a grand brave girl, and the doctor always polite like I was somebody and not just a foot soldier in an army that had thrown him in the brig."

The last of his words scattered around me unheeded. The "was" and the sorrow with which he uttered it hit me like a blow. I had feared for Tilly for quite some time but in speaking of her, Joseph, myself, the other officers and men of the fort who'd been involved in the search for her and Private Lane always referred to her in the present tense, as if, though out of our sight, she still lived. Till I heard my abductor refer to her in the past tense I'd not truly let myself believe that our vibrant, foolish, courageous little Tilly was gone. Gone forever.

"You said 'was,' Tilly *was*. Why did you say that?"

I was crying. Tears flooded down my cheeks. One splashed onto my hand, startling me. I grabbed Private Munson in that same pinching grip he'd used to propel me to this place. As I grabbed blindly I do not know what part of him I held so tightly.

"I didn't," he said.

"You did."

I felt his hands on me then, one on the wrist of the hand that gripped him, the other on my left breast. I thought he'd gone mad but he had not meant to assault me, only to catch hold of me in the dark. Both his hands found my shoulders and he squeezed so hard I knew his fingers would leave bruises.

"You quit, Mrs. Coleman. You leave this alone. Leave. It. Be." He shook me hard with each word. Not able to see and so anticipate the movement, my head snapped painfully back and forth.

"You're hurting me," I managed.

He stopped but did not apologize. "Go home. Don't tell anybody where you been tonight. Don't. Don't talk about your sister no more." Another tear—or perhaps spittle from the vehemence of his words—struck my hand.

He released me so suddenly I fell backward. I squeaked, not from the pain of striking my elbows on the floor but from the suddenness of it all. Quickly I reoriented myself and sat up. No sound of breathing, no slithery rubbing of fabric on the rough floor or walls. "Private Munson?"

I'd meant to call firmly, but it came out the barest breath of air. A terrible sense of him in that blind place, just within reach of me but silent, listening, waiting, panicked me. I crawled in the direction I thought was the doorway to the rest of the tier. My head struck something and I cried out again. I don't know whether I'd gotten turned around in my panic or when we'd first come into the powder magazine.

On my neck, my cheek, I could feel breathing, something close in the dark. I barely had sense enough to follow the wall but did so knowing in this small closed space I would reach the doorway.

Below, beyond the unfinished enlisted men's quarters, walked a lone man. Private Munson. He'd not been a presence in the hell I'd crawled free of. I had been stalked only by fear.

Knowing this did not cure me. I could not shake the sense that something horrible was right behind me. Every part of my body was shaking. When I reached the back window to our downstairs hall, it took me three tries to boost myself up that I might slip through on my stomach.

There by the open window I stripped off my clothes—Joseph's clothes—and wearing nothing but shoes, knickers and chemise, carried them to Luanne's laundry basket. At the basket I removed all but the shoes. I could not bear to have even these mute companions in folly near me. Naked, I climbed the stairs hoping Joseph and Luanne were sleeping and would not come into the hall and find me so.

In Tilly's room, I put on the clean bed gown I'd craved and lay on the sheets, the night being too warm for covers. I had thought I would sleep immediately. Back in the powder magazine, before that, even, outside Dr. Mudd's place of imprisonment, it seemed I could sleep for a month I was so tired.

When I finally had the chance, my mind refused to shut out the very things it had been exhausted by. That is why I am sitting up writing you at Tilly's desk, just as dawn is hinting at day beyond the lighthouse. Charley Munson spoke as if he knew Tilly was dead. Yet he seemed both saddened and frightened by the death, as if he had no part in it. He admitted to being the carrier of messages, and I was sure Tilly had been lured from her room that night by a message and Mr. Arnold believed one of the men who came to fetch Joel spoke with Private Munson's voice.

Private Munson first caught me crawling in my own window, struck me thinking me a thief or worse, recognized me as the captain's wife which stopped the beating, but what decided him to hide me that I mightn't face discovery was the sight of the key to Mr. Arnold's cell.

Joel worked on Charley Munson's sympathy, and he began carrying messages from Joel to Tilly. When Dr. Mudd became aware of, or became insane and deluded himself into believing he had discovered tangible proof of his innocence, he must have

co-opted Munson as a carrier either by threatening to expose
his already compromised position or won him over with charm.

Dr. Mudd pulled Tilly into his plot by appealing to her
sense of justice and drama. I don't know if Dr. Mudd in actual-
ity had this photograph proving his innocence or didn't have it
but believed he did or was simply pretending he did to get Tilly
to risk some further danger in his pursuit of freedom. I don't
think Dr. Mudd is above attempting to escape, nor do I think
he'd flinch at using our sister should he devise a plan in which
she might be of use. I came to believe that, regardless of the
truth, Dr. Mudd genuinely believes he once held the key to his
release.

Because he'd given that key into her keeping, Dr. Mudd
would have done nothing to hurt Tilly or to endanger her.
Therefore it would have been without his complicity or knowledge that Tilly either put out to sea with, or was taken away
with, or was silenced along with Joel Lane.

Mr. Arnold—if Dr. Mudd is to be believed—might have had
reason to silence Tilly, and, if Joel knew anything, to silence
Joel as well. I do not believe, however, that Samuel Arnold has
the power to do such a thing.

I spent longer than I should have working through the possible guilt of these two men, just as I allowed myself to believe
much longer than reason would have dictated that Tilly, who
had clearly fallen out of "love" with Joel, had suddenly decided
to run away with him in a sailing skiff stolen from Sinapp.

Perhaps it was hope that made me cling to the latter, but it
was cowardice that had me lingering so long with the conspirators. There remained only one person who had an interest in
keeping any proofs of Mudd's innocence from reaching the
light of day, who would not flinch at using and destroying a
lovely girl and who did not know Tilly well enough to see that
her ardor for Private Lane had cooled to the point a staged
elopement would not silence questions as to what had become
of her.

This man, of course, was Sergeant Sinapp. The sergeant
craved evil for its own sake, became rabid and vicious on the
subject of the assassination and the conspirators, lusted after,
tormented and therefore must have hated Tilly for her clear
preference for a Johnny Reb. The thick evil creature would not,

could not, harbor the sensitivity to notice when a sixteen-year-old girl was over her crush on a boy.

I am sure Sergeant Sinapp killed our sister. What I mean to find out today is if he did it with my husband's knowledge or complicity.

31

That's as good as it's going to get with a letter opener and my fingernails," Daniel announced and climbed down from the desk. The movement was punctuated with grunting so like a pig's Anna suspected he'd affected it as a tribute to Mrs. Meyers during his days as a biker, and it had turned into habit and followed him into the legitimate world.

"Let me get on with it," she said. "The thugs are gone. Whatever's happening is happening now." She sprang onto the desk and put a hand to either side of the window/firing slit. God but it was small, built small back when people were small to keep small invading soldiers from invading.

"You'll never get through that."

At first Anna thought she'd spoken her fears aloud, but it was Daniel.

"Yes I will."

"They'll be landing on the west side behind the fort at that tiny beach," Daniel said. "Away from the boats moored in the bay."

Anna nodded. She'd figured that. Though with the darkness and the rain they probably could have landed the whole Cuban navy at the visitors' dock and no one would be any the wiser.

"First priority is to get to a radio," Daniel said.

"First priority is to get to Bob," Anna said.

"Put these over your ears." Teddy shared Anna's priorities. She looked not only to Anna's escape but to her condition should she pull it off.

In the dark, "these" meant nothing. Teddy must have realized it. "I found some cardboard—three by five cards. There's scotch tape in the desk. Let me—move over, Daniel—tape them on like ear muffs so you won't cut your ears up."

Anna felt soft hands patting up her leg. She took Teddy's wrists and bowed down to guide the other woman's hands to her head. She stayed still and quiet while Teddy held first one card then another over her ears and wrapped a couple of yards of tape around her head to hold them in place.

Teddy's idea and the quick execution of it would save an inexpressible amount of pain. Still she didn't give Teddy any words of thanks or encouragement. The firing slit was not just narrow; it was deep, many feet to crawl through. Maybe six or seven. It wasn't as if she would get stuck with her head out over the moat and her fanny in the office. She could get trapped tight between the immense walls of Fort Jefferson. Maybe eight inches were enough. Maybe not. And maybe the whole slit wasn't eight inches. In a hundred and fifty years, things go out of plumb. She was afraid if she opened her mouth her fears about getting stuck in tight places, how afraid she was under the engine on the bottom of the ocean, how she'd been lost once in a cave and only wanted to die someplace she was free to move under the sun, would come spilling out.

"There," Teddy said.

Anna felt her ears. Teddy's nursing skills showed. In the dark with strange materials she'd managed to bandage the ear protectors firmly in place. A good bit of hair would undoubtedly come off when the tape was removed, but at the moment hair was the least of the things Anna had to lose.

"Okay. Good," she said. "Thanks." Pleased she'd managed that, Anna turned her back on them. They could not see her face, nor could she really see theirs. With only the firing slit, the office was cavelike in its capacity for darkness. Still, she didn't want to think about anything but her immediate task.

She took off everything she didn't need, that could catch or bunch or drag: belt, shoes, badge, watch, earrings, shorts.

The shirt she kept to protect her skin and because should any piece of it hang up on a bit of mortar or brick, she could easily rip free. Not so with the pockets and waistband of pants. Her underpants she retained because a woman requires at least a shred of common dignity under even the most bizarre of circumstances. Besides, should she become wedged and not die of fright or suffocation, without her panties she would assuredly die of embarrassment during what would have to be a prolonged rescue scenario.

Before she could come to her senses, she began. She had to go through on her side, one arm and leg up, one down, her face toward the sky, or what would be sky after several thousand tons of brick were cleared away and her bones found wedged in this man-made crack. She didn't enter the slot at the bottom with her weight crushing down on the brick sill. The opening was narrow but nearly four feet in height. Elbows bent slightly, legs vaguely froglike, she crept in like she'd seen a thousand lizards do in a thousand crevices in the Rocky Mountains. Like she'd seen Dracula do in his castle in Transylvania in some old black-and-white movie.

Squashed flat, fingers, hands and toes were her best method of propulsion. There was no room to bend her joints to use the bigger muscles. Head went in easily. The racket the brick made on Teddy's impromptu ear protectors sounded like a landslide, and Anna wondered that so much noise took up so little space. Surely there wasn't room for even something as noncorporeal as a sound wave between her ear and the brick. The cardboard-covered sides of her head slipped along easily, and she was grateful her face wouldn't take a beating. Should she survive, she had a wedding to attend. A couple of feet of space were above her eyes, the top of the slot, but in the darkness it could have been inches or miles away.

The nether half of her body was still in the office. Her hips had to be turned sideways. With her torso twisted and already in the slot, she couldn't manage.

"Daniel," she called.

"I'm on it."

Thumping ensued, then she felt her lower body being lifted up, turned gently and held level and in alignment with her lizard-on-a-wall stance.

Things grew easier. Using her fingertips, she "walked" her hands ahead, found mortar cracks to grip and pulled herself along as Daniel fed her body into the firing slit from the office side. Skin was scraped from knees, elbows, ankles. Her neck would hurt for a month from having her chin on her shoulder so long. Breasts, belly and bum were squashed into a neat line, but it went far more quickly than Anna had anticipated. When the wall had swallowed all of her up, Daniel pushed his arm in the slot so she could use his hand to push against with her feet.

In less than five minutes, with the loss of only a pound or two of flesh, Anna's hands felt the rain. There was no graceful way to crawl out, no way to bend her knees to get her feet under her, no place to grab or brace to alleviate the pressures. She cared about none of it. When her face hit the night air and she could once again turn her head, see, hear something besides the threatening scrape of brick, she placed a hand on either side of the slot and shoved. Her center of gravity moved over open air. Her legs wrenched and dragged as they twisted from the firing slit. She fell fifteen feet to strike the shallow water of the moat with all the class of a crumpled beer can tossed overboard.

When she found her feet and stood, the water was only thigh deep. Voices in her brain, shrill with urgency, shouted orders. For half a dozen heartbeats she ignored them. She was shaking like a newborn moose calf and as wet with warm salt water and blood. The joints in her legs felt like they were made of soft rubber, incapable of holding her should she move. The vicious scrapes left by her passage through Fort Jefferson's cruel birth canal, anesthetized at the time of the happening by fear and determination, were stinging. The glossy magazines were right. Beach resorts were hell on a girl's skin. Between brick, coral and an engine, Anna doubted she had much epidermis left to worry about.

She ripped Teddy's makeshift ear protectors from her head and dropped them. Littering: how low adversity had brought her. Pushing her body's complaints to the back of her mind, she opened herself to the night. The black hole of her office, the lizard crawl, the tumble to the moat, had conspired to confuse her mind. Rain and good air would cleanse it. Letting herself stand in stasis, she listened and watched and did not think. Muted by wind and distance, she could hear voices, many voices, from the other side of the fort, some sharp with command. Beneath was the guttural murmur of diesel engines. From what little she could see from down in the moat, this side of the fort was deserted: no one on the moat walls, no one on the bridge to the sally port.

Her gray matter realigned to the upright and free world, she pushed her shaking legs through the water to the moat's wall. Here by the drawbridge the wall raised a mere four feet above water level. It took her several tries to haul herself up. Her arms were as rubbery as her legs.

Wet, flayed, barefoot and in her underpants, Anna felt staggeringly vulnerable. Like one of her dad's metaphorical rabbits, she wanted nothing so much as to hop away and hide. Having just sacrificed time and epithelial cells to escape one snug burrow, she wasn't going to give in to the urge to bolt into another.

Wrapping the darkness and rain about her like a cloak, she padded quickly across the drawbridge and into the sally port.

The parade ground appeared as deserted as the harbor side of Garden Key. Anna let herself back into the office. On Teddy's desk there had been a flashlight in a charger. She felt for, found it, and clicked it on. The beam was so weak the surrounding darkness bled into the light, turning it brown.

Better than nothing. Hating the childlike slap of her little bare feet on the floor, she moved to the offices at the back. "It's me," she said, then tuned out the excited babble from behind the door. A quick survey let her know she wasn't going to be freeing them anytime soon. Six-penny nails had been driven through the solid wood of the old door and into the frame with such force the nail heads were imbedded in craters. A hatchet, left over from some chore or another, had been kicking around the office since she'd come on as acting Supervisory Ranger. For a moment she thought about trying to chop the door down but quickly gave it up. A small woman wielding a small hatchet; it would take too long.

"Sorry," she called through the wood. "I'll be back as soon as I can." Voices of protest, encouragement and advice trailed after her as she left, but she had no mental room for them. Bob

was next. A radio. And, if she could squeeze it in, pants and
shoes. The feeling of her wet hind end flapping in the breeze
was unsettling. Even Superman needed at least tights.

With a sense of being absurdly young, she ran around the
parade ground. Across the open space would have been quicker
but without shoes she didn't want to risk it. Coming up lame on
top of everything wouldn't help the situation.

Full dark had come. With rain and no lights from windows
or security lights, the fort was in true darkness. Like many a
helpless, unarmed scampering creature, Anna was glad of it
though her ears were attuned to the possibility of predators.

As she neared the west end of the parade ground and the
Shaws' house, she began to hear a mute gabbling, the many
voices kept low. Mack, Rick, Paulo and their two hired thugs
would be overseeing the unloading of their human cargo.

Ideally they'd dump the refugees and go. Then only the care
and feeding of three hundred people till the coast guard could
get enough boats to take them to the INS detention center
would fall to Anna's service. Ideally.

Bereft of power, the Shaws' house was as dark as all else in
the fort. Anna listened outside the kitchen door. Nothing. Without knocking or otherwise betraying her presence, she slipped
inside. The dying flashlight expired as she clicked it on. She left
its corpse on the breakfast table. Indoors, bare feet were a boon.
She made no noise. Cats, with more senses than mere hearing,
came meowing into the kitchen. Usually they were skittish
around non-Shaws. Nobody had fed them dinner.

Anna hurried over the stair landing and into the living room,
walking on hands and feet over the dark steps lest she fall.

"Bob?" she called softly. Again nothing. She searched the
tiny room by feel: no body, living or dead. Sharpish chunks of
the broken cast were scattered near the sofa. One she picked up.
It was sticky. Maybe blood.

Anna returned to the kitchen. Her feet made little sucking
noises as she walked across a spill on the linoleum. She rifled
through the drawers. No flashlight came to hand but she found
candles and matches. Even the single flame seemed a nova after so much darkness. It flared into red as the light touched her
hand. Blood. Bob's. Lifting her feet to the light, she saw the
red was reprised on her soles and there were scuffs of it be-

tween the living room and the door. Bob had been dragged
from the house for some reason. Possibly the body would be
taken away, dumped at sea, in the hope murder would never be
proved. Anna carried the candle upstairs. No Bob. No service
weapon in the holster of his leather gear. The thugs had one
more gun.

A defeating sadness at the thought of the proud and military
little ranger's death and the death of soul that would happen in
Teddy's eyes when she was told, slowed Anna's steps.

With a physical twist of the shoulders, she shrugged off this
mental burden. Later there would be time for it, now she needed
to be as light of foot and mind as she could get.

Forcing the deadening effects of sorrow into that padlocked
compartment of her brain already crammed with things to
grieve later, she ran upstairs to her apartment. So quickly Piedmont had time only to open one eye and note her existence, she
grabbed shorts and shoes, dressed in the darkness and, armed
with a working flashlight, hurried to the bastion said to have
housed the chapel. A breach in the wall in its northern side
overlooked the small beach where the boats would be unloading their cargo.

Because very few nights, even those cloaked in storm, are
truly dark, she could make out the activity below. Several hundred yards out to sea half a dozen sportfishing boats idled, their
great engines occasionally grunting and whining as they fought
surge and prevailing winds to stay in one place. They were all
alike, new models, three decks, the topmost housing the wheel
and navigational equipment. Donations, no doubt, from Enrico's Marine in Miami. Even given their impressive size, the
load they carried left them low in the water, wallowing like
sows in a mudhole. The decks were black with humanity.
Refugees crowded shoulder-to-shoulder, butt to belly. It was a
wonder the boats had not gone down in the rough seas on the
crossing from Cuba.

Three motorized Zodiacs, small rubber dinghies, ferried
people from ship to shore. The sea, churning and angry-
looking, was dotted with the heads of those gone overboard,
those who could swim, making for the shore.

Four of the six boats trained floodlights on the beach. The
beams were gray and sinuous with pelting rain. Their stark light

caught the backs of the floundering swimmers and ignited the flame-orange of the tender boats. In the last wash of light the beach was illuminated. Five men waited on shore, one propped with his back against a block of concrete fallen away from the foundation structure of the old coaling dock. Rick. Anna'd been so wired from her scrapingly narrow escape from the office, she'd forgotten about the wounded smuggler. Had he remained behind with the .44 Butch had lent him, Anna would have walked into it. Either the thugs didn't trust Rick alone or, despite blood and pain, he wanted to be on hand to welcome his countrymen to the Promised Land.

Waist-deep in the surf, Paulo and Mack helped exhausted swimmers to shore, men with bundles and packages strapped to their bodies. Snatches of laughter and babbled Spanish reached Anna's ears on the gusting winds. Butch and Perry waited farther back on the beach, the only two still bearing arms.

Alone, without a weapon, there was little Anna could do. Much as it irked her to let the bad guys get away, she much preferred it to a suicide charge that would end in her death and the bad guys getting away anyway. She would wait and watch. When the smugglers were gone to East Key to refuel their getaway boats, she would attend to the needs of the three hundred or so new Americans till she could turn the whole mess over to the INS.

Resigned to her role as observer, she set herself to the task of noticing and remembering as much as she could, soothing herself with the fantasy of providing damning testimony in some far-off court of law.

As she studied the sportfishing boats, her eye caught the wink of a tiny red eye, then a green, out beyond the bigger craft. In a wink they were gone and she wondered if the acid in her bloodstream had created them. Her eyes were wide and dry from staring when the ocean revealed them again.

Running lights from a small craft riding low in the water, a runabout probably, or a skiff. There was no reason the smugglers would send one of their tender boats out to sea.

The only people with reason and courage enough to brave the water in night and storm in a little boat were Donna and Patrice, the lighthouse keepers from Loggerhead Key. They must have grown suspicious of the power outage and the silence from the fort and come over to see what was wrong.

Like moths, they were headed toward the only lights showing: the floods from the refugee boats. They were running right
into the middle of Butch and Perry's game.

Once under the guns, Anna doubted Donna and Patrice
would behave in a docile and ladylike fashion. She didn't doubt
for an instant that Butch and Perry would deal with interference
swiftly and brutally. The men on the beach had their backs to
the fort. Hoping it would go unnoticed by them, Anna raised
her flashlight and clicked it on and off three times quickly, three
times slowly again and again. SOS, the only bit of Morse code
that most people knew.

The running lights, blinking their own meaningless message
as the waves hid then revealed them, came on straight as a die.
Feeling helpless, Anna kept on: three quick, three slow.

The red and green lights vanished. She waited, watching for
the ocean to raise them into her line of sight again. A minute
passed. Two. The sea remained dark beyond the fishing boats.
The Zodiacs disgorged their cargo. The beach was rapidly filling. More laughter. More Spanish. Butch and Perry, backs to
the broken concrete ringing the beach, moved close to one another, heads together, conferring.

Still no running lights. Anna had to hope Patrice and Donna
had seen her signal and were coming around to the dockside to
see who needed rescuing within the fort. Leaving the refugees
to their soggy celebrations, she ran for the sally port.

The docks were empty but for the red cigarette boat and the
three NPS boats. Anna boarded the *Reef Ranger*. Believing the
fort personnel to be secured, the smugglers had not bothered
to disable the boat radios, but there was a chance Butch or
Perry still had one of the handhelds turned on. Paulo hadn't
carried a radio and, working in the surf, it was a good bet
Mack had left his someplace high and dry. Anna decided to
chance it.

The boat radios were far more powerful than the handhelds.
Unless the storm was causing too much interference, she should
be able to raise the coast guard. She only hoped they'd not write
her off as the little ranger who cried shark. They'd come once
before at her request, only to find the search for Bob Shaw was
over.

The gods decided to throw her a bone. Though full of static, she got her message through. The weather was too filthy for aircraft, but boats were being dispatched, fast coast guard cutters. Because of high seas, there were none closer than Key West. Being wise sailors, they'd headed for safe harbor when the gale warnings were issued. It would be a couple hours before the seagoing cavalry would arrive.

Mike in hand, Anna pondered whether to radio Patrice and Donna. In the end she decided against it. If the running lights were indeed theirs and they'd not gotten her cryptic warning, they would have reached the beach and now be under the smugglers' indifferent care. If they had gotten her message, they would soon be docking.

Anna decided to give them another five minutes before she returned to her lookout in the bastion. To pass the time she removed the battery cables from the boats—the *Curious,* the *Reef* and *Atlantic Rangers* and the go-fast boat—and cached them in the toilet tanks in the ladies' lavatory.

The smugglers would have to catch a ride on one of the fishing yachts, some of which would probably be picked up by the coast guard unless they headed straight for the coast of Florida and hid out there. If they made for Cuba—and if the storm lifted—coast guard helicopters would find them.

Many ifs. Still it pleased her to annoy Butch and Perry in some fashion.

From the way the two thugs behaved and the few hints they'd let drop—the biggest being the probable shooting of Rick once the plan was well in motion and he became superfluous—Anna suspected Butch and his criminal-in-training, Perry, intended to leave the bigger slower boats for the well-intentioned suckers and use the Scarab to get clear.

There would be hell to pay when they found the cable gone and, on the tiny key, no place much for Anna to hide when they came for her. She'd worry about that later.

Emerging from the ladies' loo, Anna was met with the wonderfully uplifting sight of Donna and Patrice, their runabout in an NPS slip, walking up toward the main dock.

In an uncharacteristic burst of love for her fellow men or women or whatever, Anna ran to them like an overeager teenager and gave Donna, the first in line, a fierce hug. Donna folded her tight muttering with some alarm: "What's this? What happened? Where's the real Anna Pigeon?"

The last saved what was left of Anna's abandoned dignity. The warmth of the embrace and the joy of seeing people who were actually on her side had begun to bring tears. In front of men, unless in the grips of madness or hallucinogenic drugs and hysteria, Anna wouldn't cry. Women were much harder on her self-control. Women, touted as the illogical gender, actually believed tears were normal.

"Come," Anna said and hurried them to the shelter and sheltering darkness of the sally port. There she told them the situation and her plan to sit tight, lay low, hide out—whatever it took to stay alive and unharmed.

Donna swelled with an angry need to bust heads, see justice done. Patrice, a cop for a lot of years, just nodded. "We can always catch 'em later when the odds are in our favor."

"What if there is no 'later'?" Donna grumbled.

"Criminals are good at giving law enforcement plenty of chances. There's always a later," Patrice said.

An urgency to be back on the beach side of the fort where the refugees were landing was upon Anna. Though she could do little but observe and had made the decision to do that and only that, she needed to be there. The whole situation with the joyous refugees, the exuberance of their greetings with Paulo, Mack and Rick, their rescuers, the hanging back of the thugs, armed, conferring, was at best unstable. At worst . . .

Anna didn't want to think about at worst.

"I need to get back, get close," she said.

"We'll go with," Patrice said. "We'll be there to do whatever you need done."

"Even nothing," Donna conceded.

First they made a stop in the office. The new and brighter flashlight didn't make the nailed door look any easier to open. Donna, with her greater strength, could have chopped through it with an axe, but it would have taken time and made noise.

Over Daniel's protests they opted to leave him and Teddy incarcerated a while longer. To Teddy's repeated, "Is Bob okay?" Anna could only reply that she'd not seen him. The news regarding his blood smeared on the floors could wait.

Anna was glad to have the company of the lighthouse keepers, though it made stealth and invisibility a greater problem than had she been alone. It was quickly decided their best hope to avoid detection was to follow the moat, not along the wall but in the water.

As Anna jumped off the bridge connecting the sally port with the rest of the key, Donna asked, "Are there sharks?" It was the first time Anna heard fear in the big woman's voice, and it amused her. For no reason whatever she was put in mind of Paul Newman in *Butch Cassidy and the Sundance Kid.* "Swim hell, the fall'll probably kill yah." Sharks were the least of this night's predators.

"Not usually," Anna replied truthfully. She'd heard tales of the larger fish visiting, but the only shark she'd ever seen in the moat was the baby nurse shark. Nurse sharks had the alarming silhouette of their more aggressive sisters but were gentle creatures not much given to biting bipeds.

"In you go," Patrice said.

Anna heard a squawk, then there was a sizable splash.

Donna had joined her. Patrice came last.

The moat was uneven in depth. At no point was it over Anna's head, but along the northern side she would have preferred swimming to wading chest-deep. A desire to keep her flashlight dry kept her from it. With the rain and the sweat of her palm the metal cylinder was already running with water, but she could hope, short of submersion, it would continue to function. The light was six cells, long and heavy and encased in hard metal. She'd kept it more for its value as a weapon than a light source. One never knew what might be needed.

Reaching the corner where the moat angled south, they were just above the invaded beachfront. Behind moat wall with cover of darkness and rain and sufficient noise from wind and refugees to mask their splashing, Anna had little fear of discovery.

To the right the moat ran along the edge of the sea. To the left was a not-so-gentle slope down to the small beach. Across an open space, maybe fifty feet at a guess, the tumbled mass of concrete and timber of the ruined coaling dock provided cover.

Being smallest, fastest and, in this instance, boss, Anna went first. It was three feet from the surface of the water to the top of the moat wall. The strong arms of her companions boosted her easily, and Anna was grateful for the help. What with one thing and another, her usual strength of ten men had dwindled. She wasn't sure she could hoist herself up that far one more time this night. Bent over, moving quickly but not running, she crossed the open area without being seen. Over three hundred pair of eyes now crowded the sandy strip between stone and water, so many there was scarcely room to move, but none were interested in the high ground.

On the southern edge, cuddled up next to the rocks directly beneath where she had been boosted out of the moat, Butch was shouting for quiet. The crowd ignored him till he fired off a volley from his Uzi. Anna dove for cover. Silence fell. But for the hush of wind and rain, the quiet was absolute, with the waiting quality of an indrawn breath.

"Listen up," Butch shouted. Murmuring began. Another volley of gunfire. Everybody, including Anna, listened up.

"We got you here," Butch yelled. "Now what we got is a kind of customs levy. You're going to give us anything you got in the way of cash and jewelry, and we are going to let you stay alive to see more of America than this godforsaken sandbar."

The swell of human noise began again. Mack cried: "What the hell . . ."

In heavily accented English a man yelled: "We already give you the ten thousand dollars. You don't get no more. That was the deal."

A sharp crack of gunfire. A scream, then the long drawn out, "Nooo" of a grieving woman.

Anna took the risk of peeking out from behind the jagged slab of concrete. Between Butch and the refugees—now huddled even more tightly together on her end of the beach—a space had opened. In the middle of it, stark and stagelit by the lights from the offshore boats, lay a man. A woman knelt beside him, her hands held out in front of her as if in supplication. Her palms were a shocking bright and glistening red, the color fired by the light.

"Jiminy Christmas, the guy's a psycho."

Anna twitched with such violence she rapped the back of a hand painfully against the concrete. During the volley of gunfire, Donna had emerged from the moat and run across the open space to join her.

"Anybody else want to discuss terms?" This was Perry, a swagger in his voice, his Uzi muzzle pointed toward the mass of Cubans.

"It wasn't no ten thousand... What the fuck are you doing? My God, you killed him..." These utterances slammed together, Mack and Paulo and Rick trying to make sense of this betrayal of their dream.

Paulo and Mack, now standing shoulder to shoulder at the edge of the sea, were stunned into a stupidity that would have been funny under less deadly circumstances.

"This is what's going to happen," Butch told the cowering crowd. "Two by two like Noah's fucking animals, you're going to come up by your dead hero here and put down what valuables you got. Perry's going to see to it you don't 'forget' anything. You hold back, you get shot. You mouth off, you get shot. You do anything I don't like, you get shot."

No one moved.

A voice raised, shrill in protest, then three shots, rapid fire. A woman on the edge of the crowd nearest Anna fell to the ground screaming.

"Tell 'em, Mack," Butch said.

Mack began speaking Spanish, translating. The refugees grumbled, a swelling buzz that grew, then abruptly died. Anna guessed he'd gotten to the part about mouthing off and getting shot.

Perry handed his weapon to Butch and pointed at the nearest crouching family group, a very young mother, babe in arms and a man of an age to be her father or uncle. *"Andale, andale,"* he yelled.

Anna's sketchy Spanish education included the word for hurry. The owner of Pepe Delgado's where she'd waited tables in college used to yell it at the waitresses.

The woman clutching her child and the man with them hurried to where Perry stood near the corpse, the symbol and promise of what was meted out to those who would disobey. The woman Butch had shot was still screaming.

With brutal efficiency, Perry collected their offerings in a lawn-sized garbage bag he pulled from one pocket or another.

He patted the refugees with professional thoroughness, learned, Anna was willing to bet, by being patted down himself prior to probably more than one arrest.

"*Andale.*" The next two sheep hastened to the shearing pen.

"We've got to do something," Donna said.

Anna shared the sentiment but had no idea what "something"—at least something that didn't end like the last act of *Hamlet*—would entail.

"Why don't they rush him?" Donna hissed.

"They're used to being ruled by force," Anna said. "Peaceable citizens aren't accustomed to running headlong into machine gun fire."

"Good point."

The Cubans kept coming. The sack grew fatter. Perry, bored by easy pickings, grew ever more violent, cuffing those who were too slow or too quick or too human. He backhanded a boy of eight or nine, knocking him to the ground. The mother sprang at him. He shot her with the .44 that appeared from somewhere on his person and she fell back. More red-red and surprisingly beautiful blood spattered the sand in the wash of the floodlights. Paulo cried out. He and Mack took a step forward. Butch, an Uzi under each arm now, turned toward them and they stopped.

"We've got to do something," Donna said again.

"You're right," Anna said. "Give me ten minutes and then create a diversion."

"What kind?"

"Be creative." Overcome with the movie-bred idea of saying, "synchronize watches," Anna looked to her wrist. Her timepiece was barricaded in the office with Daniel and Teddy. No matter; salt water had probably stopped Donna's anyway.

"What's the plan?" Donna asked.

"It's a little sketchy at this point," Anna admitted.

Donna looked as if she had more questions. She didn't ask and Anna was grateful. "Ten minutes," Donna said.

Anna returned to her peephole where two chunks of concrete lay one atop the other. When both Butch and Perry were occupied with their harvest, she said, "Okay."

Donna left in a crouching walk. No one shouted in alarm or

pointed. Seconds later the big woman was gone, hidden in the fort's moat.

Anna followed, feeling the rush of fear as she entered the exposed area and a bowel-loosening relief when she reached the shelter of the moat and lay flat along its wall.

Donna was already heading back the way they'd come, forging ahead with such force she left a sizable wake in the rain-pocked water.

Patrice was waiting, chest-deep in water, next to the moat wall.

Anna hung her head over the brick till her face was less than a foot from Patrice's. Rain had plastered Patrice's thin, over-permed hair to her scalp. So close, even with what little light bled over from the beach, Anna could see the coarseness of her skin, the bluntness of her features. Patrice was there, and strong and brave, and she looked beautiful as far as Anna was concerned.

"Go with Donna," Anna whispered.

"I stay with you," Patrice replied.

Anna hadn't the courage or fortitude to argue with her convincingly, so she didn't try.

"We've got eight or so minutes till Donna does whatever it is she does. Here's the plan." Quickly she outlined her thoughts.

Patrice was silent a moment.

"Got a better idea?" Anna asked hopefully.

Patrice smiled. "I was just admiring its simplicity," she said. "It's got that classic Popeye and Brutus style."

Anna was glad Patrice had refused to leave. "Let's do it," she said.

It was a matter of less than two or three minutes before they were in place. They'd crawled on their bellies like ungainly lizards along the top of the moat wall till they were above and behind Butch. There was no cover and had either of the gunmen taken time away from their gathering of ill-gotten gains to look, they would have seen them. So close, so exposed. Anna and Patrice's lives would have been instantly forfeit. If any of the refugees saw them, they gave no sign. Once a little girl pointed, but her mother snatched her up and began whispering in her ear.

Lying in plain sight atop the moat wall like a couple of sac-rificial ex-virgins, time seemed to stop. Anna's internal clock ticked away not minutes but the quarters then halves of hours as they waited for Donna to create enough of a disturbance the two armed men would be distracted and confused for a moment.

Just as Anna was beginning to think archaeologists of the future would discover her bones splayed over the concrete cap of the wall and muse over cause of death, she heard the unmistakable sound of an engine revving. It was impossible to tell if it was one of the sportfisher boats offshore or if Donna had fired up the runabout.

The noise grew. Too rumbling for the runabout; a deep guttural roar of a piston engine with an attitude.

"Oh my God," Patrice muttered at the same moment a wild Indian cry built with the scream of an engine suddenly glutted with gasoline.

Anna looked south where the noise gathered. Suddenly the spotlight from one of the offshore vessels swung, and a vision acidic in its intensity and epic in execution came shrieking out of the darkness. Donna, astride Mrs. Meyers, throttle ratcheted down, both screaming like banshees, roared down the top of the moat wall. The Harley looked immense and black and silver and mean; Donna, wet hair streaming behind, wide shoulders bunched into muscle, a Valkyrie, an Amazon. The bike seemed to be coming at the speed of sound though it couldn't have been traveling more than thirty miles an hour tops.

Anna glanced at Patrice. Her face was radiant with love. No surprise; at that moment Anna was in love with Donna herself. Patrice's face cleared, all business now. She nodded. Anna nodded back. As one they rose.

Below on the beach all eyes were turned toward the southern moat wall, Donna, Mrs. Meyers. The Cubans were rapt, the religious seeing a vision but not sure whether it was sent by God or Lucifer. Mack and Paulo looked as men look when reality ceases to have meaning anymore, rivers run uphill, the sun sets at midday and the animals of the field speak.

Butch had turned toward Donna, but he was too close under the wall to get a good shot. Perry ran past his growing garden of dead and wounded, raised his .44 and took aim.

"Now," Anna said. She and Patrice launched themselves at Butch. As Anna left the ground she was aware of two things: the sound of a gunshot and the crash of metal on concrete. Then she slammed into Butch's back.

32

My Dearest Peg—

I am sorry for the long silence. Things here have been sadder than you could possibly imagine or than I could write about at the time. Now that the worst has passed I will do my best. I may be telling you in person before you receive this letter. I am coming home and I will be coming alone.

I suppose I should begin where I left off more than a month ago.

If I remember, at that time I had decided that I must find what, if anything, Joseph had to do with Tilly's going missing. Because of the strange and sudden ascendancy of Sergeant Sinapp I knew there was something amiss between them. Because none but Sergeant Sinapp and the men under his thrall had the necessary power and brutality—along with any reason—to remove Tilly from me, I needed to know if Joseph had been a party to it.

I had it in my mind to confront Joseph and cry, whine, threaten or shame him into telling me why he had withdrawn his protection from Tilly and me; why he had, by inaction, allowed the inhabitants of Fort Jefferson to come under the de facto control of Cobb Sinapp, a man with the moral code of a shark—and this being said, I know I have insulted the entire species of fish.

I managed to keep myself in the narrow bed in Tilly's room
till the coming sunrise turned the window from black to gray. It
was my intention to wake Joseph and have it out with him before anyone was astir to distract or interrupt us.

Given the nature of my visit to the connubial bed was not
such that a thin cotton gown felt adequate, I dressed in the clothing I had cast off the day before—not the britches and blouse of
Joseph's I'd borrowed, but my own dress and petticoat.

As I was working the skirt down over my shoulders—the
waist of this dress is narrow and the buttons down the back
don't open far enough to make donning and doffing it a simple
matter—I felt the letters. They were the same letters I had
stuffed into my pocket when Joseph came home as I was
searching his desk, reading his correspondence, and wondering
if he was being adulterous.

Having worked the dress into place, I took these letters and
sat in the old rocker we'd given Tilly for her use. It sits near the
window where what little light available would help me to
make out the writing. I lit a candle to assist the dawn and looked
at my booty.

Two of the letters were military matters; notification of
death in one case and a discussion of new supply ships and
routes in the other. The third was of great interest. It was from
Colonel Battersea of the late Confederate Army. The letter had
been sent from New Brunswick, Georgia, which, if I remember
correctly, is Colonel Battersea's home.

I believe I may have mentioned the colonel's situation. He
and Joseph were thrust into that untenable situation so common
in the late and tragic events of the war.

The colonel had been one of Joseph's instructors at West
Point. He was not a good deal older than his students, being
only twenty-seven or twenty-eight at the time of his employ-
ment there. The colonel (a lieutenant then) took an interest in
Joseph. He had him to dine with he and his wife on more than
one occasion and assisted him in many small ways while
Joseph was a cadet under his care.

After Joseph graduated the friendship continued though, of
necessity, only by way of letters. Joseph would write him often
with problems or questions concerning military matters, and
Colonel Battersea would always respond with sound advice.

Once he and his wife and their eldest daughter paid us a visit as they were passing through the garrison in Pennsylvania at which we were posted.

As fate would have it, this same Colonel Battersea ended up at Fort Jefferson, a prisoner of war under Joseph's wardship. The colonel never asked for preferential treatment and, though I knew Joseph ached to give him at least better rations and some small services to make him more comfortable, he never did. His own brand of military honor would not allow him nor would so doing earn him the colonel's respect.

They did talk quite often and played chess in the evenings on occasion. In this war of brothers and neighbors such interaction is not unusual. The colonel had been here half a year or more when he began getting letters of his wife's declining health. By war's end she had wasted away till, according to the daughter that wrote in the wife's stead, she weighed no more than a child. It seemed clear she would soon die.

Joseph attempted to secure the colonel's early release (by this time it was known the prisoners of war were to go home in peace) but for reasons I'm not privy to—perhaps nothing more than the organizational disarray the army was thrown into by the long and bloody war—permission to release Colonel Battersea was not forthcoming.

Shortly thereafter the colonel took matters into his own hands and escaped, stowed away it was surmised on one of the ships that stopped for recoaling. In his own way, I know Joseph celebrated his old mentor's escape, but he said little about it.

Anyway, that said, I read the letter from Colonel Battersea— the one I had stolen from my husband's desk—with great interest.

I shan't recopy the entire letter here. After reading it I returned the letters to Joseph's desk—an act facilitated by my breaking the latch earlier. Colonel Battersea wrote Joseph of his wife's death and of how grateful he was to have been with her at the end. Though the language was careful, for one acquainted with his story, it was clear he thanked Joseph for his escape from Fort Jefferson. It did my heart good to know my husband had been party to such a kind deceit.

Yet I believe this good and Christian act has been turned

against Joseph. Should it be made known that he, a Union Army captain, aided and abetted the escape of a prisoner of war, his career would be over. He would be court-martialed and, if not imprisoned, then drummed out of the service.

For Joseph this would be tantamount to excommunication. The army is his life, his religion. I don't think I overstep when I say it embodies his very self. As Sergeant Sinapp has long been Joseph's henchman, I don't doubt Joseph enlisted his aid in the colonel's escape. It is my belief Joseph underestimated how tamed Sinapp was and that, having been complicitous in this escape, the sergeant turned on the master. Sinapp is using this knowledge to blackmail Joseph. Joseph, an honorable man, mightn't know how those of Sinapp's ilk hate him; the more servile they are the more hatred they possess.

No wonder Joseph has lost himself. He has sacrificed his honor to hang on to the trappings of all he believes to be honorable. It's made of him a paper man, one with no core, no semblance of faith upon which to draw.

For an hour or more I sat in Tilly's room thinking on the ramifications of the letter. At length I came to believe it in no way indicated that Joseph had been party to Tilly's disappearance. I do believe that it indicates something almost as damning: that regardless of Joseph's suspicions of Sinapp, he allowed the sergeant to blackmail him into silence—inaction. If he suspected—and he must have done—Joseph looked the other way, refused to know.

Joseph became and continues to act the role of a coward. It's killing him. His spirit is crippled and even his body is wasting. He's lost weight and his uniforms, once fitting splendidly, now hang on him as if they belonged to a bigger and better man.

Whether or not I would have confronted Joseph with my suppositions—become in the supposing as real to me as proven fact—I don't know. My brown (or, given the circumstance, perhaps I should say black) study was interrupted shortly after sunrise by Luanne. She came to Tilly's room, announced beforehand by her wailing and sighing, and flung open the door.

"God has passed judgment on this evil world," she announced. "You got to come. One dead and folks fixing to die."

Luanne, for all her colorful language and even more colorful version of the Christian faith, is not given to panic or exaggeration. Without hesitation I leapt from my place and followed her.

Yellow Fever had come to Garden Key. This awful burning disease is always with us but it had descended in a way that seemed to validate Luanne's belief in scourges sent by God.

The fever lasted three weeks, Peggy. You cannot believe the devastation. Hardest hit were the officers, though I cannot say why. Within days fully two-thirds of the commissioned men were dead. One of the first to die of the fever was Captain Caulley, the fort's surgeon. The lighthouse keeper and his wife died; Charley Munson, Dr. Mudd's errand boy, succumbed. I cannot begin to name them all. Should I try my tears would blotch the ink on this page till you could no longer read the words.

Dr. Mudd was loosed from his cell and, as our only doctor, I must say he conducted himself well, valiantly, even.

The officers' quarters and the casemates behind the barracks construction were converted into hospital wards. We quickly ran out of medicines. There is little that is efficacious against Yellow Fever. It is as if the disease ignites the center of the body and burns outward until life is consumed. The effects are hideous to observe and suffer. The body is tortured and disfigured as if the disease would not merely kill but would savage. Those of us who could still stand worked to alleviate the suffering of the stricken. Dr. Mudd toiled night and day taking his sleep in minutes rather than hours. What lives were saved must be laid on his doorstep. The only man who worked harder was Joseph. No task was too menial or too vile for him to undertake. He carried slops, washed the soldiers, and spooned water into their parched mouths with the gentleness of a mother feeding a child. He held them as they died. In the quiet moments when he might have slept, he wrote of their courage to their wives and mothers.

Joseph (as well as Dr. Mudd) won the respect and admiration of all here. Well, not all. I saw not a selfless hero, not even a man trying desperately to buy back his soul. When I looked at Joseph, thin and haggard and going without sleep to minister to the sick, I saw a man who wanted to die. I believe Joseph clung to the sick, wallowed in the disease, not in hopes of conquering it that others might live but of embracing it that it might see fit to take him as well. Death refused him as it thankfully refused me. We are among the one in three who survived the epidemic.

The second week of the disease Sergeant Sinapp was taken ill and carried into the downstairs parlor of the officers' quarters there, with nine others on cots and couches, to be cared for.

I can only attribute my actions thereafter to fatigue and the mental strain of losing our dear sister Tilly. Should I not pen these excuses for my behavior I would have to admit that I had succumbed to an evil as cowardly as my husband's and as cold as that of Sergeant Sinapp.

For three days I stayed at Sinapp's side. When he cried for water, I asked him where Tilly was. When he begged to be cooled from his raging fever, I asked what he had done with our sister. I felt nothing, Peggy, nothing good. My insides were as still and cold and dark as a well. I watched without sympathy, without humanity. I gave him the water he called for after each interrogation, but I did it without thought of succor but only that he might live long enough to provide the answers I so desperately needed.

Rage burned in him as hot as the fever. Hatred for me scalded his eyes till they were suffused with blood. Had he the strength, I believe he would have risen from his sickbed and choked the life from me. He exhausted himself cursing me, screaming at me to leave. I stayed. When he went to sleep I was watching him. When he awoke I was watching.

Never once did he repent, confess or ask my forgiveness or God's.

Evening of the third day he went into the delirium that precedes death in those affected with Yellow Fever. Even then I did not allow him what peace might have been left for him. Into his delirium dreams I whispered our sister's name, questions, threats. I whispered until I was hoarse with it and he was wild, trying to fight the dream demon that was I.

It was after three in the morning, the fort by no means still or dark with the sick crying and the caretakers making their weary rounds with lantern or candle. Sinapp began to relive the night our sister disappeared. He mumbled snatches of orders, guttural grunts of pleasure, names, fragments of conversations, aborted howls that might pass for laughter in hell. I goaded and guided and finally pieced together the remnants of his ravings.

Sinapp had lured Tilly out with a note (probably delivered by Charley Munson) purportedly from Dr. Mudd. He'd then taken Tilly and, with two of his men, taken Joel as well. These children had been carried to the dungeon and slain.

The joy in the killing and the hatred of the Lincoln conspirators and Tilly's supposed proof of Dr. Samuel Mudd's innocence was not tempered by remorse even in this last madness. Before Tilly was murdered Sinapp defiled her. As he relived this, all that kept me from killing him was the sure knowledge he would die soon. I did not want to cheat him of a moment's pain and suffering.

Just before dawn he died, his soul unshriven and mine blackened by our time together and my inability to forgive him.

I suppose he was taken away and buried or burned with the other dead. I suppose I continued to fetch and carry and nurse. Nothing remains in my memory of the interval between Sinapp's death and Luanne tucking sheets around me and saying: "Sleep now or you be sick too. Sleep. Sleep."

I slept for thirty-six hours.

When I awoke there were no new cases of the fever. Those who would die had died. Those destined to live were convalescing. Yellow Fever had run its course at Fort Jefferson.

I never learned what became of Tilly and Private Lane's bodies. I was past caring. It is enough to know their souls are in heaven and Sinapp's is in hell.

Joseph received the transfer he requested. Within the month he will journey to his new post in the Nevada Territory. I will not go with him. Tomorrow I board the *Radcliff* and sail for Boston.

More than anything, Peggy, I want to come home.

Your loving sister,

Raffia

33

The jump from the top of the moat wall to Butch's back was seven feet vertically and that many or more horizontally. Wanting to inflict as much damage as possible at the onset, Anna led with elbows and knees. Patrice was at her side, shoulders touching when they left terra firma. In midair the bigger woman turned slightly to strike the smuggler with the edge of her shoulder and upper arm.

The assault was sudden and complete. The two women hit like a ton of brick. Butch went down. One Uzi flew from his hand to land a dozen feet away. The second was ripped out of his fingers and turned on him by the strong, sure hands of Patrice.

With the fall of Butch and the Uzis, Anna feared Perry would cut loose with the .44. He'd only spent one bullet she knew of. There could be five people dead or dying before he emptied the gun. This grim scenario never played out. Galvanized, refugees surged forward. Paulo, Mack and Rick were carried up to where Patrice sat astride Butch with gun to his head and Anna racked her brain in search of something to bind him with. Butch began to struggle. Patrice quieted him with a meaty fist slammed into the back of his neck. Anna's cuffs were in the office.

The crowd's roar changed tenor, and Anna decided to let Patrice worry about detaining Butch. Though Mack, Rick and Paulo had been the "good guys" to the extent of the Cuban smuggling operation, in the minds of many of the refugees they were tarred with the same brush as Butch and Perry. Along with Butch and Perry, they could be dispatched by a Latin version of vigilante justice.

Floodlights began winking out. Engines roared as the fishing boats powered up to flee. Everyone yelled, shrieked or screamed. Of Perry, there was no sign in the milling clot of Cuban refugees.

Anna ran for the Uzi lying on the sand, snatched it up, pointed it in the air and pulled the trigger. Once before, in training, she'd fired an Uzi. It bucked like a live thing, seeming to have a will of its own, a thirst for killing. "Please, *por favor, por favor, silencio,*" she shouted. The crowd fell quiet. The lights were gone. Blinded by the recent floods, she yelled "Paulo, Mack," trying to locate them before they were murdered.

"Here," she heard Paulo reply like a schoolboy at roll call.

She turned toward his voice. Her eyes were adjusting. Enough of dawn pushed at night and storm clouds that she could make him out, held captive by half a dozen men.

"Let him go," she said. No one moved. She fired another burst from the evil weapon she carried.

"Let him go," Mack repeated in Spanish. Reluctantly the Cubans loosed their captive.

"Paulo, there's a woman in the moat. Maybe shot. See to her now. Don't even think about running. I disabled your boat." Behind her, Anna heard Patrice whisper, "Dear God . . ." then a thump and a grunt as she hit Butch once more for good measure.

Paulo scrambled past and up onto the moat wall.

"Mack, come to me," Anna ordered.

The Cubans parted and allowed a newly freed Mack to walk to where she stood. He limped, and black showed at nostrils and mouth where he'd taken blows.

"Perry," she said. "Where is he? He's armed. I want him."

"Shot," Mack said succinctly. He turned and rattled off a few sentences in Spanish. The Cubans moved aside, opening a pathway from Anna to the sea. Halfway down lay a body.

"See to him," Anna said.

"He's dead," Mack replied. "A bullet tore his throat out. I saw him go down just as all this began."

Unless one of the Cubans had brought a gun with them, it made no sense. "Ask them who shot him," Anna said.

Mack did so. There was an exchange too rapid for Anna to understand, and a woman pointed up toward the battlements. Two men pointed out to sea.

"This woman swears she saw a muzzle flash from the fort. Two guys swear the shot came from the boats and the kid insists it was Butch. Sorry."

No one wanted to confess to killing an American before they'd even had a chance to become one themselves. Anna didn't care. She was grateful to the shooter.

"Paulo!" she shouted. "How's Donna?"

Two figures appeared shadowlike on the wall above the beaches. "Donna's fine" came the boiler engineer's gravelly voice. "But Mrs. Meyers is in critical condition."

Patrice began to cry, great gulping sobs of relief punctuated by a single grunt as she again bashed Butch on the side of the head to remind him of his manners.

Within half an hour Anna had things more or less organized. The refugees were in the casemates on the fort's north side where they were at least out of the rain. A Cuban man and Perry, bedfellows in death, lay side-by-side in the researchers' dorm. The wounded woman, suffering a bullet to her right shoulder, awaited Teddy in the fort's infirmary. Lack of personnel forced Anna to house the prisoners, Rick, Paulo, Butch and Mack, with the refugees, but they'd been bound securely with plastic handcuffs at wrist and ankle and weren't going anywhere soon—at least not anywhere fun. Donna was put to the task of freeing Teddy and Daniel, and Patrice, armed with two Uzis and a .44, stood watch over refugees and prisoners alike.

A semblance of order restored, Anna set about finding Bob Shaw's body. When Teddy was released, Anna didn't want her to suffer under the added burden of not knowing, of picturing her beloved facedown in the moat, eyes being nibbled by crabs. Butch and Mack denied any knowledge of what Perry had done. Anna didn't waste time grilling them. From what Teddy told her, Perry had come to the Shaws' house alone.

The sun had yet to thrust its face over the horizon, but the light had grown stronger with the shadowless clarity of a subtropical dawn. The rain had let up, and the clouds, though not gone, had lifted. It would be hot and sunny by noon.

Returning to the Shaws', Anna set about following the blood trail that began near the sofa in the living room. She'd checked the bedroom before, and Anna took her search outside. Why Perry would bother to first drag the corpse upstairs, then change his mind, drag it back down and stash the body in one of the storage casemates was a mystery. It wouldn't keep the body from being found, only delay the inevitable a few minutes. When following the twisted trail of a sociopath there wasn't much point in spending a lot of thought on logic. Anna stuck to the trail of blood.

Rain had obliterated most of the sporadic and sketchy trail. Anna found traces of what could be blood soaked into the wooden treads of the stairs leading to the second tier and her apartment. Once under the protective arches of the higher level, tracking became easy. An obvious trail where a heavy object had been dragged was left in the ubiquitous brick dust.

Bob had been taken in the opposite direction from Anna's quarters. Two casemates down, she found him. The cast had been smashed off but for a jagged-edged ring of plaster at mid thigh. The leg was rebroken, bone again breaking through the skin. Blood dyed the lower part of Bob's leg red. He lay half in the sill of the broken-out gunport facing Loggerhead Key. His service weapon was in his hand.

"Oh my God," Anna whispered reverently. Shattered leg, bleeding, Bob had dragged himself up the stairs to his bedroom, retrieved his gun, then pulled himself up to the fort's second tier. It was he who had shot Perry and very probably saved Donna's life.

He was breathing. He had a pulse, albeit a weak and thready one. "Hallelujah," Anna breathed her thanks to the ambient gods.

The whump of helicopter blades announced the arrival of the cavalry, coast-guard style. The storm had lifted sufficiently that aircraft could be dispatched, and they had outpaced the ships headed to Garden Key.

Uniformed men and women swarmed efficiently over the

fort. Bob was packaged by EMTs and whisked away. Rick, Mack, Butch and Paulo were taken into custody. The refugees were being cared for. Anna was relieved of responsibility and felt the lift as a physical thing. Light and tired and surreal, she left the bustle and shouted commands and made her way to the dock where the prisoners awaited boarding under the stern eye of two young guardsmen looking fresh and clean and strong in their natty uniforms.

Damp and crumpled, feeling old and small and frail, Anna sat down opposite but out of reach of William Macintyre. Despite his crimes—and she guessed they were even more numerous than she knew of—she felt a greater kinship with him than with any of the bright young soldiers who'd not had the night unravel and explode around them.

"Hey, Mack," she said wearily.

"Hey, Anna." If he was frightened or angry or resentful, he didn't show it. For a time they sat together without speaking, like comrades who've shared so much each knows all the other's stories and talk is redundant.

"There was no other diver," Anna said at length. "It was you. You tried to kill me, squash me under that engine."

"I'm sorry about that."

"Sorry you tried or sorry you didn't kill me?"

"As things turned out, I'm sorry I tried," Mack said.

In spite of herself, Anna smiled. "After going to all the effort, why didn't you? It would have been easy enough."

"Your feet started flipping and your little hand wiggling. I thought you were hurting. I can't stand to see anybody hurt."

Anna understood the point he made. For his cause he would kill, sacrifice the few that the many might live free. When he said he couldn't hurt anyone, he meant it literally. He could take a life but he couldn't cause pain and suffering. Maybe because, as a boy, forced by vicious beatings to reveal the whereabouts of his parents and so cause their deaths, to die meant little to him. To live in pain was the true hell.

"What happened to Theresa? Did you kill her?" Anna asked. "Or was that left to your hired thugs?"

"Trecie grew up in my old neighborhood," Mack said. "I used to see her running around on a little banana bike with pink ribbons on the handlebars when I'd visit."

It was on the tip of Anna's tongue to ask again if he'd killed her, but Mack wanted to tell it his own way. Before he could go on, Butch interrupted.

"You're going to hang yourself, asshole." Till he spoke he'd been so still both Anna and Mack had nearly forgotten about him. At the sound of his voice, Mack was transformed. Blood suffused his face, spittle formed in the corners of his mouth and he appeared to grow larger, swell within his bonds.

"You enjoy hurting people, you piece of shit. You piece of shit!"

Mack half rose, bent on attacking the other man, but the two coast guard boys stepped in. The moment past, Mack shrank to normal size. When some time had gone by, he picked up his story. He needed to tell it. Anna needed to hear it.

"Trecie—Theresa—was to seduce Lanny, get on the island and help from the inside. She was Cuban and wanted to work for her people. I guess she really did fall in love with old Lanny. She was going to tell him the whole thing; trade three hundred lives so she could be honest with her boyfriend. Rick and Paulo's brother—one of the guys killed when the fuel boat blew—came out and talked to her, but she wouldn't budge. I told 'em I'd take care of it. They don't know."

Anna waited. When he didn't go on she asked again: "Did you kill her?"

"I didn't hurt her."

"What a fucking saint," Butch sneered.

Mack didn't seem to hear him. In many ways Mack had withdrawn from the world Anna, the coast guard boys and Butch inhabited. Though he heard her questions, he answered as if speaking to himself in another place, a place not much better than where his corporal self would spend twenty-five to life.

"Trecie was going to go tell Lanny. We were down by the old dungeon in the southeast corner where we wouldn't be overheard. Trecie'd got it into her head that Lanny'd throw in with us, help our people to get to America. It was bull. Lanny's an okay guy, but he doesn't take chances. He doesn't believe in anything but a pension.

"I tried to quiet her. I needed to get her off Garden Key without her making noise. You know that sleeper hold the wrestlers used to do. I used that. It doesn't hurt."

The silence grew. From within the fort came the comforting sounds of an orderly crowd. The two coast guard men stood as still and mute as Buckingham Palace guards till Butch asked for a cigarette. Neither of them smoked.

"She never came to?" Anna said to be clear.

"Never did. Poor little girl."

"Dump the body at sea?"

"I meant to, but things got dicey. Daniel was stomping down the stairs there at that end of the fort, hollering, 'Mack, Mack.' We'd been redoing the brickwork sealing up the old cisterns. The sledgehammer was there to bust out the stuff that was crumbling. I bashed a hole, stuffed her through and was laying brick when Daniel got there.

"He stayed and gossiped for half an hour or more. There was nothing I could do but keep working. After I'd got it sealed up there didn't seem much point in changing things. I juiced Lanny with LSD to cloud his mind. He was gaga about Theresa. If he'd've been thinking clear, he'd've never let it go; screwed things up."

"And me?"

"Yeah. Why not? It worked once. And it doesn't—"

"Right. It doesn't hurt," Anna finished for him.

"Killing Trecie wasn't part of the plan, and I'm sorry it had to happen. Real sorry. Her aunt's going to feel pretty bad about the whole thing."

"Somebody always ends up hurting," Anna said.

"I guess."

More silence. Anna wanted to leave, but that would have entailed standing and moving. She wasn't ready for that. Another question came to her. "You took the pictures of Theresa from Lanny's house the other night. Why?"

Mack smiled. "You in your little dress running around at night. I thought you'd catch me for sure."

Anna didn't answer his smile. Images of her own vulnerability didn't amuse her. "Why take them?"

"Probably no reason. Lanny'd gone camera-happy after Theresa'd gone. Took a zillion pictures. I got to thinking some

of them might be of me or Paulo or Rick or something. Figured
better safe than sorry."

"You missed one," Anna told him out of spite.

He said nothing.

She stood; her back and legs had stiffened and hurt like a
son-of-a-bitch. It would take a degree of fortitude to walk away
without wincing at every step. She looked down at the murdering, poisoning, smuggling, felonious reprobate and couldn't
find any anger toward him.

"Thanks for not killing me," she said, wondering why she
should feel gratitude, but feeling it anyway. "I'm getting married," she added and realized she was too tired to filter her
thoughts or words.

"Congratulations," Mack said sincerely.

The dungeon, the old cisterns, the brickwork happening so
conveniently at a time of a young woman's disappearance:
Anna remembered her great-great-aunt Raffia's letters, the
mention of Sergeant Sinapp doing uncharacteristic physical labor himself, bricking up the ruined cistern when it had first
been done nearly a century and a half before. She thought of
Raffia feeling her way to Mudd's dungeon in the dark, how
she'd known where she was by the smell of new mortar.

Without stopping to think about what she intended to do,
Anna borrowed a ten-pound sledgehammer and a flashlight
from Daniel's shop and went to the dungeon.

"Abandon Hope All Ye Who Enter Here."

Permission to take down a wall, even one so newly and ne-
fariously constructed, could drag on forever. Bureaucracies
were good at making small problems last a long time, thus providing job security for middle management.

The blows hurt her as much as they did the brick wall, but she
was the more determined and it fell down before she did. The
stink of decomposing flesh and the scurrying sound of interrupted
diners gushed from the new-made hole, and Anna fell back. She
gave the critters a few seconds' head start, then, having kicked the
rubble away, stuck her head through, flashlight in hand.

The earthly remains of Theresa Alvarez stopped her from
going any farther. As Mack had said, she was shoved in a heap
just inside the brick wall. Fighting her gag reflex—to once start

vomiting was to have difficulty stopping till not only the smell
but the sense memory of the smell were purged—Anna pulled
and bashed away enough of the wall that she could see the
corpse more clearly, not to study it for clues, but to avoid treading on or in any way touching the pathetic thing.

She had no interest in the murder—Mack had confessed and
she believed him—but should he think better of his admission
and retract his confession before going to trial, Anna wanted to
leave what evidence there might be undisturbed.

Having created enough room to maneuver, she ducked
through the hole and stood between Theresa's feet. The body
was mashed into a rectangular opening about three by five feet
and not high enough to stand upright. At the parade ground end
was solid brick. Toward the sea narrow brick steps led steeply
down into darkness. These Anna followed. There were but eight
treads, each higher than a standard step, and then an opening to
the left, low and small like the one above.

It let into a room without a floor. The only place to stand was
a shelf no more than eighteen inches wide. Beyond this was a
great square hole the size of the casemate above and maybe that
deep. Depth was hard to gauge without proper light. Seawater
had seeped in until the old cistern was filled to half a dozen feet
down from where Anna stood.

The beam of her flashlight sank into the dark water. Beneath
she could see the brick of the walls and sand. Hidden away
from sun and storm, the water was clear, very nearly devoid of
life and utterly devoid of movement. But for water and sand, the
cistern was empty. Anna felt a crush of disappointment. It came
down on her with a weight of fatigue and she found she must sit
down on the ledge or pitch face foremost into the water. Till her
strength returned sufficiently that she could climb eight stairs
and brave the odiferous dead person, she idly played her light
across the dark water. Over the century and a half it had lain
sealed. Brick dust, lime and other debris brought down by de-
cay, rainwater seeping through from above and seawater from
below, had formed a sort of a beach on the seaward side. Either
that or the sand had fallen during a partial collapse of some kind
and remained unchanged by wind or the action of the sea from
that time to this.

As she played the light back and forth over this subterranean atoll, she noticed a darkened triangle, like a small shark's fin, protruding above the surface. The first few times she'd taken it for a shadow—or perhaps been simply too tired and dispirited to notice. Once seen it would not melt into the background again.

Finally curiosity got the better of lethargy and she scooted around the ledge on her bottom to where, with care, she could drop down onto the sand. As her fingers loosed the brick, she suffered a terrifying thought. What if the sand were viscous, near liquid and swallowed her like quicksand?

The sand gave way beneath her just enough to snatch her breath away and douse her tired body with so much adrenaline she felt as if she could have leapt the six feet to safety flatfooted. Ankle-deep in sand and gasping for air, she waited till the panic passed. Since Mack's acid trips had scrambled her brains, the center for fear in her cerebral cortex had been working double time. Normal anxiety was revved up into crippling fear that came in bowel-loosening waves. Anna hoped it wasn't going to be a permanent condition; yet one more wound that left a scar.

Recovered sufficiently that her hands quit shaking, she trained her light on the dark triangle that had lured her into the gullet of the abandoned cistern. It was a bit of weathered wood, nothing more. Because she was there and because, when the adrenaline burned out in liquid terror, she'd been left temporarily too weak to climb out of a bassinet let alone a brick tank, she knelt in the sand and began digging.

Though softened by water and rot, she could tell the board's exposed end had not been sawed but broken. As she dug and pulled, she saw sledge or boot-heel-sized indentations where it had been repeatedly struck as if someone had gone to great lengths to smash it free of a structure.

Five minutes of digging and worrying it and the sand gave up a board five or six inches wide and a bit over two feet long. Risking her fanny to the yielding sand, Anna sat and examined her find. At first her flashlight revealed nothing more exciting than an old, square-headed, iron nail. As she looked, though, letters began to separate themselves from the shades of gray where white paint had once been emblazoned on the wood. Once looking for them, they became clear enough: *rry Cay.*

"I knew it," Anna whispered. She leaned back and closed her
eyes. "You were right, Aunt Raffia. Tilly never left the fort." For
the briefest of instants, borne undoubtedly on the winds of an
acid flashback, Anna felt the presence of her great-great-aunt so
strongly she smiled. Until it was gone she didn't dare open her
eyes. Seeing ghosts at night when she was high was one thing.
Seeing them mid-morning, straight, was too much to contemplate.

rry Cay.

The *Merry Cay,* the sailing skiff belonging to Sergeant
Sinapp; the one he'd reported stolen the morning after Tilly and
Private Lane disappeared, the boat that held together the thin
fabric of lies about the supposed elopement.

It was as Raffia had said. Sinapp killed them, dumped the
bodies and the smashed skiff in the ruined cistern, then saw to
the bricking up himself. Anna didn't doubt but that she sat on
Tilly's impromptu grave. Without realizing she did so, she patted the sand with the tenderness of a mother gentling a frightened child.

Whether bones would be found, she couldn't say. Not being
a forensic expert she had no idea what a hundred and fifty years
immersed in brackish water and wet sand would do to a human
skeleton. For her, the finding of the boat was enough.

Epilogue

The refugees were taken to an INS holding facility by a flotilla of coast guard ships. According to the coast guard and INS, it was the largest single landing of illegal aliens since the British invaded in 1812. Anna had been a part of history.

The six fishing boats were stopped and taken into custody at about the same time the helicopter reached Garden Key. They had no intention of returning to Cuba. No one doubted that they were headed to Enrico's Marine Supply in Miami, but as they denied it uniformly, there might be trouble proving it. The coast guard took possession of the fishing boats as well as the captured Scarab. Not a bad haul.

Paulo, Rick, Butch and Mack disappeared into the legal system. There would be federal charges, charges by the state of Florida, and Cuban officials might want them as well. Good intentions or not, they had broken rules, laws, traditions, taboos and statutes in many jurisdictions. They would be in jail a long time. Mack and Butch faced the death penalty. Anna wished Paulo and Rick a mere slap on the hands, but they would get little leniency for being cute, young and good-hearted.

Bob and the wounded woman were medevacked out. Bob was recovering but would probably limp the rest of his life.

Anna remained at Fort Jefferson for two more weeks. Her

time was spent writing reports and retrieving personal gear and NPS property off the bottom of the ocean around East Key.

Mrs. Meyers was rescued from the moat and underwent rehabilitation in Daniel's living room. Along with a few more scars on corpus and psyche, Anna would take away from the Dry Tortugas the wonderful image of Daniel, the burly maintenance man, flitting about muttering, "Oh my dear, oh my dear," and, "Don't hurt her. Careful," as the Harley was winched up onto the moat wall.

Anna photocopied Raffia's letters and turned them over to Duncan, the fort's historian. His feelings were mixed. Excavating the cistern that entombed Tilly, Joel Lane and then Theresa Alvarez excited him. The prospect of finding fragments, the DNA of which might be matched to an actual living park ranger, filled him with glee. The prospect of dismantling the walls of the powder room to discover Dr. Mudd's innocence and, so, the negation of his book proving the man's guilt—all but three chapters of which were already completed—did not.

Knowing the glacial slowness with which a big bureaucracy moves, Anna didn't count on this question being answered in her lifetime.

She wasn't concerned. She had the answers she needed and a future full of live people to look forward to. Paul renewed his proposal via e-mail. They'd set a date, March, scarcely half a year away. Place was yet to be determined.

Anna unpacked the black velvet box that housed the impressive diamond engagement ring Paul had given her and put the ring on. She needed to get used to the look and feel—and the idea—of it before she returned to Mississippi and had to make good on her promise of matrimony.

And now a sneak preview of Nevada Barr's newest
Anna Pigeon mystery,

HIGH COUNTRY

Available in hardcover from G. P. Putnam's Sons

W ould you like baked potato or *pom frittes* with that?" Anna asked politely.

"Can't I get French fries?"

"You bet." Anna wrote *NY strip w/PF—well done* on the pad.

As the mom and dad at table twenty-nine coaxed suitable orders from a five- and nine-year-old with hearts set on pizza, Anna let her eyes drift up to the two-story windows enclosing the end of the dining room. Granite boulders the size of houses were dwarfed by ponderosa pines with trunks eight, ten, twelve feet in diameter. These in turn were made toylike by a sheer and towering cliff that served as a backdrop. In the mist on a November afternoon, evergreens showed black against the streaked gray of rock: forbidding, dangerous and, to Anna, utterly seductive. It was as if, should she leave the warm gold and russet of the grand Ahwahnee Hotel and cross the parking lot into the rocks and trees she, too, would be leached of color, would walk in the world as a ghost, a mountain breeze, the whistle of a hawk's wing.

"Do you have hot dogs?" The reality of Mom's voice cut through Anna's ghost dance with the sharp laser light of a red micro-fleece-clad arm.

"No hot dogs."

"You oughta have a children's menu with hot dogs," the mother complained.

"I'll suggest it to the chef," Anna lied easily. The chef, a veteran of many four-star establishments, was fanatical in his hatred of hot dogs and only slightly more sanguine on the subject of children.

A turkey quesadilla was settled on and Anna left the table to walk down the long gallery from the alcove. She'd always wanted to work in Yosemite National Park but in her daydreams it never crossed her mind she would be there as a waitress.

A waitress coming up on fifty might be an oddity in another establishment. At the historic Ahwahnee Hotel in Yosemite Valley, built of the very granite and pine it sheltered beneath, carved beams and great stone fireplaces warming the bones of park visitors for more than seventy-five years, much of the wait staff was wrinkled and sere. It was a plum job. Tips were fabulous. Openings were rare. Like some of the more venerable clubs, one practically had to be grandfathered in.

Anna'd washed in on a tsunami of lies and half-truths: her cover story. The phrase amused her; it was so deliciously cloak and dagger. A spy; Anna was a spy. According to Lorraine Knight, Yosemite's Chief Ranger, it was a necessary bit of drama.

Parks, even the big ones like Yosemite, Yellowstone or the Grand Canyon, were socially very small towns. Yosemite concessions workers in both the hotel and her less picturesque and pricey sister, Yosemite Lodge, along with the people minding the stores, delis and shops, numbered around twelve hundred. Nearly six hundred NPS people overwintered. In a society of less than two thousand souls, everybody knew everybody at least by sight if not by name. On the rare occasions when an undercover law-enforcement person was called for, a ranger from another park, an unknown face and name, had to be brought in.

Anna was unsure whether it was her law-enforcement status or the fact that she'd worked her way through college waiting tables at Pepe Delgado's in San Luis Obispo that inspired her own Chief Ranger, John Brown Brown, to offer her the assignment when the call went out.

She was pleasantly surprised at how fast the skills came back. She'd been wearing a dead—maybe dead, probably dead—woman's clothes literally and figuratively for less than a week and already her short-term memory had risen to the challenge. So far the hardest part of the job had been turning her tips over to the Mountain Safety Fund. As long as she was pulling in her pay as a GS-11 District Ranger she wasn't allowed to keep them. A shame; they dwarfed her salary.

A quick check of the order and she put it up for the chef. Wait staff desiring to keep the peace double-checked orders. James Wither, a man so lean his large hazel eyes bulged from nearly fleshless sockets and jet black hair hung over a forehead lined by at least fifty years of slaving over hot stoves, saw waiters and waitresses as either flawed delivery systems or malicious art vandals bent on destroying his creative visions. Anna had never seen him actually throw knives at busboys or fling trays at salad chefs, but she'd heard the stories and chose to tread lightly.

Several of the longtime servers could talk intelligently about food. These educated few Wither could see and hear. Anna, who shied away from meat but otherwise ate what was easy, cheap or put in front of her, was beneath his notice. This was good. Despite what the movies told one, a spy needed to be unremarkable. Anna was finding this and the rest of the spying business harder than she'd anticipated. Chatting, drawing people out—being downright likable—was work for her at the best of times. Doing so for ulterior motives was an absolute grind.

When tempted to give it up as a non-starter—the unapologetic opinion of Leo Johnson, the deputy superintendent—and go home to her dog, her cat and her fiancé, Anna held the photographs Lorraine Knight had shown her up to her mind's eye.

Before donning her apron and sensible shoes, Anna met with the Chief Ranger and the deputy superintendent. Lorraine had shown her three pictures of Dixon Crofter, Patrick Waters, Trish

Spencer and Caitlin Bates. These four were typical of the marvelously atypical young people who worked in parks.

Dixon Crofter, what parkies referred to as a "climber dude," lived in Camp 4, a Mecca for rock climbers from all over the world. He'd been in Yosemite three seasons. He climbed for fun. If he could get on a funded expedition to Greenland or Austria or Patagonia, he climbed for fun and money. When the park Search and Rescue team needed a climber they hired Dixon or several other of the "SAR-siters" living in the camp. Then Dixon climbed for fun, money and the good of his fellow man. Dixon was twenty-four-years old, six-foot-three, one-hundred-thirty-five pounds. From the picture Anna guessed his body was a powerful construction of cable and bone. He had long curling black hair, a smile that could melt ice, and a nose a Bedouin chief would be proud of.

Pat Waters worked trail crew. He was two years younger than Dixon. Where the climber was narrow Pat was broad: shoulders, jaw, chest. He looked strong—not with gym, bench-press muscles, but the kind that can move rocks and stumps all day and still have the energy to tell jokes over dinner. He sported a bleach-blond Mohawk and a grin that, despite the dusty rigors of his chosen occupation, spoke of expensive orthodonture. On his right bicep was a tattoo of Bill the Cat in one of his more schizophrenic poses.

Trish Spencer and Caitlin Bates were photographed together, their arms around each other's waists, their heads close, long hair twining together. Trish's was sleek and brown, Caitlin's bleached and permed with black roots. Trish had buckteeth a shade whiter than nature intended and dark eyes that nearly disappeared with the onslaught of her smile. Caitlin wore a bandanna pirate—or, to Anna's memory—hippy-style around her head and looked all of twelve years old. Neither girl would ever make a living modeling or win a swimsuit contest but they were beautiful nonetheless. Even in the flat dead medium of a photograph they exuded youth and high spirits and, Caitlin at least, an innocent wickedness that Anna found irresistible in young women.

Trish was in her third season as a hostess at the Ahwahnee. Caitlin was one of the NPS's own. She was a summer intern fin-shing her first season working in Little Yosemite Valley campground, a heavy-use area and a four mile hike, most of it straight up, behind Half Dome.

Thirteen days before Anna was brought in there was a vicious thunderstorm that dropped eight inches of snow on the park amid high winds followed by a cold snap that had yet to let up. Ten days later the high country was blanketed in another foot of snow. In the interim between these two meteorological events these four kids had gone missing.

They'd not been seen together leaving the park. None of them filed backcountry permits. They told no one of their plans. It was only assumed they were together because they'd all disappeared on the same day.

Patrick Waters left trail camp on the Illouette Trail to come to the valley for his weekend. Dixon Crofter was spotted by a maintenance worker about five A.M. that same day hitchhiking west out of the valley with a backpack and climbing ropes. Caitlin Bates had left Little Yosemite Valley camp the afternoon before, also on her weekend, headed for the apartment she shared with three other park interns near the old graveyard in the valley. Her supervisor said she'd carried nothing but an empty pack and water. He'd assumed she hiked out the Mist Trail past Nevada and Vernal Falls. It was steep—the upper half little more than a shattered granite staircase—but only a little over four miles long. Fit and agile with knees not yet forced to bend too often to the vicissitudes of life, the young intern could reach the valley floor in an hour. Trish, pleading headache, had stayed home while her two roommates left for work that morning. When they'd returned she was gone as were her pack and boots. Later it was discovered that the fire axe had been taken from its niche in the hall.

For Anna's edification Lorraine Knight had drawn the containment area of the search, the area in which, based on time, distance, physical ability, terrain and weather the missing persons had a ninety-five percent chance of being found. Outside this perimeter, Anna was amused to discover, was referred to as the ROW, the Rest of the World. To indicate even the zillionth percentile of possibility beyond that, Lorraine sketched a tiny flying saucer.

After eight days the search had been suspended—not abandoned; in spirit at least the NPS never gave up looking. We snow, ice, three weeks: if the four were lost or injured in the backcountry they were most likely dead. Unless—and this wa the deputy superintendent's pet theory—the four of them had hitched out of the park to find warmer adventures in Mexico or South America.

Anna had not been brought in as an addendum to the search and rescue effort. Yosemite had one of the finest SAR operations in the country if not the world. The park was harsh enough to provide endless challenge and the visitors foolish enough to provide the rangers with endless practice.

Lorraine Knight had brought Anna in because she was convinced the incident was far from over. She had stated her view succinctly: "I suspect foul play," she'd said and smiled at the drama of the words.

With that smile Lorraine won Anna over. They were of an age more or less and seemed to have like interests. Knight was a big woman, five-ten or -eleven, and powerful looking without being in the least masculine. Anna put her age at around fifty though it was hard to tell. Sun and wind had done more to her skin than the mere passage of years. Her hair was undimmed by either time or the elements. A braid as thick as Anna's wrist and a rich red-gold hung down past her waist. The tail of it rested on the butt of her gun like a squirrel on a branch. Out of doors when armed, the braid went up with a flick of practiced fingers to be secured in place by pins that appeared to come from nowhere.

This instantaneous affection put Anna on her guard. There were those who swore by first impressions. Anna was not one of them. First impressions could be manipulated. Anybody could suck it up and play hale-fellow-well-met long enough to impress. Few could sustain a convincing facade over time. Sooner or later cracks began to show. Anna was a big proponent of last impressions.

"Something besides the disappearances is upping the collective blood pressure of the park," Lorraine finished. Anna had felt it. A poison dripped into the small isolated community, an unspecified drift of unease that seemed to animate or enervate

warp that indefinable buzz of the human hive till it whined and
grated in the mind.

Leo Johnson, the deputy superintendent, grunted at these
feminine intuitions of dis-ease. Johnson was in his thirties and
as steely-eyed and lantern-jawed as a *Ranger Rick* comic book
character. The heroic effect was spoiled by receding brown hair
with a tendency to curl over the ears and a small mouth that, on
a young and comely lass, might be compared to a rosebud. On
Leo's broad face the comparison was more apt to be to one of
the body's other natural apertures.

Before this porcine interruption he'd had little to say, so little Anna suspected he'd been pressured into going along with
Lorraine's undercover investigation by pressure from above.

"It's a holdover from the Sunsocy killings," the deputy superintendent said dismissively.

Like the rest of the country, Anna had followed those grim
events on the news.

People managed all sorts of ways to damage or extinguish
themselves in Yosemite. They fell off the magnificent cliffs, got
lost, suffered from exposure, broken ankles and bee stings. The
brave or crazy died in base jumps from El Capitan. They
crashed hang gliders and fell out of trees, committed suicide off
Half Dome, overdosed, brawled. Search, rescue and even the
occasional death were daily fare in a park as wild and yet as
heavily visited as Yosemite. Even the odd happenstance of four
park people going AWOL would not have shaken the social
foundations as recently as two years ago.

That was before a psychopath working in the nearby town
of El Portal had sexually assaulted and murdered four women,
one of whom dwelt in an in-holding surrounded by NPS
lands.

Though the man had been caught, his evil had not stopped.
The sense of safety many enjoyed in the glorious stone heart of
the Sierras died along with the women. In the most graphic
way the monster had brought home the fact that there is no
place evil cannot reach. Because of this the disappearance of
the park people raised fear levels in the valley till there were
times the small hairs on the back of Anna's neck fairly prickled
with it.

Talk would have it that the Sunsocy murders were happening again, that a copycat had taken up residence in Yosemite Valley.

Chief Ranger Knight had brought Anna to Yosemite because she too feared the killings had just begun.

ABOUT THE AUTHOR

Nevada Barr is the award-winning author of ten previous Anna Pigeon mysteries, including the *New York Times* bestsellers *Hunting Season* and *Blood Lure*. She lives in Mississippi, where she was most recently a ranger on the Natchez Trace Parkway.

Visit Nevada Barr's website at
www.nevadabarr.com

GET CAUGHT READING AT SEA

getcaughtreadingatsea.com

Join top authors for the ultimate cruise experience. Spend 7 days in the Western Caribbean aboard the luxurious Carnival Elation. Start in Galveston, TX and visit Progreso, Cozumel and Belize. Enjoy all this with a ship full of authors, entertainers and book lovers on the **"Get Caught Reading at Sea Cruise"** October 17 - 24, 2004.

PRICES STARTING AT $749 PER PERSON WITH COUPON!

Mail in this coupon with proof of purchase* to receive $250 per person off the regular **"Get Caught Reading at Sea Cruise"** price. One coupon per person required to receive $250 discount. For further details call **1-877-ADV-NTGE** or visit **www.GetCaughtReadingatSea.com**

*proof of purchase is original sales receipt with the book purchased circled.

Carnival
The Most Popular Cruise Line in the World

- -

GET $250 OFF

Name (Please Print)

Address   Apt. No.

City   State   Zip

E-Mail Address

See Following Page For Terms & Conditions.

**For booking form and complete information
go to www.getcaughtreadingatsea.com or call 1-877-ADV-NTGE**

Carnival Elation

7 Day Exotic Western Caribbean Itinerary

DAY	PORT	ARRIVE	DEPART
Sun	Galveston		4:00 P.M.
Mon	"Fun Day" at Sea		
Tue	Progreso/Merida	8:00 A.M.	4:00 P.M.
Wed	Cozumel	9:00 A.M.	5:00 P.M.
Thu	Belize	8:00 A.M.	6:00 P.M.
Fri	"Fun Day" at Sea		
Sat	"Fun Day" at Sea		
Sun	Galveston	8:00 A.M.	

TERMS AND CONDITIONS

PAYMENT SCHEDULE:
50% due upon booking
Full and final payment due by July 26, 2004

Acceptable forms of payment are Visa, MasterCard, American Express, Discover and checks. The card-holder must be one of the passengers traveling. A fee of $25 will apply for all returned checks. Check payments must be made payable to **Advantage International, LLC and sent to: Advantage International, LLC, 195 North Harbor Drive, Suite 4206, Chicago, IL 60601**

CHANGE/CANCELLATION:
Notice of change/cancellation must be made in writing to Advantage International, LLC.

Change:
Changes in cabin category may be requested and can result in increased rate and penalties. A name change is permitted 60 days or more prior to departure and will incur a penalty of $50 per name change. Deviation from the group schedule and package is a cancellation.

Cancellation:

181 days or more prior to departure	$250 per person
121 - 180 days or more prior to departure	50% of the package price
120 - 61 days prior to departure	75% of the package price
60 days or less prior to departure	100% of the package price (nonrefundable)

US and Canadian citizens are required to present a valid passport or the original birth certificate and state issued photo ID (drivers license). All other nationalities must contact the consulate of the various ports that are visited for verification of documentation.

We strongly recommend trip cancellation insurance!

For further details call 1-877-ADV-NTGE or visit www.GetCaughtReadingatSea.com

----

For booking form and complete information
go to **www.getcaughtreadingatsea.com** or call **1-877-ADV-NTGE**

Complete coupon and booking form and mail both to:
**Advantage International, LLC,
195 North Harbor Drive, Suite 4206, Chicago, IL 60601**

NOW AVAILABLE IN HARDCOVER

NEVADA BARR

High Country

PUTNAM

From the *New York Times* bestselling author

NEVADA BARR

HUNTING
SEASON

An Anna Pigeon mystery

'An engrossing and deftly written thriller."
—*San Diego Union-Tribune*

"Genuinely thrilling."
—*Lost Angeles Times*

"Park Ranger Anna Pigeon is back."
—*Rocky Mountain News*

0-425-18878-7

Available wherever books are sold or
to order call 1-800-788-6262

B012

New York Times bestselling author

NEVADA BARR

BLOOD LURE

An Anna Pigeon Novel

"All is not well in Grizzly Country...
Barr's red herrings and sly twists culminate
in one huge payoff."
—*Entertainment Weekly*

0-425-18375-0

Available wherever books are sold
or
to order call: 1-800-788-6262

B011